A Tattered Curtain novel

PHANTOM

GREER RIVERS

Blue Ghost Publishing, LLC
BGP Dark World

Cover Design: TRC Designs

Editing and Proofreading: My Brother's Editor

ASIN: B09WSVTHP4
Paperback ISBN: 979-8-9861242-2-3
Hardback ISBN: 979-8-9861242-3-0

PHANTOM

GREER RIVERS

Phantom

She is my muse, and I am her demon of music.

A year ago, I witnessed sweet Scarlett Day's dark side. She's been my obsession ever since.

I was content with being her secret. Content with protecting her from afar... until an enemy from my past sets his sights on her.

Our families have a deep history of hatred, and Scarlett is caught in the middle.

Meanwhile, her mind plays tricks on her. When a panic attack goes horribly wrong, I emerge from the shadows to save her.

Now that she's mine, I can't let her go.

I've mastered the darkness. She tempts me with her light.

But when my mask is gone, will she fear the monster underneath?

Playlist

"Darkness" by X V I
"Twisted" by MISSIO
"Voices In My Head" by Falling In Reverse
"The Devil is a Gentleman" by Merci Raines
"Billie Jean" by The Civil Wars
"Bad" by Royal Deluxe
"Power Over Me" by Dermot Kennedy
"Primavera" by Ludovico Einaudi
"Your Heart is as Black as Night" by Melody Gardot
"Good Things Come To Those Who Wait" by Nathan Sykes
"Monster" by Willyecho
"Beautiful Undone" by Laura Doggett
"La Vie En Rose" by Emily Watts
"Play with Fire" by Sam Tinnesz, Yacht Money
"Pyrokinesis" by 7Chariot
"Scars" by Boy Epic
"How Villains Are Made" by Madalen Duke
"All Is Lost" by Katie Garfield
"Sway" by So Below
"Up Down" by Boy Epic

Get the full playlist here:

A Note From The Author

The Tattered Curtain series can be read in any order and is a series of complete standalones inspired by classic stories and stage productions. Phantom is a dark and spicy retelling of Gaston Leroux's Phantom of the Opera with mafia and stalking elements set in modern-day New Orleans. Guaranteed HEA.

TRIGGER/CONTENT/TROPE WARNING

Phantom is a dark romance. It should only be read by mature readers (18+).

Full list of triggers/content warnings and tropes can be found at the QR code below.

Protect your heart, friends. Reader discretion is advised.

If you or a loved one needs help, there is hope. Call the National Suicide Prevention Lifeline: 800-273-8255, or go to suicidepreventionlifeline.org and save a life, maybe even your own.

Once Upon A Time...

AUTHOR WITH BIPOLAR DISORDER
EDITION

In 2014, I suffered my first full blown manic episode. I had to be hospitalized in a psychiatric ward and thereafter began my bipolar journey. And it has, in fact, been a *journey*. An adventure sometimes, but a damn odyssey most.

I've struggled with my mental health for as long as I can remember and I've been going to therapists and psychiatrists since 2009. Even still, there are many ups and downs in my battle for a healthier mind, combatting my manic alter-ego (who I've jokingly named Athena), enduring various medications that doctors have prescribed "just to see" how my brain would react (usually poorly), and severe incapacitating bouts of depression.

I pulled much from my own experience to write this story, and every symptom Scarlett has is something that I've personally experienced. You, or someone you know, may have bipolar disorder that presents differently and that's okay. As with most things, bipolar disorder is not a monolith, and there's no one-size-fits-all solution. For me, writing has been an extremely therapeutic outlet. I honestly don't know where I'd be without it, my husband, and my therapist. Oh, and medication, of course.

All this to say, if you have been searching for answers to the secrets your brain insists on hiding... *keep going*. It's hard. It sucks. But, your health and happiness are worth it. *You* are worth it.

Never, ever forget: You are loved. You are wanted. You matter.

To my manic side, Athena, you crazy bitch.
Get some sleep, girl.

"If I am the phantom, it is because man's hatred has made me so. If I am to be saved it is because your love redeems me."

Gaston Leroux
The Phantom of the Opera

Prologue

I float on the musical notes hanging in the air. Each one is loud and percussive as they all dance out of the open doors of the Bourbon Street bars. When I spin around, I can capture the high ones and sing them at the top of my lungs.

The tempos are slower versions than I'm used to. But *everything* is *so slow* right now.

Even the laughter around me sounds sluggish, battling with the upbeat jazz radio that started buzzing in my head a week ago.

All the words and beats and melodies jumble together. The ones in my head clash with the ones in the street. I'm not sure which I'm hearing loudest at the moment. They're all blending together into a harsh cacophony.

I stop spinning and stick my tongue out, wondering if I'll be able to taste the powdered sugar scent that wafts out of Café Beignet, despite it being a few blocks away.

"Get her the fuck out of here, Jaime."

I stutter to a stop and whip around to face the voice that rumbles low, yet can still be heard above all the chaos in and around my mind. It raises the hairs on the back of my neck and makes me shiver as I curve my long black curls behind my ear.

But when I spin toward the deep bass, I can't find the owner, only my best friend, Jaime. My poor bestie bites his fingernails and glances around us. Weariness and defeat dull his usually vibrant brown eyes.

"What's wrong?" I ask, only my voice comes out strange. It takes me trying again to realize my tongue is still out. I roll it back up into my mouth like a chameleon and giggle.

Jaime only curses in Spanish under his breath, looking more defeated than ever. "She's sick, man. I can see it in her eyes, like you said."

Who is he talking to?

Confusion tries to filter through the fog in my mind, but I physically wave it away. "You're no fun."

"We have to go, Scarlett," Jaime answers with a wobbly smile, obviously trying to put on a silly face to distract me as he waves my high heels at me. "Let's put your knockoff Manolos back on—"

I stomp the dirty ground with the balls of my feet and whine, "But they *hurt*."

"Too bad, girl. I told you not to wear them to the Quarter, but you didn't listen to me, so now here we are. Either put them back on or I'll have to carry you. Hurry up, though. The cops are already thinking you're straight up *loca*."

"Well, that's rude—"

He reaches for me as I pout, but I twist away, nimble on my bare feet.

"No way, *High*-may! *High*-may! *High*-mayyyy," I belt his name out in an off-key tune and keep my eyes peeled to find a date for my friend so he'll finally lighten up tonight. A superhot, short, college-aged touristy looking guy passes by at the perfect time and I grab his hand.

"Come here! My bestest friend in the whole wide world desperately needs to get laid. He's no fun when he hasn't gotten a good dick in a while."

"*No joda*, Scarlett." He snatches my hand away from the other guy's and wraps his arm around my shoulder, keeping me flush to his side. "Of course you'd find the sexiest guy on Bourbon Street right when I have to get you out of here. Where the hell is this wingwoman energy when I actually need it?"

"All the fun in me died with my dad." A high-pitched laugh escapes me, even though a sharp, knifelike pain in my chest tries to break through my euphoria.

"*Meirda*, Scarlo, I'm sor—"

"Nope!" I roll out from underneath his arm and shove my hand into his apologetic face. "No, no, no. No more sadness! I already did all that. I couldn't get out of bed for a month and now I feel free! I'm going to fly... dance... no, wait!" I stab my finger at the nearest glowing neon sign. "Let's get a drink!"

"You spent all your money in less than twenty-four hours, Scarlo. You're broke."

My bottom lip pokes out. "Please? Pretty, pretty, pretty please? I'll pay you back, I swear!"

"Dominguez!" that sexy, grumpy voice shouts between us again. "I'm on my way. Don't let her out of your sight."

I try to pretend like I don't hear it because I'm not sure whether it's just another frequency joining the jazz radio in my brain, until I realize Jaime's got someone on speakerphone.

He grimaces and puts the phone to his ear just as a mobile DJ wheels a cart down the center of Bourbon Street. I squeal and clap like one of those cymbal monkey music boxes. Without a glance back at my Debbie Downer friend, I get lost in the dancing, gyrating crowd traveling with the DJ.

Hot guys lean over the railing of the balcony above me, demanding to see my tits. I giggle wildly and rip off my brand-new black lace see-through crop top that I *borrowed* from a Royal Street boutique today once I'd realized I'd spent all my stipend money. Winding my arm back, I throw it up to them and cheer when they fight over it, ripping it to shreds. I'm still covered by my black bra, but the boys don't care. The sky rains beads down on me anyway. I try to catch them all but end up tripping and falling over the plastic balls onto the gross pavement, landing on my knees. A burst of laughter rolls out of me, until a burning sensation stings my skin. My black curls spill over my eyes and I pull them back to see better.

"Oh no..." I gasp quietly at the sight of tiny glass shards embedded in my kneecaps.

It's fine. I don't *really* feel it. I'm *invincible*. A little glass doesn't hurt, and any pain I feel inside—or out—will all disappear once I *finally* start drinking.

Jaime reluctantly agreed to go to Bourbon Street to dance my restless energy out, but since we stepped onto the street itself, he's been nothing but a buzzkill and trying to drag me back into the dorms at the Bordeaux Conservatory of Music.

The school and the New French Opera House take up the whole block from Toulouse to St. Louis and Dauphine to Bourbon. We haven't gotten far at all. Hell, I bet if I tried hard enough, I could sling one of my new beads and hit a corner window.

As fun as that sounds, I decide against it, not wanting to risk reminding Jaime that he could literally sling *me* over his shoulder and take me back, no sweat.

A big sigh from deep within my lungs makes my bare shoulders sag in the sticky summer night air. With the exhale comes a huge wave of exhaustion that nearly has me collapsing the rest of the way to the ground.

But I fight it. I've been fighting it for four days straight. No sleep means no nightmares. No nightmares mean only happy Scarlett. I figured it out just a week ago and it's been magical, taking me out of my mopeyness in no time.

To combat the urge to close my eyes, I focus on the pretty strobe light shining from the top of the bar in front of me. It sparkles into the midnight sky, making the stars shine magnificently with the kaleidoscope of colors.

I lie back with my elbows resting on the raised sidewalk and get comfy, ignoring the lumpy shard that's keeping me from straightening my leg all the way out and has the audacity to try to ruin this moment. A commotion behind me breaks my concentration as I'm about to get situated, and I'm brutally yanked up by both arms.

"Hey! Let go of me!"

"Ma'am, you have the right to remain silent..."

Two hot New Orleans cops read me my rights while they carry me to a parked police SUV at the corner of Bourbon and Toulouse Street, right outside the New French Opera House.

"Fuck!" Jaime curses from somewhere behind us and my eyes widen. My New Orleanian best friend never curses in anything but Spanish, French, or his own personal combination of *Spanglench*. Not unless shit's really hit the fan.

"Stop fighting us, ma'am, or we'll have to tase you."

"Let go of me and I'll stop fighting!" I screech and kick. "Jaime! Help!"

"She's a junior at Bordeaux Conservatory. Her dorm is right behind me. I can take her home," Jaime offers, having finally caught up to us.

"No can do. She's hurting herself at this point and we've already made the arrest while she was screaming at us."

"What are you arresting her for?"

People gawk and I glare at them. They only laugh in response. *Assholes.*

"Drunk in public and disorderly conduct. Usually we let those types of crimes slide in the Quarter, but she's out of control, sir. We have to at least stick her in the drunk tank for her own good."

"Drunk!?" I scoff, trying to escape their hold, but the cops squeeze tighter on my biceps. "I haven't even drank anything!"

"Yeah, fucking right," one of them grumbles. "Let's see what the breathalyzer says back at the police station, sweetie. We've still got you on disorderly conduct."

I growl back at the cop, but stop when Jaime gives me a pointed look and mouths for me to "shut up."

"She's actually telling the truth," he answers out loud. "I don't know what's going on with her, but she needs help, not jail.

Can you help her?" He shoves his phone in his pocket and carves both hands through his thick, dark-black hair, messing up his pompadour.

Jeez, the guy's *really* bent out of shape. His hair is *always* perfect, and his normally Broadway-worthy timbre has an annoying pleading quality to it.

But a tiny voice rising over the jazz radio in my thoughts tells me he's right.

Something's seriously wrong with me.

Nah. Fuck that voice.

"Let me... *go!*"

To evade them, I suddenly go limp. The cops don't expect it and drop me on my ass. I immediately get up and sprint like my life depends on it.

The wind whizzes past me... I'm way too fast for the loser cops yelling at me to stop... I'm moving so quickly, I could win any race... Hell, I should've gone to college for track and field instead of singing... Oh, shit... maybe I can go to the Olympics after I graduate... Unless I become a huge star on Broadway... Maybe I could even do both... But no, fuck Broadway... I want my *own* stage—

My face meets the ground violently as something crashes me to the pavement, breaking me from the thoughts that were racing as fast as I was. I don't feel it. I'm only pissed that someone had the fucking nerve to stop me.

I roll to my back, cursing, spitting mad until I realize it's fucking *Jaime* who caught up to me.

"What the hell, jackass? What the actual flying fuck?"

The jerk has tears in his eyes but *I'm* the one he just fucking trampled like a goddamn linebacker. Jesus Christ.

"I'm so sorry, Scarlo. I had to. They were going to tase you." He whispers watery apologies but still hands me to the two police officers.

Once I'm in their custody, they slam me against the cold metal of the police SUV.

"Oh, god, be gentle with her, *please*! She's not okay. This isn't her." He keeps begging them not to hurt me, but they don't listen as they brutally wrench my hands behind my back to cuff me, forcing a scream from my throat.

"I'm sorry, Scarlett. So, so sorry. He didn't want me to do this, but you *need* help."

"Who the fuck is 'he'? And fuck their help. Tell them to leave me alone, Jaime!" I scream, furious that tears flow down *his* cheeks, when he isn't the one being fucking *arrested* right now.

He shakes his head as I'm brutally thrust into the SUV's open door. The cops are talking to me, but I can't take my eyes off my traitor of a best friend and the jazz radio in my head is up to full blast, tuning them out.

"Scarlett Day?"

I tear my eyes away from Jaime toward the driver's seat to see one of the cops that was *just* in front of me.

"How the fuck did you get there so fast?"

The police officer frowns as if he's confused. "We're taking you to the hospital to get your knee checked out. If what your friend says is true about you being sober right now, they'll have you evaluated and might have you committed instead of going to a drunk tank."

I snort. Fucking idiots. They don't know a goddamn thing about being crazy. *I* grew up with crazy, until my mom finally did what was best for everyone and ran off. Good fucking riddance to her.

"I'm not crazy," I hiss back and twist toward the window to berate Jaime for getting me into this mess. Only he's already getting yelled at by someone I don't even know.

But, oh shit, would I like to get to...

The man is *gorgeous*, despite the fact that anger reddens his fair cheek. He's got inches on my over-six-foot-tall friend and I lick my lips because *fuck* is he the kind of man I'd love to pop my cherry. I'd make him take that stupid mask off the right side of his face though. Granted it's pretty hot, too. My mind keeps racing, imagining all of the positions I've watched on porn sites this week for the million times I tried to get off by myself.

But when he faces the police car as we drive off, the fury melts from the uncovered side of his face and everything hushes around me. My chest expands with much-needed air and my vision tunnels to focus solely on him. He mouths something I can't make out, but the way his lips form an *O* shape makes me do the same with mine. His dark, mesmerizing gaze has me relaxing against the seat until the SUV turns off of Toulouse Street, leaving him in the dust.

I keep trying to imagine his shadow in the tinted window, wondering about the stranger who made my mind quiet for the first time since my dad was murdered.

Overture

PRESENT DAY

When she laughs, I imagine shoving my cock down her throat, sparkling tears glistening down her gorgeous face until I come.

But when she sings... *fuck*, when she sings... now *that* is true ecstasy.

From my perch in the theater's box five, I can hear the gorgeous soprano perfectly as she flawlessly executes "Je veux vivre" from Charles Gounod's *Roméo et Juliette.* My eyes drift closed in pure relaxation as my pretty little muse hits every note.

It's the last night of this particular opera for the theater majors at the Bordeaux Conservatory of Music. They've been performing it at their home theater in the New French Opera House for weeks, but this is the first time my angel has been the lead. It's been a hard year for her, and she's practiced constantly in the privacy of her own room to be promoted from her under-study position.

Tonight, with the spotlight shining on her, Scarlett is proving to her sleaze of a director—and the rest of this auditorium—that she should've been the lead all along.

"Sol," my twin brother, Ben, urges quietly beside me, pulling me away from the show below and back to our meeting at hand.

His bone-white skull mask covers the right half of his face, just like mine. I can't see his black hair or warm-blue eyes in the darkness of our theater box, so I don't bother turning to him. Looking at Ben is like looking into the mirror of a future that never was. That reality has never been so flaunted in my face as it is right now, with the brother of the man who burned that future away sitting right in front of us.

Ten years ago, I had to murder Rand's brother to escape his clutches. I was only fifteen. Rand knows what his brother did was unforgivable. I'm shocked he has the balls to ask for this meeting after all these years, as if our families' histories haven't been irreparably stained by blood.

I sure as fuck can't get over it. Rage has been simmering in my veins ever since this meeting began, but the pathetic blond fool across from us is completely oblivious.

In his defense, he shouldn't expect unprovoked violence tonight. Not here. Although it will be fun fantasizing about hanging him from a curtain rope during intermission, it's not like I'll be able to act on it. The opera house is our side's neutral ground, so he has nothing to be worried about. Besides, my fucked-up fate isn't Rand Chatelain's fault, exactly. It's his family's.

Despite the fact that Rand is the last Chatelain and the heir to their fortune, he fled New Orleans after everything happened between our families. He's been going to school in New York and gallivanting across the world for the better part of a decade, running away from his responsibilities and leaving the care of his side of New Orleans with his dead father's second-in-command, Jacques Baron.

Or at least Baron *was* in charge. Definitely not anymore.

At the pleasing thought, I smirk behind my drink until I notice Rand smiling hopefully at me. His brilliant-white teeth glint in the New French Opera House's dim lighting and his blond hair gleams gold, like the innocent cherubs painted above the grand crystal chandelier in the center of the House's ceiling. It's annoying as fuck.

"She's pretty, isn't she?" Rand's stupid grin winks back at me while he acts like he's in on some inside joke. "The singer? Amazing voice."

"Pretty?" I ask as I swirl my Sazerac. Madam G's bartenders always keep me supplied during my meetings, but not even the heady cocktail can help me endure this idiot. "Pretty is an insult." The last word spits from my mouth before I can stop myself and I tip the rest of my drink back.

"Sol," Ben's gentle admonishment is barely enough to remind me of my position. But Rand's calculating look seals the deal. Especially when he leans forward like he's finally got something to bargain with.

"I have a proposition, but it'll be in exchange for building a Chatelain hotel in the French Quarter and unhindered access to Port NOLA, of course."

Before I can snap at him, Ben whispers back harshly. "We've told you, Rand. The ports and the French Quarter are ours. Port NOLA, aside, anything on the other side of the expressway is Chatelain land, like Central City, the Garden District—"

"You get all the pretty little flowers," I offer with a smug look that Rand frowns at.

Ben shakes his head and continues, "It's been that way for the past decade, thanks to your brother. Your family agreed to the truce—"

"No, my brother Laurent agreed to the truce," Rand corrects. "And then *he* killed him right after." He thrusts his thumb in my direction and I cheers my empty rocks glass.

"It was a pleasure, Chatelain."

That happiness I *know* is a facade slips as his eyes narrow at me. "You mother—"

"All within the bounds of the truce, I'll add," Ben interjects, obviously trying to silence us before I fuck up the meeting I don't give a shit about. "Do you want to dishonor your brother's name by violating his own truce? He was the one who wrote the clause that any attack on a family member may be repaid in equal blood."

"I'd say your brother got off easy," I grunt.

As if my body blames me for my fate, a phantom itch flares on the scarred skin of my right arm. But all my attention is focused on challenging Rand. I've struck a nerve, but he knows I'm untouchable right now. It's neither of our fault that his brother signed the truce while actively breaking it, earning his punishment. If Rand were to retaliate, he'd be dishonoring his dead brother's word. Not to mention that if Rand attacks me first then I can respond with equal blood. As per his brother's truce, of course.

My brother's disapproval is tangible. It's not that he trusts Rand. Ben just wants this meeting over and done with, no drama. But, it's the first time our families have spoken in a decade. It was bound to get uncomfortable.

Ben's never been one for the more unsavory details about what it takes to keep a city safe, thriving, and loyal. I'm used to this part. He shakes hands. I use fists. The wheeling and dealing is his forte, protecting our people by financial and legal means. I run security and rule with physicality and knowledge. My shadows work in tandem with Madam Gastoneaux from the speakeasy below. Together, we're unmatched at gathering secrets from all over the French Quarter and beyond. Blackmail works just as well as fists. Sometimes better.

"The Bordeauxs don't go west of the expressway," Ben reminds him. "Chatelains don't go east or to Port NOLA. The hotel in the French Quarter won't work because our people don't conduct business on opposite sides. Not without invitation and not unless there's harm by one side to the other."

I smirk. "And to think, I didn't even have to wait for an invite *or* leave the Garden District to get my justice since your fucking brother *kidnapped* me—"

"The point *is*," Ben jumps back in, "the truce was made to protect our own. Our mothers tried to smooth over our families' centuries-long feud by sending the three of us to the same boarding school, and that failed miserably. Laurent may be dead, but we all know that Sol is living proof that our families are *even* now."

The right side of my face burns underneath my mask and Rand winces, although for his loss or mine, I'm not sure. Just because we were friends as kids—before I was used as a bargaining chip—doesn't mean those loyalties survived the death of his own brother, no matter how much of a monster the elder Chatelain was.

Rand sighs contritely and I go back to trying to tune him out to listen to the aria. But his voice has a nasally quality that's hard for me to ignore.

"I know. I've been out of the loop for ten years, but we weren't *always* rivals. I thought I'd at least offer to introduce her to you, if you're interested."

"How the fuck do you know Scarlett Day?" The question growls out of me before I know I'm speaking.

Rand's lips curve into a proud smile. "Didn't you know? Lettie and I go way back. I guess you could say we're childhood sweethearts."

Every word he utters makes my grip tighten around the empty drink in my hand. As I think about how to respond, I relax my fingers, one by one. If I break another piece of antique glassware, Madam G will skin me alive and cook me, and I won't even have a dead Chatelain to show for it this time.

"How?" I finally reply, my mind still unable to work around the news. "The three of us are all a few years older and studied in France while Scarlett's family is originally from Appalachia."

Rand's brow rises and I can feel Ben stiffening beside me. I've overplayed my hand.

"Know a lot about *my* Lettie, do you?" The urge to smash my glass in his satisfied face is strong, but I wait impatiently for his explanation. "Scarlett's dad was a traveling musician. She went with him everywhere, including when he played his summer tours in the French Quarter. I'm surprised she even has money to pay for this school. You Bordeauxs aren't cheap."

"We host many scholarships here at Bordeaux," Ben offers to my disapproval. "Miss Day won a scholarship after her father passed away."

"That's right, he was murdered. Poor Scarlett." Concern crumples his face as he glances briefly to her again, but I won't let him get off that easy.

"He was murdered in the *Garden District*," I answer, my left brow raised. But Rand doesn't seem to notice my accusatory tone. "*Your* district."

"It's awful. My father and brother took a liking to him when they saw him play, you know, *before* they would've been relegated to west of the expressway. I met her at one of his shows one summer, and then we were inseparable until I had to leave for school. It's too bad they aren't around to see her." He gives me a pointed look before wistfully watching Scarlett on stage. "They would've loved to see Little Lettie thrive. She deserves it, too."

When Rand twists in his velvet armchair to see us both again, Ben's eyes flicker to me through his mask. He steeples his fingers and moves on.

"This feud has taken many from both of our families. It's why our truce is so imperative. And why we have to say no to the Chatelain hotel in the French Quarter. Aside from the steep history your buildings would destroy, our families are better off doing business on separate sides of the city. As we agreed."

Rand's thin lips press into a straight line and he returns his gaze toward the stage. A look akin to the hunger I feel inside shows in the tension around his eyes. I stare daggers at the side of his head. If he knew what was hanging in the vaults below the stage, it'd wipe that dazzled look right off of his face. Scarlett Day is mine. One of his own men had to learn that the hard way.

Rand shifts back to us and studies the inside of box five. "I've always thought it curious that your family holds meetings here. But I must say, with a show like Miss Day, I can see why you'd want to set the opera house as your neutral ground."

And because I never leave it.

My family has called the New French Opera House their home since we bought the charred land of its prior namesake in 1920. The original burned down to nearly ashes, and when the original owners couldn't recover with insurance, the lot went vacant. My great-grandmother was distraught over the demise of the original French Opera House and Bordeaux men can never say no to their wives. Ben is the perfect example with his wife, Maggie, Madam G's daughter.

But, not only did my great-grandfather want to please his wife, he saw a golden opportunity with Prohibition going into effect. He bought the old French Opera House's plot of land and rebuilt a near replica with better safety measures. They sold the old Bordeaux mansion in the Garden District, and Jeremiah Bordeaux made the *New* French Opera House a conservatory for art students so my great-grandmother could teach and live out her passion full time. He even designed dorms for the students and a family wing that Ben and Maggie live in now.

But beneath, he utilized the French Quarter's slightly higher elevation to his advantage and engineered a flood-proof maze of cellars and tunnels to use during Prohibition. He ran his illegal distillery through the speakeasy, Masque, built below. Madam G's ancestors struck a deal with him and they've owned and run it ever since. The masquerade theme set in place then protected patrons from potential prosecution if they were ever caught—which, they never were. Now, it protects me.

As soon as I was released from the burn unit of the hospital as a teenager, I left the family wing upstairs and repurposed the cellars and tunnels for my own home. My only haunts now are the cellars, the tunnels, the opera house, and Masque. I never go anywhere without a mask, so this is my home. It's where I'm most comfortable and where my shame isn't on display for the world.

It's why I've been able to hear Scarlett's sweet voice day and night. My angel of music works hard at her craft. She's inspired me, a veritable demon in my own right, more these last few weeks than any other voice or composer I've studied over the years. Gounod, himself, would kill to hear her sing his songs right now. I know I have.

The last few notes of the aria reverberate throughout the auditorium and my fingers itch to join the roaring applause. Thanks to the spotlight, my poor eyesight can still make out the golden-red sheen in each wild black curl. Her ivory skin glistens under the hot beams, and the look of wonder on her face is fucking breathtaking.

After countless rehearsals and vocal drills, I knew she'd bring down the house. I want to cheer for her, but showing any sign of weakness in front of a Chatelain will only paint a target on her back. I've done that too much already.

Giving a Chatelain—*any* Chatelain—the upper hand can mean a death sentence. I won't allow Scarlett to be caught in the middle of our minefield.

That doesn't stop Rand though.

"Bravo! Bravo!" He leaps to his feet and leans over the golden railing, clapping and calling for her with the same fervor I wish I could. Her gaze lifts toward my theater box, and her silver eyes sparkle in the spotlight. The cavernous hole in my chest begins to beat with life as she gazes up and her smile widens.

Does she see it's me? Does she know I'm here for her?

I've always hidden within the shadows, but the thought that my muse has finally *seen* me has me moving to stand. But Rand begins to wave like a fucking maniac and realization sinks in.

It's him. She only sees him. Her *childhood sweetheart*. I've remained in the darkness, behind my mask for far too long.

Ben and I require that those we do business with show their faces, while our men—my shadows—wear masks, ensuring anonymity for those who work for the Bordeauxs. Not only does it protect our men and their families, it also prevents insurrection. And while it's always been a policy I've benefited from, I'm regretting it now.

The way Scarlett smiles at Rand leadens my stomach. No doubt he's soaking in the way she's looking at him and understands the way it affects me because he glances back at me with a satisfied smile. The opera house is meant to be a safe zone, free of violence. Today though, jealousy has me fantasizing about throwing the smug piece of shit over the railing.

"I think she recognizes me!" he calls triumphantly.

I'm silent, but Ben replies quietly as the crowd dies down and the stage lights go out. "Seems like it."

"Yeah?" Rand nods with excitement. "I should go to her, right? Say hi?"

"*No*," I growl. My right hand clenches into a fist and my tungsten skull ring warms as I imagine bloodying Rand's pretty face.

"What I *think* Sol is trying to say is that there is still the rest of the performance. Not to mention, we're not finished here," Ben points out, desperately trying to keep us on task.

"And the truce," I add. "She's *mine*."

I feel Ben stiffen beside me and I don't blame him. Even I can hear the obsession in my voice. It's dangerous.

"He's right, she's off-limits," Ben cuts in with a lie. "She lives in the Quarter under our protection."

Rand shakes his head and hushes his voice as the opera continues. "I may have been gone a while but I remember the parameters of the truce well. Living in the French Quarter alone doesn't make her *yours* explicitly. I see no branding or amulets to signify her allegiance. The truce is only to make sure no crimes occur by one of ours on the wrong side of the line, or against someone you specifically protect. I'm not going to hurt her. I've always cared for Scarlett and I haven't seen her in over a decade. I just want to say hi, maybe take her out for a drink. You can't keep her from me, Bordeaux. I'm not one of your *shadows*." He spits out the word like a curse.

"At least my shadows know who leads them," I counter.

"That's a fucking low blow," Rand steps forward as I slowly stand from my seat, my six-foot-four frame towering over him. To his credit, Rand tries his best to meet my eyes before Ben steps between us.

"You're making a scene," Ben hisses. "And there's already one that people have *paid* to see. Let's not ruin the show." He turns to the open doorway. "Sabine?"

Our second-in-command, a tall brunette with light-brown skin and a curvy athletic build, appears from the shadows. Her mask is one of my favorites, a horned demon's face wreathed in flames covers the top half of her face, revealing only her charcoal eyes. Her hand is ready at the dagger that never leaves her side.

Sabine is good. Fucking great even. No one else in the box can see how ready she is to end Rand before his next breath. In a bright room, even I'd struggle with that knife-wielding vixen. But when the lights are out, no one is my equal.

"Need me to take out the Chatelain trash?" Sabine asks casually.

"Trash?" Rand hisses. "You didn't think my *brother* was trash."

A barely perceptible sneer curves her lips as she carefully avoids my gaze. It's the most emotion she ever shows. "That was before Laurent showed his true colors. As far as I'm concerned, Chatelains should get dumped in the Mississippi River with cement shoes, like the good ol' days."

Rand's face pinches in disgust. "I don't know what he ever saw in you."

"An easy target. But now, I'm a threat. So what do you need?" she defers to Ben, the Bordeaux moral compass. If she asked me, we'd end up gleefully throwing Rand over the railing together.

"Escort him back to his seat in the audience. We're done here."

"With pleasure. Come with me, Randy Boy."

"Shut up," Rand grumbles, but follows her out as he straightens his lapels and cuts a haughty glance toward me. "I've got a soprano to see anyway. Oh, and, since she is technically unaffiliated, I'm declaring her. Consider her a Chatelain. Who knows, maybe she will be one day."

I'm halfway out of my seat when Sabine closes the door behind her. Ben's insistent grip on my forearm is the only thing that stops me from stalking after them. My body vibrates, anxious to strangle another Chatelain and remove his pompous ass from this world.

It's not a new feeling by any means, but I haven't been face to face with a Chatelain since I was fifteen, and this time there's a different drive pulsing in my veins. Instead of the steady drumbeat of revenge, something else clashes like a cymbal with the percussive beat I'm used to.

Fear.

My skin crawls. A Chatelain getting inside my head is unacceptable.

"Not worth it, brother. You've already given him one message down in the cellars with that bastard Jacques." I glance to my twin, a dim glow lights his face from his phone. "I'm texting Maggie. Chatelain might want to get backstage. I want her to be prepared."

I nod once. Our operation thrives on hiding in plain sight, but we never involve innocents. Many of the stagehands are on our payroll since the New French Opera House and speakeasy below are neutral ground. We've made a vow to never start anything on the grounds, but we'll sure as fuck finish it.

Every muscle in my body rebels as I calmly take my seat, deciding to listen to my brother. Ben settles in beside me, and I try to watch the rest of Scarlett's performance, despite the anxiety welling inside me.

"Do you really think he'll go backstage?" I ask when the feeling makes it hard to breathe.

"You can't have her, Sol."

I flick my eyes in Ben's direction before dismissing him. "I don't know what you're talking about."

"Scarlett Day. A woman like Scarlett loves the light. The *spotlight* to be exact. You'll have to stop capitalizing on all the rumors and emerge from those shadows you cling to."

"Relax, brother. I just don't want an innocent in the firing line. I'll stick with the eager-to-please tourists you bring me." The lie burns on its way up, turning my tongue to ash and forcing me to swallow. "She's nothing."

"I've never seen you so agitated over *nothing* before," Ben scoffs. "And I can't remember the last time you even looked at another woman, let alone spent time with one of the tourists that's begged for your attention. But the fact of the matter is, if Scarlett Day is affiliated with the Chatelains, she's off-limits. It's safer that way."

In her white-as-snow gown, Scarlett is luminescent as she sings alongside her costar and best friend, Jaime Dominguez. Knowing she has someone I can trust to protect her when I'm not around gives me peace that's never come easily. But I'll be there if Chatelain visits her. And if he doesn't, then I'll have her all to myself. My cock twitches behind my zipper at the prospect.

"She's. Off. *Limits*," my twin mutters more insistently.

The left side of my lips lifts up with my arrogance. "We'll see about that."

I feel Ben's eyes on me, studying me, like he doesn't already know everything I'm thinking. Finally, he answers with a sigh. "I'm sure she'll be at the after-party at Masque. Chatelain will likely attend just to fuck with you. I guess you'll have to come out of the shadows, after all."

A scowl pinches my face, drawing the skin on the right side tight. I fucking hate crowds. Scarlett doesn't go out like I know she used to, instead staying in to study or practice in her free time. But I'll be damned if she goes and I'm not there. "I have something urgent that needs my immediate attention once the show ends. Perhaps I'll meet you down there after."

I'm not surprised by the knowing, raised eyebrow on what used to be my mirror image.

"Something... or some*one*?"

I don't bother with a response. As usual, my brother already knows the answer.

Act I

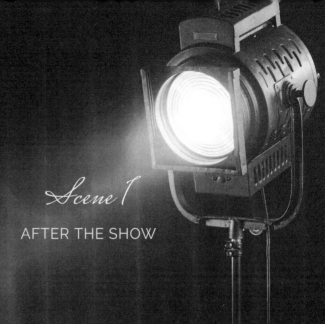

Scene 1

AFTER THE SHOW

My heart races as the crowd cheers. It's a rush that I could never describe, even though I've been dying to feel it for years. I should be exhausted after the way I've been rushing around, getting ready for the show, but energy vibrates through my veins. My nerves have been working in overdrive ever since Jilliana called out sick at the last minute, leaving the lead role for her understudy.

Me.

I bow again with my fellow castmates, reveling that I've finally achieved the dream my father worked so hard to get for me.

"It's going to be you in the center of that spotlight, Lettie, bowing to your adoring masses."

And I am.

It's exciting and thrilling and feels like I've accomplished everything he wanted.

But still... it's everything *he* wanted. I thought it would be everything I wanted too, but it's not enough. I haven't figured out that missing piece, but when I do, holy shit it's going to feel like heaven. Which is slightly terrifying considering the way I feel now.

Definitely can't forget to take my meds tonight.

My best friend squeezes my left hand. Jaime's gorgeous smile blazes on his bronze face and his dark-brown eyes sparkle in the spotlight.

"Soak it in, Scarlo. You've earned it." His voice carries over the cheers and my smile widens on my already aching cheeks. All at once we bow one final time before rushing backstage.

As soon as we get past the open curtains, Jaime and I wade through the cheering and celebrating cast to sneak to my nearby dorm which doubles as my dressing room. Once I'm inside the door, I immediately look toward my makeup desk, only to find empty space on the corner. I barely have time to hide my frown before Jaime shakes me by the shoulders playfully.

"Scarlo, baby doll, you nailed it tonight. I've been listening to you practice for months but where did *that* come from? We have the same vocal coaches, and they never taught *me* to sing like that!"

"I don't know." I chuckle, a little uncomfortable with all the praise. "Just all the practicing paid off, apparently."

If he knew the truth he'd totally freak out. It was just me and my dad my whole life, so Jaime is the brother I've always wanted. He hasn't just protected me from the world's dangers, he's protected me from myself, too. Ever since I had my first full-blown manic episode last year, he's made sure I'm taking care of myself. If he found out that I was practicing with a voice and music *inside* my head, he'd lock me right back up in the loony bin. And that can't freaking happen.

"Well, whatever you're doing, keep doing it, *cher*." His unique mix of Latino and Louisiana accents is always strong when he's excited or has been drinking. Honestly, right now, it could be both, since he likes to take a shot or two of tequila before a show.

As excited as I am about my debut at the New French Opera House, I still can't shake my nerves so I go to my makeup desk and begin to search through my drawers.

"Shit, are you feeling up?"

Jaime knows me so well, it's scary. I shake my head slightly at his question of whether I'm feeling like I could be on my way "up" to a manic episode.

"No... I think? I slept fine last night but these nerves are going to keep me up. It might be the start of something if I don't get them under control. Nothing to worry about yet, though."

I place my plastic pill organizer on the counter before popping one of the as-needed anxiety meds I'm prescribed to slow down my racing heart at times like this. I take a long swig from my water bottle on my desk to wash it down.

"Proud of you, Scarlo."

My eyebrow rises. "For what?"

"Taking care of yourself. Rocking the stage tonight. Take your pick, babe. You're gonna be better than your dad ever could've dreamed."

Jaime didn't know my father. We only met after my dad died and I was deep in a depressive stage. He bulldozed his way right past my defenses and now that my dad is gone, Jaime has been my personal motivational coach and my voice of reason.

But now there's one other voice I desperately wish I could hear from. It never appears when others are around, so I'll have to be patient. And I'll *definitely* have to make sure no one finds out I'm hearing shit again. It's been months of hearing the voice and music and I've had no other trouble. Maybe auditory hallucinations aren't so bad so long as everything else is under control?

A throat clears from the open doorway and I shift to find a man I haven't seen in *years*.

"Oh my god, *Rand*? I thought that was you up there!"

"Scarlett, it's so good to see you."

My friend from childhood throws his arms around me. I fight the urge to stiffen at the all-but-forgotten touch and force myself to hug him back, water bottle and all. He squeezes me close and the scent of gardenias itches my nose, reminding me of the pungent gardens where he grew up. I pull away to evade the smell but grin at him.

"What are you doing here? It's been, what? Ten years?"

"Yup..." He chuckles warmly. "Ten whole years. It's been way too long."

"Yeah, jeez. That's forever." I step back and take a moment to drink him in while he seems to do the same.

His thick blond hair is gelled back and as tidy as ever, going well with his perfectly tailored suit. Those handsome boyish looks I had a crush on when I was twelve have aged well into preppy male model features. He's freaking gorgeous. When his hand rests on my lower back, my nerves skyrocket.

"I saw your performance and wanted to come tell you how stunning you were out there. But I didn't realize you'd be..." His clear-blue eyes flick to Jaime before resting back on me. "Preoccupied."

"Jaime? Oh, god no. He'd be more interested in you than me." I laugh and turn to Jaime for confirmation, but my friend has a frown on his face and his arms crossed.

"Who are you, again?" Jaime asks abruptly, making my eyes widen.

"Sorry, I got caught up in the moment." I point my water bottle between my past best friend and my current one.

"Jaime, this is my friend, Rand. Rand, meet Jaime."

Jaime bows with a flourish that stretches the long white sleeve of his ruffled poet shirt, revealing his leather skull bracelet he stubbornly refuses to take off, even during a performance.

"Jaime Dominguez, a.k.a. her best friend. And from the way you're looking at me, I guess I should clarify that I'm her *gay* best friend. No need to go pissing on her."

"Rand Chatelain," he replies and winks at me. "And there's no need to mark my territory. Scarlett knows where we stand. She and I go way back. My family helped support her father's music career down here." He tugs me in for another hug and I sink into it this time, much more prepared than the last. "And, oh, Little Lettie, how I've missed you."

My dad's endearment rolls into me like a freight train. This whole night has been a cluster of emotions and a damn tear wells in my eye. Ugh, what an emotional mess. So embarrassing.

"I've missed you, too," I automatically answer before extricating myself from his hold and trying to get a grip. My heart still hasn't calmed down and seeing my childhood crush has it going off the charts.

"So you're a Chatelain?" Jaime asks, his voice nearly a monotone. "What *are* you doing here?"

"Um, Jaime, he's *from* New Orleans," I whisper harshly. "He has every right to be here."

"Not on this side," Jaime adds cryptically.

"*Jaims*, what does that even mean?" I chuckle and narrow my eyes at him to cut the attitude. But his expression is guarded and strained, and his gaze is solely on Rand.

Thankfully, Rand doesn't seem fazed by my friend's sudden rudeness, instead observing the room with that piercing gaze of his.

When we used to sit and people-watch during the day on Bourbon Street growing up, I thought Rand's clear eyes made him practically omniscient. He seemed to know everything about everyone, even the tourists. As he studies my dorm room now, I wonder what he's thinking.

There's the small living room, my makeup-slash-study desk corner, and a kitchenette. In the other room is a simple bedroom and an adjacent bathroom. It's not much, but it's more than living out of a suitcase and after traveling with my dad all my life, that's all I need. Still, that old girlish habit of trying to impress him rears its ugly head.

"Sorry, Rand, I don't know what's gotten into him. The guy just needs a good tequila shot after a show. He's a shadow of his normal self when he's already given everything to the stage."

"A shadow of his normal self, huh?" Rand really focuses on Jaime for the first time and glances at him up and down. "The New French Opera House is neutral," he states without further explanation, confusing the hell out of me, but Jaime seems to understand as his eyes narrow slightly. It's like they're speaking in some kind of strange boy code.

"Okay... well, to be fair, you *do* hate opera. Or at least you used to." I elbow Rand in the ribs and he rubs his side playfully.

"I don't *hate* opera. Your warbling as a kid wasn't ideal, but tonight? Fuck Lettie, you were a vision."

His eyes rove over my white lace dress and I shift on my feet from the intensity of his gaze. I can't stop my nervous smile as I silently wish my anxiety medication would freaking kick in already.

"Thank you. I've been practicing a little bit since my warbling days."

Rand laughs heartily and the tension breaks in the room. Sort of. At least until he walks toward my desk. When he picks up my pill organizer and shakes it, the air in my chest freezes.

"Are you sick? I saw you taking medication."

"Wow. So not your business." Jaime tsks.

A blush heats my cheeks. I totally agree, but I answer anyway, "Oh, yeah, I'm fine. It's nothing. Just a little anxiety."

He shakes my pill organizer for emphasis again. "That's a lot of drugs for just anxiety—"

"*No joda*, Chatelain—"

"It's okay!" I interrupt before my old best friend and my new one are at each other's throats for no reason again.

These types of conversations make me want to crawl in a hole and hide, but I've promised myself that I would normalize it. The cast knows. The whole school practically knows. Why not my childhood friend?

"The medicine is because... I have bipolar disorder. Type one, to be exact." I shrug my shoulders and resist the urge to curl the rest of the way into a ball.

Rand's jaw goes slack and his tan cheeks redden as he sets the pill organizer down. "Oh, shit. I'm... Scarlett, I'm sorry. I didn't–"

I wave away his apology. "No big deal. Or at least I'm trying to make it not a big deal. It's just like any other illness. If I don't take my meds, symptoms can flare back up. The only difference is that sometimes my symptoms mean I can go a little cray." I smirk at my friend who's seen it all. "Jaime knows."

"Yeah, no need to get a suite at Château Psych anytime soon."

Rand shifts uncomfortably at our jokes. His blond brows have nearly shot up to his hairline, but I can tell he's trying his best to be nonchalant as he not so casually wraps his arm around my waist. A shudder races up my spine like a cold chill. "Sounds like you've got a lot to tell me, Little Lettie. What do you say we catch up over drinks?"

While I practically worshiped him as a kid, that abruptly ended right before he went back to boarding school. We've both grown up now, though, and things are way different than they were back then. Our age difference doesn't matter anymore, for one. Honestly, he's a catch, and I should be ecstatic over all the attention he's paying me right now. But ever since Dad died—and everything that happened after—it's been hard to get excited or even be around people at all.

That's why I like the voice.

I shake the thought from my mind, remembering that I'm supposed to be answering the very *real* people right in front of me.

Before I can open my mouth, a crash from the hallway makes me jump from Rand's grasp.

"Shoot. Sorry about that." A chuckle echoes from the hallway. I recognize Maggie Bordeaux's soft pitch instantly. She's a constant presence at Bordeaux Conservatory of Music and while she may be the theater school's assistant director, she might as well be promoted at this point, since the real one, Monty Arquette, doesn't know what the hell he's doing. "Sorry, y'all. I dropped my walkie-talkie—*Oh.*"

Maggie stops midsentence and digs into her back jeans pocket for her phone.

"You're Rand Chatelain. What're you doing in the French Quarter?"

"That's what I said," Jaime grumbles.

"Why does everyone keep asking that?" I try to laugh to defuse the situation but it comes out flat as Maggie and Rand eye one another.

She breaks her gaze first, glaring down at the phone in her hand. Her cloud of tight, springy corkscrew curls tries to fall into her eyes, but she pushes them back. In the dim hallway light, her screen glows against her dark-brown cheeks as she grimaces and mutters, "Guess that answers my question. I should've been more worried about my texts than my walkie-talkie."

A cocky smile I've never seen on Rand before flashes across his face. "Let me guess, your husband texted you? Go ahead and tell him that Scarlett was just about to say yes to drinks tonight. Weren't you, Lettie?"

Alarm flares in Jaime's eyes. "But what about the after-party?"

"After-party? Where?" Rand asks. "That could be fun. I don't care where we go. I just want to catch up—"

"Cast members only," Jaime interjects and it's on the tip of my tongue to argue with him, but I catch a glimpse of something white on my makeup table.

Excitement spikes through me again and now all I want to do is shoo everyone out of here so I can be alone. I look away quickly to not garner suspicion and I catch Rand's pout. His disappointment subdues my excitement into guilt.

I was about to blow him off when I haven't seen him in years and he's gone out of his way to reconnect. It really would be good to catch up. I've shunned so much of my past to protect myself from my own emotions. Maybe it's time to open up again.

"It's in Madam G's speakeasy, Masque," I offer. "You should come."

The warmth in his eyes and the gentle pressure on my hip where his hand squeezes me tells me I've done the right thing. But my focus isn't on him anymore as I try my best to keep my eyes off my makeup desk.

"I'd love to, Lettie."

My own grin wavers, and I extricate myself from his hold. The nickname feels too soon to hear again, but I'll do my best to take it one step at a time.

"Great! I'll just, um, I'll meet you down there, if that's okay? I need to freshen up a little and get out of these clothes."

"Freshen up if you want," Jaime cuts in. "But you look fabulous and the rest of us are wearing our costumes with our masks since it's closing night. Come on Rand, let's give the lady some space. Mags and I will escort you down there."

I can feel the air around Rand thicken. "I don't need an escort."

"Of course you don't. But we know the password and I'm *sure* you don't since it's a cast secret."

Rand turns to me with a small frown. "Are you sure? I can wait so I can walk you there."

"Trust me," Jaime answers for me. "She's safe here."

"I'm good, I promise. I'll see you guys down there. Ten minutes, tops."

Rand searches my face until Jaime lands a loud clap against his shoulder, making him wince.

"Come on, Rand. Let's give the poor girl some space. It's not like she'll get lured away by the Phantom of the French Quarter."

I roll my eyes as Jaime wags his brows and Maggie turns the sterling silver skull hanging from her necklace.

"You New Orleanians and your superstitions. There's no *ghost*. This place isn't haunted, it's heaven. There are no ghosts in Heaven, just angels."

"You always did believe in angels and demons." Rand's smile is genuine and warm with nostalgia.

My dad used to sing me stories for hours, playing them on his keyboard or guitar to a jazz riff he'd been working on with whatever band he played with at the time. His favorite was about how he'd sold his soul to a devil and that he'd been stalked by demonic shadows ever since.

Selling your soul for talent isn't a *new* idea, obviously, but at seven years old, I took my dad's word as gospel. He made the devil, demons, and angels sound like muses in their own right. I asked him about when I'd get my own once. He'd laughed and kissed my head, saying I was too good for a demon, but someday, if I practiced hard enough, I'd get my own angel. I used to even believe him.

But the day he died taught me something very important. With the hatred I felt that night and the wild emotions I experienced afterward, there's no way I'd get an angel. An angel wouldn't want anything to do with me.

A demon, however...

"Well if you're sure you're okay to stay, I guess I'll go." Rand's voice trails like he's expecting me to change my mind, but the fact that he's still questioning me grates on my nerves.

"I'm a big girl now, Rand." I smile and wink as I step back, trying to hide why I want everyone to leave. "So shoo! I'll see you in a second."

Thankfully, Jaime pulls him away before he can protest anymore and starts down the hallway. Maggie grabs the handle to my dressing room door.

"My daughter, Marie, has a babysitter tonight, so I'll head out earlier than everyone, but hopefully I'll see you down there in time."

"You will. I'll be there before you know it."

She nods and steps out, shutting the door behind her. As soon as the door is closed, I whip around to face the prize on my makeup table.

Scene 2

THE LETTER

Anticipation bubbles up as I see the envelope, cream and pristine. My fingers carefully brush over the white rose lying beside it, a bloodred ribbon delicately tied around the thornless stem. Lifting the flower to my nose, I soak in the scent, loving the subtle earthy smell, like it'd been freshly picked from the sender's garden.

Letters just like this one have appeared in my room sporadically for months, always right here on the corner of my makeup desk. I have no idea who they're from, or how they get here. That's obviously a red flag, and the first time I received a random mysterious envelope, I should've reported it. But they'd started showing up when I was at my lowest, and I didn't want to question one of the few things that got me out of bed at the time. Now, I hate it when days go by without one. I wasn't sure if a letter would arrive tonight, but with this being my first performance as a leading role, I'd hoped. Thank god that hope wasn't in vain.

I lay the flower gently back down beside the envelope before picking it up next. Like always, written in near-perfect cursive on the front is "*Ma belle muse.*" The first time I received a letter almost a year ago, I did a quick internet search to verify the translation.

My beautiful muse.

A staccato beat pulses in my chest as I open the envelope, careful not to destroy the bloodred wax skull sealing it shut. Once it's opened, I reach inside for the first of two letters I know are there.

Ma muse,

You were magnificent tonight. Congratulations on your debut. The spotlight is dim compared to your radiance. I envy the light that touches you. It makes me question remaining in the dark.

Tu me verras bientôt,

Ton démon de la musique

"My muse... Your demon of music."

I whisper it aloud, wondering if my demon is somewhere listening as I say the parts I know in English and butcher the French sign-off. My French diction and language courses taught me enough to read, speak conversationally, and sing, but I have no confidence in my knowledge. I always double-check myself when I read something new.

I hold the letter to my chest and my demon's leather and whiskey scent drifts up to my nostrils, settling me. Even though I *know* no one is here, I swear I can *feel* the heated gaze I imagine he possesses. Or that he would possess... if he were real. Looking around, there's nothing to convince me I'm not going crazy, only my cluttered and slightly messy dressing room.

I sigh and reverently store the letter with all the others in the bottom drawer of my musical jewelry box before extracting the second letter from the envelope. Sheet music.

The pretty words of the first letters are lovely, but his *music* is divine. Every envelope contains thick cream paper with hand-written songs that I rarely hear, or I've never heard before. The ones I'm unfamiliar with are always in the perfect pitch for me to sing, almost like my demon of music wrote them specifically for me. Sometimes, I even hear piano music and his deep bass drifting into my room. Or... at least I think I do.

This music is all I have of him. If it weren't for the letters, I'd worry I was making the whole thing up.

The fact that *he* calls himself a demon in his notes should obviously scare me. But it's what I called him out loud when I read the first letter that had no signature. All I could think of then was the angels and demons my dad sang about. My demon must have heard me because the next letter that came had the name he uses now. It should freak me out, and it's crazy—maybe literally —but my brain can't shake the idea that whoever my mystery pen pal is, he's good. Or at least he's good for *me*. Sometimes that's all that matters.

I begin to hum the notes to myself before retrieving my journal from my bedside table. My nose scrunches as I concentrate to remember what lyrics I've scribbled down that will fit the beat. As soon as I get to the page I'm thinking of, I see the corner has already been folded.

"That's weird," I murmur. Bending pages is a no-no for me— bookmarks all the way, even in my music books. But sometimes I write in a sleepy daze in the middle of the night so maybe I did it then?

That feeling of being not quite alone has only heightened, and I scan the room. It's not an uncomfortable feeling, necessarily. If anything, I'd say it's almost like a guardian angel is watching over me. There's just my nightstand, the bathroom's open door, and my full-length mirror beside the foot of my bed. Nothing out of the ordinary.

Maybe my demon of music is watching over me.

Shaking my head with a chuckle, I do another once-over of my lyrics and mentally combine them with the musical notes from the letter. A rush, unique and different from anything I experience when I'm acting, courses through me. I've always wanted to sing my own songs like my dad used to. But I've never had the courage.

Going solo means the entire show is based on me. No under-study, no one to rely on if I mess up. What if I have a manic or depressive episode and can't perform? Fear, doubt, and uncertainty have held me back, but writing my lyrics brings me joy like no other.

I sing the words while sight-reading the sheet music. Before long, I'm swept along with the gentle swells and descents of the melody, until a buzzing noise sparks me from my focus.

Whipping my head around, it takes me a second to realize it's my phone buzzing on my makeup counter in the other room. As soon as I answer, Jaime yells into my ear over the background music.

"Scarlett! What the hell? Where are you, babe?"

My eyes dart to the clock on the wall. I've been lost in the music for over an hour.

"Shit. I'm sorry Jaims, I'll be there in a few."

"Good. This puppy dog of yours is getting on my last nerve. If he makes one more rude comment to a waitress, I will kick him."

I snort. "You can't kick puppies, Jaims. Everyone knows that."

"I think the world would make an exception for this one," Jaime grumbles.

I toss my journal back on my bed. "Don't worry. I'll be down in a sec."

"Good." Jaime hangs up without another word. The man never says "bye" like a normal person.

I tuck my phone in the pocket the goddess of a seamstress sewed into the white Juliet dress. After touching up my makeup, I'm ready to go, but something in my full-length mirror catches my eye. The frame looks as if it's been broken apart at the seam, so I pop it back in.

"Gonna need to get that replaced," I mutter to tell myself as I grab my white lace masquerade mask.

My eyes catch the white rose on my makeup counter and before I can stop myself, I take some scissors from one of my drawers and cut the long stem. As I work one of my sewing pins through the thick fabric of my dress, I poke my finger.

"*Shit.*" Blood wells up and I pop my finger into my mouth to soak it up before it gets on my dress. Thankfully, I'd already gotten it mostly attached before I pricked myself, and I'm able to get the rose the rest of the way on one-handed. I check the mirror one more time before I leave and curse.

The rose has a barely noticeable smear of blood from when I pricked myself. The garnet speckles are the only color I'm wearing and totally stand out, but it still looks pretty so I keep the flower on. Other than the blood, the white petals nearly blend in with my white dress, but I don't care. If I can't work on the lyrics to my demon's music like I want to, at least I can wear the rose he gave me.

Stopping by the doorway, I gaze wistfully through my bedroom door at the sheet music tucked into my journal lying on my bed. I'd *love* to stay in and just work on the new piece my phantom pen pal sent me, but I promised Jaime I'd go to the after-party this time.

My pocket buzzes and I know he's calling me again. He's practically the only one who ever does. So with one last peek at my journal, I resolve to work on it later and close the door, not bothering to lock it. Bordeaux Conservatory of Music is one of the safest places in the French Quarter, if not *the* safest.

As I walk the dim halls to Masque, I use an internet search to translate the sign-off of the letter, "*tu me verras bientôt.*" It's a new one he's never signed off with before and it has me curious.

But when the words appear, I stop in my tracks. Staring at the bright screen, my heart rises to my throat as alarm bells desperately try—and fail—to override the hope and thrill flooding through my veins.

"*You'll see me soon.*"

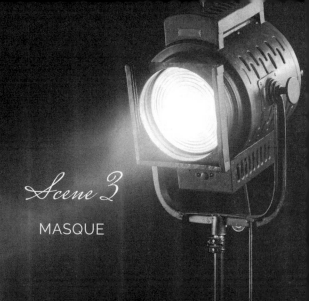

Scene 3

MASQUE

With the crowd inside Masque, it's hard to imagine there's anyone left on Bourbon Street. Thankfully, Jaime has already secured us a table near the rest of the cast. As soon as I walk in, he leaps up from his chair beside Rand and waves wildly, confirming any question I may have had as to whether he's been drinking yet.

"Scarlo! Over here!" Jazz and blues versions of current popular songs blare from the speakers, but I can still hear Jaime over it all.

The dimly lit room is a maze of eclectic furniture surrounding a dance floor and a currently empty stage. Small lamps glow at each table, showing off the patrons sitting in their velvet mismatched couches and chairs. Once I get to our section, Rand pulls out a seat next to his, but Jaime tugs my arm to sit beside him against the velvet booth across from Rand.

I barely hide my giggle when the lamp illuminates Rand's face. The poor guy sports a sour look, made all the more ridiculous by the red-and-yellow jester mask covering the top half of his face. I have no doubt Jaime loaned it to him, especially since Jaime, in his stunning gold feather masquerade mask, looks quite pleased with himself.

He turns slightly unfocused eyes to me and points at the flower pinned to my chest. "Pretty. From a fan?"

"Yup." I nod quickly, thankful for the out as I pivot the conversation. "Sorry I'm late, guys. What did I miss?"

"I was just showing your dear childhood friend this skull bracelet I got in the French Quarter." Jaime admires his leather bracelet with its metal skull totem attached. "Don't you like it, Rand?"

"He *loves* that thing," I whisper-yell to Rand over the music, pretending like he and I are conspiring in order to lighten whatever mood the two boys have gotten themselves into. "He even keeps it on during performances."

"Yup. I'm loyal to the Quarter. Just remember that." Jaime gives him a broad Cheshire smile, and I can't help but feel lost.

"Am I missing something?" My nerves huff out in a chuckle. "Are we still talking about bracelets?"

"Yup. Skull bracelets and the French Quarter." He pokes my ribs and I squirm away. "*Outsiders* wouldn't understand."

"Hey! No fair. Just because I didn't grow up here full time, doesn't mean I'm an *outsider*. My dad would argue with you on that one."

"Speaking of your dad." Rand points his thumb toward a speaker. "A die-hard jazz and blues fan like him would've had a fit if he heard these covers, am I right?"

I listen to the "Billie Jean" cover by The Civil Wars for a few bars, barely resisting the urge to belt it out before shaking my head with a nostalgic grin.

"No way! He was a sucker for blues and jazz versions of popular songs. According to him, every good song has the same heart. He would've loved it here." The sultry vibe in the speakeasy makes me sway in my seat and all I want to do is climb on that empty stage and take over the mic. "God, *I* love it here. I know that much. I've been at Bordeaux Conservatory for four years now and I don't come down here nearly enough. It makes me want to stay forever."

"Stay? Here? In New Orleans?" Rand asks, surprise in his voice.

I shrug. "I've been thinking about it. I'm, um... not sure that opera is my passion anymore. I kind of want to go solo for a bit."

Rand frowns. "Can you even do that? You know... with your condition? What if something happens and you can't perform? There are no understudies in solo acts."

Warmth creeps over my skin as he voices the exact fear that keeps me silent when all I want to do is sing.

"I've been doing well with my medication. I think I could manage it," I hedge with zero confidence in what I'm saying. Having someone from your past tear down your future feels like your hopes are violated before they've even begun.

"You can definitely manage it," Jaime insists and rolls his eyes. "Don't listen to him, Scarlo. After that performance tonight no one doubts you could take on the world with your high *C*."

"Of course. Of course," Rand backtracks before he smiles again. "It's just that your head's always been in the clouds, Lettie. No harm in keeping it in check."

"I think society is good enough at doing that all on its own," I giggle. "But thanks for your concern."

Rand opens his mouth to say something else, but the music dies down to a low rumble and the lights brighten. A few tables away in the corner of Masque's lounge, Maggie stands from her seat beside her husband and raises her glass to our director, Monty, at the opposite end of the room.

"A toast!" Maggie's purple sequin mask glints in the light as she addresses everyone. She lifts up her martini and the rest of us follow suit. "To a great closing night... and to starting the whole process all over again next week with a brand-new show." Groans fill the room as we collectively lament over our hectic schedules here at Bordeaux Conservatory. Maggie just grins and ignores our complaints, tipping her drink toward me and Jaime instead. "Scarlett, you stole the show. I'd say you and Jaime are our new dynamic duo."

She continues on, thanking the rest of the cast and crew, but the room buzzes with whispers. Eyes dart in my direction and I have the distinct feeling that people are talking about me even though Maggie is still giving her speech.

I shook in my heels tonight as I tried to measure up to Jilliana. Frankly, without my demon of music's encouraging letters and help practicing, I don't think I would've had the confidence to actually do it. Maybe Rand's right. I've always wanted to be on the stage, but maybe I'm better as a background character.

I shake my head to get rid of my anxiety and focus back on Monty, who is preening like a peacock over Maggie's praise until Jaime butts in.

"And don't forget about you, Mags! We *really* couldn't have done it without you. An amazing direct–I mean, *assistant* director."

Monty's pale face reddens around his silver masquerade mask, but Maggie just rolls her eyes at Jaime's antics and smirks.

"Just drink your tequila and try to keep your clothes on this time, okay? We don't need to hear another country ballad coming from a naked Jaime anytime soon."

Jaime feigns annoyance as the rest of the cast snickers at the memory. "Hey now, that was *one* time!"

The room erupts into laughter, but mine falls short when a dark shadow glides along the back wall. I'm entranced by the new arrival, a man in an all-black suit with a bone-white mask covering the right side of his face. Even stealthy, his movements are full of power that's only enhanced by his well-over-six-foot frame. He slips into a seat on the other side of Benjamin Bordeaux, Maggie's husband and one of the trustees of Bordeaux Conservatory of Music. I can't make out every detail in the darkness, but I'd swear I'm looking at Ben's mirror image, all the way down to the same skull masks.

As he settles into his seat, his dark eyes scan the room briefly before halting... on *mine*. A fluttering fills my lower belly at the intensity in his stare, and I can't seem to look away. Warmth fills my core and I cross my legs, squeezing them together underneath my white dress. The tempo of my heartbeat has gone from *adagio* to *vivace* and this man is directing it effortlessly with one piercing gaze.

"Who is that?" I murmur to myself under my breath.

"That's Sol."

I jolt at Jaime's reply, surprised that he even heard me, not to mention his answer.

"Sol? As in *the* Sol? Solomon Bordeaux?" My voice is barely audible, but Jaime nods anyway.

"The one and only." He avoids more than a glance in Solomon Bordeaux's direction, which is fine, since I've gawked enough for the both of us. "Word on the street is that Maggie got the good twin. Sol never goes out. He's a total recluse."

I snort and Rand glances at me. "What're you guys laughing about? These speeches are so boring, I need to hear something funny."

"*Scar*-lo's crushing on Sol Bor-*deaux*." Jaime's whispered, drunken singsongy delivery makes my cheeks heat. "Rumor has it he's a god in bed."

Rand's brow furrows. "You have a crush on the Phantom of the French Quarter?"

"No, no, no," I sputter, but a nervous thrill runs down my spine as I slowly register what he said. "Wait... the what?" Jaime chokes on his drink. "Sol isn't *the* Phantom. He's just a hot recluse. The Phantom's not *real* real, Scarlett. Don't listen to him."

From Jaime's tone, he obviously thinks Rand's claim is ridiculous. But hell, with the way I was just enthralled by Sol's gaze alone, I'd believe he could be the most powerful man in New Orleans. *If* the Phantom were real, that is.

Rand shakes his head. "Oh, is that what they're saying these days? And here I thought the Phantom was an actual threat."

"Wait, Rand," I interrupt before my scowling best friend can open his mouth to argue. "You believe the Phantom of the French Quarter is more than a legend?"

Rand scowls. "I know he's real."

My mind is blown that my logical friend would believe in something so far fetched. "Okay, but then how can Sol Bordeaux be a 'total recluse' and the Phantom of the *entire* French Quarter? It doesn't make sense."

The Bordeaux family and Rand's family, the Chatelains, own everything in this city. My dad and I visited every summer while I was growing up, but I never paid attention to the city's politics. I still don't, to be honest. I've always thought that the Phantom of the French Quarter, the alleged enforcer of the Bordeaux family business, was a myth. But even if Sol Bordeaux is the bogeyman of New Orleans, there's no way he'd attend a party, right? He's a glorified mobster.

"He has his minions do his dirty work, of course. They're his shadows when he can't be around," Rand answers. Concern whitens his knuckles around his rocks glass. I wish I could tell what his expression is underneath his jester mask. His worry seems to have undertones of... *anger*, for some reason. "Believe me or not, Lettie, but Sol Bordeaux is a thug and a fucking assassin. Don't go anywhere near him."

I bristle at the command. "You know, *Little Lettie* doesn't like to be told what to do." I smirk and cross my arms. "What's so bad about him anyway? It's not like all those stories can be true. Whether he's a vigilante or an *assassin*, I'd hardly think he'd come to a masquerade speakeasy for a night out on the town."

"He normally doesn't," Jaime agrees, his brow furrowed. His fingers twist his skull bracelet as he squirms in his seat. "I'm kind of shocked to see him."

My gaze shifts to the *Phantom* again. The dim light hits his face just right and even from tables away, I swear I can see midnight blue sparkling back at me. My silver eyes are drawn to his dark ones, like the moon to her night. The way his gaze immediately locks onto mine makes me wonder if he ever broke his stare.

Transfixed, it takes me a second to realize that his left eye is the one that is glittering back at me. The other on the masked side of his face doesn't seem to take on the same ethereal quality.

He leans back, causing his suit jacket to fall open, revealing a broad chest straining against a black button-up shirt. He rests his elbow on the table, and his large metal ring catches my eyes, but when the tip of his long index finger brushes over his mouth, I lose all focus. A pang of need twists inside me and I lick my own lips, wondering what his taste like—

"Seriously, Scarlett." Rand's scolding snaps me away from my lustful thoughts. "Stay away from him. I can't even begin to tell you the awful things he's done to my family."

That catches my attention.

"What do you mean? What has he done?"

"I believe the boy said he *can't* tell you, Scarlo."

I narrow my eyes at Jaime, but his are on Rand. My old friend doesn't seem to notice as his fingers wrap around mine. When he squeezes, I don't hesitate to squeeze back, finding comfort in the gesture.

"He's right. I can't tell you, Lettie. It could put you in danger. Just stay away from him. For me? He's bad news, especially for a good girl like you."

My face blanks as his words hit a raw nerve.

... a good girl like you.

He's always seen me as helpless and innocent, but he knows nothing about me now. I try to pull my hand away, but he holds tight. I relent, just to appease him.

Like I've always done.

Shaking my head slightly, I push the thought away, not wanting to dwell on it.

"Okay, Rand. I promise."

He finally lets go as the crowd claps at the end of Maggie's speech. When he looks away, I can't stop myself as I glance at Sol again, the mysterious Phantom of the French Quarter, if Rand can be believed. His gaze feels hot on my skin and nothing like the cold nature I've heard he has.

"You didn't even hear the end of Maggie's speech, did you?" Jaime laughs at me. "You're gonna start drooling if you don't get it together, *mi amiga*."

"Shit." I wipe my mouth, because for once, Jaime isn't exaggerating.

He snorts at me. "I don't know what you want me to tell you, Scarlo. He's a run-of-the-mill hot white dude—" Jaime glances between the two of us and does a double take. He curses as he straightens. "Scratch that. If a guy looked at me like that, I'd let him make me sing falsetto any day, and I'm not even into broody men. Who knew you could still eye fuck with a fake eye?"

I twist toward him. "*Fake* eyes?"

Jaime shrugs. "Well only the one behind the mask."

The dull one.

"I heard it's got X-ray vision or some shit."

I roll my eyes. "Psh, yeah, *okay*."

Jaime shrugs. "Hey, the guy's so rich, it could be true for all we know. But if it is, then maybe that accident wasn't such a bad thing. Although, I'm sure that mask is hell on his complexion. I wonder what he uses—"

"What accident?" I ask, trying to keep my fellow skincare lover from getting derailed. He's usually much better about staying on task when we gossip. Unless he's drunk, of course. Which—I watch him lick the inside of his glass for the last remnants of liquor—okay, yeah, I should be expecting this.

He comes away with the glass, smacking his lips before finally answering me. "He and Ben are identical twins but no one's seen Sol's true face in years, so it's hard to say whether they still look similar. I'm not sure what happened. It's all very hush-hush. He might be hideous under there now for all we know."

"Whatever he's hiding behind his mask can't be worse than that cold, black heart of his," Rand mutters.

I'm *dying* to ask more questions, but someone rushes in and hands Monty a letter, catching my attention. The music is still low and it's bright enough in the speakeasy that it's easy to hear Monty's gasp when he opens the envelope. His shocked face pales further as he looks it over.

"Hold on," Jaime says as he sits up and props his chin in his hands. "I smell dramaaa."

I giggle until Monty turns the letter over. There on the back is a distinctive black wax seal that shines in the light, revealing the skull imprint.

My heart stops. I recognize it easily. I should, since it's exactly like the one I've been receiving for months.

It's *his* seal. My demon of music.

As Monty opens the envelope, his hands shake so badly that I can see them all the way from here. I have no idea why I do it, but I risk a glance back at Sol. I no longer feel the weight of his stare as he takes in the scene with what looks like practiced disinterest on the left side of his face. Ben's uncovered side is looking at his brother with a hint of frustration.

"Is this a joke?" Monty yells and the light background music stops altogether.

"What's wrong?" Maggie asks from her table. Her mother, Madam G, emerges from the shadows near the bar. She's unmistakable in her peacock-feather mask. It's the only color she has on and her arms are crossed over her long black dress as she watches over her domain.

Monty tosses the letter onto the table before sneering. "Okay, very funny. Who the hell did this?"

Maggie leaves her seat and plucks the letter from the table. Her mother comes up behind her and reads over her shoulder as Maggie speaks.

"Uh, Monty. I don't think this is a joke. It's signed by the Phantom."

Whispers erupt over the low music and a few people glance in

Ben and Sol's direction, making me wonder whether Rand is onto something after all.

"Oh, so I'm just supposed to believe that the so-called *Phantom* of the French Quarter gives a fuck that Scarlett Day is chosen as the lead role for the rest of the year?" Everyone shifts their attention to me. Embarrassment heats my cheeks and I sink farther into the soft velvet booth. "Do you have something to do with this?" Monty asks me with a mean chuckle. "Did the quiet little mouse finally find her backbone?"

"No, I—"

A glass breaks near where the Bordeaux brothers sit, giving me a small reprieve.

"Sorry, I dropped my glass," Ben offers apologetically. "What else does the letter say, Mr. Arquette? Obviously the bastard is just messing with you."

"He'd better be," Monty agrees.

"I don't think he is," Madam G offers and taps the letter still in her daughter's hand. "It says you must stop with Jilliana and let a true prima donna sing."

Maggie narrows her eyes at Monty. "What is he talking about, Monty? What're you doing with Jilliana?"

"Nothing! I can't be responsible for the delusions of a ghost!"

"What about this part that says all that is behind the scenes shall be brought into the spotlight if you don't come clean?" Madam G asks.

"Crazy, obviously. Or a prank. Scarlett, Jaime, are you behind this?"

I stutter, afraid to speak. Give me a script any day and while I may sweat my ass off from nerves, I'll still deliver my lines. But put me on the spot and I become a wordless puddle. Thank goodness Jaime comes to my defense.

"Get over yourself, Monty. We earned our spots on the stage fair and square. We don't *need* to resort to blackmail."

Monty huffs. "Well, I'm not a fan of practical jokes so whoever's behind this, come forward now. I don't have the patience..."

He continues to accuse various people throughout the room when Rand leans over the table.

"Want to know what Sol and his family are capable of?" he asks me quietly, making it so that only I can hear him.

The question catches me off guard. I don't answer, but merely looking in Rand's direction is enough of a yes for him.

"Ask Madam Gastoneaux, the supposed 'owner' of Masque. She's under the Bordeaux family's thumb. They make her pay so much protection money that she's nearly bankrupt. They're just itching to take Masque from her."

"But Ben is married to Madam G's daughter," I point out, shaking my head and glancing at Jaime, only to see that he's too interested in what's happening at Monty's table to add anything. "Why would they blackmail Ben's mother-in-law?"

For the first time, I'm kicking myself for how oblivious I've been over what goes on in this city.

Rand shrugs. "Evil doesn't always make sense, Lettie. But if I had to guess, I'd blame that infamous Bordeaux greed. It's always about money with them."

Disgust crinkles my nose. My father was bullied his whole life by thugs, mobsters, and people who ran the clubs where he performed. He might not have actually sold his soul to the devil, but he knew enough demons to damn him. Brushing elbows with the criminal underworld was *all* my father knew. I would never go about my career the same way, but different times and opportunities exist for me that he'd never dreamed of for himself, growing up dirt-floor poor in the foothills of the Appalachian mountains.

"I can guarantee you whatever's going on with that letter, Sol Bordeaux has a hand in."

Rand's theory tightens my heart in my chest. Satisfaction seems to creep over the small smile on his lips, as if my confusing disappointment is exactly what he wanted. But it's not like he could have any idea of what that envelope means to me. My eyes dart to Sol as I begin to wonder whether my own demon of music might not be the devil himself.

"Shit. Who the hell is texting me..." Monty mutters as he pats at the phone in his inside breast pocket before digging it out. As he reads the screen, his eyes widen and he frantically looks around the room. "Someone! Go check the cellar! Madam Gastoneaux, call 9-1-1!"

"What's going on?" Madam G asks loudly over the new commotion. Ben scowls at his brother, whose hand slowly moves to cover his mouth, hiding what I swear is a smirk.

"Jacques... Jacques Baron," Monty chokes out.

That name brings cold goose bumps to my skin. The guy is an animal. He's always making the women in the cast uncomfortable backstage. Last week alone, he cornered me on the way to my room and felt me up.

My fingers flex into a fist again, just like they had then. I'd wanted to scream. To hit him. Something to get him to go away, but I'd just stood there, shaking.

Like a scared little mouse.

The shame over *letting* him grab my ass and thrust against my jeans makes me almost feel worse than the actual touching did. The thought of his hot breath, moist on my neck, still makes me cringe. If it hadn't been for Maggie coming to look for me... I don't know what would've happened.

"What about Jacques?" Rand asks with an edge to his voice.

"You know Jacques Baron?" I ask, but Rand ignores me.

"He's a Chatelain man," Jaime provides unhelpfully. My blank stare makes him sigh. "Girl, you really should know this city. Your head is so in the sand, you're bound to get it chopped off around here. Being a Chatelain man means he works for Rand's family."

My jaw drops at Jaime's statement and out of the corner of my eye, I see Maggie grab Monty's phone. She gasps before glancing over to her husband, then addresses the rest of the room. "Jacques Baron is dead."

Scene 4

INVITATION WITHDRAWN

"A text message, hm? I thought you were more old school than that," Ben mutters behind his glass before taking a large mouthful of the drink. I shrug. The room is frantic as people try to see the text message I sent Monty from a blocked number.

"Jacques is *dead*?" someone yells as commotion and hysteria spreads.

"—suicide—"

"—he hung himself—"

"—with a stage curtain *rope*?"

A picture is worth a thousand words, even over the phone, and this one speaks volumes, revealing Jacques Baron hanging from the ceiling in the cellar below the stage. I thought it was fitting that a rat die with his brethren where they scurry through the basements. Ben knows it had to be done. After seeing Jacques paw at Scarlett last week, he practically wrote the suicide note himself.

"Also, not great timing with the Phantom letter," my brother points out.

Okay, I admit sending the text immediately after Monty opened the letter was a little rash. I'd previously intended the letter to be my only surprise tonight, but once he began to accuse Scarlett of being the sender, I had to change my plans. Texting Monty the picture I took earlier today was the only thing I could think of to get the heat off of her in the moment.

Besides, I've been getting bored waiting for someone to find him. He needs to be cut down before the body starts to stink or the rats decide to make a meal out of his corpse.

The staff begins to mill around again and I welcome the new Sazerac from the waitress, since I was actually the one who broke the last glass. That's the thing about Masque. Despite the fact that a crisis is taking place in real time inside the speakeasy, the service is still on point, even if Madam G is glowering at me for breaking another one of her glasses.

"What if someone connects the letter with the picture?" Ben asks more blatantly, but still quietly enough that no one will hear him over the bedlam.

"Let them add fuel to the wildfire of rumors surrounding me. People worship the heroes protecting them until they realize the cost of their safety. Whispers in the dark keep the worst of my justice from coming to light. You know reputation means everything. No one is afraid of an ordinary man with a horrifying face. Let the Phantom be terrifying in their minds."

"Your face wouldn't be what terrifies people. At some point, the citizens of this city are going to figure out that not all the whispers are rumors." Ben sighs. "And then the NOLA PD who are on our side will be forced to turn on us."

"It had to be done," I insist.

Ben wants more than that, I can tell. He purses his lips and narrows his eyes, shifting his skull mask. My face makes the same movements when I want an explanation, or at least the left side does. Ben might be frustrated now, but he knows that if I've made a kill, the person deserved it. It's the same moral code I've had since I was fifteen.

I watch Scarlett out of the corner of my eye. A delicious mix of confusion, concern, and satisfaction swirl on her face over the news. Her last emotion makes my cock swell with need. My little angel is more savage than she looks. I love her innocence, but her darkness is what calls to me. Jacques Baron's death was a gift from me to her, and I knew she'd love it. If Monty doesn't heed my warning, I have no doubt she'll enjoy that one, too.

"Sol, are you listening?" Ben asks with a huff.

"No," I answer honestly.

He sighs again. "Why do you play with your food, knowing you're not going to eat it?"

I frown. "What do you mean?"

"*Her.*" He tips his head toward my muse. "You act like she's yours. It was bad enough when we both knew you'd never go after her, but now that Rand has declared her, she's completely off-limits. Besides, she's not like the women you bring home in the dark. She'll want to be with you in the light. Women like Scarlett Day want to see the man behind the mask. Are you willing to reveal that to her? Are you ready to *show* yourself? Or will you just watch your pretty doll from afar?"

I fidget with my ring. His questions hit home more than I'd like to admit. Scarlett and her voice have been my fantasy for months. But no matter how dark my angel of music is on the inside, I'm certain she'll never be able to accept how ugly I am. Inside *and* out.

"You're right," I finally respond. "She won't be interested as soon as she sees what that bastard did to me."

Ben snorts and shakes his head sadly. "If you think I'm only talking about your skull mask, you haven't been paying attention."

Confusion twists my face and pulls the skin tight. I take my eye off Scarlett to question him, but a throat clearing makes me face the man who's approached us.

One of my skull-masked shadows dips his head before speaking. "Rand Chatelain to see you, sirs."

I didn't know which one of my men it was until he opened his mouth. Masks ensure that no one knows who works for the

Bordeauxs. Not knowing who they can trust outside of me and Ben also prevents my men from betraying us to our enemies.

Ben relies on his vision too much, so he is at a disadvantage in the dark. But our shadows answer to me and as soon as they get close enough for my other senses to catch details, it's easy to deduce their identities. Ben is the face of our operation, our mask, so to speak, and I am everything underneath.

I nod to the man and he steps aside to reveal a deliciously furious Rand with a garish red-and-yellow jester mask covering the top half of his face.

"You wish to speak to me?" I ask. "Bold, considering you're trespassing."

"I was *invited* by Miss Day," Rand insists with a smug sneer on his lips.

My jaw threatens to tic at the jab. Despite my wish to keep my feelings private, I fucked up in box five earlier tonight, showing my hand. Now Rand is testing me to find out just how valuable his taunts are. I can't fucking stand it, but what's done is done.

"Invitation trumps the truce," he spits back when I don't reply. "But it's not like you respect it in the first place."

"I'm sorry, what was that? I couldn't hear you over how loud your ridiculous mask is," I point out and smirk.

He tears off the jester mask, revealing his fury in full force. His emotions are unchecked, so unlike his normal charming presence and the opposite of the cold calculation his brother had. Interesting.

Ben angles forward, making sure no one at the adjacent tables in our corner can hear us. When he speaks, the uncovered part of his face is neutral, but his words are laced with cold anger. "What do you mean we don't respect the truce?"

"Jacques Baron," Rand bites out. "You hung a Chatelain man, my former proxy. No doubt the police will rule it a suicide, as they normally do when you're involved. But do you really expect *me* to believe my second-in-command killed himself underneath *your* opera house? I thought this was a fucking safe zone."

"Chatelains are only as safe in the House as they are rule abiding. One wrong move means reprisals. You know that," I answer.

"One wrong move? What did he do?" Rand leans in so closely I can see the vein in his temple throbbing. I haven't missed his fists clenching and unclenching at his side. He's losing his composure.

Good. I've been waiting for him to crack.

"He was a spy for you." I give the partial truth.

Baron wasn't an actual threat since all my men knew he couldn't be trusted, but I don't want Rand Chatelain to know that I'll kill for my muse, not yet.

"I demand evidence." He stabs the table with his finger.

"Do you dare *question* me, Chatelain?" I ask carefully. "In my own home?"

Just then, a vision in white catches my eye and stops the conversation cold as Scarlett's slender fingers brush Rand's forearm. My eye doesn't leave the place where their skin touches until they're apart again, the briefest of moments that feel like an eternity too long. She's close enough that even with my poor eyesight, her white rose shines like a beacon in the dim light. But a red tinge makes me frown.

"What happened to your rose?" I ask, unable to stop myself.

The world quiets around us. Her eyes widen before darting down to the rose and she fingers the petals delicately.

"I pricked myself putting it on," she answers. Her voice is low, but our interaction has created a cocoon of silence around us, so I hear it perfectly.

"Why didn't you take it off?" I ask.

A small smile curves her lips and she covers the flower protectively before looking at me again. "This came from someone special. And I love white roses, so I couldn't bear to part with it."

"Not even after it hurt you?" My lips purse and her brow furrows as she tilts her head to the side with a tentative smile.

"No, I guess not. Not even after it hurt me."

Her confession stirs something deep in my chest and all I want to do is whisk her away. She turns to Rand, breaking our gaze and bringing back all the noise in the room, the sensation akin to coming out of a tunnel.

"I'm, um... heading up to my dorm." Her lyrical voice is soothing to my ears, despite the fact that it's nearly drowned out by everyone's hysterics over Jacques Baron's demise. "The party is clearly over."

Rand turns on a hungry smile that makes my fist tighten. "Let me walk you up."

Her bright-moonlight eyes flick to mine. "No, um, that's okay. It's just upstairs."

Rand opens his mouth but Jaime interjects. "I've got her. Go on home, man. I'll protect her from the big bad Phantom of the French Quarter." He smiles, studiously ignoring me.

She beams up at her best friend like a sister to a brother, and not for the first time I'm thankful that Jaime took his assignment as seriously as he did. Since they were already cordial, it was easy enough for him to befriend her when she was at her lowest. His daily updates have become unnecessary thanks to the fact she's moved to her dorm, but he's stuck around because now he's her true friend. It calms me to know that in those few moments when I'm not around, she's still safe.

Rand sputters for an objection, but she squeezes his forearm and wishes him a good night before leaving.

I watch her unabashedly as she navigates the crowd. Just when I think she doesn't feel it, this gravitational pull like the moon to the night, she glances back. Her silver eyes flare and her gorgeous pink lips part. My cock jumps to push inside them, but I slowly settle farther into my seat. She breaks eye contact first as Jaime irritatingly guides her away from me and around the corner to the exit.

I glare back at Rand. He's still staring where Scarlett disappeared, and the frustration reddening his face pleases me. He's now seen the undeniable chemistry I have with his alleged childhood *sweetheart*. Even though Scarlett doesn't realize my connection with her yet, and even though I'll never act on these emotions, fuck does it feel good for *someone* to know Scarlett Day is mine.

When he finally drags his eyes away from the empty space and back to me, he's failed to conceal his anger and I can't resist toying with the prick.

"Leave, Rand. Your invitation has apparently been withdrawn. Don't come around again until our next meeting. Our business is done. Your request for access to the port and a hotel in the French Quarter is denied."

Rand's lips morph into a tight line before he finally speaks. "This isn't over, Bordeaux. I *will* get what I want."

"You can try," I answer with a bored sigh. "But just like your brother, you will fucking fail. A little advice? Make sure your failure isn't at the same cost." I cross my ankles under the table and my arms over my chest. "Or don't. I don't give a shit. I've always got more rope handy. Just ask your second-in-command— oh... *wait*. You can't."

Rand's eyes burn with fury before he stalks away in silence. Satisfaction courses through me, a sensation not too different from the buzz I get when I indulge in my Sazeracs.

"First Baron, then Monty, now Rand?" Ben's words carry an edge. "If you keep fucking up and threatening these Chatelain men, you're going to get burned, brother. Again."

I smirk before taking a sip of my drink. "I'll have fun while it lasts, though."

I couldn't give a fuck about me. I haven't cared about my fate since I was fifteen and learned my entire life could be taken away from me in an instant. That realization was shortly followed with the revelation that the same fatal truth applied to those who harmed me and the ones I loved. My enemies and I have been living on borrowed time ever since.

But now that a certain soprano has appeared on my stage, all of my time has belonged to her. Nothing else matters.

Speaking of which...

"I have to go." I stand from my chair, ignoring the fact that

Ben has apparently been talking to me this entire time. Right now, my one-track mind doesn't allow for anything other than thoughts of white roses and moonlight.

Ben doesn't try to prevent me from going. He hasn't for months now. At this point, neither of us could stop me even if we tried.

My little muse is my addiction, and her voice is my drug. If there is a cure to my madness, I don't want it. I'd rather welcome blissful oblivion.

Scene 5

THROUGH THE MIRROR

As soon as Jaime drops me off at my dorm, I close my door and sag against it. Thank God he volunteered to escort me to my room so I didn't have to go with Rand. I'm ready to collapse on my bed to finally relax, and I don't know if it's because I crushed on him for so long, but his presence puts me on edge.

And the way Sol stared at me? Like he wanted to *consume* me? Yeah, that sure as hell didn't help. When he asked about my rose, my heart leaped into my throat. His voice caressed me more lovingly than any hand ever has, and I'd nearly become breathless myself. A flutter in my core drags out a small moan from my chest at the memory, but a thump somewhere in the walls snaps me out of it.

You'd think I'd be able to tune out all the things that go bump in the night in this building. With thousands of students, faculty, and staff milling around, Bordeaux Conservatory is never silent, no matter how good the soundproofing is.

I push away from the door and unpin my rose before laying it gently on my makeup counter. Once I peel myself out of my heavy Juliet dress, I take a deep soothing breath and go about my nightly routine, thoughts of tonight racing through my head.

Before I head to the bathroom, my eyes drift to the rose again and catch on the sight of the envelope from my demon of music.

Monty received the same type of letter that my demon sends me, down to the wax skull seal on the back. Although the seal on mine is a seductive red rather than an ominous black, could the envelopes be from the same person?

Mine are also signed off with "*Ton démon de la musique*," but Monty's was signed "Phantom." Is my secret admirer a demon of music? A phantom? Or both?

Does it matter?

I guess it doesn't. Objectively, both have major stalker vibes, but I've never felt creeped out by the roses, notes, and sheet music from my demon. They've felt more like love letters than messages from a villain, like delicate promises instead of the alarming threat Monty received.

And while I should be feeling upset over Jacques's death and the fact that Monty accused me of threatening him, my chest actually feels lighter knowing that I haven't been making my own notes. Our letters have gone on for so long, a defeatist part of me was beginning to think they were a figment of my imagination to deal with the guilt of my dad's murder last year.

Even though my logic says I couldn't have written them myself, it's validating to know that *someone* is actually behind them. My brain has played tricks on me for longer than I've been medicated, and even though I haven't had an episode in months, enough insecurity can make even the strongest mind question reality. But I got definitive proof tonight that I'm still sane. I also have proof that I have a real-life pen pal who is admittedly on the stalker side of secret admirer, but I'm still sane nonetheless.

As soon as I finish scrubbing off my stage makeup in my en suite bathroom, I return to my makeup counter to find my pills... only they're not there.

I scan my desk, cursing myself over the untidy mess I've always maintained and groaning at the prospect of trying to find my medication among the many bottles of foundation, eyeshadow pallets, and hair accessories. I always put them in one specific spot for this reason, but the aftermath of the show caught me out of my routine. When I finish searching the surface, my drawers prove just as fruitless. I render my organized chaos into a tornado of disaster, until I finally give up. Resigned, I turn to my last resort. Old meds.

I've been on a journey to control my inner demons for the past year, ever since I was hospitalized for my manic episode. Even after I was diagnosed with bipolar disorder, it still felt like my psychiatrist was guessing at what meds would click for me. Some were worse than others, sending me straight to sleep, making me gain weight, or turning me into a raging bitch. One even changed my vocal cords and I stopped that one immediately, despite the fact that it worked in every other aspect. My psych and I have finally nailed down a combination of meds that works for me.

Normally, I wouldn't go back to the old meds, especially not the ones that make me feel worse. But after all the events of tonight, I can't deny that my mood is elevated and I want to cut off a manic episode before it starts.

My thoughts are racing, I'm energized, and the urge to go downstairs and do something reckless—like, I don't know, confront Sol and his piercing midnight gaze—is nearly overwhelming. It could all be totally harmless, normal emotions.

But it could be the beginning of the end of my sanity.

Especially considering the *triumph* I felt over Jacques's suicide? It's not lost on me that as someone who experienced terrifying suicidal thoughts for nearly a month after my dad died, I should have more compassion for someone who likely ended theirs.

Maybe I'll find empathy tomorrow, but I can still feel where his hands groped me so brazenly last week, like he'd done it hundreds of times before. What if it wasn't suicide at all? I can't help but think he might've gotten what he deserved from someone less cowardly than me.

That last self-righteous thought makes me pause, solidifying my decision to take an old medication tonight and calling my doctor about getting new prescriptions tomorrow. The drug knocks me out and gives me bizarre dreams, but next-day grogginess is better than winding up in a psych ward after failing to stave off a manic episode.

Anything but that.

I go to my small bedroom and dig in my bedside table through the many old orange medicine bottles I should've thrown out months ago. My fear of getting sick again due to this exact situation made me keep them in the bottom of my drawer, so once I find the right one, I pop a pill into my mouth and sip from the water bottle that stays on my nightstand.

I quickly finish my nightly routine, knowing I don't have long until the drug will quite literally make me pass out wherever I stand.

One time, months ago, I curled up on the floor of my dorm room, not caring or lucid enough to drag my ass to bed. Thank goodness Jaime has a key. I'd texted him earlier in the night and he must've picked me up and carried me to bed. I was tucked in all nice and cozy the next morning, but I was too embarrassed to confront him about it and he's too much of a gentleman to bring it up.

I toss on a thin white T-shirt and slide underneath my plain pink quilt with my Kindle, eager to read at least one chapter before I pass out. Until I remember that I left off on a steamy scene.

Oh shit.

It's a particularly sexy scene between a vampire king—my favorite—and the woman he *technically* kidnapped. A few lines in and I'm already squirming under my sheets, trying to resist the urge to live vicariously through the heroine and pursue my own pleasure. But I'm weak and before long, my free hand is trailing down my torso toward my cotton panties.

Midnight eyes blink in my vision as the need to create my own fantasy takes over.

"*Sol...*" I breathe.

My nipples harden, begging for attention, and I answer their call with my other hand, letting my Kindle fall to the bed as I pinch each peak over the fabric of my shirt. Arousal floods my panties and my fingertips finally find their way to the elastic and dip underneath to find my clit. The pebbled peak between my thumb and forefinger tingles as my mind conjures up Sol's broad and powerful form stepping through my mirror.

A part of me—the very small, stupid, prudish side—nags me to stop, telling me that something isn't right. But the saner part of me knows the medication is only beginning to run its course, probably because I haven't taken it in a while. And after this lucid dream, I'm going to crash and wake up feeling hungover at eight a.m. on the dot.

My index finger zeroes in on that small bundle of nerves. If I had more time, I'd bring out my vibrator, but I don't know how long I've got until I succumb to sleep. Using my pointer and middle fingers, I quickly caress my clit until I find the rhythm that sends a jolt through my body. My left hand molds and teases both breasts and my body undulates under the covers as I begin to race toward my finish, tantalizingly close, but just out of reach. In my mind, Sol stares at me from the mirror and I reach out to him.

"Come, please. Help me. I need you," I plead with my mysterious phantom.

His movements seem hesitant as he steps closer. Or is he gliding?

"Are you real?" Knowing somewhere in my psyche that I'm talking to an empty room, I giggle. "Are you my demon of music? Or the Phantom of the French Quarter?"

No, he's a figment of my imagination, is what he is.

My eyes widen when he opens his mouth.

"I am your Sol." His voice is deep and rich, just like it was earlier tonight. He spoke with only a hint of a whisper but it resonates loudly in my mind.

I know his name is Sol, but my heart pounds in my chest at

the thought that he is my *soul*. He's the fabrication I've concocted to heal from the trauma of losing my father. Maybe this voice is exactly that. My soul.

"My soul," I whisper back. "Sing to me, Sol. My demon of music."

He doesn't sing, but music comes from somewhere and I *know* it's the song my demon wrote for me. His hand gives off a dim light, seemingly summoning the music from somewhere. The glow shines on his bone-white mask. Even though it covers half of his face, it can't hide the five o'clock shadow dusting his strong jaw. My eyes trail down his body over his unbuttoned collar and the rolled-up sleeves of his black dress shirt. His dark pants do little to hide the hardening bulge behind his zipper, and I love the fact that he's not trying to hide it from me either.

Then again, why should he? This is my medically induced fever dream. Why would he hide his need for me?

Even as I think it, my mind fights itself, telling me something is off here, but I shake my head and plead again, wanting to give in to the sensations.

"Please touch me, Sol."

His midnight eyes scorch my skin as he stares at me hungrily in a way that has me writhing underneath my fingertips for that crescendo that remains infuriatingly out of reach.

His warm hand brushes against my cheek and I lean into the touch like a cat in heat. As I do, he sits down, knuckles still touching my skin, until he stops suddenly.

"Did you take this shit again?" he grumbles and grabs my medicine bottle from my bedside table. "After the way it made you pass out last time?"

"H-how... do you know about that?" I ask, confused. But of course he'd know. *I* know and that's the extent my dream state can provide.

"Why?" his voice demands gruffly. If it weren't for the gentle way he's stroking my cheek, I'd be afraid of his tone.

"I lost my medication."

"*Lost* it?"

"Yes." I wince sheepishly, embarrassed that I can't remember where I put my pill container. "But I don't want to go back there again."

"Where?"

"The ward. I can't be crazy again."

Understanding wars with the protective concern wrinkling his brow. He nods once and pockets the meds.

"No more of this, Scarlett. I'll find your other medicine before you resort to taking old ones. I'll take care of you."

"Th-Thank you," I moan just as my single-minded fingers find a very sensitive spot. "Please, Sol..."

He twists to see me better, but his fingers don't leave my cheek. I can see his other hand grabbing his cock through his pants, but not stroking, almost as if he's having to stave off his own release.

"I will not touch you the way you want, but show me how you give yourself pleasure and tell me how you like it as you do."

"I... I've never." His eyes flare. "I mean, I know how to do it myself, but I've never... in front of someone... or *with* someone."

His knuckles flow along my jawline and down my neck until he reaches my collarbone, uncovered by my baggy T-shirt. "You've never been with anyone before? Not even before this year?"

The phrasing of the question is odd, but when I shake my head "no," his left midnight eye sparkles down on me, causing a delicious shiver to erupt through my whole body. I lie on my back and wantonly spread my legs for his view, loving the way he raises his brow and growls when he asks his next question.

"When you fuck yourself with your fingers, *ma belle muse*, who do you think of?"

"You," I whisper over the soft song playing on repeat. "My demon of music. *Your* music."

"Ah... think of me, *ma chère*. Touch yourself. Stroke those slender fingers against your pretty clit and think of the music we'll make together one day."

I moan at his words as I obey him and my fingers work furiously.

"Good. Now stop—" I whine in protest, but listen to his command. "Massage your nipples with your wet hand until they're glistening pink for me. I can see your pussy dripping from here. Dip your finger deep inside and feel how much you need me."

I raise my shirt and drench my nipples with my desire while my other hand curves two fingers into my entrance. His hungry gaze widens and his fingers keep stroking the sensitive skin of my collarbone, never going past the stretched collar of my T-shirt. The hand on his clothed cock stretches angrily before fisting himself through his pants again.

"Please, Sol. Touch me. I need to feel you."

"No," he finally says. "I want to hear that pretty voice tell me what you like until you come."

I'm so turned on and I'm beginning to worry that the medication is going to stifle my orgasm like it has in the past. It keeps feeling like it's drifting away, and if I lose it while this need still drives me, I'll fucking scream.

"It's going away. Please, Sol."

"I can't touch you yet, but I love to hear you beg, pretty muse."

I moan and close my eyes, getting lost in the haze. Who is this woman that's pleading for her phantom to pleasure her? At least he doesn't seem to mind, even though he's making no moves to listen to me.

It's because he's not real. He's a hallucination.

Oh god... *am I going crazy again?*

My throat feels tight and it takes me a second to realize Sol is cupping my neck. I should be freaking out, but I'm calmed by his touch, especially when concern softens his eyes.

"You're not crazy, Scarlett."

Did I say that out loud?

"You're just medicated with the wrong drug, which you will never take again. Do you understand? It's not good for you."

"O-okay."

His fingers gentle before leaving my neck to play with a curl of hair.

"Close your eyes. Give in to the darkness. Let my voice guide you until you come."

I shut my eyes again and a wave of exhaustion washes over me, like the drug is finally kicking in. My need to come is still overwhelming yet has never felt more out of reach.

"I... can't," I groan and pull my hand away as I roll to my side, feeling stupid at the tears pricking my eyes. One escapes and falls down my face, but he catches it swiftly with his index finger. "I need to come but I can't, Sol. Please, you have to help me come."

Hunger and indecision mar the unmasked half of my phantom's face. He finally swallows hard and his voice is rough when he speaks.

"You need me to help?" When I nod, he growls. "Fuck, okay. I could never deny you, *ma petite muse.*"

The bed dips as he squeezes in behind me on the twin mattress. His essence—whiskey, sugar, and leather, like a Sazerac in a lounge—washes over me as his arm slides underneath my neck and rolls me closer to cradle me, my back to his chest.

My mind is sluggish as the sleeping drug works its way through my system. His warm breath flutters the tiny hairs on the back of my neck and I tremble. Lips brush against the sensitive skin, drawing a moan from deep within my soul, mixed with the frustration of my tired limbs and the ache between my thighs.

"Close your eyes, Scarlett."

I blink quickly, not even realizing they were still open. My eyelids finally drift closed like he commands. His fingertips skate lightly down my arm until his large grip trembles over mine, covering me in such a way that no part of his hand actually touches the rest of my body. He begins to control my body masterfully, like a conductor in his own symphony, and leads my hands where I need them.

Under his direction and fingertips, I trace my arousal-soaked nipple with one hand. With the other, my new guide travels us back down to my pussy and we delve underneath the hem of my panties.

When I feel my own desire, my phantom curses behind me, and I squeeze my breast almost to the point of pain. My hips grind against the hard length branding my ass and I wish I could feel him from the inside. Our fingers find my clit at the apex of my legs and Sol uses the pressure of his own finger to flutter over the delicate bud.

"Sol, yes," I moan as he pulsates my finger like a heartbeat. "More."

"Tell me what you're feeling."

"Good... so good..." My sentence drifts off but he shakes me.

"Give me more than that or I'll stop." The edge in his voice only heightens the thrill.

I whimper as I search for my words and an orgasm in the same moment. "Y-your hands on mine... they're warm... strong. Safe."

His movements pause. "Safe?"

I nod and his ministrations pick back up, this time with less furious urgency and more... reverence. So I tell him that, too.

"You're my pretty little muse, Scarlett. I worship your voice. Your body, mind, and soul are no different."

"Even the darkness in my mind?" I ask, not sure why it matters if my phantom accepts my madness.

"Especially your darkness."

His whispered confession relaxes me further and triggers the beginning of my orgasm. My muscles tighten as our fingers play my clit like a duet piece. Somehow, he knows exactly how to strum me into release.

"I feel like my body knows your touch and the song you want to play with it. My core already knows the right key."

"Do you like the music I give you? The songs I've written just for you? They won't compare to the ones you sing when you come."

My breath hitches when one of his fingers guides mine inside my channel and he begins to pump my hand.

"*Yes...* I love your music. Some days it gives me reason... purpose. My heart thrums every time I see your white rose and letter."

A grumble of approval vibrates against my neck, as if this phantom, my demon of music, loves praise. It emboldens me to keep going, but he presses the heel of my hand into my clit, snapping my attention to the aching desire building in my core. The walls of my pussy contract against my finger as my own palm kneads my bundle of nerves frantically.

I give up trying to move on my own and he takes over, pulling me tight against his chest and grinding the heel of my hand against my pulsing need. He keeps pumping my finger in and out, and all the while, his cock thrusts against the thin cotton covering my ass.

"Sol... it feels so good. Your hands—"

My muscles tighten from the top of my spine down to the curl of my toes and I cry out as I ride the very tip of the swelling crescendo... and fall, wave after wave, like a cascade of octaves playing over my skin as I come.

His fingers keep up that rhythm until the song is too much to bear and I'm pushing him away while pulling him close at the same time.

Minutes, maybe hours, pass as I try to catch my breath. When I completely recover, Sol's lips brush against the shell of my ear, sending tantalizing ripples of warmth down my body as he drags his fingers up my feverish skin.

Whiskey and sugar scents drift under my nose as his lips caress my ear. "I always knew pleasure would make you sing so pretty. I need you to know that no one but me will ever hear this song from you. The world can have Scarlett on stage, but only I get to hear *ma jolie petite muse* when she hits those high notes. Tell me you understand."

I don't... and I do at the same time. Exhaustion is finally winning out though, so instead of asking my phantom, my demon of music, what he means, I go with instinct and nod. "I sing for you, Sol. Only for you."

He hums with approval. The soothing pitch drifts into varying musical notes until it becomes a familiar song. I want to sing it, but the entire embrace—his lullaby, his warmth, his scent, his *power*—lulls me to sleep better than any medication alone.

Scene 6

FITTINGS AND FRENEMIES

When I woke up this morning, not only did I feel like I had a hangover from hell, my panties were damp and I swear I could smell sugar and whiskey. It's one thing to have auditory hallucinations, but visual and olfactory? I didn't even know the last one was a thing.

Needless to say, I called my doctor for refills and then I promptly freaked the fuck out.

For months, I've been hearing music coming from a vent in my room. I thought it was someone practicing and it took me searching high and low for where the music could be coming from to finally realize I was having auditory hallucinations again. At first, it worried the hell out of me, but oddly enough, there were no other symptoms of mania. So I took the beautiful piano tunes and the sexy crooning from the bass singer as a reprieve from all the emotions still whirling inside me from my dad's murder.

Then I began to receive letters from the mysterious pianist and even interacted with him while I sang his music. I didn't know what to believe, and frankly, by that time, I didn't want to ruin what I had by looking into it. It sounds crazy in and of itself to just *ignore* what's going on around me. But, whether my demon of music was real or fake didn't matter as much as protecting the idea of him and the comfort he'd given me.

Now that my hallucinations have escalated to literally getting turned on by my visions, I'm not sure what to do. If I bring any of this up to my psychiatrist, I'll no doubt be getting a one-way ticket to my own room with a barred window and a blurry view of a dumpster I'll wish I could throw myself into.

Again.

I stare blankly into the fitting room mirror, fingering the thick fabric of my new costume, and sigh. Monty suddenly decided this morning that for the next opera we're performing, *Faust*, I should be Marguerite, the female lead character, instead of Jilliana. Now I'm going to have to be refitted for the dress she was supposed to wear. All I'll have to tell the seamstress later today is that it's a few inches long. Other than that, it fits perfectly.

But it feels all wrong.

We already had auditions and, while I thought Jilliana sort of half-assed hers, I know she would do anything for this position. After being the star of the show for a night, I've realized that although I love the theater spotlight, just like this dress, it's not exactly the right fit.

The truth is, I don't want to be the lead in this opera. More and more lately, I've realized writing my lyrics is where my heart lies. My own words, my own music, my own stage. I'm not sure what to do with that revelation, especially since one lead performance has turned my mental state on its head.

"What the fuck am I going to do now?" I mutter.

"Um... get out of my way, for starters."

I jump at the lovely soprano voice, tinged with anger, and immediately move to the side so Jilliana can check her dress—my old dress—in the mirror.

"Sorry Jilliana. I didn't realize you were there."

She huffs. "Of course you didn't. You're too busy blackmailing the director into kicking me to the curb."

Monty sent us the announcement this morning via email since he's still nursing his hangover. I've been dreading the moment I would see Jilliana ever since. I'd selfishly hoped she'd stay sick for at least a few more days. I'm silently cursing my luck until Jilliana's accusation finally hits.

My eyes widen in my reflection as I gape at her. "What did you say?"

She shrugs a shoulder, her natural red, perfectly ironed curls fall effortlessly over her shoulder and I twirl one of my wild ones self-consciously.

"You're blackmailing Monty into making you Marguerite." She stops examining her dress in the mirror and turns to me with crossed arms. "Do you know how much I've had to sacrifice to get that spot, only to come down with a damn stomach bug the night casting directors from all over the country came to visit?"

"Casting directors were here last night?"

Jilliana's brilliant green eyes flare. "Oh my god, you didn't know?" She scoffs. "You didn't know, and still sang the best performance of your life. That's... infuriating if I'm honest. Monty and Maggie are meeting with some today to talk about casts for their upcoming shows. Where have you *been*, Scarlett? Do you even care about your future, or are you just stealing the spotlight for your own amusement?"

Heat rises into my cheeks and I know my light skin is beet red. But she's right, I've been going to Bordeaux, fulfilling the dream my father wanted—the one *I* thought I wanted. Since I achieved a taste of it last night, I'm truly at a loss for what's next. I'm more confused than ever as to whether I want to do anything theater related, or whether I've been hiding in my understudy position, too afraid to take charge and audition for the main character in my own life.

"Listen, Jilliana, I swear I didn't blackmail Monty. I don't even know where his letter came from. I was at Masque along with everyone else when it was delivered."

Jilliana's face scrunches in thought before she sighs. "Okay, fine. I guess that was a little far fetched. It's just weird that whoever the sender is said to keep *you* as the lead. Like, why would they care? Besides, I think I'm more mad about Monty rolling over like a wet dog after everything I've done for—"

Her mouth clamps down and I frown.

"What have you done, Jilliana?" I ask quietly.

Her eyes glisten and she shakes her head with her lips tight. I've known Jilliana for years but we've never been close. Still, my heart hammers at the distraught look on her face and every girl code alarm is blaring loudly in my mind. I glance around the fitting room before taking her hand.

"Follow me," I order and lead her through the dark recesses backstage. My room isn't far away, so it takes us no time to get there.

Once I do, I shove us inside and close the door.

My room is slightly less messy since I cleaned up this morning, but the couch is still covered with my costumes from closing night. I point to my makeup chair for her to sit while I perch on the arm of my couch.

"Okay... talk to me. Did you do something for Monty?" At my question, Jilliana's gorgeous full red lips thin so much that they whiten and I rephrase the question. "What has Monty *made* you do?"

The change in wording seems to strike a chord and that bottom lip begins to wobble. Realization kicks in. I've always heard rumors about how Jilliana *earned* her role as Juliet after her crappy audition. That one day wasn't her best, but she's an amazing singer and a phenomenal actress. I never doubted she deserved the role, but I did doubt the rumors.

Until now.

"Oh, Jilliana..." I lean my shoulder against the wall and hold myself back from hugging her. I know what it's like to feel violated, so I refrain from comforting her physically until I know how she wants to be consoled. "Does he... does he hurt you?"

She wipes her cheeks as tears spill down them and shakes her head vigorously. "No, nothing like that. He just, um, said that if I wanted the role I had to... *show* him how much I wanted it. On my knees."

Disgust for that awful man slithers over my skin. "What a fucking pig."

"Right? That's what I said... but then he told me that if I didn't do it, he'd tell everyone I came onto *him* and that I'd get kicked out of Bordeaux."

"Jilliana, you *have* to tell Maggie. She's the assistant director and can tell her husband—"

"No!" Jilliana yelps before gentling her voice again. "Just... no. All I want is to get through my senior year unscathed. No one will hire me if they think I accuse directors of... you know."

I nod reluctantly, not comfortable with the forced limbo Jilliana is in. But I totally get it. I didn't report Jacques last week and he was just one of the temporary stagehands, not our *director*.

"I'm sorry Jilliana... if I can do anything—"

"You can't," she murmurs. "Not unless you can find the blackmailer. Whoever he or she is, is ruining everything."

"Believe me, if I could find him, I would." Even though I have no idea who is sending the letters, I still feel weirdly responsible and wish I could do more than just comfort her. "Can I give you a hug?"

She gives me a watery smile, and as she stands, I embrace her taller form underneath her arms and whisper. "I think you should report him, but I get why you're afraid. I'll help any way I can, even if it's just holding your hand while you come forward."

"Thanks, girl. I don't want to do anything, yet. I just—" Her hug stiffens right before she pushes me away so hard I almost fall. She snatches a paper off my desk and my heart freezes in my chest as cold panic grips me. "What the hell is this, Scarlett?"

She flips over the envelope from my demon of music, revealing the crimson wax seal I'd carefully opened around to keep intact.

"Jilliana, I can explain—"

"You said you had nothing to do with Monty's blackmail."

I take a step forward, but she raises the letter above her head, making it impossible to reach.

"I didn't. I—"

"Then why the fuck do you have the same envelope?"

I stop trying to retrieve the letter and riffle through my jewelry box to find the sheets of music from my other letters. Part of me wants to keep my demon to myself and own up to a crime I didn't commit. But my fingers shake on the paper because I'm more terrified I'll get kicked out of Bordeaux if I keep him a secret any longer.

"What game are you playing, Scarlett?"

"It's from... the envelope is from my..." I hesitate, not knowing how to out him and not seem crazy.

"Spit it out. Who is sending you letters?"

My demon of music.

"It's from a secret admirer," I finally blurt out.

Boiling my demon down to such a simple moniker feels like a betrayal on my tongue, drying my mouth like ash. But it's the best I can come up with without sounding off my rocker for corresponding with what is essentially a very musically talented stalker.

I hand her the many pages of sheet music before I can stop myself. She takes them warily, eyes narrowed.

"A secret *admirer*?" Her words are carefully measured before she studies the papers. After a moment, she hums one of my favorites until a high note cuts her off with a squeak. She clears her throat and those angry emerald eyes shoot daggers at me. "Nice song. And how convenient it is that it's perfectly in your register. Tell me something, Scarlett, whenever do you find the time to compose, what with all your backstabbing and blackmailing?"

My jaw drops. "What? No, I—"

"Did you give me the stomach flu too? So I'd have to miss the one night casting directors come to scope out the talent?"

"Jilliana, you have to believe me—" I take a step forward and Jilliana gathers all the sheet music up before power walking out my door.

"Believe what? That you're a lying bitch who is so pathetic she writes herself love letters?"

She twists the papers in her hands, ripping up a page of music, and I run after her to rescue my gifts. Thanks to her dance experience, she easily pivots away from me before picking up her pace and throwing handfuls to the ground. My throat tightens as each piece drops.

"Jilliana, stop! Please—"

I bend to the ground to collect them as we go, ignoring all the ogling spectators drawn to our drama. She continues to march toward the stage and hot tears burn my eyes. I do my best to keep them from rolling down, widening my eyes so that I don't embarrass myself even more by getting too emotional, but it's nearly impossible to stay composed.

By the time I've caught up to her, she's already in the middle of the stage, ripping all the music sheets and my heart into shreds, scattering them both to the ground like confetti.

"What is all this supposed to prove, Scarlett?" she spits out bitterly, straightening her posture when she seems to realize we have an audience. "Because all I'm seeing is a jealous psycho coming for my spot. The spotlight *I* earned."

It's on my tongue to be vindictive and correct her, but that would undoubtedly make things worse.

"I swear, I had nothing to do with Monty's message. That's what I was trying to show you. That I've been receiving my own letters, too—"

"What's going on?" Jaime appears from backstage with Maggie not too far behind. "Jilliana, what the hell are you going on about now?"

"We've got rehearsals and not a lot of time to make this show flawless," Maggie joins in. "Let's get back to our places, people."

Reinforcements. Thank goodness.

"Oh, great. Let's ask her best friend, shall we? Jaime, why don't you fill us in?" Jilliana turns around in a circle like an announcer for a fight, stopping at Jaime. "Maybe you can tell us who blackmailed Monty. I'm sure Scarlett's bragged all about her little *secret admirer.*"

"Her what?" Jaime snorts before Jilliana's eyes narrow and he realizes just how pissed she is.

She slaps a torn sheet of music and the envelope into Jaime's chest. He catches them and a bewildered expression wrinkles his face as she questions him.

"Looks just like the so-called Phantom's, right?"

Jaime chews his lip as he inspects the sheets, and Maggie reads around his shoulder. When Jaime turns over the envelope to the seal, his eyes flare with recognition and flick to me. Either confusion or indecision wrinkles his brow, neither of which is good for me.

"So?" Jilliana asks, her hand propped on her hip. "Tell us all about her little admirer. I'll be the first to apologize if you can tell me who wrote these. Who threatened Monty and sent *her* love notes?"

Jaime gulps and his grimace shows how concerned and uncertain he is. My chest aches as soon as I realize he's not going to stick up for me. And why would he? I never told him about the letters because I was afraid of the exact look he's giving me right now. His face is one I vaguely remember him making only once before, right before the cops took me to the hospital.

"Um, Scarlett, are you feeling okay?" he asks quietly. "I know you were excited last night—"

Maggie winces. "I'm sure there's another explanation—"

"Oh that's *right*. How could I forget the most important thing about our little Miss Perfect Scarlett? You're bipolar, aren't you? Doesn't that mean you're crazy as fuck?"

"Jilliana, shut the fuck up. You don't know what you're

talking about," Jaime reprimands while he glances nervously at Maggie.

But Jilliana barrels ahead, like she's finally found the missing clue to her mystery. "You've even been committed once before. You went cuckoo bananas and the cops had to take you in. What does your psychiatrist have to say about you sending yourself little love notes to brag to all your friends? Did you somehow make Jacques hang himself, too? I know he had a thing for you."

Have I gone crazy again?

The question rings in my mind and the burning tears finally leak from the well of my eyes, trailing down my cheeks. I let them fall, refusing to call any more attention to them by wiping them away.

"Scarlo—"

"Aw... Scarlett," Jilliana interrupts my friend and mocks me with a fake pout. "There's no reason to get so *emotional*. They're just questions. I just want to know why you're writing these notes to yourself and blackmailing Monty."

Am I writing these notes to myself? Is it all in my head?

I shake away the thought because it *can't* be true. I know how to write music, but I've never been as talented as my demon. Or maybe I have been and I'm just realizing it now in a manic state?

"No," I say out loud and focus on Jilliana. "I didn't blackmail Monty. Obviously Jacques was having trouble of his own, and I didn't send these notes and music to myself—"

"Then who did?" Jilliana asks as she crosses her arms.

"I... I don't know."

No way in hell am I going to explain my theories that sound wild even to me. That my demon of music wrote them for me, or that he's the muse my father promised me, *or* that I dreamed he and Sol Bordeaux were one and the same in a drug-induced stupor and that I had the best orgasm of my fucking life with only my fingers and a dream.

Shit. Maybe she's right.

"All right, that's enough of that," Maggie yells over the

crowd's growing whispers. "Everyone, we have a *lot* to do in very little time, alright? All this will get sorted out soon."

I bend to pick up a few more sheets, keeping a wide berth away from the fellow student I once thought could be my friend. There are a few pieces left that I leave alone as embarrassment stings my skin. All the while, people snicker and gawk. No one helps me. Not even Maggie or Jaime.

By the time I've gathered up enough to hopefully put most of them back together, I turn on my heels and walk back to my room, trying to hold my head high.

"Make sure you take your meds today, Scarlett! You're already so upset. Don't want to have to lock you up again!"

"*Cállate la puta boca*, Jilliana. Goddamn," Jaime fires back as the dark hallway swallows me up.

I desperately wish I could disappear. My friend is calling for me to stop, but I don't wait for him. Instead, I pick up speed until I get to my room and shut the door, careful not to slam it in case someone thinks I'm being *moody*.

Taking a steadying breath, I try to ignore Jaime calling for me from the other side of the door. If he can't stick up for me in public, then he can sit out there all by himself. I lock the door and collapse right on top of the clothes covering the couch. I spread the sheet music pieces on my small coffee table, trying to organize them, but angry hurt has blurred my vision to near blindness. Blood rushes in my ears, muffling Jaime's—and now Maggie's —pleas.

I know they were just as blindsided by this whole fiasco as I was. Still, not being able to adequately stick up for myself, and then not having anyone stick up for me, stings like hell and I'm not ready to see them again.

My mind flashes back to my dad comforting me, talking me through what we hadn't yet realized were episodes. The depression or mania would come on slowly back then and last for weeks. But he'd always remained patient, just joking that I had my mother's wild fighting spirit.

He'd meant it as a compliment, but my mom left us because she didn't have the tools to understand herself, and we certainly weren't equipped to handle her. We had to find out from the officer on our doorstep when that fighting spirit left this world entirely. She'd been in the middle of what must have been a depressive episode and alcohol had always been her cure. It'd been her damnation the night she'd gotten behind the wheel with it.

Ever since, my "wild fighting spirit" has scared the shit out of me. It wasn't until my first full-blown manic episode after my dad died that I was forced to get help. Jilliana just cruelly threw my worst moments in my face.

But is she right? Am I going crazy again?

From my seat on the couch, I peer inside the open door to my bedroom, to where I *know* I left my orange bottle of old medication last night. The container is nowhere to be found and has been missing since I woke up this morning. The only explanation I have is that the dream version of Sol Bordeaux I conjured last night took it.

Fuck, what if I am losing it again?

More than anything, I wish my dad was here... or, ironically, I wish I could hear the music that caused this whole mess.

Vibrations buzz against my thigh and it's only then that I realize I'm still wearing my costume over my leggings and thin T-shirt. I unzip the back and slide it off quickly, just in time to retrieve my phone from the pocket on the side of my leggings and answer without looking at the caller ID.

"Little Lettie!" Rand's voice sounds so wrong to my ears, especially when I was just wishing for my dad's. But maybe Rand's the exact distraction I need right now. Someone who knew me before my diagnosis. Someone who knew my dad.

Hope for a reprieve flutters in my heartbroken chest as I mask the wobble threatening in my voice. "Rand, hey! What's up?"

"I'm in the Quarter on business. Want to go get your favorite while I have a break?"

I jackknife up. "Beignets?" I pause and narrow my eyes with suspicion even though he's not in the room. "From where?"

His chuckle warms my chest, reminding me of a time when twelve-year-old me craved to make him happy. The fact that he's laughing now does wonders for the throbbing pain in my heart, especially when he answers correctly.

"Café du Monde, obviously."

Scene 7

JUSTICE IN THE DUNGEON

T he coward in front of me died with pain permanently etched into his miserable face. He knew once my shadow brought him down here that there were only two ways out of my dungeon, trial by water or combat.

The first means risking the runoff channel that flows on the far side of the stone room. It's one thousand feet to the mouth of the Mississippi River in dark, murky water that requires one to hold their breath for many feet at a time through the tunnels. It's treacherous, especially if the water is slow that day, but I've done it several times in the middle of the night, just to ensure the fairness of my options.

The second is by far the more dangerous alternative: a duel with choice of weapon.

He didn't even put up much of a fight.

Many people look at me and somehow assume I didn't train for years in everything I've supplied in this room. They see the river and think I'm the safest bet, but every single victim has been sorely mistaken, and this one was no different. I even gave this sad bastard my knife once I realized how poor of a shot he was with his gun. He still didn't stand a chance with my fists.

"Brother?" my twin's voice echoes down into the cellar. "A word?"

I don't answer, continuing to wipe my hands on the wet washcloth, annoyed that there's blood still in the crevices of my ring.

"It's always so dark down here," he complains for the millionth time in a decade.

"It's how I like it," I explain again. With my poor eyesight, I'm at a better advantage in the dark.

Ben takes the last step on the staircase and enters the room. "Yeah, well now it smells like piss too. The combination is—" He rears back, turning his face into the crook of his blazer's elbow as he sees my kill in the middle of the room. "*Shit*, Sol. You didn't tell me you had another one."

"I don't tell you a lot of things," I reply simply.

Us Bordeaux brothers may be identical in DNA, but what made us who we are at our core is entirely different. His soft, compassionate, thoughtful personality was molded by loving parents and the best French boarding school money can buy. That was me too, until I turned fifteen and I was stripped of everything I knew.

I saw our loving father get murdered, our saintly mother fall into a psychotic depression from which she never emerged, and I was tortured mercilessly. Only murder set me free. Just like my victims down here, if they ever beat me, that is.

So if I told my diplomatic brother all the unsavory things I have to do behind the scenes to keep our people safe and to make those who hurt us pay, Ben might not fare much better than our poor mother.

"What did this one know that saved him from the usual Phantom suicide?" he asks, trying to cover his nose.

Phantom suicide.

It's what I am—or the Phantom of the French Quarter is—known for. Phantom suicides are reserved for the men who are so guilty that I don't need their confession and they don't deserve a chance to fight for their lives. The mysterious deaths are made to look like suicides so that our contacts in the police department have easy and *uncomplicated* reports.

"This one is a little message, to show our dear Chatelain friends their business needs to stay the fuck out of our French Quarter."

"Is that why you left your calling card?" He points to the crude skull imprinted into the man's forehead and I shrug.

"It suits him, don't you think? He chose a gun and was so terrible at aiming that I gave him my knife and resorted to fists." I scrub the fine indents of my skull ring to clean any remnants left during our fight to the death. "It'll be good for Chatelain to realize I'm behind this one. He's gotten too comfortable. Good Ol' Randy Boy needs to know his place."

"'Randy Boy,' huh? Never knew you were one for nicknames."

"I don't see how you could've missed that part of my personality. I have several myself, if you'll recall."

Ben gives a mirthless chuckle. "Someone's got a sense of humor today. What's got you in such a good mood?"

Not what...who.

I feel the twitch of a smile lift my lips, but I quickly school my face. It's just my brother, but if I show him my true feelings, he'll try to make me stop what I've been doing. I can't let him stand in the way. Not of this.

"Nothing," I finally answer. "I just enjoy administering justice. And this one..." I tap my victim's loafer. "He had info on an unsolved case right here in New Orleans."

"Seriously? I don't remember a recent case in the French Quarter. Was it from Dad's time?"

"Nope. A year ago. In the Garden District."

Recognition flickers on Ben's face and I know I've been caught. There's a reason he runs the front of our business—he's sharp as a tack.

"Sol, what the *fuck*? We can't be in Chatelain business."

"This *isn't* Chatelain business. Gustave Day—"

"Scarlett's dad's murder is *not* Bordeaux business. It happened on the Chatelain side, ergo, it involves Rand's police force, his people. This is Rand's cold case to solve."

"She's not one of his," I hiss. The fury that boiled up so quickly surprises me, but I don't tamp it down.

"She's not one of ours, either."

"Not yet," I promise, my nostrils flaring.

Ben simply shakes his head. "I'll repeat it again. Gustave Day's murder is *not* Bordeaux business. the truce—"

"Fuck the truce," I spit back.

"Sol, I know you think it's bullshit, but it's an agreement between our families all the same. I made it with Rand's brother, Laurent, and when you killed him, you sealed the accord. Now it extends to Rand and we should abide by the rules. We must if we're to keep this city and our families safe."

"You were coerced to enter that *agreement* by Laurent. And *now*... he's gone," I point out smugly. "There's no need to keep this farce of a truce going."

We had all of New Orleans at one point and the Chatelains were simply a thorn in my father's side. Then one night when I was fifteen, during our boarding school's equivalent of spring break, all hell broke loose.

"We can't have a repeat of that night," Ben pleads. "I lost my father, mother—"

"And brother," I finish, knowing the young man I was, never came back after that night.

Ben swallows but doesn't argue with my claim. "I know. But the truce keeps our families safe, so that something like that will never happen again. You already took out Jacques Baron—"

"He was a spy who deserved to hang for all the harm he caused our families. Not to mention the fact he was assaulting women in *our* home."

"I don't disagree. But if you rile Rand up—"

"It's just this one case," I argue. "Aside from the fact that it's a cold case, something about Gus Day's murder doesn't make sense."

"How so?" Ben asks.

"Well, if the Chatelains and the Days were on such good terms, why would Rand not be outraged about his death? It was on his turf."

Ben snorts. "That's a weak opening statement, brother. They might have had a close relationship *ten years* ago, but that doesn't mean Rand would turn over heaven and earth to find a suspect in what seems to be a random mugging, even if it was for his childhood friend. Any other details, Mr. *Holmes*?"

I glare at him. "Someone attacked Scarlett that night. He tried to assault her." My fingers bite into my palms at the memory. "Her father attempted to stop him, but the attacker turned on him instead. The bastard never pulled a gun on Scarlett, saving it for the confrontation with her father. Almost like he was waiting for him and Scarlett was merely a distraction."

"And you got all this from police reports and this snitch?" I don't elaborate and just nod. Ben frowns and rubs his eyes. "So the attacker was waiting for him because... why? It sounds far fetched, Sol. Who would murder Gus Day? He was a beloved jazz musician, for fuck's sake. And hell, the perpetrator wouldn't have needed a gun with Scarlett. She's practically a waif."

I wince at his observation, but he's not wrong. Watching her spark dim this past year has been torture. She's taken care of herself mentally, but everywhere else in her life she's a shadow of the bright light I've seen her to be, hiding away from the world. I'm *this* close to intervening. Hell, I did a lot more than "intervene" last night.

Physically shaking my head to push the delicious vision away, I turn back to our conversation and point to the dead man between us. "I'm not sure who would want to murder Scarlett's father, but this guy seemed to think Day was struggling more than he let on. He was apparently in deep debt with a Chatelain man or involved in some shady shit connected with the Chatelains somehow."

"Did he say that? That he owed someone who worked for the Chatelains?"

My jaw tics in frustration, not wanting to show my hand yet. "No, but it's not a far stretch."

Ben huffs. "Not a far stretch? Sol, it's a running leap. Rand would've been *in charge* of that hit. He and Scarlett are childhood friends. Do you really think he'd make that call? He's not a monster."

"*All* the Chatelains are monsters," I growl.

Ben's nostrils flare and I suddenly realize I'm inches away from his face. I don't wear my mask down here, so he's seeing the ugliest side of me. The side of *him* that could've existed if he'd been the one to sneak out that night and get kidnapped nearly a decade ago.

"I'm not your enemy," Ben says, his voice calm and admonishing at the same time.

I jolt back and almost run my hand through my hair until I realize it's still not perfectly clean. I go to wash my hands, leaving them under the rushing water even as it becomes scalding.

"You're not my enemy," I finally agree on an exhale. "I wish I could apologize, but I won't stop until I get answers."

"Why? What does this have to do with us? If Day was connected to the Chatelains and he died in the Garden District then he's not our problem. What's your end goal here? Find the murderer?"

My hands clench around the bar of soap underneath the spigot as I consider my answer. "Something like that."

"Seriously, Sol. You have to give me a reason—"

"I can't see Scarlett suffer anymore, okay?" I give him the partial truth. "Maybe if she knows the circumstances around her father's death, then she can live again."

Numbness has crept into my hands and I dry them off on another washcloth. The old spigot squeaks its protest as I shut off the water with the towel. When I turn around, Ben is staring at me with a thoughtful look.

"What?" My voice is stern and unforgiving. I don't like to be examined, and Ben's studious nature never ended after law school.

He shakes his head. "You like her. *Really* like her."

"I don't know what you're talking about."

I turn away to avoid his inspection and awkwardly look for something to do with my hands. But there's nothing. I already cleaned myself up and I can't move the body yet. It's got to drain so it'll be easier to cut him up and dissolve identifiable pieces before dumping the rest in Chatelain's precious garden.

"Scarlett Day," Ben insists. "I've seen you get obsessed, fixated, stalk your prey, but I've never seen you like this over a *woman*. You've got to let her go, Sol."

"Why?" I ask, wheeling around on him and giving myself away in the process. "You have Maggie and Marie. Why can't I have Scarlett?"

"Aside from the fact that Chatelain has made a claim to her? Because I *dated* Maggie." He enunciates each word like I'm an idiot and all I want to do is break his flawless nose. "We fell in love. Got married. Then we had our daughter. And we did all that in the daylight, which you avoid like the plague. *That's* the way things work. You don't go outside, brother, and you use informants along with whatever Madam G hears from Masque to build this Phantom of the French Quarter facade. But when was the last time you even *saw* Bourbon Street?" I open my mouth to argue but he tsks. "*Not* through a security camera. Real life."

That caveat clamps my mouth shut, and I'm too stubborn in my own fears and shame to prove him wrong. I do what is necessary to run the security side of our operation, but I don't venture outside the comfort of the House often if I can help it.

What happened to me is one of those French Quarter tall tales, like the legends behind the Sultan's Palace and Romeo spikes on balconies. The kidnapping and torture of Sol Bordeaux is a ghost story. A cautionary tale to New Orleans boys not to go out in the middle of the night. But no one knows the whole story, and I never go out without my mask on to confirm theirs.

I don't give a fuck what I look like, though. That's not why I stick to the shadows. Half of my face is a grotesque ruin and my eye was stolen from me, but I cover the right side of my face because I'm ashamed the Chatelains got the best of me. And I'm horrified over the collapse of my family in the process. If I hadn't been a stupid, impetuous child, my family would still be intact. We'd still *rule* New Orleans, and maybe even all of Louisiana. We wouldn't be desperately holding on to the NOLA Port to keep it away from the sick Chatelain bastards.

"Listen," Ben continues, more gently. "If I knew you'd step in the daylight for her, I'd fucking *encourage* this fantasy. Hell, I'd set up the reservation at Arnaud's myself. But it's just that, Sol. A fantasy. And your obsession is going to get one of you killed."

That has my attention.

"How so?"

"You'll break the truce and Rand will retaliate. You've already toyed with the clauses. There's to be no harm in the opera house, and yet Jacques—"

"*Unless provoked*. The clause is 'No harm in the opera house unless provoked.' As Rand's former proxy, Jacques Baron's very existence here was a provocation." The words growl out of me, emerging from somewhere deep in my chest.

"Okay, what about your latest victim? He's a Chatelain man but you and I can't breach sides except by invitation."

"I haven't done that, either. I've been waiting for this one to make the wrong move." I nod at the corpse.

One of my shadows found him selling drugs to one of the drumming kids on Bourbon Street last night. The bastard was peddling the same poison that caused a child's overdose death just last week. I'd been watching over my angel and I'd hated to leave her, but it's my job to protect my people. It's a good thing I left, because according to my security feed, this was the exact man we were looking for.

"He was already on my radar as a Chatelain man," I explain to my brother. "He had information that I needed about the night of Gus Day's murder. But then he came to the Quarter and committed a crime that resulted in death. See? No breach."

"Seems almost convenient, don't you think?" Ben's eyes narrow at me.

His words make me pause. "What does?"

"That you'd so obviously reveal your obsession with Miss Day in front of Rand, and then the perfect snitch appears at the right time and right place. Do you not think Rand is tempting you to make one wrong move yourself?"

His points make me hesitate, but I shake my head. "No fucking way. That posh idiot couldn't figure out how to tie Velcro shoes."

Ben shrugs. "But what if he *is* smart enough? He hasn't been in town since he buried his brother in Lafayette Cemetery No.1. Now he's back from New York requesting to build a hotel in the Quarter and access to New Orleans's port? You know Laurent was trying to reintroduce human trafficking after our father eradicated it here. Who's to say Rand isn't trying to fill big brother's shoes?"

All the math is adding up except that it's *Rand*, not Laurent, who would have to be the mastermind.

"Not possible."

"You still see Rand as the goofy blond kid from school. The annoying suck-up we loved to hate. You were trapped by Laurent, but *I* was on the outside, witnessing Rand watch his older brother's every brutal, calculating move. He had to have learned *something* before he ran away to New York. He left his side of New Orleans in the hands of his proxy for too long, but he's back with a plan and I think your obsession with Scarlett Day has given him an opening. Think about it. We lost *half* of this fucking city to them over one calculated incident. Either you and I can't live up to our father's name, or the Chatelains are actually *dangerous*."

I shake my head and point at my brother as I try to get him to see reason. "You were a child when you were forced to sign that bullshit truce. You only went along with it because you thought Laurent would return me if you did. Our father had been murdered days before and I was held as ransom at the time. No one expected you to live up to our father's legacy at fifteen."

"While that may be true, I, for one, choose to err on the side of caution. Rand is formidable, Sol, and he has an interest in Miss Day. What if he's using her to get to you? That makes her a threat to our family and all the loyal people backing us. You need to accept that. Leave her—and all this—*alone.*"

My hands squeeze into tight fists that make my knuckles ache more than the fight I just won. Ben has always been the twin with the logical brain and I've always been the one with the emotional brawn. I trust him with my life, but even as he states his case against getting involved with Scarlett, I can't shake the compulsion to check my many security cameras set up all throughout the House to see what my obsession is up to.

I had my trusted shadows install, or rewire, every camera on the Bordeaux side of New Orleans. Ben may be the legal protection for our people, but I'm responsible for the physical and that includes knowing every meticulous detail about my city.

Fuck, maybe Ben's right. What if she is a distraction?

A chime dings from the security room down the cellar hallway and I spin on my heel to go check it.

"Sol, have you been listening—"

"I've heard you," I snap right before I enter the darker room. A message blinks on a far computer and I pull it up on the screen.

She left. I couldn't follow.

Alarm pounds in my chest, but I try to calm down as I search the security footage spanning the French Quarter, hoping she's still on our side of the city.

The shadow would've told me where she'd gone if he knew, but I have a suspicion. My little muse has a sweet tooth like me and she's also a beautiful creature of habit, which I've come to be thankful for.

Ben is wrong. Rand isn't using her against us. I know everything about Scarlett Day, so I would know whether she was one of his pawns.

Wouldn't I?

Refusing to dwell on questions I can't answer, I switch the screens to my first guess and nearly smile when I see her wild, gorgeous black curls haphazardly piled on her head. A powdered sugar grin curves her pink lips. Someone is blocking the camera, but it looks like she's just sat down with her white paper Café du Monde bag and hasn't yet poured the remaining sugar into her chicory coffee. I tried the concoction last Halloween. It's cloyingly sweet, just like her.

Except I've witnessed the dark side she possesses. It was only once, but that night changed everything, sparking my obsession. Ever since, I've craved to learn everything about my angel of music. I desperately need to know if her darkness matches mine.

Just when I'm about to sit down and appreciate watching Scarlett as she enjoys one of her favorite things, the person who'd been blocking the camera finally moves.

The warmth I'd been feeling turns to ice in my veins.

"What the fuck is she doing?" I grumble.

"Fuck, I knew it." Ben appears in the room beside me. His muttered curse embodies everything I feel. "Do you still think he's incapable of manipulating you, Sol?"

I don't answer as my brain tries to drum up a plan to follow her. To hear what she's saying to him. Is her smile for him, or the pillowy powdered donut that Rand Chatelain is currently wiping from her lips with his *fucking* thumb?

"Quit growling, you beast. Living underground has made you a goddamn animal," Ben mumbles. I hadn't even realized the rumble was coming from me. "She's not yours, Sol. She's not even one of *ours*, loyal to our family. We can't afford her the same protections. You know the parameters of the truce. Only those loyal to our families are protected. Whether she knows it or not, her loyalties lie with Rand."

I pull my fists into my lap to keep them from sending my keyboard flying. I want to get up, run to Café du Monde, and demand Rand's seat. My face and shame burn in protest.

"What're you going to do about it, Sol? Go get her?" He's reading my mind again, mocking me.

But he's also making a point. It's broad daylight and not Halloween, Mardi Gras, or any other celebration that would warrant a mask. Going out and about in public—even with one of my more realistic prosthetics on—would be admitting defeat to the Chatelains in the eyes of those who believe the rumors. That Laurent did, in fact, scar me for life. That I made the Bordeauxs weak with one impulsive decision and that we can be taken down in one swift move.

"I can't." The whispered admission crawls out of me. I wonder if my defeat sounds as pathetic to Ben's ears as it does mine.

"Then you have to let her go, Sol," Ben answers back, his voice both soft and firm at the same time. "She could ruin us. And Rand knows it."

"Beignets from Café du Monde are everything good in this world and you can't change my mind." I take another sugary bite and moan before meeting Rand's clear-blue eyes. His clear-blue *hungry* eyes.

My smile falters and I squirm in my seat. His gaze is different than the one Sol Bordeaux gave me at Masque last night and the one I imagined in my drug-induced dream. Sol's intensity made my core throb, my breath freeze in my chest, and need overwhelm my skin in an explosion of goose bumps.

Rand's feels... odd? I can't quite explain it. It's not *unwelcome* I guess, but it's certainly not giving me the same intoxicating desire that I felt last night. His elbows are propped on the wobbly white table, and his chin rests on thick, interlaced fingers. I study them, remembering featherlight touches by a completely different set of fingers from my dream, long and powerful—

"Do you still have a crush on me?" Rand asks, snapping me from my dirty imagination.

"Wait, what?"

"We were childhood sweethearts, Lettie. I'm the boy you ate beignets with while people-watching on Bourbon Street. Don't tell me you've forgotten our epic love story," he teases.

"Oh." I laugh and wave a powdered sugar–covered hand. "Childhood crushes are so silly, right?"

"And why do you think that? Hm?" He smirks and trails a finger down my hand. "Don't you remember those hot summer nights together? I don't think I could ever forget your touch..."

My smile grows brittle at the edges and I move my hand to take another bite of beignet, trying to hide my discomfort. Ever since I realized those *touches* back then were wrong, I've tried hard to forget those confusing nights. I'd had a crush on him, sure, but at twelve, I wasn't mentally or emotionally ready to act on it like he apparently was.

"Well, you were sixteen and I... wasn't. I guess looking back I see it a little differently."

He scowls and sits up straighter before sipping his chicory coffee. That's all the man got. Whoever goes to Café du Monde and *doesn't* order beignets has a screw loose somewhere.

Takes a crazy to know a crazy, right?

I blanch, but he doesn't seem to notice.

"Well, I was a kid, too, y'know. But it's a good thing we're older now, right? No societal standards to hold us back."

His brilliant smile is back and I try to meet it. My heart is pounding as I search for what to say. I don't want to hurt his feelings, but I'd rather not think about that particular part of our past.

"We've definitely both grown. Now I know that you were meant to be more like the brother I always wanted."

That grin disappears again and I'm sure I've annoyed him. Or maybe I'm just reading into things.

I have been paranoid...

I swallow a sugary gulp and close my eyes, knowing the truth. I'm going to have to suck it up and call my doctor for an earlier appointment or things could get much worse from here.

"Are you enjoying your beignet?" Rand asks and I nod, thankful for the small talk.

"Yup, almost finished actually—"

Rand reaches out and brushes powdered sugar from my lip with his thumb. I jolt back. I can't help it. My admittedly messy fingers swipe my lip, no doubt making it much worse, but I have a real need to get his touch off of my skin.

"Shit, Scarlett, you don't have to act like I'm diseased. I'm not some Bordeaux." Hurt mars his handsome face and I wince.

"Sorry, I didn't mean to... I just wasn't expecting—"

"For a friend to help you when you have something on your face? Jesus Christ."

For you to touch me at all.

He glances around as if he's checking to make sure no one noticed my embarrassing reaction. Seemingly satisfied by the lack of nosy onlookers, he clears his throat.

"Well, I think you should get used to me helping you out."

"Um... why?"

"I'm going to be around more. I've moved back home from New York to finally take over the family business. I've put off my responsibilities for long enough."

"Oh. That's exciting." I bite my lip as I try to think of how to broach my next question. "How are you holding up? You know, with Jacques..."

His neutral expression darkens. "What do you know about Jacques?"

"Nothing. Nothing at all, really," I reply hastily, not liking his change in mood. "Just that he worked as a stagehand at Bordeaux Conservatory and he also worked for you in some capacity—"

"How do you know that?"

It's on the tip of my tongue to answer him, to try to appease his anger, but I don't want to get Jaime in trouble if Jacques's employment was some kind of secret. "That's just what I gathered from last night. You know, since we found out he committed—"

"It wasn't suicide," Rand spits back. "The Bordeauxs were behind it."

I dart my gaze around to make sure no one's listening before I whisper. "You think the Bordeauxs... *murdered* Jacques?"

"I do. And now one of my men has gone AWOL. It's why I'm in the French Quarter today."

"AWOL?" My brow furrows as I try to keep up with all the accusations and information. "As in, he's a missing person?"

Rand sucks his teeth and nods. "Yup. I met with some of my contacts earlier today to try to find him, but I can't. I'm afraid he might be in trouble, what with him being on the Bordeaux side of New Orleans and all."

"I'm sorry, Jaime's already scolded me for being so out of the loop. But what do you mean by the Bordeaux side?"

He narrows his eyes. "The Bordeauxs think they run this town, but they're sorely mistaken. Like I said last night, they're thugs, Scarlett. And dangerous. They hurt and harass innocent people in the French Quarter all the time. I'm just hoping my man didn't get caught up in their criminal exploits."

My eyes widen. "That's so scary. Are you going to call the police?"

He shakes his head. "They're in the Bordeaux's pocket. If I can't find him myself, there's nothing I can do."

I'm touched, but also a little surprised that he's confiding in me. I can't help but want to comfort my friend. "Rand, I'm so sorry. Is there anything *I* can help with?"

A small smile curves his lips again. "You're a good distraction, Lettie. If you want to help me, I think we should go on another date."

Rand's timing is impeccable as I take a final bite of beignet. Powdered sweetness goes down the wrong pipe and I cough, sputtering up more fine sugar with each hack.

"Jesus." He gets up to slap my back and I try my best not to squirm away from his touch while focusing on not dying. "Here."

He hands me my unsugared coffee. I take a few sips of the bitter drink, making a face as I try to stop choking.

Finally, I settle down and he kneads my shoulders once before moving his seat *right* beside me, thigh to thigh.

I wish I'd just choked.

Suicidal ideations? Or just a horrible first "date?"

Oh my God, brain, just shut the fuck up. I don't need this right now.

"You okay? You've always been a messy eater, wolfing down your food like an animal." He laughs at my expense.

"I'm okay," I answer, not having the energy to stick up for myself.

Do I ever?

My mind pauses at the thought, but I tune back into Rand's weird version of... flirting, I guess.

"Next time we go on a date, I'll choose something healthier and less messy, and fancier obviously. There's a great sushi place on my side of town."

Sushi... I like sushi but with all of the eclectic food New Orleans has to offer, sushi's not usually my go-to. Then my mind snaps out of it to argue the *real* problem here.

"Rand, did you think this was a date?"

He stops short and I *swear* he's trying not to glare at me.

"Did you... not? I thought it was pretty obvious, since I paid for everything. Why else would I invite you?"

I jerk back. "Um... because we're *friends* and you wanted to catch up?" I can't hide the edge of disappointment in my voice. I'd been looking forward to just that and he's ruined it by trying to make it more.

Rand's eyes narrow before he clears his throat again and concern plasters his face. "Are you feeling okay, Little Lettie? You seem like you got mad all of a sudden. I hate to ask, but did you take your medication today?"

My jaw drops. *"Excuse me?"*

His hands shoot up as if he's innocent and didn't just gaslight the shit out of me. "I'm just asking. I'm worried about you. You seemed happy a few minutes ago and all of a sudden you look pissed, like your bipolar meds aren't working."

Shock, embarrassment, concern, and anger run through me

like a dissonant chord and I'm not sure which note to listen to, which emotion sounds and feels right for this situation.

"What you're describing *isn't* bipolar disorder, just what everyone thinks it is. Not that it's your business, but I *did* take my meds."

Just not the right ones last night.

Reality begins to shift on me again as I try to catch the truth in all the windy chaos in my mind. I *know* I took medication last night that would stave off an episode. I *know* I've been taking care of myself. And yet, Rand has the audacity to look at me like I don't know what I'm talking about.

"Listen, if anyone should know about what's going on inside *my* head, it's me, okay?"

He shrugs, obviously not believing me. "Okay. If you say so."

"I do. Say so, that is," I add awkwardly. There's a moment of silence for the death of mediocre conversation and I end it by dumping the remaining powdered sugar into my chicory coffee.

"Scarlett," he admonishes. "That's *so* bad for you."

"What can I say? I like a little chicory in my sugar," I joke as I stand up and collect my bag.

"Hey, where are you going?"

"Home. Thank you for the beignets. They hit the spot. I've got rehearsal tonight and I really should practice."

And now I need to go before I smack you, I finish in my head.

"Wait, I'll drive you—"

"It's only a couple of blocks," I insist with a wave of my hand. "I need the exercise... especially after all these calories." I pat my stomach for emphasis with my sarcastic response.

He frowns and wraps his hand around my arm, stopping me. "I think you're getting the wrong impression. I didn't mean to offend you. I'm just worried about you. I've always cared about you. You know that. It's why I paid for your room and board at Bordeaux."

"What?" My stomach drops. "*You* did that? I thought I won that scholarship—"

His smile is warm as he reaches for my hand. "That was me, Lettie. I sponsored it after your dad died so you could still attend. And now I'm making sure you're taking care of yourself during your schooling."

"I... I had no idea."

Confusion and questions cloud my mind, but guilt that I've been harsh with him creeps in. It's almost unbelievable, but the more I think about it, the more it makes sense.

Jaime had found out about the scholarship and suggested I fill it out, but I'd been depressed and half-assed the form. When the school reached out to tell me that I'd won, I'd been surprised as hell. Getting to live in a dorm and keep going to school was a dream come true. I'd previously been renting a classic, New Orleans-style shotgun house with my dad off campus, but I was on the verge of being homeless after he died because I couldn't pay for tuition and housing. The scholarship covered both.

"I thought you didn't need to know, but if telling you keeps you from seeing me as the bad guy then I'll spill my secrets."

His confession and concern unruffles my feathers and I relax in his grip. "You're right. I'm sorry. Thank you so much. I guess I've been a little... irritable today. I do need to go, but you could walk me?" I suggest, trying to smooth things over.

Glancing down at his feet, he grimaces. "Sorry, but I'm wearing Armani. I can't walk on Bourbon Street."

A good-natured chuckle mixed with relief huffs from my chest. "No worries. I'll be fine. Like I said, it's just a couple of blocks. Bye, Rand. Thanks for the beignets."

"Wait, is tonight's rehearsal open to the public? Maybe I could cheer you on."

I appreciate his support but I shake my head. "They're closed to the public, and I think you'd make me more nervous."

"Aw, do I make you nervous, Little Lettie?" His hand curves over my shoulder and squeezes.

Yeah, actually, now that you mention it.

I dip out from underneath his grip and laugh awkwardly. "Something like that. See ya, Rand."

I'm already turning toward Bourbon Street and back to the New French Opera House when he calls to me.

"Well in that case, I'll text you ASAP about our next date."

Resisting the urge to both turn around to set the record straight that this *wasn't* a date, and also run for the hills, I settle for shouting over my shoulder. "We'll see!"

I lose myself in the crowded streets, letting the bustle of people swallow me up. My skin itches I'm so mentally irritated and all I want to do is run off this extra energy.

Am I getting up again?

Jesus.

Not everything is a symptom. Groaning outwardly, I latch on to my therapist's mantra for when my anxiety tries to take over. My next psych appointment can't come soon enough, but I can hold out until then.

Hopefully.

Scene 9

CHANDELIER DOWN

The rehearsal tonight is closed to the public. Thankfully, owning the building has its perks.

Monty has been dying to know whether the Phantom of the French Quarter is real and who is blackmailing him. I've heard he's convinced that the Phantom will attend rehearsals, so in theory, I could be risking my anonymity by showing up. But aside from staying in the shadows of my box, I've made other assurances to hide my identity as well.

All the theater boxes are locked, but I stationed one of my men on this floor as security to prevent anyone from trying to break in. Another is in charge of lighting and sound in the control booth so that the lights never darken enough to reveal me to those on stage. Not to mention that when Madam G dropped off my Sazerac, she used the same hidden stairwell I did to travel through the tunnels from the speakeasy.

Along with the smoke and mirrors act, I have one more trick up my sleeve to ensure Monty behaves. The Phantom will strike tonight, which is why *my* appearance must go unnoticed.

Though Ben may not approve of my fun, I have altruistic motives for harassing the director. A few weeks ago, I'd been navigating the old Prohibition tunnels when I heard rhythmic slapping and the redheaded soprano's Tony Award–worthy fake orgasm through the walls of his office.

He's a theater professor and director fucking a student at my family's school. I wanted to kill him then and there for the disrespect, but I hadn't known the extent of the circumstances yet. Maybe she was a more enthusiastic participant than she'd sounded.

But after Jilliana got the lead role despite her horrendous audition, I knew something was off. Now that I've spoken to my shadows doubling as stagehands, it's clear Monty is taking advantage of the young woman. My plan of action took a more deliberate turn last night, starting with his letter.

Threatening Monty has secured Scarlett's rightful place as Marguerite, the lead female role, but according to the performance I heard on my way to my muse's dorm this afternoon, he still hasn't kept his disgusting hands off the redheaded soprano.

I hadn't had the time, or the prep, to punish him then, so I'd resumed my course, silently promising my target that I'd finish my business with him tonight. At that moment, it was more important for me to visit Scarlett's empty dorm to try to find her medication and any information as to why she left with Rand.

If my second-in-command pulls through, I should be getting more answers on that front shortly. My impatience and nerves are firing through my veins as I wait, triggering fidgeting tendencies that I didn't even know I possessed, and now I can't get my knee to stop fucking bouncing.

Trying my best to focus back on the rehearsal, I study Jilliana as she adjusts to her new supporting role. She's running through her part individually at the moment, just like Scarlett is slated to do afterward.

I tip my head over the railing to see Monty studiously ignoring Jilliana, as if pretending she doesn't exist would erase the fact that he fucked her only hours ago. Meanwhile, Maggie is working her ass off backstage which happens to be perfect for my plan. I just need to wait for the right moment.

The faux door in the column across from me opens slightly, letting Sabine's lithe form slip inside. Her signature black outfit and fire mask makes her almost as terrifying as me. She doesn't sit, always preferring a ready posture.

"What do you know?" I ask, leaning forward to allow my whisper to carry.

"I spoke to my IT contact in NOLA PD. She can meet you with the videos you need." Her velvet voice is more hushed than mine. All my shadows know my hearing is excellent. It's had to be since the day half my vision was brutalized all those years ago.

Expecting a different conversation, my brow furrows as I try to figure out what she's talking about until it dawns on me. "She found the footage of Laurent's basement?"

She nods. "My contact didn't watch more than a second to confirm, like you asked, but there's more than just the clips he sent to taunt your brother. She's going to compile it all before you meet, but that bastard seems to have videotaped the entire encounter. Potentially hundreds of hours of video have been collecting dust on the shelves since it was an open and shut case."

Curiosity and rage swell in my veins. I was aware that Laurent videotaped my torture to torment Ben and trick him into agreeing to the terms of the truce, but I'd had no idea he'd recorded twenty-four seven. I *thought* I already knew everything there was to know about my kidnapping, but trying to exhaust all resources to figure out how the Chatelains and the Days are connected has me turning over every loose pebble.

My latest victim only confirmed what I'd already suspected. That there's more to Gus Day's affiliation with the Chatelains than I thought. I just have to figure out what that is.

"Will she be able to meet tomorrow night?" I ask.

"She will. By that time, she should have all the videos compiled into one format for easy transfer."

"Good."

I wait for Sabine to continue, but she doesn't. She knows why I really wanted her here, but she's hiding the ball for some reason.

"And what about earlier today?" I finally relent.

When I visited Scarlett's empty room this afternoon, not only could I not find her medication, what I *did* find made my stomach drop.

There on the coffee table were nearly all the music sheets I've given her over the past year. Ripped to shreds.

I'd crumpled to the couch and sat for way too long, just sifting through the pile. My heart pounded in my throat the entire time as I tried to piece together both the actual pages, and why she would do this. Was what happened last night the catalyst?

The thought had nearly made me sick, and I'd called my second-in-command to get to the bottom of it. If something I did caused that reaction, then I'm sure as fuck going to fix it. Somehow.

Sabine sighs and sucks her teeth, looking more than unwilling to tell me what she found out. I'm about to do what I never have to do and prompt her again when she finally answers me.

"There was an incident today while Scarlett was trying on her dress."

"What kind of *incident*?"

"Jilliana got angry at Scarlett for blackmailing Monty."

Well, that's unexpected. Why anyone would assume Scarlett is involved is bewildering. My muse may have a darkness in her that only I can see, but she'd never stoop to my depths.

"Where did Jilliana come up with that theory?"

"Jaime says she found your correspondence." My heart sinks. "Your letters to Scarlett and the one to Monty have the same wax skull seals, so Jilliana put two and two together."

"Shit," I mutter, not caring that my second sees my disappointment. "Anything else? How did she end up with Chatelain?"

"Jilliana took your letters and tore them up in front of everyone, then accused her of sabotaging her and Monty. She… also blamed Scarlett's disorder."

"Fuck. Why didn't Dominguez stick up for her? He knows his position."

"Jaime said he and Maggie didn't want to out you and were at a loss of what to do. Heat of the moment indecision."

"Unacceptable."

Sabine shrugs. "We don't all get to hide in the shadows and it's harder to perform in the spotlight."

My eye darts to hers, but I know she can't see my reproach. I feel it oozing from my every pore though, so I have no doubt she can tell my displeasure. I don't like being scolded with backhanded metaphors.

Sabine, of course, doesn't care. It's no good to have a bootlicking second and her measured boldness is why Ben and I trust her with our lives.

"Apparently, Jaime tried to console her after she ran to hide in her dressing room, but she wouldn't open her door. He heard her talking on the phone and making plans, but she refused to stop and listen to him or tell him where she was going when she left. He would've followed her, but he had class."

I shake my head and sit back, setting my drink down before my clenching fists fracture the glass. My own actions have cascaded to this point and now Scarlett has suffered. I have to fix this. I've already made an effort to remedy the torn pages, and she was able to get new medication today, but I need to cure the rest of the pain I've caused her. I didn't humiliate her and push her to Rand directly, but I toppled the first domino.

My mind drifts back to Ben's observations about Rand's plans for the city port. The Chatelains have dealt in women, drugs, and blood money from the beginning. The Bordeaux agenda has always been to thwart the Chatelains' access to the port. In the process, we've financially, legally, and physically protected New Orleanians who are loyal to us. After Prohibition, when alcohol became legal again, the Bordeauxs began to deal in information instead, and when necessary, like this morning, there's the occasional violence to secure it.

We've always been smarter, keeping them from ruining the

city and only ceding ground when our mothers' attempt at peace backfired and Laurent Chatelain decimated my family.

But unlike his ambitious brother, Rand cares more about his style than his reign. He's been in New York doing God knows what with who the hell knows. The unknown is what makes me the most nervous. If the impressionable fool found someone else to follow on their coattails, then he very well may have come back to finish what his brother started.

I'm shaken from my musings as Jilliana finishes her piece with an overly dramatic flourish and arm raise. She waits breathlessly, only for Monty to ignore her.

He's scared. Good. Let him fear the Phantom.

"Scarlett Day," he calls out. "You're up. *Il était un Roi de Thulé* from the top. Let's see if you can surpass Jilliana's rendition since you have such a *huge fan* in the Phantom of the French Quarter himself."

My jaw tics at his jab. Clearly he is not fearful enough. I glance at the shadow in the control booth in the center balcony. He nods before exiting the booth toward the far wall, and I shift my gaze onto the stage again.

"What're you up to, Sol?" Sabine asks with an edge to her voice.

"Not your concern, Sabine," I growl.

Scarlett responds to Monty softly, stoking the flames of my anger at this piece of shit for making her feel small. My spine straightens as I shift to keep an eye on the beauty, while still careful to remain in the darkness.

Scarlett is a vision in blush and gold, flawless in every way as her gown drapes loosely from her shoulders and hugs her breasts in the shape of a heart. Her dark curls fall down her back and twist over her chest to kiss her neckline. She is perfection.

But she wrings her hands as if she's nervous or uncomfortable on the stage. My brow furrows and I itch to go to her, to calm whatever discordant notes are causing her worries. As Jilliana walks off stage, Scarlett tries to make a wide berth, but Jilliana won't let her. The bitch I've been trying to help goes out of her way to bump into her so hard that Scarlett crumples to the ground.

I jerk to my feet but Sabine grabs my arm. Even her viselike grip couldn't stop me, but I glare down at her anyway. I yank free and barely resist the urge to leap over the fucking railing.

"Do you want to reveal yourself? Your interest in *her*?" she asks coolly.

I don't argue. I can't, because she's right, goddamn it. Revealing my interest in Scarlett, showing my hand in this game of cat and mouse, will only further put a target on her back. I've already done enough damage. Ben's right. As much as I crave my obsession, that's all she is. An obsession. I need to let her go.

But I don't know if I can.

Scarlett gets back up on her feet and carries her head high and proud. She stands in the middle of the stage right underneath the spotlight and takes a deep breath.

"Hurry up. We don't have all night," Monty barks, making her jump and revealing the anxiety that's plaguing her right now. I want to hurl my Sazerac glass at him but I snatch it up and pull a drink from it instead, keeping it in my hand for something to do while I remain standing to listen to my pretty little muse, my siren.

"Sorry. Okay, I'm ready."

The music begins and as she starts to sing, I lean back against the real column in the box and watch her. My eyes follow every note's trail as it begins and escapes her body. Her palms face up, seemingly drawing emotion and energy from the very air around her. The melody starts in her diaphragm, making her soft belly expand and contract. Her breasts rise and fall with each belted breath and the lyrics travel all the way up her delicate, fair neck. My free hand flexes and my cock twitches.

I'm aching to hold her in my arms right now, but I can't let my resolve disintegrate already. This will have to be the last time I see her perform—

"Leave," I command my second, not wanting an audience to witness my last moment of joy as I watch Scarlett take flight with her music for one final time.

Sabine doesn't hesitate, disappearing into the faux column again.

Scarlett's perfect bow lips surround each word, a small circle that would strangle my cock should she keep the shape. Her cheeks are flushed with exertion, no doubt exactly as they'll look the first time she's ever fucked. It's an image I'll have to take to my grave should I actually leave her alone.

"Cut!" Monty yells abruptly, forcing Scarlett to halt. "I've heard enough!" He stands in the center of the auditorium seating and screams at her. "That Phantom has got to be out of his mind if he thinks you deserve the lead over Jilliana! Are you even trying? Your high notes make my ears bleed—"

I glare at my shadow, now near a hidden pulley on the far wall, and raise my fist. At my signal, he grabs the lever with both hands, having already unlocked it, and pulls it to the side, letting the lever go free. A loud tinkling begins as the crystal chandelier above us shakes. Monty stops his tirade when the sound crescendos and the links holding up the grand fixture groan.

Suddenly, like ice in a glass, the chandelier tumbles to the seats below while Monty scrambles away, screaming for his life. Right before the fixture causes a definite crash, it stops midair. The crystals clink together like wind chimes as they settle.

Scarlett's jaw is slack and I can't read her expression. It's either stunned horror or guilty satisfaction, possibly a combination of the two.

From the stage, the poor thing doesn't have the delicious benefit of seeing Monty plastered to the ground, his face stark-white as he hyperventilates at what would've been a brutally painful death.

My great-grandfather heard a horror story from Paris about a chandelier falling in the middle of the Palais Garnier, killing a woman. He put a stopgap in place, allowing the chandelier to be lowered enough to clean or change the crystals by ladder, but not so low as to endanger patrons. Or in tonight's case, shitty directors.

Monty scrambles out from under the chandelier, unscathed, like my great-grandfather and Ben would've wanted, and stands up to brush off the imaginary dust clinging to his ridiculously cliché tweed blazer.

"Th-th-that's it. N-no more. I'm done! I quit!"

Triumph rolls through me. Monty quitting is the best-case scenario for him. Mediocre directors and professors are a dime a dozen and Bordeaux Conservatory of Music deserves the best. I'll have fun blacklisting him across the country. He'll never have a job where he can leverage his position of power over his students again.

Curious and shocked onlookers filter onto the stage. Maggie pushes through the fray and shields her eyes from the spotlight with her hand over her brow. "Monty, what the hell happened? Are you okay?"

"I'm done, Maggie! I quit! I won't risk my life for the show! Tell your husband that after all I've done for this school, I refuse to be terrorized by some monster!"

"Monty, wait!" Maggie, the kind soul that she is, jogs stage right down the stairs leading to the auditorium to follow him as he stomps out of the house. "What are you talking about?"

"The Phantom of the French Quarter! Obviously he has it out for me and I won't tolerate it—"

His voice cuts off as the doors slam shut behind him. Everyone on the stage begins to talk over one another, at a loss of what to do next. Jaime raises his hands to settle the crowd.

"Is everyone okay? No one got hurt?" They shake their heads and Jaime smiles wide. "Then it sounds like we're off for the rest of the night. Drinks at Masque?"

The cast and crew cheer and whoop, high-fiving as they exit the stage en masse. My shadow has returned to his station at the control booth, like he never left, and shuts off the big spotlight, leaving only the dim lights to illuminate the stage.

And my muse.

Without the spotlight, actors on the stage can clearly see the auditorium seating, a fact I realize much too late.

Scarlett's gasp makes my cock twitch and my eye catches her stunned silver ones, sparkling from the low lighting remaining in the hall. She takes a tentative step back—*away* from me—even though I'm a story up and three box lengths away.

Her words are barely a whisper, but thanks to the acoustics, I hear them perfectly.

"It *is* you."

Act 2

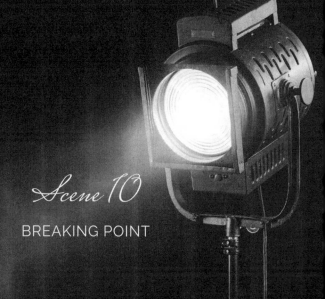

Scene 10

BREAKING POINT

I saw him.

Sol Bordeaux. The sexy man from my dream, the brooding one from Masque, and, apparently, the Phantom of the French Quarter.

He watched me from box five with sensual need plainly visible on his face, even with a bone-white mask covering half of his expression. My core clenched from just one look, while I stood in shock right there on the stage.

Does seeing him now mean that everything I know is real? Or was he an apparition? A true phantom that's only a byproduct of a wild, manic imagination? Questions barrage my brain and I can feel the aura of a panic attack coming on.

I'm so fucked.

The air in my chest can't come fast enough. I hyperventilate while staggering through the halls backstage, narrowly missing a senior baritone. In my panicked state, I push past him and collide with my dorm room door, shoving it open quickly. It's only once I'm inside that I realize I haven't taken a deep breath since I gasped onstage.

I swallow, trying to calm down, but it's no use. My vision is fading on the edges and I know it is only a matter of breaths before I pass out.

Sol Bordeaux.

One minute he was there, but in the blink of my eyes, he was gone. Like a hallucination.

But this time, I'm sober. There are no drugs in my system like last night.

Shit.

Taking the wrong meds before bed suddenly feels like one of the worst things I could've done. After I left Café du Monde today, I stopped by the pharmacy to retrieve another round of all my medications. When I got back, I took the right ones immediately. Was that not enough to stave off an episode? Or is this just a garden variety panic attack?

I've never visually hallucinated before. Auditory, yes. But my drug-induced dream last night was so vivid. Was I hallucinating then, too? Or was it real?

I try to catch up with my need for oxygen, even as I throw open drawer after drawer of my makeup counter to search for my meds. It takes riffling through each one to figure out the new prescriptions have been on top of my desk the whole time.

Panicking has clouded my thoughts. It buzzes through me, gripping my chest like a vise. If I don't get relief soon, I know I'll pass out, or worse.

Do panic attacks alone cause mania?

I grunt in frustration at the anxiety and hopelessness scratching at my lungs right now.

I'm not thinking straight.

I know this.

One side of me says everything has an explanation. It desperately begs me to lie down and chill out, that this will all pass soon enough.

The other side is just as loudly screaming that I conjured up a vision in the middle of my rehearsal and is instructing me to do everything in my power to feel better as soon as possible.

Despite all the logic trying to break through the barrier of hysteria controlling my mind right now, I listen to the side that promises immediate relief and snatch one of my pill bottles up. As soon as I wrench the top open, pills clatter to my makeup desk and I frantically collect them in my hand.

It's too many.

I know this.

And yet...

I can't stop myself.

I swallow them whole, choking until I grab my water bottle from my nightstand. When I'm finished, I slam it back down onto the surface... right next to a spotless white rose with a bloodred ribbon tied around the thornless stem, and an envelope adorned with a crimson wax skull seal.

The rose and letter halt me in my place. My mind finally slows for once. With shaking fingers, I carefully open the envelope, keeping the skull intact like I have with every letter over the past several months.

The past. *Several*. Months.

Oh my god, what have I been doing? Why the hell have I been avoiding looking into this lunatic? My caring, thoughtful demon of music could be a fucking *serial killer* for all I know. The Phantom of the French Quarter, the enforcer to the modern-day New Orleans Capulets against the Montagues, two glorified Mafia families. Rand says the Bordeauxs are dangerous. What would happen if I've *blindly* fallen into the middle of their feud? Why have I been so naive about this man? Is it because I'm afraid of what it means if he's real? Or is Jilliana right? Am I terrified I've been doing this to myself all along?

I gulp, trying to push out my racing thoughts to investigate the newest letter. A folded wad of paper rests inside the envelope and I gingerly pull it out, already dreading what I'll find.

One by one, my trembling hands set out sheet after sheet of music, all from my so-called demon. All perfectly intact. Like Jilliana hadn't ripped them to shreds hours ago. I swivel around to the coffee table, hoping to see those scraps of music sheets piled high, evidence of what I *know* happened today. My stomach flips at the sight of the perfectly clean coffee table.

My heart lodges in my throat and I fall to my knees, the music sheets scatter around me. Tiny drops of water smear the carefully handwritten notes. It's someone else's writing. Not mine. It can't be mine. Right?

Puddles of tears form on the page like watercolors, wiping out whole measures of the songs. My vision darkens as the world presses in. I clutch my throat, trying to breathe but something is lodged there... no... it's just my own voice.

I'm screaming.

Someone pounds on the door behind me as I rock back and forth. I curl up on my faux fur rug that covers my dorm's carpet, trying to take comfort in its softness, hoping *something* will calm me down.

A crash and a thump batter my senses as whoever was at my dressing room door bulldoze it open, causing it to slam against the wall.

"Shit, Scarlo—"

Voices from the hallway talk over one another.

"What the fuck is wrong with her?"

"Is she okay?"

"Wait, who is—"

"Close the door, Dominguez." My fingers clutch the rug until a familiar deep bass croons to me. Strong hands curve around my shoulders. "It's me, *ma petite muse*. Listen to my voice, it's just me."

My ravaged mind doesn't know who "me" is, but my body does. Leather, whiskey, and warm sugar fill my nose, giving me the oxygen I've searched for ever since this panic attack started. The man—my demon—pulls me into his chest. I cling to him instantly. He's my port in this storm and relaxation settles deep into my bones as a song vibrates against my ear from his chest.

My savior sings in French. I don't know the lyrics off the top of my head, but my addled mind still recognizes the tune. It's one of the songs my demon sent me, "La Vie en rose," only the way he sings it makes it sound like a lullaby.

"Get them out of here," my savior hisses.

A door slams and the bustle of voices and questions disappear.

"Try to sing with me, Scarlett," he whispers into my hair. The song resumes and I open my mouth to obey him, but my chest hurts too much.

"I c-can't. My chest—"

"It's because you're not breathing. Come on, Scarlett." Concern creases his brow as he pierces me with his midnight gaze from behind his skull mask. "You were born for this. Sing for me." He places a large hand across my belly, below my rib cage. "From here."

The combination of his embrace and the drugs are starting to calm my senses and I'm feeling lighter. Muscle memory engages my diaphragm right underneath his palm, and I suck in much-needed breaths to sing the English version of "La Vie en rose" while he hums. My eyes flicker open and closed as I attempt to keep his intense gaze. Together we sing about roses blooming and angels singing and my heart rate starts to slow down... until it gets *too* slow.

On that revelation, my mind tries to panic again, and as if on cue, my friend's voice, laced with worry, interrupts us.

"She took these, Phantom. Is that why she's acting like this?"

Phantom.

"*Fuck.* No, *this* is a panic attack, but those drugs will be working soon enough. Count them. Quickly. She got them today so hopefully they're all in there."

Pills fall silently onto the rug and my eyes beg to open, but they've finally closed for good. My senses are already too overloaded, so I rely on the others to calm down and assess. Like smelling whiskey, sugar, and leather, or listening to the soothing voice I've heard in my dreams. If I open my eyes, will those things go away?

"How many did you take?" I'm jostled and brought to a sitting posture, one strong hand cups my face and shakes me not too gently. "Scarlett, baby." My demon's voice is harsher than before. "Answer me. How many did you take?"

"I-I don't know." My lips are numb and my tongue is thick. I can't seem to hold myself up, but I want to tell my demon that I'm fine, that I know what I'm doing. But the words don't form.

"It's a thirty-count bottle," my friend answers for me. His name is on the tip of my thoughts... but it's slipping away. "There are twenty left, but she's got more brand-new bottles I'll have to count and there are pills everywhere."

"*Goddamnit.*"

"She should go to the ER, sir. She needs to be evaluated by a psychiatrist, maybe even get her stomach pumped."

I feel a scream build up and escape, but once it leaves my lips I only manage a whimper. "Please... no... no psych ward. Can't go back..."

"*Jamais, mon amour.* I will take care of you." He speaks with such authority that even though I don't know what he meant, I relax in his hold, trusting him. "Call my brother, tell him to bring Dr. Portia to me."

"Where will you be?" my friend asks, although the question seems slower than his usual cadence.

"He'll know. Just do it."

The world moves underneath me as my demon stands up, giving me the same queasy feeling I get when I'm on a boat. I try to push away but the arm cradling my upper back rights me and clutches me tighter while my demon sings to me again in French.

"I... I don't know the words," I complain numbly. My savior huffs a laugh, interrupting his sweet lullaby, and he kisses the crown of my head while squeezing me close, now with one arm surrounding my back and one underneath my legs.

"You don't need to know the words when you inspire them,

ma muse."

"But I w-want to know them," I insist. My frazzled mind and emotions are clinging to his music as deep slumber threatens to swallow me.

"I'll teach you, but for now, hum along. Let the music free you from the darkness in your mind."

My eyes peek open and burn in bleary focus at lamps ensconced in stone walls as we move through a tunnel.

Where are we?

I want to ask the question, but my mind is everywhere and nowhere, kind of like wherever we are...

The leather and whiskey scent is joined by the smell of damp earth. The lamps do little for lighting but my demon seems to have no trouble. It feels like we're descending. Lower and lower we go until we finally stop.

I open my eyes slightly to see a terrifying devil made of fire with black pits for eyes standing right in front of us. My heart thuds in my chest until my own demon speaks, letting me know whoever this is can be trusted.

"Ben and Dr. Portia will be here shortly. Let them in. But only them."

"What about her handler?" the devil responds in a smooth alto. "Can he come in?"

My handler? What does that mean?

My savior pauses for a second, like he's asking the same question, but I feel the thick muscles in his chest tighten and his body say no before he does.

"Ben and Dr. Portia. No exceptions."

My head is spinning and I'm exhausted, but whether that's because of the pills I took, or the panic attack still trying to stiffen my muscles, I'm not sure. I desperately want to know what's going on, who's saving me, where I am, but my mind can't hold on to more than the gentle lullaby whispered by the deep voice above me. It's soothing and exhilarating. Heavenly and sinful, like a true demon of music, lulling me to trust him. I don't fight it.

For the first time since my dad died, I feel comforted despite the roiling pressure in my mind. I crave the acceptance of my demon's embrace.

He ends the conversation with the flame-wrought devil and we enter a heavy steel door. It shuts behind us immediately, sucking all the light back into the tunnel. The lack of visibility doesn't deter him though, and he walks several paces through pitch-black darkness.

"I will always protect you, *petite muse*. But with that being said, this is going to hurt both of us."

Before I can really register his warning, bright lights blind me and I'm gingerly placed in a sitting position on cold tile and draped over porcelain. I open my mouth to complain, only to have two long fingers shoved down it.

Surprise, embarrassment, and revulsion rush through me like a freezing cold deluge of water. My body rebels against the foreign source. Without giving me a chance to fight back, he twists me to face the toilet I've been laid across and I violently cough out the contents of my stomach.

He kneels behind me and pulls my hair back, cradling me with one arm around my waist when he's not forcing his fingers down my throat.

"That's it, baby, you're doing so good. I don't know if the amount you took is fatal, but I know we've got to get that shit out of you. "

"No. I can't—" I shake my head but his large hand invades my mouth again while his body keeps me facing the bowl. Tears, snot, and vomit spew out of me and I scream at the expulsion. All the while that soothing voice tries to calm me even while my body fights him. Somewhere deep down I know he's doing this for my own good, but god do I hate it.

Every time my body tries to hold back, his fingers stimulate the gag reflex I didn't even know I had until now. We go back and forth like this for what feels like hours until the only thing coming up is bile.

I collapse against his chest, sobbing, exhausted, and thoroughly spent, my muscles in agony already.

"Shh... shh." His gentle bass vibrates my back and he washes my face with a cool cloth. "You did good, baby. So good, *ma chérie.*"

His fingers caress my cheek and I shake my head limply.

"Please, no more... I can't."

"It's okay. It's okay." He gathers me up in his arms. "No more. I think we got everything out."

I nod dumbly and let him pick me up again, settling me on my feet but keeping a strong arm wrapped around my waist for support. Thankfully, he turns off the light, soothing the migraine exploding in my head caused by all the purging. He turns on the sink faucet, even though the bathroom is barely visible. I don't know how he can see to help me take a greedy sip from the glass he brings to my lips, but he does it easily.

"How can you see?" I ask, my voice is hoarse as it leaves my raw throat.

"I don't need to," he answers. "I've lived here for so long that I know where everything is."

"Okay, well how can you see *me*?"

A low chuckle huffs from his chest. "I've studied you for so long that I know almost everything there is to know about you."

He cups my cheek before I can respond. Concern rolls off of him and although I barely know this man, my heart aches that I caused his worry. "What I don't know is why you took so many pills. Tell me, Scarlett. Were you..." He swallows. "Were you trying to—"

"No! No, no, no." My objection ends on a squeak. "I was just... scared. I... I *needed* the panic to stop."

I sense him nodding and he kisses my forehead, sending the butterflies in my lower belly fluttering wildly.

"Never again. You'll never put yourself in danger like that again. Say you understand."

"I understand," I repeat immediately.

Exhaustion weighs me down and I lean into him as he guides me through the darkness.

"Where are we?" I ask, my brutalized voice wavering with uncertainty.

"My home. You are with your *démon de la musique, ma jolie petite muse.* You have no need to fear me."

He walks us farther into the dark space before helping me lie on a deep, soft bed and tucking me underneath the cool covers. I curl on my side while silk sheets rustle beside me. A thick, heavy quilt is piled on top of me and I ball up into a fetal position, my arms wrapped around my knees as I lie sideways.

My savior's comforting, large body curves around mine protectively. He scoops his arm underneath my neck to situate my head on the silk pillow while squeezing me to his chest. The fluid move is familiar, like everything with my demon, and it's easy to trust him and give in to fatigue.

Before I let go, my lips move and the thought I still can't wrap my head around falls out.

"You... real?"

A rough chuckle against my neck warms my insides as he squeezes me closer, molding my body to his. "As real as you want me to be, *ma chérie.*"

"Good," I whisper. Relief floods through me, washing away the absurd worry I've had over the last couple of days that all this has been in my head. "Don't leave."

"*Jamais, mon amour.*"

Never, my love.

The words flutter into my chest as he continues. "I thought I could once, but that lasted less than five minutes. It took you seeing me to realize I could never miss your songs again."

I open my mouth to mumble thank you but he shushes me again. The lullaby I almost know the words to whispers in my ear as I finally give in to darkness.

"Sleep now, Scarlett."

SHE'S NOT A TRINKET

Scarlett is finally safe in my arms, but I still can't relax. Instead, I desperately strain to hear every breath and count the beats in between like a metronome. The rhythm is slow, but its steadiness reassures me. Every fermata in between breaths seems way too long and I have to resist the urge to shake her awake to make sure she's alive.

I should've let Jaime take her to the hospital. No... *I* should have said fuck it and gone to the hospital with her, mask and all. But I'm banking on the hope she's been diligent with her medicine like I know her to be.

The multitude of questions I have flooding my mind are enough to drive me mad. I make it my business to know everything there is to know about Scarlett Day. All I want to know right now is *why*?

Seeing my muse sobbing on the floor was like looking a decade into the past, to when Laurent murdered my father right in front of me and my brilliant mother lost her mind. Those nightmares collided into the present and I couldn't hold back anymore.

Without a second thought, I'd pushed open the hidden mirror door in Scarlett's room and rushed to hold her against my chest to calm her. I sang the only lullaby I could think of to keep her breathing normally. When she finally sank into my embrace and sang the English version, my heart tripled in time.

Thank goodness Jaime was there and found her medicine bottle. I'd thought it was solely a severe panic attack at the time, but I'm hoping our family psychiatrist can shed light on the effects of the medication Scarlett took. If I have to, I'll take her to the hospital, but I'll do everything in my power to keep her away from the psych ward. I wasn't able to get to her in time during her first full-blown manic episode, but I won't let her down again.

A soft knock signals the doctor's arrival, interrupting my guilty conscience.

I'm loath to leave her, but I have to brief Dr. Portia on Scarlett's condition, so I peel myself away. When her hand tries to catch mine, a fluttering in my chest makes my heart swell to the point of pain. As gently as I can, I roll her to her side and slide off of the mattress, closing the black curtains of the four-post bed behind me.

Padding lightly across the thick carpet, I travel down the hallway and answer the door. Sabine peers back at me behind her fire mask with a plain plastic bag in her fist.

"Jaime gave me these," she whispers and hands the bag to me. "Apparently she got these prescriptions filled at the pharmacy today."

I nod, already knowing that. I'd been planning to get them myself after visiting her dorm, but the pharmacy said she'd taken care of it.

"How many were missing?" I ask.

"All but seven pills are accounted for in one bottle, and there's one missing from every other bottle."

Relief floods my veins. Worst-case scenarios have been flying through my mind ever since Jaime said he had to count them. Seven is a lot, but it seems manageable.

Ever the silent shadow, Sabine sidesteps into the darkness,

allowing Dr. Portia's short frame to pass by. My brother follows behind her with her large medical bag hanging from his shoulder.

"Come in, but stay quiet," I order in a hushed tone as my guests walk past me.

By the time I turn back to Sabine, my second-in-command has disappeared into the darkness, no doubt resecuring the tunnels. Normally, my security cameras and shadows operating outside the opera house are more than enough to prevent unwanted visitors, but I'd texted her right before bringing Scarlett to my home to ensure I had yet another safety measure in place.

Up until my meeting with Rand, I had no reason to think Scarlett wasn't safe inside the Bordeaux Conservatory. Unfortunately, if anyone realizes just how much my obsession with Scarlett Day consumes me, my enemies would tear her apart to get to me.

The dim lamps inside my foyer barely illuminate the concern clouding Dr. Portia's face. Ben's frustration rolls off of him in waves. Even without good lighting, I can tell he's pissed, but I'll have to deal with him after I know Scarlett will be okay.

"Sol, where're the goddamn lights? Not everyone has cave vision—" I flick the switch next to the door, setting the overhead lights ablaze. Ben winces as they flare throughout, revealing the small entryway and hallway leading to my kitchen, den, office, spare bathroom, and bedroom. "Shit, that's bright after those dark tunnels. But, thanks—"

I lift my hand to silence him, making sure I can still hear Scarlett's heavy, labored breaths. Each pause causes anxiety to spike my heart rate, but the fact that she's breathing at all settles me a little bit.

I lower my hand, unveiling Ben's frown. "Sol, what is going on? Why did I have to leave my family late at night?"

Ignoring him, I turn to the psychiatrist our family has had on standby for the past decade.

"There's a woman in my bedroom—"

"Well that's a first," Ben huffs.

Dr. Portia's eyes widen as she waits for me to continue. They both know how protective I am of my space and Ben at least knows that I've never entertained a woman in my quarters.

I push past their shock and extract a pill bottle from the bag Sabine and Jaime used to collect Scarlett's medication.

"She took these..."

Dr. Portia dons her glasses before accepting the bottle. The wrinkles around her inquisitive dark-brown eyes crinkle further as she examines the label. "Epilepsy or bipolar disorder?"

"Bipolar type one." I rattle off the medical reports I memorized after she was released from the hospital nearly a year ago. "History of psychosis and auditory hallucinations during severe manic episodes. She also experiences irritability, reckless tendencies, and alternating periods of depression. Episodes are made worse or triggered by lack of sleep, missed medications, and extreme stress."

"Jesus, Sol, you sound like a goddamn medical infomercial," Ben scolds but I just shrug. "I had no idea you were in this deep."

Scarlett and her mental health have been my top priority ever since her father was murdered. I'd only been watching over her for a month prior to her hospitalization last year, but I realized then that my fascination with her ran deeper than mere infatuation. I thought it'd peaked at obsession, but the tangible grip she has on my chest is indescribable, completely different than any fixation I've had before.

"If she takes this, what seems to be the problem? Is she in the middle of an episode?" Dr. Portia asks.

"That's the thing, I don't think so. As far as I know, she's been in remission for months, but tonight she took well over her prescribed dose."

"Fuck." Ben swipes his hand on his face, a habit I broke a long time ago thanks to my mask. Right now, though, my hands itch to do something—anything—to get the restless energy out.

"Do you know why?" Dr. Portia turns the bottle over. "And how many?"

"She claims she just wanted the panic to stop? She was coming down from a panic attack when she explained herself. I'm not sure how many she took. But her bottle is new and there are seven missing. I forced her to vomit them up because I wasn't sure how toxic they could be at that level."

"Hm... the issue date is from today. Has she been taking her medication as prescribed otherwise?"

I open my mouth to say yes, that I've made sure of it, but what about just last night? I'd arrived to her room late after getting held up at Masque so I missed most of her nightly routine, but she'd taken an older medication that makes her exhausted.

"I... I don't know," I finally admit, hating that I don't have all the answers. "She mentioned last night that she lost her medication."

Ben scowls at me the entire time I explain to the psychiatrist what it is I *do* know about Scarlett's disorder. Dr. Portia, to her credit, keeps whatever judgments she likely has hidden behind her mask of practiced concern.

"I see..." she replies once I finish showing her Scarlett's other bipolar prescriptions, vitamins, and allergy meds.

I've got to hand it to Sabine and Jaime, they were thorough. My poor little muse's proverbial medicine cabinet is like a goddamn drugstore.

"That's so strange. She sounds attentive to her health, how could she just *lose* them?" Dr. Portia asks under her breath, more to herself than to me, which is good since—once again—I'm out of answers.

She hands me back the bag full of medicine after studying each one and looks up to address me from her short stature.

"I will examine her, but if *she* is as dutiful to her medicine regimen as *you* are..." Those judgments she hides so well finally leak through. Her sentence drifts off, thick with reprimand as she peers over her glasses at me.

I refuse to feel ashamed, though. Without me, Scarlett could very well be dead thanks to whatever her father was mixed up in with the Chatelains. Not to mention what happened tonight.

Then again, without me, she might never have overdosed in the first place.

The look of horror she had on her face when she saw the intact music sheets crushed my chest. She'd always looked at them with a coy happiness, her excitement unbridled and addicting to see. I don't know what sparked the terrified look this time, but it cut me to the core.

Dr. Portia huffs at my lack of response before patting her sleek, gray bun, and resuming her professional demeanor. "If she is diligent, then our best-case scenario is that she only took those missing pills. Which means she'll be fine. Expect grogginess and a horrible migraine in the morning. Perhaps nausea, but all in all, nothing more than a hard night on Bourbon Street."

My heart lightens and the breath I've been holding escapes me like a balloon until my brother speaks. "And the worst-case scenario?"

Dr. Portia grimaces. "Worst-case scenario? She needs to go to the hospital as soon as possible and get her stomach pumped."

Ben curses but I shake my head. "I made her vomit almost immediately after she took them. I would've done it even sooner but I wanted to get her away from prying eyes. That had to have helped, right?"

Dr. Portia nods. "Absolutely. With that in mind..." She blows out another breath and quirks her thin lips to the side as she thinks. "I'm guessing since I'm here, the hospital is a last resort? As per usual?"

"Yes," I answer without hesitation.

"Sol, you can't be responsible for her if things go south—" Ben chides, but I hiss back at him.

"You've seen what they do to patients. It's a prison in there." I don't need to tell him Scarlett begged me not to. He understands well enough how traumatizing bad mental healthcare and psych wards can be.

Dr. Portia clears her throat. "In defense of the hospital, it really is much better than when your mother—"

"Oh, so do *you* want to stay there, then?" I challenge. Her lips flatten into a line. "Didn't think so."

Ben still shakes his head with disapproval, but Dr. Portia continues. "Fine. Is the guest room available in the family wing upstairs?"

"Yes, it is," Ben provides this time.

"Very well. I'll stay there tonight. After I check her vitals and examine her—"

"She's asleep," I argue.

Dr. Portia frowns at me like she used to do when I was a teenager. I frown back.

"I won't do more than a bedside check unless I feel it's absolutely necessary. And if I do believe that a more thorough examination is in order, you can't stop me, Mr. Bordeaux."

I scowl but don't argue further. She's doing me a favor as it is and I need her on my side.

"If you hurt her—"

"I won't," Dr. Portia snaps back.

Very few people can talk to me that way, but with her, I let it slide. The older woman has worked with our family for over a decade and has seen us through it all. If any outsider can scold me, it's her.

The tense muscles in my shoulders relax as she continues our standoff, and I finally relent. I grab her heavy bag from my brother and lead the way to my still-dark bedroom without turning on the overhead light. When I get to the bedside table, I click on the dim lamp so that when I open the four-poster bed's curtains, Scarlett won't be accosted by harsh lighting. Once I've finished drawing back the black fabric, my chest tightens at the sight of my sleeping little muse.

She'll be okay, I tell myself, hoping I'm right. I set the medical bag next to the bed and hover beside Dr. Portia. She pauses before beginning her examination.

"A little space, Mr. Bordeaux?"

My face twists, but I honor her request, backing away to join my brother. Dr. Portia pats Scarlett's shoulder and she wakes with a start, but the doctor's calming presence settles her. When her worried eyes search for me, a smile that's more confident than I am lifts my lips.

"It's okay. Dr. Portia works with my family. She's here to check on you."

Scarlett nods slowly and the bed rustles as she sits up to address the doctor. Her sweet voice floats to me and I cling to its softness while Ben wastes no time barraging me with his angry whispers.

"What the fuck are you doing, Sol?" Ben's usual frustration has an edge of anger that I rarely ever hear. "First you drop the chandelier on Monty—"

"Oh, did he end up quitting?" I ask, making Ben's brow furrow.

"Goddamnit, yes. But that's beside the point. He thought the Phantom was out to kill him."

I wave away his concern. "You know as well as I do that our great-grandfather rigged the chandelier's pulley system to prevent it from crashing."

"Yes, we know that. But Monty didn't. Now I have to find another director last minute and hope the last one doesn't sue us for emotional distress."

"We've got enough dirt on him to persuade him out of court." I shrug. "And just promote your wife, obviously."

"Maggie?" He pauses his tirade. "You don't think the board would cry nepotism?"

"Not if they've seen her in action," I scoff. "If they haven't, they're not paying enough attention to care one way or another. She's more than qualified. Promote her."

"That's not a bad idea. Of course, she might say no herself because she never wants to feel like she's being favored..." I can practically hear my brother's gears turning inside his mind, right up until the moment he realizes that I've derailed the conversation. "Back to my other point. What about Scarlett? Tell me what's going on here. Why do you have Rand Chatelain's childhood sweetheart in your *bed*?"

"They weren't childhood sweethearts," I insist, barely containing the growl threatening in my chest over the way Ben describes *my* muse. "She needed my help. What was I supposed to do?"

"Oh... I don't know, maybe don't stalk her in the first place? Hell, *maybe* your notes were what drove her insane—"

"Enough," I command through gritted teeth, preventing him from saying aloud what I've been worried about from the moment I saw her tears fall on the new music sheets.

The only thing keeping me together is the knowledge that I've been sending her letters for almost a year and this is the first time she's suffered like this. I'd even say the letters *helped* her, at least in the beginning.

After her father died, she was a wreck. I watched over her during her depressive and manic episodes at a loss for what to do until she was committed into the hospital and finally diagnosed. When she came back, I realized one day that she could hear me as I practiced piano down here. Her angelic voice drifted back to me and before long, I was singing along.

That duet sparked an idea. Watching from behind her mirror and listening through the ducts wasn't enough. I had to get closer to her, learn everything about her.

Letters have always been my method of communication with those outside my family, but this time, I hadn't wanted to be the Phantom of the French Quarter. I sent them unsigned, desperately hoping she'd be amenable to the idea of a secret admirer. When she interacted back with me and I heard her sing to herself about her demon of music, the name stuck.

"She loves my notes," I insist. "Something else happened. Something started all of this anxiety she's been struggling with. I just have to figure out what."

"You don't *have* to do anything but leave that girl alone."

In direct opposition to his order, I edge closer to the bed, trying to see what Dr. Portia is doing as she digs through her bag. Scarlett's silver eyes flash toward me and she gives me a curious half smile. As if drawn to her, my foot takes another step, only stopping when my brother roughly grabs my shoulder.

"Focus, Sol. Do you plan to keep her here under the guise of protection? What about Rand? He's all but declared his intentions in making her his."

"She's *mine*," I growl.

"No. She. Is. Not. She's a *person*, Sol. Not a trinket you can polish and set on the shelf. Neither of you seems to understand that. You have to let her go. Leave her alone."

My mouth works in a fury over his demand and accusations but the fact that Scarlett has lain down again under Dr. Portia's calm ministrations eases my nerves.

"I can't keep her, I know that," I finally admit. "But I will keep her safe. Beyond that, I'll let her decide."

Ben looks as if he wants to argue more, but he must realize the ground I've afforded him. "Fine. If this gets out of hand any further, though, or if Rand calls for war over her, *I* will be the first to stop you. I have to protect Maggie, my daughter, and our people above all else. She's not one of ours."

"Not yet," I repeat my answer from the first time we had this disagreement.

Dr. Portia closes the curtains, symbolically silencing our conversation before she turns toward us. "Her vitals are good. She's tired and complained of a headache, but that's normal. I wouldn't be surprised if she's already back to sleep. I've left some over-the-counter pain pills for when she wakes back up. Keep watch over her, although, it seems that whatever she took was purged from her system quickly enough to not take root. I've also hooked her up to an IV drip. That should lessen the harsher side effects tomorrow, if there are any. Once you get through the bag, there's no need for another. If you come across any problems just give me a call. I'll be right upstairs."

Relief sags my shoulders and I swallow to wet my suddenly dry throat before speaking. "Thank you. Thank you for helping her."

Ben's eyebrows rise, but Dr. Portia just nods. "Of course."

My brother loops her medical bag over his shoulder and she follows behind as I lead her to the bedroom door. But before I can cross the threshold, Ben stops me from entering the hallway.

"We'll just be a moment, doctor," Ben tells her and juts his chin toward my foyer, indicating she go on.

I wait until she's relatively out of earshot before questioning him. "What?"

At this point, I'm annoyed I even asked him to be here. I was worried and frantic when I ordered Jaime to contact him, but I needed my brother, not someone who would judge me and make the situation worse.

"Look, I'm sorry I was harsh." Ben's voice is gentler this time as my twin seemingly reads my mind again. "I just want to make sure you know what you're getting into. What you're getting our *family* into. I needed to know you understood the risks."

"You've no reason to worry. I won't put anyone in danger."

He raises his free hand, surrendering the argument. "All right. I hope that's true. I won't say anything else. I trust you."

He claps me on the shoulder and walks out. The hallway is a straight shot to the foyer, so even though it's dark, they don't need a guide to the door. He opens it and allows Dr. Portia to walk through first before closing it behind him without saying a further goodbye.

I lock the dead bolt and turn off all the lights, not minding the fact that I'll have to walk through darkness to my bedroom. Through the open doorway, the lamp seems to blaze like a sunrise against the garnet carpet. I'll leave it on in case Scarlett wakes up in the middle of the night and wonders where she is. But if she does, I'll be there to soothe her.

Before I slide into bed, I adjust the curtains to prevent the fabric from pulling the IV from Scarlett's skin. Once I finish, I strip off my dress shirt, blazer, and pants in favor of a long-sleeved white T-shirt and gray sweatpants.

I wish I could help Scarlett out of her blush and gold costume and into more comfortable clothes. Unfortunately, after the trauma of the night, I'm afraid waking up in a new place with the realization that a relative stranger stripped her while she was unconscious would send her careening over the edge she nearly toppled from already.

Then again, waking up in the arms of said stranger may have the same effect.

No. Sleeping beside her is nonnegotiable. I've wished for months that I could hold Scarlett in my arms as I drift off to sleep. There's no way I'm giving up the opportunity now.

I peel back the curtain on the other side of the bed and slide under the covers until I'm inches away from her. Afraid I'll rip the IV out of her arm, I don't dare move her, so I settle for lying on my side and watching her sleep on her back.

The lamp glows through the slim cracks between the curtains, revealing her profile to me perfectly. Her fair skin has a golden hue thanks to the dim light's warmth, and her dark lashes fan over her cheeks above the darkened bags underneath her eyes.

Has she not been sleeping well? How did I not know this? Did I miss the signs that suggest she's on her way into a manic state, or did something else happen?

Either way, she'll sleep like a damn baby in my care, I'll make sure of it. I've learned through my own research that for people with bipolar disorder, sleep is the best medicine to stave off a manic episode.

Hopefully, we've caught this one in time.

I lean into her and kiss her temple over her fine baby hairs and brush them back so they don't tickle her face.

"*Dors bien, mon amour.* Tomorrow is a new day."

COME IN, PETITE MUSE

M y head... isn't killing me.

The thought has me frowning before I even open my eyes. Something tells me I should have a huge migraine right now, but other than the extreme exhaustion weighing down every muscle, I feel... fine.

Why do I feel fine?

Visions of last night flicker across my mind like a slideshow at three times speed and it's hard to grasp one moment over any other. All I can remember is a sweet lullaby and the soothing way the singer's strong chest vibrated against my cheek as he sang to me. His whiskey, sugar, and leather scent envelopes me still in an intoxicating embrace. And even now, I imagine piano music playing in the background.

Wait... there *is* piano music playing.

The notes are less muffled than they usually sound through the vent in my room. My eyes flutter open to take a look. They burn with fatigue, but I do my best to blink slowly until I'm finally peering out into the world.

The very *dark* world.

Am I in a box?

My breath quickens until I see a gap in the wall, revealing a gentle glow beyond that.

Wait, no. That's not a wall. It's curtains.

Red fabric surrounds me and I sit up as I realize I'm snuggled in a king-size bed of silk sheets and thick quilting. The bed underneath me is heavenly cozy, no doubt contributing to the incredibly refreshed feeling underlying the weariness in my bones.

Where am I?

The gentle notes from my dreams flow through the curtains, caressing my senses. I pull the quilt aside and climb out of bed, sinking my bare feet into a thick, plush crimson carpet.

An IV stand is placed by the bed, but whatever bag that might've hung from it has been removed. I search my arms to find a small Band-Aid covering a cotton ball over the crook of my elbow. *I was hooked up to the IV... but why?*

A vague, hazy image filters into my mind of an older woman with kind, dark-brown eyes.

Dr. Portia. That was her name.

Answers piece together and break apart back into questions, creating and dismantling a confusing jigsaw puzzle of memories. Instead of staying put and trying to build a picture of what happened last night, I push open the curtains fully to assess my new surroundings.

The alluring scent of powdered sugar almost seduces a moan from me. I glance around to find the source and excitement zings through me at the sight of the white paper Café du Monde bag sitting on the bedside table. Beside it, an alarm clock reads six o'clock... *p.m.*

Holy shit, I slept all day.

My eyes widen at the revelation and I resist the urge to dig into the beignets so that sugar can solve all my problems. Instead, I observe the rest of the room.

The stone walls, recessed lighting, dim lamps, and rich black, crimson, and gold hues make the bedroom look like a modern version of the king's room in every medieval movie I've ever seen.

The thick carpet is actually one large rug that takes up the entirety of the walking space in the room. And stunning photographs of the world's most impressive sites line the walls. I spin around to see them all until it dawns on me that there are no windows.

Am I underground?

Unsure, I continue my inspection by wandering toward the pictures in awe, slowly taking in gorgeous snapshots of places I've always dreamed of visiting, like the Colosseum, Machu Picchu, and the Sphinx. Scattered among the global wonders are photos of France and even New Orleans.

My fingers trace the gold filigree of one photograph in particular. The pianist in the band looks so familiar and my heart twinges when I realize—

"That's your father."

I jump back as if the photograph itself had spoken in the deep bass tone. Twirling on my heel to face the speaker, I feel my eyes widen on the man filling the doorway.

And I do mean *filling.*

The ceilings must be nine feet tall, which if I'm still in New Orleans like I think I am, is really freaking impressive considering the city is barely above sea level in most places. The door seems to be an ordinary height, and yet the man staring back at me nearly touches the top of the frame.

His broad shoulders are covered by a loose-fitting white T-shirt but the corded muscles in his arms stretch the width of the long sleeves. Dark lines of a tattoo on his muscular chest and right arm bleed through the thin material. Gray sweatpants cover his strong lower body, but bare toes peek out from underneath his pant legs.

That little detail calms me for some reason. It's a weirdly comforting vulnerability, but I'm not sure why.

My gaze travels up to meet midnight eyes. One sparkles like the stars in a moonless sky. The other is dull behind the bone-white skull mask that I've somehow already grown accustomed to.

Strands of his thick black hair fall over his forehead, almost veiling his right eye, but he doesn't seem to notice.

The uncovered left side of his face is striking. His skin is a pale ivory and unmarked, smooth but for the light scruff of a beard trying to form. That jawline is harsh, and it tics under my perusal. When I get to his lips they too form a hard line, but a slight twitch tells me he's pleased with something.

Sol Bordeaux, the supposed Phantom of the French Quarter, and maybe my demon of music, is *pleased*. My pulse quickens at the thought that he could be pleased with *me*.

Somewhere along the way, during my examination, I lost my breath. My stomach tightens and I begin to feel hot all over.

He takes a step forward, but uncertainty over the desire pumping in my veins forces me to mirror his move backward. That twitch of a smile sinks to a frown before his delicious voice carries to me again. This time, concern laces each word.

"Are you alright?"

"What?" I croak painfully. My hands shield my neck protectively, as if whatever is hurting me stems from the outside. I try to swallow, but the saliva I can manage to muster feels like lava going down my throat.

"Sit on the bed," he commands with a scowl.

My body obeys before I can stop it and I watch him from my place on the bed as he disappears through an open door on the right side of the room. He doesn't turn the light on, but water flows on and off from a faucet and he emerges again with a full glass.

"Here, drink this. Dr. Portia said you'd be thirsty today."

I take the cup with eager hands and bring it to my lips, not caring that I'm slurping the contents down. When I finish, I take a breath like I've been underwater for minutes and wince when my throat aches again.

"Throat hurting?"

I nod and he pivots to the bedside table, retrieves two pills from a small bottle, and holds them out to me in his large palm.

"Take these."

My eyes narrow and dart from the pills to his waiting face. I shake my head slowly.

"You don't trust me?"

"I don't *know* you."

He takes one of my hands and deposits the pills into my palm. I inspect them, sniffing them like an idiot before I swallow down what I'm pretty sure is just run-of-the-mill aspirin with another gulp of water.

He fixes his heated gaze on me. "You know me, *ma belle muse*. You just don't want to admit it."

My heart stutters and my eyes widen again. "W-what did you call me?"

He smirks. "My pretty muse. I would've figured you'd know what it means by now."

"I do..." My pulse races in my veins as my slow brain tries to add it all up. "You *are* my demon of music."

That smirk widens to a half-cocked smile. The satisfaction there springs a fluttering sensation in my lower belly.

"Very good, *ma chérie*. I've always enjoyed your nickname for me. I find it quite fitting." He bows low with a flourish. "But from now on, you can just call me Sol."

"Sol..." I taste his name on my tongue, loving the feeling until I remember what Rand told me. "But you're also the Phantom of the French Quarter. You... you *hurt* people. Like Monty... and Jacques Baron."

He frowns and straightens. "Monty was never in any real danger because the chandelier's chain is too strong and short to break or reach the ground. As for Jacques... he was a disgusting rapist who disrespected women. Anyone who receives my punishment fucking deserves it. Jacques Baron was no different. Surely you understand vigilante justice better than most."

My heart thunders at his last sentence. I have no idea how Sol so accurately pegged my own moral code, but he's right. There was also no judgment against me in his statement, just fact, and the rest of his answer satisfies my curiosity. Hearing that Jacques got the end he deserved validates the satisfaction I felt when I first heard he was dead. Sometimes, literally fighting for justice is the only kind we get in this world. But I don't dare agree with him out loud.

"But... you're not—you're not supposed to be real, right? I thought..." My shoulders drop with a confused huff as realization trickles in like water droplets through a hole in a dam.

All the rumors... all my friends who I thought were just superstitious when they rubbed their skull jewelry like a totem and spoke of the phantom like a bogeyman... my own suspicions and what I thought were hallucinations...

They're all true.

"I'm very real. I'm sorry I ever did anything to make you think I wasn't. That was never my intention. I figured you were content with keeping me your secret."

"I was," I admit as my thoughts run wild. "And if you're real... that means I wasn't hallucinating. I was beginning to wonder if I was slowly going insane again and I was just along for the ride. But you're *real*." That realization should scare me, but I can't muster anything but relief. A question sparks hope in my chest and my eyes widen. "What about my first manic episode? The past several months I've been hearing piano music, but during my first manic episode, it was nonstop jazz playing in my head like a constant radio on low volume. Was that you too?"

He winces and the hope that I was never actually crazy deflates like a balloon. I half expect to hear that squeaky leaking sound.

"Of course, it wasn't." I curse on a sigh. "*That* was only as real as hallucinations get."

His fingers twitch at his sides, like he's trying to figure out if he should comfort me, but I bristle, still unsure about who I'm talking to or why I'm here. As if he can already read me like a book, he stuffs his hands into his pockets instead and leans a broad shoulder between two gold frames on the wall. The move makes his biceps look impossibly chiseled and my core heats. I squirm to cross my legs on the bed, but I can't find it in me to stop staring as he answers me with sad sincerity.

"That was *not* me, I'm sorry to say."

"But you know about it? My bipolar disorder?" I ask. He nods carefully, like he's not sure where I'm going with the line of questioning. "How do you know about it?"

He pauses for a moment, examining me with a tilt of his head and a warm, intense gaze. I squeeze my legs tighter.

"I didn't become the Phantom of the French Quarter without knowing everything that goes on in my city, *ma chérie.*"

"Okay, but why do you know so much about *me*?"

"Because you are everything," he answers simply.

I take another sip of water to bide time while I think of my response. After the cool liquid massages my sore throat, I finally reply. "That's, um, very flattering, Phantom—"

"Call me Sol, please."

"Okay." I swallow again. "*Sol*... like I was saying, that's very sweet and... admittedly creepy, but it doesn't exactly answer my question."

His head shakes as if he's truly baffled, too. "It's something I can't explain, no matter how many times I've tried to make sense of it myself. Maybe one day we'll both be able to understand what you mean to me."

My mouth falls open and I want to question him more, but his shoulder pushes from the wall and he gestures to a dresser across the room.

"There are clothes you might find more comfortable than your costume. Meet me in the den when you're finished with your morning routine."

At his word choice, my gaze snaps to Sol again, only to see his sculpted back muscles and dark-ink design pressing against his thin shirt.

"Wait! How did you get my clothes?"

He spins on his heel and half smiles underneath his skull mask again before walking backward out of the room. "The Phantom has his ways."

With that, he leaves and closes the door behind him. My eyes drop to my outfit as I finally realize that I'm still in my blush-and-gold Marguerite costume from rehearsal. The rehearsal where he was watching me.

How long has he been watching? And why the hell does that bring an odd thrill of pleasure up my spine when I should be scratching the stone walls to escape?

Piano music plays lightly through the door, like an echo from a memory, prompting me to hop up and change my clothes. While the events of last night are a haphazard jumble in my mind, I'm thankful that whatever happened didn't involve him changing my clothes himself, *or* sending me to the psych ward, both of which might've been necessary considering the hazy fog over my brain right now.

I put on a matching black bra and thong. My cheeks warm at the thought of Sol touching my unmentionables, but I'm more grateful for the fact that I'm not being force-fed antipsychotics right now than I am embarrassed about my underwear. I slide into a simple pink scoop neck T-shirt, dark jeans, and black fuzzy socks —not grippy, thank God.

Once I change, I head to the bathroom Sol used earlier to fetch a glass of water and relieve my full bladder. Upon quick inspection, all my morning and nighttime routine products are perfectly lined up on one side of the double vanity's black marble countertop.

All of them.

I use the extensive regimen as a way to keep my own sanity in check. Great sleep, a routine called social rhythm therapy, and medication have been my stay-sane cocktail ever since I was diagnosed.

How did he know?

I'm not sure I want to find out the answer to that, to be honest. Not yet. I'm still wrapping my mind slowly around the fact that my moment of panicked insanity last night, when I took those pills, didn't kill me. My mouth tastes like something died inside it and my throat burns like hell thanks to being forced to purge the drugs.

Not wanting to think about the severity of my actions just yet, I shake my head free of that truth. Instead, I open up a still-packaged toothbrush to begin my morning routine, pretending like I'm not holed up in a rich guy's basement that's God knows where. I don't know how I'm supposed to be reacting to the fact that a near stranger stole me from my room, saved me from being committed to a psych ward, and probably kept me alive. I doubt relief and gratitude should be overwhelming my fear.

Is the reason why I'm not scared to death right now because my mind has been through hell and back in the past forty-eight hours? Or is it because Sol is a smoking-hot, droolworthy, demon-at-a-masquerade vibes kind of attractive?

No, he's been my own muse for months. I can't be afraid of him. He cares about me.

Which is even creepier!

Okay... so maybe the Sol-is-hot factor has something to do with it.

I agree with my inner monologue until I get lost in my routine and tune it out. The music outside the bathroom has changed pace to something that sounds like *Clair de lune* by Claude Debussy but with a lively jazz beat. Intrigued, I quickly complete my last steps and take my morning medication so I can go listen.

Once I'm done, I grab the bag of beignets from the bedside table and do what I've always done. Follow the music.

It leads me through the bedroom door and into a hallway, where each note dances and bounces off the stone walls. The lack of windows everywhere I go seriously has me questioning where we are. Last night, I remember being carried down, not driven or flown out of the city. But despite the fact that New Orleans is notoriously below sea level, here I am in what appears to be an underground castle home with electricity and running water. I pass by a modern kitchen, a fully equipped personal gym, and even more stunning photography from all over the world.

If Sol took these himself, his talent doesn't stop at music. Each photo sucks me in and makes me feel like I'm actually there.

I slow alongside another photograph beside an open doorway. This one is a stunning black-and-white picture of graves inside St. Louis No.1, the cemetery tourists flock to in droves, like bees to honey. But this one is different than any I've ever seen, depicting a grand raised plot with the Bordeaux family name inscribed in the stone—

"Come in, *petite muse.*"

Sol's voice echoes from the room I'm standing outside. How he knew I was here, I have no clue. I thought I'd been pretty quiet on the plush rugs, but I guess the phantom really does see and hear everything.

I round the corner into a living room with the same aesthetic as the rest of the home. There's photography, soft rugs, stone walls, but this time there's also an inviting black leather couch and an ottoman with two matching chairs. The seating curves in a semicircle and faces the back corner of the room where a sleek, black grand piano sits in all its glory. A big-screen TV hangs above a lit gas-log fireplace on the right side of the room, but unlike every other home I've been in, the piano—and not the TV—is the room's focus.

The piano is angled away from the door, making it so that Sol's back is turned slightly to me. His long, strong fingers skillfully roll over the keys, and I can't help but stare as his inked upper back muscles flex underneath his thin white shirt. Mesmerized, I set the beignets on a small table next to the door, unable to step farther into the room for fear of breaking the spell.

But he knows I'm here, a fact he confirms by seamlessly segueing the current song to the one he sang to me last night. My chest aches to know the words to the French version, but they're just beyond the tip of my tongue.

I listen for a few more minutes, letting my eyes close as I hum along to the music. When I open my eyes on what I know is the last note, I look up to see Sol's midnight eye blazing on me. He slowly drops his hands from the black and ivory keys.

We hold each other's gaze until my rapidly increasing heart-beat thrums in my chest. I swallow down the sudden need to throw myself at him. The overwhelming sensation is so foreign, I have trouble fighting against it.

I've never had much luck with guys. Obviously, taking someone home from Bourbon Street to my dad's rental house was absolutely out of the question. But even after I moved into my dorm, no one has ever kept my interest. If I did express wanting to get to know someone more, the guy would inevitably run for the hills without so much as asking for my number. Not to mention the fact that Jaime is the worst wingman ever. Every time I thought I had a real shot at someone, he'd assume the big brother role and scare them off.

So I have no experience to shed light on what to do right now.

No man—not a single one—has *ever* looked at me the way Sol is right now. It fuels a need in me I've never felt, not even on my wildest manic nights. It's exhilarating and terrifying at the same time.

"I told you that you knew it." Sol's voice breaks me from my thoughts.

"Knew what?"

"The song." Sol nods to the piano. "You were singing the words under your breath. I told you that you knew it. You seem to know every song I play. Even the ones I've written myself."

"Oh." I shake my head, faintly remembering asking for the words during my panic attack. "I don't know the French lyrics. But I've always had a knack for predicting music. My father used to joke that 'Little Lettie's never let a song pass her by without knowing it first.'"

Sol's smile lifts up faintly. "My mother was the same way."

"Your mother?" I ask, trying to remember what I've heard through the New Orleans rumor mill. For all Jaime's love of gossip in the Bordeaux Conservatory, he hates talking about the Bordeauxs themselves.

"She's gone."

My heart clenches at the gravity in those two words, and I grip the doorframe to stop myself from going to him.

"I'm sorry. My dad is gone, too. My mom ran off when I was a kid."

God, shut up. He does not care.

"I'm sorry, too," he offers. His sincerity hits straight to the bone in that way only people who've experienced the same grief can understand. "Your father was a great musician. New Orleans loved him."

"You knew my dad?" My voice cracks on the last word.

He shakes his head sadly. "No. But I listened to him plenty of times. I used to sneak off with my brother to Frenchmen Street to hear him play. Ben's never been much of a music fan. He takes after my father." The left corner of his lips lift up like he's told an inside joke and I can't help but smile back.

But then my smile falters. "Why am I here, Sol?"

Without answering, he stands up from the piano and shoves his hands into his sweatpants pockets before walking slowly toward me. My pulse races faster and faster with each step until he stops with only a few feet between us. The intensity in his gaze never wavers, and I suddenly have to fight the urge to flee. But I stand my ground and raise my chin to meet his sparkling midnight eye.

"Last night, you had some sort of breakdown," he answers, searching my face. "You took too many pills and I had to bring you here, to my home beneath the opera house. It was the only way I knew to get you help without taking you to the hospital. I wasn't sure how many pills you took, so I made you throw them up and I had our family doctor assess you."

The facts don't hurt my pride as much as I expected them to, thanks to his gentle tone. I knew most of the information, but hearing it all laid out is a lot to unpack.

"I saw you watching me from box five. Then you vanished. It freaked me out and I had a panic attack. But how were you in my room so quickly? How did you know I..." I don't finish the sentence, too embarrassed to say the actual word for what I did when I took too much medication.

His eyes roam over me, like he's looking for any sign that I'll run away before he answers.

"Because I watch you."

I nearly prove him right as my fight-or-flight response kicks into high gear, only to settle on *freeze*.

"You... watch me."

"Yes."

I wait for an explanation but when he doesn't elaborate, I scoff. "What do you mean, you *watch* me?"

"When you moved into your dorm, I realized quickly that you could hear me practice through here." He points to the vent above the piano. "The first time you wrote lyrics to one of my songs and sang along..." He drifts off and the reverence in his voice makes my heart flutter. "Your voice is ethereal, Scarlett. I needed more of you."

"That's when your letters started." I glance around the room, not sure what I'm looking for until I find a small desk with candles of various colors and sizes surrounding stationary and a laptop. It's a juxtaposition of past and present, just like him. "You really are real. My demon of music."

"I heard that in one of your lyrics. It fits. The world already knows me as the Phantom of the French Quarter. But being your *démon de la musique* is what I didn't know I craved. Hearing your voice singing my music is... perfection."

Pride swells in my chest, but I try my best to focus on what his words actually mean in this situation.

"So you... what? Break into my room?" I scowl at the thought. "Do you watch me undress?"

"No, of course not." He frowns back at me. "I only stay long enough to hear you sing the lyrics you come up with and write in your journal. Your nose does this cute little scrunched thing when you concentrate." His accompanying chuckle seems to surprise him and he cuts it off abruptly. Appreciation twists my heart in my chest, threatening to derail my resolve to be mad at him. "Except for what happened the other night, whenever you're in a compromising position, I look away for your privacy."

"Well, how *gentlemanly* of you to stop looking long enough for me to—wait..." My eyes widen as realization creeps in. "The other night? Holy shit, it *was* you! Not a dream. You were actually there when I... Oh my god, you're *sick*."

His lips flatten and he narrows his eyes. "Scarlett—"

"No." I wave my hand and spin around to the door. "How the hell do I get out of here—"

"You're not leaving—"

"Yes, I am," I call over my shoulder as I march toward my freedom.

Two impossibly large hands latch on to my shoulders and pull me against his chest. Sol's whiskey-and-sugar scent immediately floods my senses, but I fight against the intoxicating aroma.

"No! Let go of me!"

"I can't do that, Scarlett. You need to listen to me."

"No, damnit!"

I twist and dig my heels into the carpet, but with the combination of fuzzy socks and my unyielding captor, my efforts are futile. Once he wraps his long, muscular arms around me, my attempt to escape is completely hopeless, and he holds my writhing, cursing form until I've tired myself out and my chest is heaving for breath.

"Calm down and listen to me, little muse," he murmurs above my ear. "You *know* me. You know I would never hurt you."

I'm plastered to him with nowhere to go. His heart pounds at my back and like my own stuttering pulse, I can't tell if his is due to fear or desire. My lungs adopt the same cadence of his breaths and my fight leaves me after several deep inhales and exhales. All the while, he never lets up on his strong embrace, which is somehow soothing in and of itself.

I *know* I should be pissed. Any other woman would be in this situation. But unlike any other woman, even though I'm angry, hurt, embarrassed, and confused, I can't deny the glaring truth. I've known and trusted my demon of music for months, and if he *hadn't* been in my room last night... I might've died. Or if anyone else had found me I'd be locked up in a psych ward again right now.

"There you go. That's it, *ma petite muse.*" His whispered encouragement flutters my hair, and I lean into his embrace completely. "Relax against me."

My skin grows sensitive where his arms envelop me, but I push past the warmth flowing in my veins to remember why I'm frustrated.

"You've... you've been *stalking* me and... you *pleasured* me—" I cough out when a shiver of desire rolls down my back.

"And you begged me to," he purrs.

My entire body pushes against him again and for some reason, he lets me go.

"I was *drugged,* Sol. I couldn't have given consent. I thought you were a dream—"

His bark of laughter makes me stop.

"What's so funny?"

"You were not *fully* drugged yet, *ma chérie.* That medication takes a while to kick in all the way. I wasn't planning on you seeing me through your mirror, but you did. What am I supposed to do when you *beg* me to make you come? Should I have left you there, keening and moaning my name with no release? I helped you come using your own fingers because even though it was agony not being able to give you that release myself, I could never deny you anything you need. You can believe what you want to believe, but I only gave you what you demanded."

I shake my head, determined to hold fast to my version of the truth, but... he's right. On some level, I wondered if the medication hadn't hit yet, but does that mean I really wanted him that night? What does it mean if I *still* want him, even right now? Am I not supposed to hate him for doing something like this?

He takes a step forward and I retreat again, only for him to keep stalking toward me.

"When I came to your room, I wasn't expecting to see you like that. I almost left once I realized it, but your voice *called* to me, like it always does, *ma jolie petite muse*. But this time, you called my *name*."

I swallow as we continue our dance and my lower belly tightens.

"Your fingers weren't doing the job," he continues. "You *needed* me."

My back hits the stone wall, but the human one in front of me doesn't stop his pursuit. He raises his forearms to rest them against the wall on both sides of my head, caging me in. My breaths come in heavy pants as I focus on his sparkling midnight eye. He dips his head low and his nose caresses where my scoop neck T-shirt reveals my bare collarbone. Tingles and goose bumps erupt over my skin. Without second-guessing myself further, I clutch the loose hem of his shirt in my hands and twist the fabric taut as I tug him closer.

His nose skims my neck, continuing up my jawline to my ear before his hands clench into fists against the stone. The muscles in his thigh are rock hard as his knee pushes between the apex of my legs. My body instinctually grinds against his thigh, searching for release, and I know my panties are soaked.

"I could *smell* your arousal then." His sharp inhale draws cool air over my fevered skin and his low chuckle heats it right back up. "Just like I can now. Do you know how fucking hard it is for me to know *exactly* what you want... exactly what you *need*, and deny us both the pleasure of me giving it to you?" His lips and teeth nibble my earlobe as his right hand threads through the curls in my hair. He arches my neck to the side, leaving my throat vulnerable to his light-as-air kisses. "Tell me, my pretty little muse. Tell me how I'm supposed to deny you when you beg me to make you come?"

His left hand strokes down my side and slides behind my lower back to help me find my pleasure against his thigh. I'm practically riding him and his hard length pushes against my stomach, reminding me that delicious release—like what he gave me the other night—is just within my reach.

"I'm not good, little muse. My obsession with you is the only pure thing about me. Never forget that I'm your *demon* of music, Scarlett. You can't expect me to behave like a gentleman when you beg like my whore."

He lifts me and wraps my legs around him as he pushes me flush against the wall. The new position has me straddling his thick length, lining the head of his cock up to massage my clit. I moan at the sensation and cling to his shirt, hanging on as he controls my every move. I'm already so close, all I need is just a few more of his subtle thrusts against my center.

"Answer me, Scarlett." His warm lips brush mine as he speaks.

I want to please him, but I've completely forgotten the question because I'm... al...most...*there*—

He suddenly pushes away from the wall, dropping me to my feet and taking all my breath, composure, self-righteous arguments, and *orgasm* with him.

"Sol! What the hell?"

"I won't have you accusing me of giving you another orgasm without your *consent*." His mischievous smile tells me he knows exactly how close I was and my mouth falls open.

"Was all that just to prove a point?" I straighten my shirt and cross my legs in a desperate attempt to ignore how wet I am between my thighs.

But the damp indigo-dyed patches on his gray sweatpants where my jeans rubbed against his thigh and cock give me away. He follows my embarrassed stare to the evidence he bears of my arousal and that infuriatingly smug look on his face beams back up at me.

"Prove a point?" he asks as he lifts a shoulder and crosses his arms. "And what point would that be?"

The cotton fabric straining around his chest and biceps looks like it could burst at the seams with one heavy breath. He does nothing to hide the raging erection in his sweatpants and all his entire cocky demeanor does is get me more flustered as I try not to gape at his impressive size, because good god is he huge.

"Scarlett?" he prompts me, bringing my eyes back to his. "What point do you think I'm trying to make?"

"That I—" I cut myself off when the left side of his smirk lifts higher, taunting me. "I have no idea." I finish and cross my own arms haughtily.

"Deny it all you want, *ma chère*. But I was more than a phantom to you that night. I was exactly what you needed."

I growl in frustration and push against the wall to head toward the door, snatching the Café du Monde bag up as I stomp out.

"Where do you think you are going now?"

"Back to my dorm," I yell back as I enter the hallway.

"I'm sorry, I can't let you do that," he replies in an infuriating, singsong voice. "Even if I did, you can't escape me in my own city, *ma belle muse*, and I don't think you really want to."

His laugh may be teasing me as it echoes from the den to my place in the hallway, but his words strike a chord in me.

This is *the* Phantom of the French Quarter. The man that everyone fears so much, they talk about him in hushed whispers. And I...

I'm being a brat.

The fact that I even feel comfortable talking to him this way shows how unafraid of him I actually am. I'm claiming I'm mad and disgusted by him watching me and making me come the other night, and I know I should be terrified of the man who has stalked me through my bedroom mirror for months. After all, I'm the quiet, scared little mouse who never sticks up for herself, too afraid I'll hurt someone's feelings, or I'll get emotional and wind up in a bipolar episode.

But I'm none of those things.

I'm alive with the rush his attention gives me. I feel protected that he's been watching over me all this time. And I'm obviously more than a little turned on that this mysterious man wants—no, *needs—me.*

Despite my revelation, I refuse to deviate from my course as I march down the short hallway, passing another bathroom on the way and ending up at what I'm assuming is the front door since it's the only closed one I've come across. I unlock the two dead bolts, ready to leave, but I'm confused that he's only just now emerged from the den and walking toward me at a leisurely pace.

"I'm leaving," I warn him again.

"No, you're not." His calm voice shows how undeterred he is by my threats, and he moseys toward me with his hands nonchalantly in his sweatpants pockets.

"Watch me, since you're so good at that." I glare at him as I twist the knob to swing the door open.

Only it doesn't budge.

I pull again while Sol leans his shoulder against the wall in what must be his signature not-a-care-in-the-world posture. As if it's plotting against me too, the door doesn't even move a fraction as I jiggle the handle. I growl at Sol, but his only response is to glance at the top of the door. I follow his eyes to see yet another latch, but this one is way too high for me to reach.

"Come *on*," I groan and kick the door with my fuzzy-socked foot. "Son of a—" Shooting pain radiates up my leg and I drop my bag of beignets to grab my foot. "Holy shit. *Ouch*, that stings."

"This game is only fun if you don't hurt yourself, Scarlett," he scolds me with a furrowed brow.

"It's not a game at all!" I yell and limp to rattle the door again. "Let me out of here."

He sighs like *I'm* the annoying one when he's the freaking jailer. "I'm afraid I can't do that."

"And why not?" I snap.

The uncovered side of his face grows serious. "Because last night you had a panic attack and overdosed." That *word* is like a needle, painfully effective at bursting my self-righteous bubble. "In any other circumstance, you'd be locked up and monitored in a psych ward right now for the next seventy-two hours. Longer, actually, since it's the weekend. I'm keeping an eye on you instead."

Gratitude eases tension in my shoulders as his logic sinks in. But I don't want to give up just yet.

"Gee, Sol, am I supposed to be thankful for your hospitality?" I shake the doorknob in vain. "Why is being here with you so much better than a psych ward? At least there I get watercolor paint and a busted Cable TV."

That lopsided grin that makes my core throb is back as he tilts his head. "I can think of quite a few things we can do that are way more fun than watercolors and TV. Speaking of which." He checks his watch. "Ah! You have impeccable timing." He picks up the Café du Monde bag I dropped on the floor and hands it to me. "Eat your beignets and get dressed. We'll leave in less than an hour."

"*What*?! I did all this arguing for my freedom and now you're saying we're just going to leave?" I huff, but he's already turned his back to me. "Wait a minute. What am I getting dressed *for* exactly? Where are we going?"

He spins around with an impish grin on his face and points to his skull mask.

"The masquerade, of course."

Scene 13

TREME'S WHITE ROSE

By the time I've stomped back into Sol's bedroom, he's nowhere to be found, but a rose gold satin gown lies across his king-size bed. Something tells me the dress will fit like a glove.

Up until a few minutes ago, I was certain I was going to be locked up in this medievalesque underground lair for the rest of my days, so the fact that he's wanting to go to a *masquerade* of all things silences my questions. For now.

While I'm getting ready in the en suite bathroom, I apply mascara, a little blush on my cheeks, and lip gloss. My curls can't be tamed, so I leave them down to do their thing. When I'm finished, I slip into the trumpet gown and nude strappy heels.

The off-the-shoulder neckline kisses the top of my breasts. My hands move with a mind of their own as they smooth along the curves I suddenly have. The shimmery fabric flares out where a thigh-high slit rests just below my hip. It's gorgeous, decadent, and easily the most expensive piece of clothing I've ever worn.

But not only is the zipper impossible for me to reach by myself, the off-the-shoulder straps are supposed to crisscross down my spine to tie into a bow at the small of my back. I take a steadying breath, knowing I'm about to have to let Sol touch me again so he can do the job.

Hopefully I can control myself this time, Jesus.

I leave the bathroom while holding the back of my dress together awkwardly and find Sol sitting on the bed, scratching the right side of his face while he looks at his phone. He's already changed into a charcoal-gray suit and white button-down with a rose gold satin tie that matches my dress.

"Ah, all done? Let's go—" He lifts his head up from his phone and does a double take.

His lips part in shock. Mine do the same, although, at the moment, I might be more stunned than he is. The mask he wears tonight doesn't even look fake. It fits him like a second skin, as if he's rolled it onto his face and adhered to it. I've seen plenty of talented makeup artists in the industry, but if I wasn't as close to him as I am right now, I wouldn't know it was a mask at all.

I bite my lip and his gaze darts to my mouth. The hunger in that vivid midnight eye makes my core clench and my barely there thong is already getting soaked.

He swallows, seemingly gaining the composure that is still evading me. "You're breathtaking, Scarlett."

Heat blooms to my cheeks and my gaze falls to the ground. He's there in an instant, lifting my chin to meet his sparkling midnight eye. The right one is extremely dark, though almost identical. But *I* can tell the difference between the man and the fake.

"Don't hide from me, little muse," he murmurs, searching my eyes. "Own your beauty."

If the eyes are a window to a man's soul, then my demon of music has starlight in his dark depths. Everyone else says his eyes are black as coal, so does that mean I'm the only one who can see the man inside the phantom?

Settle down, girl. You barely know him, and from what you do know, he's your stalker.

And my savior.

I can't tell anymore who's winning these arguments, my head or my heart. But I'm relieved to know that I haven't been steadily losing my mind over the past several months.

What I thought were auditory hallucinations was actually Sol's very real piano playing. The music sheets and roses didn't just appear out of thin air, he'd left them after moving silently through my mirror in my room. Sol was behind it all, which means I haven't relapsed into a manic episode. I'm still healthy, in remission, and *not* on the verge of psychosis again.

"I um... I can't tie this by myself."

He releases my chin as I turn around for his help. Through the open bathroom door, I can see our reflection in the mirror and easily read the reverence in his gaze as his fingers skate down my bare back.

"Mmm... yes. When I told the boutique owner to send their finest, this was exactly what I envisioned. Heads will roll if they stare at what's mine for too long, but goddamn am I a lucky bastard for getting to look at you all night."

My heart flutters at his words while my logic tells me I should correct him. That I'm not *his*.

But I want to be.

His fingertips send electric shivers throughout my body while he zips me up. When he finishes, he takes his time to tie the dress's ribbon straps at the small of my back. Once I'm securely in my dress, he pulls my thick black curls over my shoulder and looks at me in the mirror as he leaves the lightest of kisses on my nape.

I'm *this close* to being totally okay with remaining his captive and living in this modern medieval lair forever. But he pulls away, leaving me bereft of his touch, and mad that I almost gave in so quickly again. Sol Bordeaux is quickly teaching me that even when I'm sane, I'm one complex bitch.

I swallow and turn to face him, studiously ignoring the desire on his face, even though it's tempting me to throw all caution to the wind.

"Exquisite, *ma chère*."

"You don't look so bad yourself, Mr. Bordeaux."

He grimaces. "Sol, please, little muse."

"So that's a no to calling you my demon of music? And what about the Phantom of the French Quarter?" I tease. "How did you get that nickname by the way?"

His lips quirk up. "You'll see me in action tonight. Come on, we should go before it closes."

"Before what closes?"

"Miss Mabel's shop."

I frown because that answer means absolutely nothing to me, but I don't ask him to elaborate, instead, resolving to just go along for the ride for once.

He walks down the hallway and I follow close behind him. When we get to the door, he pulls out his phone and types in a code. The door *whirs* and *clicks*, and all three latches unlock simultaneously, even the highest one. I'm afraid to ask why he has one so high up.

"It's so intruders on the other side don't realize there's another lock to break. Doors are at their weakest where the lock connects to the frame. It makes the door easier to kick in if the lock is only in the center, but when the dead bolt is also at the top, it's much more difficult."

"How did you know I was wondering that?"

Right now, his smirk is one of the only ways I can tell that he's wearing a mask because while the left side lifts up, the right remains unnervingly still, frozen in a neutral state of bland disinterest.

"I watch people, Scarlett. It's what I do. I deal in secrets and protection. Knowing what people are up to is my job." He brushes his fingertips against my cheek and I barely resist the temptation to curl into his palm. "And *you* have a *very* expressive face, at least to me. If I didn't know you better, I wouldn't believe that you have even an ounce of darkness in you." He bends low and brushes his lips against the shell of my ear. "But we both know better, don't we, *mon amour*?"

My lips fall open, and my heart pounds with questions and the endearment. Before I can ask him how he knows my darkest secrets, he pushes me aside gently with his arm across my chest.

"Get behind me, Scarlett."

I do as I'm told without thinking of defying him and as he opens the door and peers out, it takes me a second to realize I have no desire to even try to run away.

"Follow behind us," he orders crisply.

I peer out from behind Sol's waist and see a figure with flames on its face, emerging from the dark.

My heart races at the stranger's arrival, not to mention how harsh Sol's tone was. It makes me realize how gentle he's been with me.

"Yes, Phantom," a husky alto responds. The woman is tall, maybe six feet, although that's got nothing on Sol. Her long, sleek black ponytail falls down her back and her mask of fire, intricately painted to shimmer and shine with reflective light, glows against the dim illumination from the corridor behind me.

"I remember you from last night. Um... thank you for, you know, helping," I whisper dumbly. "I'm Scarlett."

The mask only covers the top half of her face, revealing a twitch of a smile. "And I'm Sabine. But let's keep that between us, shall we?"

"Come, Scarlett," Sol commands in that tone I'm realizing he saves just for me.

He takes my hand and leads me out the door. Sabine closes it behind me and Sol presses a button on his phone screen to rotate the locks back in place. I follow him blindly through the dark tunnels while Sabine's light steps pad behind me.

The stone passage is lit by industrial-style Edison bulbs, protected by metal caging, the same ones that line Sol's hallway in his apartment. Rushing water resounds in the distance as we stick to the left side of the dim walkway.

"Is that a river? *Underground*?"

"We're below sea level down here," Sol explains. "My great-grandfather wanted dry pathways for his ventures during Prohibition, so he had an architect and city planner in his pocket who helped divert the runoff and flood waters into these underground channels that lead to the Mississippi River. The French Quarter is already slightly above sea level compared to the rest of New Orleans, and in the past, these channels have helped prevent disastrous flooding in the streets above us."

"Whoa, what happens if I fall in? Will I get swept into the Mississippi?"

Sol tugs my hand against him, as if he's afraid I could speak that accident into existence.

"*Never* get too close, pretty muse. I can't lose you," he mutters so low under his breath, I doubt Sabine heard him. "The channels reroute excess water to pipes that span like a labyrinth underneath the French Quarter and end at the mouth of the Mississippi. While there are sections of the maze where you must hold your breath, you could survive the thousand-foot distance as long as you move swiftly with the current and keep your head close to the oxygen at the pipe's ceiling. But most people don't know that."

I snort. "Do a lot of people like to swim down here?"

His silence makes the hair on the back of my neck stand at attention.

"Some are given that choice, yes. Others choose to fight their way out."

I gulp as I try to piece together what he's saying. "So when people come down here they either swim... or fight. Who do they fight, and why?"

Minutes go by where I only hear the ominous rushing water a mere few feet away from me.

"They fight me, Scarlett. As for the why... let's just say people don't *choose* to come down here. But when they do, I've made sure they deserve it. That's the Phantom's—"

"—moral code," I finish for him, remembering our conversation about justice earlier. "What's, um, the success rate for choosing to swim?"

He pauses and I swear he's literally trying to calculate the numbers before he finally answers.

"Low."

"And what about the second choice?" The option where people *fight for their lives.* "What's the success rate there?"

"None," he answers quickly, not even needing to do the math. "So far, the latter option has a zero percent success rate."

"And yet, the bastards keep choosing it," Sabine sneers.

Damn... the Phantom of the French Quarter really is *the Bordeaux family's enforcer.*

Questions bombard my mind, but I'm not sure I want to know the answers yet. He's said before that whoever gets his brand of justice deserves it, but just *how many* people have deserved it over the years?

My chest aches, but my heart is a glutton for punishment when it comes to Sol because I don't feel bad for the people who have lost their fight down here. For some reason, I trust the Phantom's judgment in choosing a criminal's fate. Especially, since he gives them a way to earn their freedom while still being guilty. No, I don't feel bad for them.

I feel bad for *him*. My demon of music.

How many deaths can someone be responsible for in their lifetime before their soul is black as night? Is there any coming back from that?

We continue down the walkway, and I try my best not to observe everything with my head on a swivel. But I can't help my curiosity, even in the dark, so when we finally stop in front of a wrought iron spiral staircase I nearly crash into Sol.

"Careful, little muse," he murmurs warmly before climbing the steps, still holding my hand.

"Where does this go?"

"All the way up to the roof, but we won't need to go that far."

He settles on the first landing outside another steel door, and keeps my hand in his as he presses another button on his phone screen. Once it's unlocked, he opens it, and Sabine and I fall back in step behind him.

The cool, damp stone smell is immediately replaced by that of wood and varnish. The darkness still prevails as I try to see in the small corridor.

"Where are we?"

"We're inside the walls of the opera house. These hidden paths were how patrons and liquor traveled in secret from the house to Madam G's speakeasy. Of course, it was her grandmother's then."

"Madam G's family has owned Masque this entire time?"

My conversation with Rand feels like a lifetime ago, even though it was literally just yesterday. He'd said the Bordeauxs are extorting Madam G, but with everything I know about the Phantom of the French Quarter so far, I'm not sure I believe that anymore.

"Yes, Madam G's family, the Gastoneauxs—formerly the Laveaus—and the Bordeauxs have a long, beneficial history together. My great-grandfather rebuilt the burned-down French Opera House for his wife. Madam G's grandmother wanted a safe place for trusted family and friends to gather without scrutiny. Building the hidden speakeasy at the same time as the New French Opera House was the perfect answer."

"If Madam G's family owns it, why do they have to pay you rent and protection money?"

Sol snorts and narrows his eyes at me before taking a left turn. With each passing step, the cacophony of sounds from Bourbon Street filters in louder and louder through the walls, but I hear Sol over it all.

"You think anyone can tell Madam G what to do? Her family has been running this town before mine even stepped foot on its soil. We've always worked together. And why would she ever pay rent on what she rightfully owns? Who told you that?"

It's on the tip of my tongue to out Rand, but there's obviously bad blood between the two of them. Getting in the way of either is the last place I want to be, even though it seems I've somehow already landed smack dab in the middle of their feud.

I let several steps pass by before giving the most noncommittal, true answer I can think of. "You know... just heard it around town."

Sol grunts. "Well you've been misinformed. Always verify your sources, Scarlett. My brother and I provide legal, financial, and physical protection to those who are loyal to us. There are always factions in the city trying to rise up and harass business owners out of the French Quarter. Some will do anything to steal the success this city can provide. Ever since Hurricane Katrina, we've grown and we're thriving again. Some people want to take it all for themselves, and some simply don't want us to flourish at all.

"But beyond all that, Madam G is family. Her daughter, Maggie, is my sister-in-law and her granddaughter, Marie, is my niece. Ben and I would run security for Madam G for free, but her family line has always been proud and powerful. She's no different and she refuses the 'family discount,' as she puts it, so Ben and I just put all the money she gives us in a trust for Marie when she turns twenty-five."

"Oh..." That's all I can come up with after Sol thoroughly demolishes Rand's accusations.

Sol doesn't seem to notice my silence as his phone lights up again. He pushes through a door that I hadn't even realized was right in front of us.

"Wait here," he whispers before slipping inside.

"They're different than the rumors, you know."

"Ah! Jesus." My hand flies to my chest at the sound of Sabine's voice behind me. "Scared me to death."

"I get that a lot. But seriously, don't believe everything you hear. The Bordeauxs are honest to a fault, so whatever you *do* hear, be sure to ask one of them first. I know I wish I had." She mutters the last part, but I still manage to hear.

Sol reappears and grips my hand again. "Coast is clear."

He leads me out of the dark corridor into a garage. A shiny, black Aston Martin is parked inside, and he rounds the trunk to open the passenger-side door for me.

"Get in, please, little muse."

Something about the word please coming from this huge enforcer's lips nearly makes me laugh, but I bite it back and slide into the car, waving goodbye to Sabine as I do.

Before he closes my door, I hear him call out to her. "We will be back shortly."

He closes the door before I hear her respond and then the next moment he settles into the driver seat and presses the lift on the garage door remote, revealing the intersection of Toulouse and Bourbon on the other side.

It's been a year since I let loose and partied on Bourbon Street. Now Jaime has to practically force me to leave my dorm. I can't remember the last time I ventured into the chaos. Nausea churns my stomach at the thought of braving it again, but the feeling dissipates as Sol steers away from the parade of people in the road.

As if he knows what I'm thinking, he squeezes my hand.

"I'm sorry, little muse. But the good thing is you were diagnosed and you've been working hard on your treatment. It's paid off. You're getting stronger every day. Trust me."

His words warm my chest until a parked cop car's blue light shines in the rearview mirror. That, plus his words, flood my thoughts like a deluge, filling in the gaps of one of the many holes in my memory that I haven't been able to access since that night.

Until now.

A dark-haired stranger with a mesmerizing gaze calls to me from outside the police SUV.

"I'm sorry, little muse."

I blink back into the present and snatch my hand away from his.

"Wait a second... were you... were you *there* that night?"

The fact that I can't see the expressive side of his face right now is frustrating as hell, but his tense posture tells me what I need to know.

"Scarlett, I can explain—"

"Oh my god, you *were*! But that was only a week after I moved into the dorm. I hadn't even heard you play yet. It was still jazz music and mania back then. Why were you there?"

He swallows before taking a right. "I'm the Phantom of the French Quarter. It was brought to my attention that you were sick—"

"By who?"

He shakes his head. "That doesn't matter. My men are everywhere and one of them was concerned enough to involve me. I did my best to get you out of there before you got in trouble... but I failed."

Those last three words fall between us like a boulder, crushing my chest.

"So, one of your men called and you tried to save me? From myself?" I swallow to get past the lump in my throat. "That's... that's it?"

He pauses to merge onto Basin Street before he answers. "That's it."

"Oh..." I sag into the seat. "You've been trying to help me this whole time?"

"I failed you once, Scarlett. I refuse to fail you again. You just have to trust me."

I nod slowly and my nose scrunches while I try to organize all this information in my mind. While I'm thinking, I stare out at the shops and restaurants whizzing past my window, one by one, until I finally make my decision.

Sol's methods may be completely unorthodox—a.k.a. illegal —but everything he's done has been in my best interest. When he speaks, my heart and body trust him completely, sometimes obeying commands before I even register what he's said. It's just my mind that's hanging on to those last threads of doubt. It's time I trust him there, too.

"Okay..." I exhale out all my tired objections, ready to turn over a new leaf. "Where are we going?"

He shifts slightly and I can see the lopsided grin lift the left side of his face. "Treme. I have some business to take care of—"

Business? Like what? And with who—

No. Nope. No more questions. Just trust the man for once.

"Sounds... good." And with that, I finally give in.

As if to punctuate the end of our conversation, Sol activates the Bluetooth speaker and a beautiful piano piece by Ludovico Einaudi filters through the speakers.

"I love *Primavera*! It's one of my favorites—" I stop midsentence when I see his right ear lift, as if that side of his face is trying to smile, too. "Let me guess. You knew that, didn't you?"

"Guilty."

A chuckle escapes me. "Is there anything you *don't* know about me?"

"Not for long, if I can help it."

I laugh outright at his honesty and sit back to hum the music. We take a few turns into the Treme neighborhood, and somehow Sol patiently resists ramming the drunken revelers that permeate New Orleans this time of night.

After a few more songs, we both get lost in humming a rendition of "The Flower Duet" from the opera *Lakmé*. I've used it as an audition piece before, so the words come easily to me, but when Sol finds the low harmony in his deep voice, our own duet gives me goose bumps and my stomach flips with excitement over our sound. When the song finishes, we let the next begin, but we're too busy grinning like fools to sing.

"So tell me, my demon of music. Where the hell did you learn to sing like that? Did you go to Bordeaux Conservatory too? Or does talent just run in the family?"

He huffs a laugh. "It definitely does *not* run in the family. My father couldn't carry a tune in a bucket, and my brother's even worse. My mother loved to sing, and I wanted to please her, so I learned music at the French boarding school Ben and I attended."

"Seriously? Rand went to boarding school in France. Was it the same one?"

Sol sucks his teeth and I immediately regret the question. The anger that rolls off him makes me shudder, but when he answers me, his voice is just as soothing as ever. Not a trace of that underlying rage is aimed at me.

"Yes, we went to the same boarding school. Rand's attendance was meant to be an olive branch between his family and mine. Our families were competitors during Prohibition and thanks to some shady business dealings on *both* sides, the Bordeauxs and Chatelains have been rivals ever since. My mother wanted things to be different with us, and my father could never say no to her, so they struck a deal with the Chatelains. They forced us to go to school together, *away* from their feud, so that our generation would be the first without conflict."

"But that didn't happen," I hedge.

"We have a truce." He squeezes my hand before resting our clasped fingers where my dress's slit reveals my thigh. "But that's not your concern. Not tonight, at least."

A truce... I like the sound of that. Could that mean their hatred for each other can be set aside? I'll have to wait and save those questions for another night.

"Okay... so tell me about boarding school. What was it like?"

"Ahh, boarding school, where rich kids learn how to work hard and play harder. When I wasn't being a hellion, I studied music and martial arts. Also fencing, but that was just so I could beat my brother. He never trained as much as I did. Still doesn't. But Ben was an overachiever everywhere else. My passion was to make music and travel the world. Ben wanted to save it. When we quit boarding school at fifteen, we turned to private homeschooling. After that, Ben went to LSU and Loyola College of Law. I took up the security side of our family business and I compose music whenever I can, jazz and blues mostly."

"Ugh, I *wish* I'd studied jazz. That's my dream. Jazz and music composition. I've always wanted to go solo, but I... I haven't yet,"

I finish simply, not wanting to go into all my inner doubts right now.

"You would be amazing at it," Sol answers. "Your vocals are a dream for opera, but with your voice and your knack for writing lyrics... Scarlett Day, you were made for your own spotlight."

My cheeks heat. "My dad always talked about how hard it was—"

Sol snorts. "He's right. It *is* hard. But you work hard at what you love. That combination will make the difficult things worth it when you achieve your dream."

His words sink in as he keeps driving, and our conversation settles into a comfortable silence with the music playing in the background until the car slows.

He pulls into a parallel parking spot on a street with a mix of shops and cozy shotgun houses.

"We're here."

He's already out of the car and rounding the hood to open my door before I can ask where "here" is. He helps me step up onto the sidewalk and rests his large hand on the small of my back, sending tingling warmth up my spine.

"Hopefully this will answer some of your many questions."

Finally.

He leads me to a small shop with a cute sign hanging over the door. Saint's Petals is written in cursive in the center of a pink hyacinth. Sol opens the door for me, letting me enter first, and I inhale deeply as the earthy scent of fresh-cut flowers fills my nose. Sol wraps his arm around my waist and ushers me in. A bell rings to signal our arrival and he promptly lets go before taking a step away from me. The air inside feels chilly without his warm touch.

"I'm coming, hold your horses." A woman with a thick New Orleans accent warns us from the back of the shop. Only a second passes until a rotund, elderly woman with sun-weathered skin appears, smiling at us before putting on her glasses. When she does, she claps.

"Oh, well don't you two look prettier than a picture? Mr.

Bordeaux, I was wondering when we would get a visit again. I've just been sending those roses through errand boys, but I know they've appreciated the tips."

"She loves them, Miss Mabel. I'd like to get her another dozen today."

'She' can speak for herself, I think. But I watch in silence, trying to figure out where this piece of Sol's life fits in the puzzle I've been putting together.

The woman's rheumy eyes crinkle as her smile grows wider. "Well isn't she a lucky lady? Consider it done. I know my Simon will be disappointed he missed you, but he had treatment today so he's feeling under the weather."

"I'm sorry to hear that. Anything I can do?"

She fiddles with her sugar skull necklace as she shakes her head. "Oh no, it's just treatments and time right now. Thank you though, sweetheart, you've always been such a thoughtful boy. You take after your momma that way."

Sol smiles again. "Hey, don't tell anyone, though. You'll ruin my reputation."

"Oh, no need to worry about that. Your secrets are always safe with me. But tell me, who's your friend, honey?"

I hold my hand out to shake hers and open my mouth to answer but Sol interrupts me.

"This is Maggie's friend, Miss Mabel. I thought I'd show her the shop where the Bordeauxs get all their flowers, but if you don't mind, we're on a tight schedule. I'd hate to keep you open past closing. Is everything ready for tonight?"

Maggie's friend? I press my hand to the sudden ache in my chest.

"Sure is. All delivered and set up."

She begins to chatter Sol's ear off as she prepares a bouquet of white roses in a vase, going on about anything, everything, and nothing in between. The woman has to be the Jaime equivalent of Treme's neighborhood gossip. To Sol's credit, he listens, asks questions, and seems genuinely interested. When she's finished, Sol hands her his black card and she turns around to ring him up.

"I've got your regular Sunday bouquet of burgundy snapdragons just about ready for delivery bright and early in the morning, too. People don't buy fresh flowers like they used to. I'm hoping once the economy picks up that more husbands will treat their wives like you do, Mr. Bordeaux."

His wife?! He's been talking about sending flowers to his wife?

Jealousy pricks my heart, but when I try to step even farther away from him, he reaches out and tugs on the ribbon straps of my dress, effectively keeping me in place unless I want to unravel.

"Things will look up soon enough, Miss Mabel. Have a good night and make sure those bouquets keep arriving to the house. I know my wife, *Maggie*, loves them," he says with a pointed look to me.

He must want her to think he's Ben! But why? Her glasses' lenses are thick, and at this distance with his mask, Sol looks just like his brother. But why would he need to walk around town looking like Ben?

I immediately feel a weird mixture of relief and embarrassment that I was jealous of Ben's *wife* and the Bordeaux men's affection for her. First of all, I adore Maggie. After the shit Monty's put her through this year, she deserves a daily flower delivery. Second, I have absolutely zero claim over this man walking me out of this gorgeous flower shop. The fact that I care at all has me confused as hell.

Sol lets go of me to grab the flower vase before telling Miss Mabel good night. After we walk out, he moves to open my door and helps me slide inside, placing the vase on the floorboard safely between my legs so it doesn't spill. When he closes my door I hear a low whistle outside.

Sol straightens and presses his key fob. The doors lock with a chirp and he walks briskly toward an empty space between two shotgun houses. His head is on a swivel, taking in his surroundings, and his hand hovers over a bulge on his right side.

Is that a gun?

My heart rate picks up and my breathing comes in pants as I try to remember any and every rumor I've ever heard regarding the Phantom of the French Quarter.

He glides to the house and stops feet from it. I maneuver in my seat to try to glimpse around a tree in my way, but I can only make out a short, skinny man in a hood. When he turns his head, his face reflects off of the lamp light and I gasp.

Ben?

But, no... it can't be. Is it a mask? Do other people have the same mask Sol has? Is this one of his *shadows* dressing up like him?

I try my hardest to hear, but of course, I can't make out a thing when they're twenty feet away. Sol nods at whatever the guy is saying and digs in his pocket before handing the guy a wad of cash. The Bordeaux look-alike takes it and counts it as he runs off toward Saint's Petals.

What the hell is going on?

Once the other man is gone, Sol glances around before striding back to the car.

Shit, I have twenty feet to decide how to play this. Do I ask questions? Do I want to know the answers? What will he do once I know them?

I've had a macabre sense of justice for as long as I can remember. My dad wasn't always on the right side of the law, and the police never did us any favors. When my father was murdered, I hadn't been able to tell the cops the *whole* story, but they'd known enough to try to find the murderer. And yet, the case is still unsolved after a whole year.

But my instincts tell me I can trust the man who saved my life rather than turn me over to a psych ward. I can trust the man who protects his city, buys women flowers, and genuinely wants to know how well an elderly couple is doing.

When he hops into the car, I only have one question.

"Why did you let her think you were Ben?"

He starts the engine and the glow of lights in the car lets me catch a glimpse of a smile reflecting off of his tinted window. "Have you ever seen a phantom?"

"No," I reply slowly.

"Neither has Miss Mabel." He lifts his face and that smirk kicks up his lips. "And yet, somehow the Phantom of the French Quarter knows everything there is to know about Treme."

I nod before it finally clicks. "So if you're Ben in public, then you can keep a beat on the city, but the Phantom of the French Quarter can stay just that. A phantom. One that runs on rumors and the smoke and mirrors act. And since you rarely go out, it would be news around town if you did, so you like to stay in the shadows."

"Exactly."

I smile, feeling like I've finally figured this man out, at least a little bit. "So where to next? I can't be this dressed up with nowhere to go."

His shoulders relax, as if he's grateful not to answer more questions right now. He pulls out of the parking space and flashes me another sexy, lopsided smile.

"Masque."

I t would've been easier to get dressed up for the masquerade after visiting Saint's Petals, but to ensure Miss Mabel's safety, I always meet with her right before her store closes. That way, one of my men can guard her when she leaves.

Scarlett and I waste no time once we get back to the opera house, though. As soon as we're out of the Aston Martin, I lead her through the tunnels so that we can drop off the flowers and change masks. She grabs her rose gold butterfly masquerade mask and I take off my itchy prosthetic mask in exchange for my charcoal-gray skull one that also covers the right side of my face. After that, we head through the tunnels to the speakeasy.

A man in a mask like mine stands guard outside as the bouncer. All of the bouncers who work for Madam G also work for me, so he opens the door before Scarlett can even give the password.

Inside Masque, the lively jazz music blares down the stone hallway and my ears ring in protest. I normally wouldn't be here. Ben is the one who covers the business deals held at Masque. The speakeasy is where we hold meetings for our side of town, while box five is where we conduct business for everywhere else.

Tonight, I am purely here for pleasure, or rather, Scarlett's plea-sure. I wanted to show her she's not a prisoner in my home, and going out will hopefully prove that.

When we navigate the winding turns into the speakeasy and come up to yet another steel door—no guard, this time—I open it. Her little gasp makes the whole night—putting on that godfor-saken itchy prosthetic face mask earlier, going outside, and conducting my nightly affairs—all worth it.

Her moonlight eyes flash to mine and the astonishment that shows through her butterfly mask makes my chest swell with pride.

The theme for the masquerade is Dark Clouds and Rose Gold Linings, like a play on words for "every cloud has a silver lining." The entire speakeasy is awash with metallic gray, rose gold, and white, and everywhere you look are the roses I ordered from Saint's Petals, white with hand-painted flecks of metallic rose gold. I'm not one for parties, but Madam G and Miss Mabel really outdid themselves this time.

"When you asked Miss Mabel if everything was ready, this is what you meant?" She points a slender hand to the lavish decora-tions inside, but Madam G interrupts before I can answer.

"Miss Day, Mr. Bordeaux," she calls me with a smirk that flut-ters the feathers on her peacock mask.

My eyes narrow at the formality. We're family for god's sake, but she's always loved playing up our roles for the community. Like I told Scarlett, the Bordeauxs and Gastoneauxs work in tandem for the French Quarter. Over the years, the Bordeaux reign wouldn't have been possible without the Gastoneauxs' ability to obtain secrets. Blackmail is one of the easiest ways to ruin those who try to fuck us over.

"Welcome to the party," Madam G continues. "Your table is reserved as per your request, Mr. Bordeaux."

"Thank you, Madam G. I'll have my usual and the lady will have the same, plus a Cinderella mocktail." Madam G nods and

walks away, leaving me feeling smug and Scarlett with that perpetually shocked look on her face that I've grown to crave. Spoiling
my little muse is so goddamn satisfying.

"You know I don't drink? And you know my *favorite* drink?"

"Of course I do," I answer simply as I lead her through the
crowded room.

After learning that alcohol can screw up sleep patterns for a
person with bipolar disorder, I spent hours trying to come up
with ways to get her to stop drinking. But she did it on her own.
According to the shadow I have on her, she never wanted to feel
out of control again.

As I wind us through the metallic and rose gold-masked
guests, I sneer at every man who looks at her a little too long,
silently memorizing each asshole's mask for a personal shit list to
give one of my shadows later. When I peek back at her, Scarlett is
oblivious to the looks she's getting. Her eyes are bouncing left and
right at the bouquets and draperies of roses.

Smug pride swells my chest, and I peer easily over the crowd
and find my brother in his corner. He's hard to miss since his
mask looks just like mine. I catch his attention and he nods back,
settling into his chair with his sweet Maggie. It looks like the night
is boring for business, but that's all the better. On a bad night,
Ben needs me because he can't stomach the discipline sometimes
required to keep people in line. It looks like we can fully relax and
enjoy the party. For now, at least.

Once I finally get Scarlett to the corner booth reserved for us
on the opposite side of the lounge, I let her slide in first so that I
may be the buffer between her and all the people on the dance
floor.

Candles illuminate each table, rather than lamps, and the
high-backed booths and tall wall separators muffle the music,
making it easier for guests to speak to one another within the
booth. The candle glows against Scarlett's ivory skin, and the
moons in her eyes shimmer within her rose gold butterfly mask.

"Do you like it?" I ask, hating how much I want her approval. But when she gives it freely, a ripple of pleasure flows down my spine.

"Are you kidding me? Obviously! This is amazing. I rarely come down here, but when I have, it's been nothing like this. The flowers were an amazing touch, Sol."

I'm damn near preening, but I remember where the credit is actually due. "Miss Mabel has needed a little more cushion financially this year due to her husband's illness, so the business should do her good. All I did was pay for the flowers and my shadows set it all up for Miss Mabel and Madam G. It helps that some of them are already stage hands for the opera house."

She stills, and I know that inquisitive brain of hers is churning. "Your... shadows? That's what you call your men, right? The ones who work for you?"

"Yes. They help me around the city. They are the Phantom's body—my eyes, ears, and mouth."

"Are they sometimes... your fists?"

I smirk. "They rarely have to be, but yes. Though, I am usually the one who dispenses justice."

She nods and glances past me to the dance floor, studiously not looking at me.

"Does that bother you?"

She takes a moment to think about her answer, and I lay my arm across the back of the seat, subtly scooting her closer to me in case she tries to flee somehow.

"No," she answers with a sincere shake of her head, and I relax around her. "I already knew that. I'm mostly surprised you're telling me anything at all."

My gaze flicks over her face before I pull her fully underneath the shelter of my arm.

"I trust you, Scarlett. I know you're good at keeping secrets."

It's true. I'd be an open book if I knew she wouldn't run away. After all the time I've watched her, I'm confident that the nature of my work would be the least of her hang-ups. But there are a few people in her life that if she realized how they'd first crossed paths, she may never forgive me.

Her eyes widen and her lush pink glossy lips part in a way that makes me want to thrust my cock between them and stretch them to their limit. I shift beside her and face the crowd, trying to adjust. My cock has no hope of deflating completely, and hasn't since she put on this tight-fitting gown. The slit more than halfway up her thigh is tantalizing all on its own. Before going out, I had half a mind to tell her to change. But then the thought of being out on the town, even if it is just Masque, with Scarlett on my arm made me more excited than I've been... *ever*.

A waitress slips by almost unnoticed but for the drinks and two plates of gumbo she leaves on our table. Scarlett's eyes round like saucers and she digs into her food, loving the hell out of it so much that she nearly drops some on her dress. I'm prepared though, and I catch the small droplets with a napkin before smoothing the clean side over her lap.

Her cheeks pinken as she mumbles her thanks. "Sorry. I didn't realize how hungry I was until it was right in front of me."

"I enjoy watching you eat."

A shy smile creeps across her face, and I begin to eat my own gumbo, satisfied that she's not embarrassed anymore. When I've finished, I promptly reach for my drink and take a cool sip of my Sazerac.

"Can I have a taste?" Scarlett asks.

I frown over the lip of my drink. "Are you sure? I thought—"

She waves away my concern. "It's just a theory I'm testing."

I nod once and slide it to her. She gingerly takes the tiniest of sips, making a sour face before smiling wide.

"I can't tell if you love it or hate it." I chuckle.

"I suppose it doesn't matter since I don't drink. But if I did..." She smiles at me and meets my eyes. "I've already come to crave the smell. I definitely think I could grow to love the taste."

Her words send a curious jolt of hope in me, but she doesn't linger on them, instead adjusting her position to better watch the party. I bite back the urge to question her about any possible hidden meaning, not wanting to confront the crushing disappointment if I'm wrong. So rather than face my fears, I take advantage of her preoccupation and study her wistful look.

Madam G chose the best band on Frenchmen Street for the event. The songs are a blend of pop and R&B, modified to have a blues and jazz rhythm. The singer croons into the microphone like he's holding a lover and there's no escaping the sensual energy coming from the music. The dancers on the floor grind and ride against each other in unison, like a damn orgy in the middle of the room. I hope to Christ Scarlett doesn't want to dance. I will if she wants to, but if anyone so much as breathes in her direction, I'll send them to form a line outside my dungeon to deal with tomorrow.

"I used to dream about singing at places like this."

I turn to Scarlett to see her eyes twinkling and focused solely on the band. I knew she loved to write lyrics, but I also thought she loved theater. Earlier in the car, she'd surprised me when she'd mentioned going solo, revealing to me that for once, I *don't* know everything there is to know about this woman. Not yet.

"Yeah? Why don't you? Like I said, you're certainly made for it."

She opens her mouth but clamps it shut. Her alabaster cheeks redden. "I'm... I'm afraid."

I frown. "Of what? You go on stage all the time for your shows. What's different?"

She sighs and her eyes dip away from the band to the candle on the table.

"In theater, I either am the understudy, or I have one. The show must and can go on because there's always backup... Even if I, you know, go utterly batshit crazy."

I scowl at her phrasing, but I know better than most that masquerading your own problems with humor is an easy coping mechanism, so I bite my tongue about it this time and confront the topic at hand.

"And you're afraid that if the show or performance only revolved around you, that you'd what? Let people down?"

She nods.

"So let me get this straight. You're willing to hold back on living your dream because you're afraid of letting people down?"

She huffs a good-natured laugh and begins to rip her drink napkin into small pieces. "Well, when you put it that way, it sounds silly."

A small smile lifts the left side of my face and I can feel the skin on the right side tingle and tighten at the movement. "Is that the only reason?"

"No. What if I fail? Or people hate it? What if I try this new thing and I'm totally bad at the songs I've written—"

"I've heard the song lyrics you've written, Scarlett. That should be the least of your concerns. So what is it, really?"

She blinks at me and huddles away like prey to a predator, hunching her shoulders and crossing her arms over her chest. I fucking hate it. "Answer me. Don't hide yourself, *ma petit muse*," I murmur.

I wrap around her tighter and reach for her with my free hand to tug her away from the corner. She sighs and unfolds from her cocoon. My chest expands with pride that I've coaxed her from her shell.

"The reason why I freaked out recently is because of how good I felt as the lead the other night. I haven't felt that... *euphoric* since my first full-blown manic episode a year ago. It terrified me that I could've sparked another one. Even though I've been doing everything right, I could still get thrown for a loop and the last one nearly ruined my life."

The look of defeat on her face twists my heart, but I won't stand for her beating herself up over something she's controlled as well as she can.

"Did you?"

She stops shredding her napkin and looks up. "Did I, what?"

"Did you become manic?" Her mouth falls open and works on empty air as she tries to answer, so I fill in the blanks. "It seems as though your anxiety and fear of the unknown got the better of you this time rather than mania. That fear that you were going 'batshit crazy'"—I give her a pointed look to show my dislike for that particular phrase—"that was why you took so much medicine last night, right?"

She nods slowly.

"Well, how do you feel today?"

She pauses, seemingly assessing herself from within. "Other than some fatigue earlier... I feel fine. Good actually."

I nod confidently, having already guessed the answer. She doesn't need to know that I've studied her descent into madness with the same fervor I do studying sheet music like *Gaspard de la nuit* by Maurice Ravel, one of the hardest songs to play in the world. I mastered the intricacies of that piece and I'll master the intricacies of Scarlett Day the same way. I've had a decade of learning how to predict another person's moods. She's had barely a year to understand her own. I understand her anxiety, but diligence and continued remission will help her be confident in her own ability to judge her future.

A curl falls in her face and I push it to the side behind another. "Sometimes happiness is just happiness, *ma jolie petite muse*. There's no need to second-guess it. Just enjoy it."

Her brow rises, lifting her mask with it, as she looks up at me with hope. But just as quickly she shakes her head and challenges me with a huff. "You're so confident. How do you know I wasn't on the verge of a manic episode? How do you know that after every solo show, I won't get psychotic again?"

Even while she fights me, she longingly admires the stage, as if her dream was miles out of reach instead of just across the room. The singer of the band announces a break and an idea percolates.

"Come with me."

She narrows her eyes and watches me warily. "Why?"

"It's just a theory I'm testing." A smile quirks my lips and I grab her hand, not giving her any further opportunities to second-guess herself or panic. "Follow my lead."

Entr'acte

Scene 15

BLACK AS NIGHT

"Sol! What're you—" I squeal as he practically picks me up to whisk me away to God knows where.

Wait, no... I *know* where.

The stage.

"Sol, stop!" I hiss as we pass through the throng of dancers. He lifts me up by my waist and plops me onto the stage. I lean in to yell at him and stop in my tracks.

The left side of his face, the expressive side, is so *happy*. He's excited about this. But...

"I can't, Sol—"

"If you're so worried about disappointing people, what about me? I'll be disappointed if you don't sing your heart out right now."

"I can't, Sol. I can't do this," I insist, wringing my hands and barely resisting the urge to swipe the sweat already gathering there onto my new dress.

His hopeful grin makes my heart race even faster than the prospect of singing onstage right now. "Please, Scarlett? Trust me."

I want to.

I bite my lip and look out at the crowd. Most are hardly

paying attention to me, still swaying and dancing to the house music now that the band has stepped off for a much-deserved drink. But a few are looking at me with curiosity, including Sol's brother, Ben.

Maggie sits beside him, and I catch Jaime just a table over. I give a timid wave to them both, just now realizing that I haven't even had my phone since my rehearsal yesterday. It's usually glued to my hand, but I don't even miss it.

Focus! You're about to sing solo in front of all these people...

Jaime is swaying in his seat, obviously drunk already, but he seems subdued, and his eyes are tense as he smiles. Maggie is grinning like a supportive big sister, her tight curls bounce as she nods at me and mouths, "go for it."

I sigh and look back at Sol. Sincerity has replaced the mirth and he grabs my hand before stepping easily onto the high stage. He bends low and whispers in my ear as his fingertips lightly caress my bare lower back, making me shiver.

"I'll be with you every note of the way, pretty muse."

I haven't even agreed yet but I know before his eyes meet mine again that I'm going to give in. With one final squeeze of my hand, he walks stage right to the speakeasy's upright piano. I tentatively step toward the old-school microphone, trying my best not to let my wobbly knees topple me over on my heels.

It shouldn't be so different, singing in front of an audience in an opera performance versus now. But in one, I'm dressed up as a character, with a cast and crew to have my back. If something goes wrong, it wasn't *me*, it was Juliet, or another member of the cast. All by myself is completely different.

But so is the rush I have right now.

That's what I'm thinking about when I wrap my hand around the microphone stand and blink to adjust to the brilliant spotlight. I use the blindness to my advantage and just focus on the thrill racing through me as the house music dies down. A quick glance to the right at Sol shows him beaming back at me in encouragement. I shake the nerves from my hands and turn around as he plays the first note. A brief shock of panic jolts through me as I realize I don't even know what song I'm singing, but it only takes the very next measure for me to realize it.

When Sol, my demon of music, sent me sheet music, there were never any words. I realized quickly that it was a game, and all I had to do was figure out what the song was. I'd sing it back and when I got it right, the far-off piano would join in.

Now that I realize my demon is very real, I can't believe I let myself freak out for so long. At this point though, I'm glad I didn't come clean. I might not have been crazy, but the story sure sounds like it.

I wait the few measures until the first note and then I begin to pull from within to belt out the lyrics to "Your Heart is as Black as Night" by Melody Gardot. It was one of the first songs my demon ever sent me, and I know it straight away.

The words flow from my diaphragm and feel like they're vibrating through every pore before they emerge from my lungs and throat. I close my eyes and let the music take me as I caress the microphone. When we finish the first verse, I inhale to start the chorus but the rich notes from a trumpet and saxophone shake me into opening my eyes.

The band members nod to me, telling me to keep going as they play, and I glance back at Sol. His lips lift in an encouraging smile, giving my core a delicious twist of excitement that's very different from the way the stage makes me feel.

I pivot back to the crowd and sing about how my lover has perfect timing, how I'll lose my mind over the way his black heart makes me feel. When I glance back at the man who started this all, my gaze catches on the way his strong hands lovingly brush against every ivory and black key. When I raise my eyes to meet his, midnight heat bores into me and desire pulses in my core, keeping time with the drummer that's now playing with us.

Every acting coach I've ever had would be screaming at me to face the crowd, but I don't even care if they're enjoying it when all I can see is the hungry way Sol is eye fucking me right now. My skin prickles and craves for those long fingers to caress me inside and out. All the while I'm singing every note and even though the key is a little low for me, the lyrics are designed for us and couldn't have been a more perfect fit for this moment.

When the final words flow from me, I hold the last one longer than normal, allowing for the saxophonist and now the drummer to add a flourish. When they finish, there is a pause, one where the whole world is silent and it's just me and Sol under the spotlight. The nerves and energy that scared me before are a distant memory as everything snaps into place inside my chest, almost an audible click as my dreams and realities align.

The room erupts in applause.

I spin around, having entirely forgotten in that moment that there was more than the two of us in the entire world, let alone this speakeasy. Everyone is on their feet, and that jittery excitement that always scares me settles into a deep calmness in my bones. Euphoria expands my chest with pride.

This. This just feels fucking *right*.

A hand claps on my shoulder and jolts me out of my reverie to see the lead singer with a cocktail and a wide smile across his weathered, dark-skinned face.

"Damn, girl. You've got pipes."

"She's the spittin' image of Gusty Day, too. Prettier obvious-ly." The saxophonist winks a rheumy-blue eye. "Any relation?"

"He's... he *was* my dad," I finish. "You knew him?"

A host of emotions cross the singer's face. "Yeah, we knew him. Played with him quite a few times. Shame he got mixed up with the wrong crowd, but at least you've figured out the right one." His words make me frown but when he keeps going, I lose all train of thought. "If you ever wanna sing with us again, just let us know. There's always an openin' for Gusty Day's kid."

Tears prick behind my eyes, but I smile and nod. This whole experience has been overwhelming, and I can't decide whether to run off the stage with Sol, beg to play another song, or shout "yes" to the lead singer at the top of my lungs. But I just stand there like an idiot until a strong arm wraps around my waist. I instinctively turn into the whiskey-and-leather scent, seeking the peace I know it brings me.

"Arrange it with Madam G, Zig, and we'll chat about another show," Sol offers before waving at him and helping me off the stage. "Maybe the Red, White, and Black Party next weekend."

"Will do, Mr. Bordeaux."

I wave goodbye to the band as Sol whisks me away. The lead singer calls for another round of applause. The cheers lift me up, making me feel weightless with more pride than any and all of the shows I've performed on the opera stage combined.

The crowd quiets behind me as Sol pulls me through the halls. The darkness is a stark contrast to the spotlight that was just beaming down on me, and I have to blink several times to see before we arrive at a darkened alcove. As soon as we stop, I open my mouth to thank him, but the warm taste of Sazerac cuts me off.

Sol's lips mold to mine, and one hand splays across my back while the other cradles my head. I melt into his embrace, moaning into his mouth.

He breaks the kiss with a chuckle. "Kiss me back, Scarlett."

It takes his prompting for me to realize I'm just standing there, dumbstruck still like I was on stage. I immediately wrap my arms around his shoulders and curl into him.

"Fuck, yes," he growls into my mouth and delves his tongue inside. I savor the warm whiskey-and-sugar flavors as I taste him back. My hands thread into his hair and his hand on my waist pulls me in tighter.

"You were everything up there, Scarlett. Fuck, the way you came *alive*." His lips pepper down my jawline. His mask isn't hard on my face like I thought it would be, but I'm careful with it still. He obviously doesn't want to take it off yet, not even to kiss, and my pulsing inner muscles will revolt if I screw this up.

His nose grazes over the sensitive skin on my neck before nipping my collarbone. I yelp but love the little bite of pain.

My fingers are still threaded into his hair so I dare to pull him up and bring him to my lips. He growls with urgency when I do and ravages my mouth with his before I break away.

"I need you, Sol."

He doesn't hesitate, not even for me to finish begging him before he gathers me into his arms. I'm vaguely aware of my dress ripping up the slit, but I couldn't care less as he picks me up. He holds me like a bride being carried over a threshold, like he did when he carried me to his underground home last night.

"Don't let go, Scarlett."

"Never," I whisper back.

I encircle my arms around his neck, and he pushes against a wall beside us, revealing a secret door.

Act 3

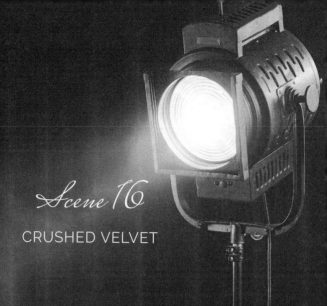

Scene 16

CRUSHED VELVET

We enter one of the Prohibition tunnels Sol's great-grandfather commissioned.

The Edison bulbs provide just enough visibility for me to see. We glide through the hallways as quiet as ghosts, taking turns and stairs. I can't get my bearings until I hear rushing water and find that we're somehow already back to his home. He fiddles with his phone and the door hisses open.

Not wasting another second, he barrels through the door and closes it behind us, locking it from his phone. He slams his hand against a switch on the wall and all the dim Edison lights and lamps light up throughout his home. Now that I can see the desire reflected in his face, I need him even more, and I'm attacking him before he can get us any farther than the foyer.

He pulls something from his waistband and it *clunks* against the entryway table as I wriggle from his hold to set my feet on the ground. His suit jacket is in my way, so I shove it back, pushing it off so he can shrug it the rest of the way to the floor. I unknot his tie and toss it to the ground, but when I reach for his button-down, he grabs one of my arms and drapes it around his neck. I cling to him while he wraps my legs around his waist.

His hands cup my ass cheeks before traveling up to the ribbon straps laced down my back. He unravels it, and the off-the-shoulder neckline falls between us, catching on his chest before it can reveal my naked breasts.

He captures my lips, and his fingers dig into the muscles of my ass cheeks in a deliciously painful massage. As he marches us down the hall, I'm kissing his mouth, biting his bottom lip, and pecking his left cheek, anything to get closer to him. My heart races and my core floods with need. His hard abs contract against my fluttering clit as he moves.

His footsteps are silent and my back is to the bedroom so I don't know we're there until he's swung the curtains open. The move is so forceful, they fly back from the railing they're secured to and land on the bed, mixing the velvet curtains with the velvet comforter. Without fixing the pile, he flings me on top of it all onto the bed.

A yelp escapes me before rumbling into a giggle and out of habit, my hands fly to my dress to keep my breasts covered. He prowls onto the bed and pushes my knees apart with his, causing another rip underneath me.

"My dress is going to be ruined," I pout playfully.

"I'll buy you another." He kisses my lips before caging me in on both sides of my head with his forearms. His fingers gently strip me from my masquerade mask before he explores my mouth.

"What if I want *this* dress," I tease against his lips. "It's one of a kind."

"Well then you can always cherish its memory as the night I ripped it apart to make you come on my tongue."

His fingers curl around my satin neckline and pull it down, unveiling my breasts. A sudden bout of shyness threatens with a lump in my throat until he takes total control. His long piano fingers mold my breasts and push them together as he kisses down my chest and around each areola.

"Do you know how hard I was all night, knowing you weren't wearing a bra under this thin fabric? The way every man salivated over you made me proud... and murderous."

"I didn't see anyone drooling over me, Sol."

I lift my hips up as his tongue swirls around my nipple. He sucks it into a peak and caresses the other with his finger, so softly the light touch has my core fluttering.

"Are you telling me you only had eyes for me, then, *ma belle muse?*" His wicked smile makes my cheeks hurt with one of my own.

He licks my other nipple before leaving wet, open mouth kisses down to where my dress still circles my waist. That entrancing midnight eye winks back at me, sparking a thrill down my spine. I bite my lip as he grabs the split hem at the top of my thigh and rips the entire dress up the middle. He doesn't give me a second to react before he's dragging my thong down inch by slow inch.

I close my eyes as his breath skates across the sensitive skin of my thighs. Goose bumps spring up all over and my heart stutters at the tingling sensation. I squirm underneath him until he captures my legs with his hands. My breath quickens as he peels them wider and settles his broad shoulders fully between them. Warmth surges from my core when he hooks his arms around my thighs and uses his thumbs to spread me apart. Even though I *need* him there, my hand reflexively tries to cover my pussy.

He nips at my fingers with his teeth, forcing me to snatch my hand back with a yelp. "Sol!"

His dark chuckle fans warm air against my most sensitive place.

"You don't get to hide from me, my pretty little muse. Next time my warning won't be so gentle."

I swallow and pinch my eyes closed, refusing to look at him as I confess. "I... I've never... I've never been with—"

"I know," he replies back and my eyes snap to his.

"You *know?* How the hell do you *know* I've never done anything but kiss a guy—*ow!*"

The bite on my inner thigh makes me sit up on my elbows to scold him, but he laves it, making it feel better.

"Don't talk about other men. Ever," he growls.

"Okay, but that doesn't answer my question." My eyes narrow at him.

He seems to hesitate before shrugging a broad shoulder farther underneath my leg and resting his hands around my upper thighs, as if to keep me from escaping.

"You told me the other night. When I made you—"

"When I was *drugged* and thought you were a *dream*?" The memory shoots into my head and I frown, considering if I should even be doing this with him at this moment at all.

"*No*... when you were so desperate to come, I freed you from your sexual frustration. That's what good dream lovers do."

That makes me laugh outright. "I'll admit, I've never had dreams quite as good as that one."

"No more dreams, little muse. Only memories. I'm going to make sure you never forget the first time I taste you."

I open my mouth to keep up the conversation, my nerves getting the best of me, but one swipe from my phantom's tongue and I'm a goner.

He starts in the center and laps up the arousal I know is pooled at my entrance, stroking all the way up to my clit. His warm tongue circles the nub and I moan. My fingernails claw for something, anything, for purchase and I find velvet in my grasp. Hopefully it's the quilt and not the curtains, but one more graze of his tongue makes me forget about caring at all.

Sol removes one hand as the other props up my ass cheek, bringing me as close as possible to taste me. His tongue spears inside me, sending shooting tingles of pleasure over my skin. My legs squeeze his head as my muscles tense with pleasure, but he keeps my left leg spread well away from his mask. He zeroes his tongue onto my clit, pulsing against it, and I gasp when something prods my opening. I peek down at him to see that one long finger is teasing my core, asking for entry.

"Yes, Sol. Please, I need your finger inside me."

I might've tricked myself into thinking I was drugged at the time, but I remember Sol guiding my fingers to find that perfect spot inside me. If he set me on fire without even touching me, I may combust when he does it on his own.

My hands tighten around the fabric I'm clutching, and the curtain rings clack together. The canopy rails creak above us, but Sol doesn't seem to be concerned.

His long nimble finger strokes my inner muscles and his tongue swirls around my clit until the pressure inside me builds to a fever pitch.

"Yes, Sol, please. Right there..." I whisper over and over, loving the way each encouragement seems to spur him on faster.

The need to come rises and rises, pushing me to the brink of bliss until he sucks my clit between his lips and focuses his midnight gaze on me. I jerk the velvet closer until it's taut and a sharp *snap* resounds against the walls. His name stutters from my lips as I finally hit that peak and tumble down, down, down back to earth.

All of a sudden, wood above me cracks and something collapses, threatening to crush me. I shriek through my orgasm, bliss and terror warring in the adrenaline flooding my veins, but Sol leaps on top of me, protecting me. One of the bed's canopy railings lands with a *thump* and he grunts above me. In all the commotion, my body still tremors with euphoria and his finger stays focused on the spot inside me, letting me ride the secondary notes of my orgasm even as he shelters me.

When I finally come all the way down on a sigh, I realize Sol has completely shielded me. My hands clutch the lapels of his white dress shirt and we're surrounded by what must be pounds of heavy velvet. As he gently withdraws his finger from my center, a breath stutters from me at the way each knuckle brushes my sensitive muscles. He catches my gasp between his lips in a scorching kiss. My hand strokes the uncovered left side of his face, but when I reach the right, his hand snatches mine.

"Don't." His voice is a threat but there's an air of pleading to it that makes my heart ache.

"I won't," I promise quickly, changing the trajectory of my left hand to thread into his hair instead. In the dark, I'd almost forgotten he'd even had his mask on due to its soft material. He moans back into my mouth as I tug his dark, soft strands and the mask presses into my face as our passionate kiss melts into tenderness.

When the velvet cloud enveloping us begins to become stiflingly hot, he breaks the kiss and sits up. The fabric tents over his powerful frame, allowing air to caress my cheeks. He tosses it off his back, and it's only then, in the dim light of the room, that I realize what I did.

"Ah! I broke your bed!"

"Just the canopy and curtains. They can always be fixed." He bends down to kiss me again and laughs against my lips. "Besides, there's not much higher achievement for a man than breaking his bed while making a woman come in his arms."

I giggle and swat at him. He deftly dodges it and stands up to remove the thick pile of curtains and one beam that'd landed across his back, careful not to bump me in the process.

"Are you okay?"

"I've been through worse," he murmurs. "It won't even bruise."

My eyes narrow as I watch his back muscles move underneath his dress shirt, as if I could see a possible bruise forming right beneath the fabric. But I get mesmerized by the ink swimming underneath the thin cotton shirt.

Cool air skates across my bare chest, breaking me from my reverie and giving me a cold chill. I sit up and gather my dress together, suddenly taking note that he's completely clothed while I'm vulnerably naked. Insecurity warms my cheeks as I try to cover myself with scraps of satin, and I know my pale skin must be beet red right now.

"What're you doing?" I hear him ask, but I don't look at him until one of his hands suddenly captures my wrist. I look up to see him holding clothes in the other. "Did you think I wouldn't take care of you? Lift up your arms."

He releases my wrist and I raise my arms like he asked, letting the satin dress scraps flutter down my skin. Ever so gently, he slides the white T-shirt down my arms and over my head. Whiskey, sugar, and leather envelop me, and I take a deep inhale as the cotton drifts past my nose.

When I've settled into the undershirt, I meet his warm gaze and smile shyly. A possessive glint in his sparkling eye catches me, reminding me of the look he gave me when other men allegedly dared to glance at me in Masque.

The truth is, he was right. There was no way I could look at anyone else when his fingertips were caressing my lower back all night. Why would I want anyone else's eyes or hands on me when I can't get enough of Sol's?

"I won't have my pretty little muse be shy in my bed. You'll either be confident and bare, or looking at me just like this in my shirt. Understood?"

I nod slowly and a grin spreads across my lips at the possession clouding his expression. The thick length in his pants seems to get even harder.

"What about you?" I ask tentatively, not entirely sure how to broach the subject. I glance at the steel tenting his suit, but when I look back to his face, a mischievous smile greets me.

"After you sang for the crowd, I just wanted to hear you sing for me. And what a gorgeous song it was." He steps closer and traces his finger down my throat before whispering in my ear. "I want no one else to take pleasure in hearing the sweet music I draw from you at night."

I swallow underneath his fingertips and nod, not sure what else to do in response. His tongue licks the shell of my ear as he says something else, making my skin tingle.

"Promise?"

I have no idea what he just said, but I'm quickly realizing I'll agree to anything while Sol Bordeaux touches me.

"I-I promise."

"Good." He pulls away. "Now get ready for bed, Scarlett. I know you have a routine and you need to get a good night's sleep."

The reminder is the first one I've had about my bipolar disorder and my nose scrunches as I take stock of my body and mind.

There are no jitters. No nerves. My brain isn't racing a million miles a second. Other than wanting Sol to get right back into bed with me—which I think is totally normal considering the smoldering man in front of me—I have no desire to do anything else reckless. And if this man has only encouraged me, protected me, and given me the best night of my life so far... is wanting to sleep with him really reckless at all? It feels delightfully inevitable.

"What're you thinking about so hard?"

"I feel... *fine*," I finally answer. "I feel *good*, but not euphoria 'high in a manic state' good. My happiness just feels like... happiness."

"Sometimes that's all happiness needs to be." His smile softens and he caresses my cheek. "You can see madness in the eyes, you know. And there's absolutely nothing but sated relaxation in your silver moons." I give in to his touch and am one caress away from purring like a kitten when he stops. "Now, go get ready for bed. If I have anything to do with it, I'll keep you this way."

Sol leaves me be as I shower in his gorgeous black marble bathroom and get ready for bed. Once I finish my nightly routine with all the products Sol apparently had one of his beauty-conscious shadows fetch from my dorm, I go back to his bedroom.

He's sitting up against the black wood headboard, waiting for me in another loose black long-sleeve T-shirt and silk pants. The underground home is quite chilly, so I'm a little jealous of his pajamas, but I have no doubt I'll be just fine underneath the covers.

I walk slowly to his bed, wondering when he'll look up from

his phone. But he continues to stare at it like it's offended him, and a frown mars his face. Then I notice that his hair is slightly damp, and I frown, too.

"Where did you get ready for bed?"

"In the bathroom, down the hall," he mutters and types furiously on his phone.

"You didn't want to get ready with me?" I ask hesitantly.

I don't know the etiquette with this stuff. I don't know why this is hard for me to ask. And I don't know why I care. But something about the fact that he knows almost literally everything about me and he won't even brush his teeth around me puts me off. But then *again*, I shouldn't care... right?

"I didn't want to interrupt your routine with mine," he answers casually.

I snort. "Aren't boy routines step one: wash your face, step two: brush your teeth. Rinse and repeat? That was my dad's anyway. Everywhere we went, he had that damn bottle of three-in-one shampoo, conditioner, and body wash. Years of neglecting my own skincare and hair is one of the reasons why I'm so religious about it now."

He huffs, still not looking at me. "Mine's a little more involved."

I want to tease him more, but my eyes narrow when I realize his brow is still furrowed.

"Is everything okay?" I ask.

He looks up at me and lays his phone face down on the nightstand.

"Yes, everything is fine. Just business." He gestures for me to come to him and pats the bed.

I crawl in beside him underneath the thick quilt, trying not to think too much about that answer.

How many times had my dad said the same thing? Only to go off and be gone for hours, leaving me in random hotels or rental homes in strange cities? I've often wondered if the men my father associated with were responsible for his death. If so, then he put me in danger that night too.

Will Sol do the same?

"Business huh?" I finally ask, not able to hold the question in. "What kind of business?"

He chuckles and lies on his side, facing me. He's now back to his usual white skull mask, and he rubs his right eyelid as he chuckles. "So inquisitive, little muse."

I shrug, attempting to play it off. "I've got questions for my kidnapper. So sue me."

"I didn't kidnap you, Scarlett." The scowl on his face only makes me giggle. "I couldn't let you be alone without knowing the extent of what you took and I want to make sure you're still in a good headspace before I let you venture back out into the world alone."

I sigh. "I know. You probably saved my life. But when can I go back to my dorm? I've got another rehearsal on Monday, y'know. I realized just tonight that I don't even have my phone with me. Jaime's probably worried sick."

"I figured it would be good to be radio silent while you recouped. If you want your phone, I can send someone to retrieve it. As for going back to your dorm... we'll see how well you sleep tonight. If you feel relaxed and healthy tomorrow, I'll consider it."

A pang in my heart confuses me. I'm not sure why what he said hurt my feelings... or maybe it's just because I don't really *want* to leave yet. I turn over to hide my emotions from him either way.

"Perfect," I lie.

For once, Sol doesn't seem to notice my fib, and for once, I wish he would. With my back to his front, he pulls me into his chest. His hard length presses against my backside and he does nothing to hide it. I wiggle against it to tease him, but Sol nips the shell of my ear, forcing a yelp from me. He squeezes me close so I can't escape him as he growls into my ear.

"Good night, Scarlett."

We lie on our sides and Sol scoops his arm underneath my neck before curving his forearm over my chest. His other hand pulls me closer to him by my hip bone. It's comfortable and secure, and for the first time ever, I feel... safe.

"Good night, Sol," I finally whisper back.

S carlett's deep, restful breaths arrive in minutes, no doubt contributed to by medication, the excitement of the night, and the orgasm I gave her. A sense of pride swells in me that I've sated her and that she feels safe with me despite my having *kidnapped* her.

My watch lights up on my wrist where I'm holding Scarlett to me. A lone glance at the screen tells me Sabine's contact has finally gotten back to her with answers. If they're ready to meet then I must go, no matter how much I loathe leaving her.

I pull my arm out from underneath her and roll her so she's comfortably on her back before I slide out of bed. The Edison lamps beam a warm glow over her curly raven strands fanning around her head like a halo and her angelic face is still rosy from her orgasm.

Normally my curtains would block the light out, but my little muse is a fucking vixen in bed and tore them down. Despite the fact that the railing had fallen on my back at the time, I'd still wanted to shove my cock in her right then and there. The way her tight cunt sucked my fingers was so enticing, I would've given almost anything to feel the pleasure on my shaft instead.

But she's a virgin, and no matter how fucked up I am in every other situation, I know Scarlett deserves more for her first time than a quick fuck, and that's all I would've been capable of after her stunning performance. I hadn't known that her heart wasn't in theater, but I would have if I'd ever heard her when she puts her whole fucking being into the song, like she did tonight.

I check my phone to make sure there's another delivery ready for her in the morning while padding across the carpet to the bathroom, grabbing my clothes along the way. I change out of my sleep pants and into my boxer briefs, but before I put on my dark jeans, I fist my stiff cock through my boxers, to the point that a jolt of pleasure and pain zaps down my spine.

Part of me wants to relieve the pressure, but the part of me that lives for delayed gratification has me squeezing tighter and tighter until I finally let go. The blood pulses throughout my shaft and I hiss a breath, reminding myself how much more rewarding it will be to wait until I can come inside Scarlett instead. I inhale a fortifying breath before jerking my jeans up my legs and tucking my still-hard cock inside.

After donning socks and shoes, I take a swig of mouthwash. I hate removing her taste, but it has to be done if I'm to keep a level head for what's next. There's no way I'll be able to concentrate with her scent right underneath my nose.

I exit the bathroom and make the few strides to take one last look at Scarlett. I'm tempted to linger, but my watch lights up, reminding me that I have other matters, matters that involve *her*, that need my attention. I brush a soft curl off of her face and leave a featherlight kiss over her forehead.

"I'll be back soon," I murmur, silently hoping she'll wake up and catch me so I'll get to crawl back into bed.

Her breaths remain slow and consistent, though, like a melody in *larghissimo*. Scarlett needs her sleep more than most and I sure as fuck am not going to be the one who sends her head-first into an episode by destroying her sleep patterns.

With that in mind, I leave the bedroom and grab my gun

from the entryway table to holster it before leaving home. I activate the security feed inside through my phone, so I can monitor my sleeping beauty while I'm gone. In nearly a year, there hasn't been an hour that's gone by that I don't know what she is up to and I won't stop now, even though she's in my own bed.

Obsession.

That's what my brother calls it.

But the ache I feel when I'm away from her is much more than any obsessed revenge I've embarked on. It's the feeling you get when you find the *perfect* song, the one you could play for eternity, never getting tired of a single note, and still not want to get to the final measure.

I'm still refusing to believe our song will end. I can't kill the hope that my muse will write our lyrics someday.

While I walk a city block underground through my great-grandfather's tunnels, I use the security app on my phone to turn off the Edison bulbs lining the stone walls until I'm closer to my destination. My awareness is at its peak in the dark. When I reach one of the tunnels I took with Scarlett earlier, I bear right.

Even though I know I'm the most formidable thing in my pitch-black tunnel, I never go the same route twice in a row. It's why I'm traveling above ground for most of my journey tonight. That, and it's good for my people to know I'm not *actually* a phantom.

When I get topside and wind through the hidden Prohibition route with bars on either side, the aboveground hallway that lines the restaurant comes to a stop in front of a heavy wooden door. I open it and immediately pass into a different world.

The brick alleyway is packed with people enjoying the outdoor bar of one of the most popular restaurants in New Orleans. Fleur-de-lis spikes line the back wall, and a green trellis with vines and plants threaded through the lattice work mostly blocks the bar patrons from this particular entrance to the passageways. The lights strung up on the brick provide shadows and darkness for me to disappear in. Music blares from speakers in the back corner, but they're no match for the crowd as they boo at whatever sports game is playing on the big-screen TVs set up throughout the restaurant.

"Hey man! Mask dude!"

I bristle at the attention in the small alcove, but I turn around slowly to see a middle-aged man dressed like a frat boy facing the far corner of the small vestibule to my hidden halls.

"Yes?" I ask, an edge to my voice.

Normally plants and other shrubbery growing over the trellis are enough to deter people from exploring back here. Not for this asshole apparently. And as the alcohol reeks from his pores, I can smell why.

The man has piles of Mardi Gras beads around his neck and he sways so precariously as he urinates against the painted brick that it's a wonder he's even hitting it at all.

He hiccups as he points to his dick. "I'm pissing here, dude. Fuck off."

I glance to the left, through the shrubbery, where a clearly marked restroom is two doors down.

"This is not your property to piss on, *dude*," I answer.

"I can piss wherever I want, motherfucker." He zips up and tries to glare at me through unfocused eyes.

No doubt his confidence is sky high thanks to the hurricane drink he's almost finished. I've easily got half a foot and fifty pounds on the guy and from the beer belly he's showing off through his sweaty, half-open pastel button-down, there's no way he trains like I do.

But there are other things on my agenda tonight besides putting a drunken fool in his place, so I roll my eyes and turn around.

"It's your lucky day, asshole. I've got shit to do."

But the imbecile has a death wish.

"Fuck you, dude. You don't own this shithole. I can piss wherever I want. You can't tell me what to do." His words warn me half a beat before he grabs my shoulder with all his drunken strength.

I don't budge.

He tries to tug me back, but I dig my heel into the ground and scout my surroundings. The garbage human and I are secluded, but for the camera at the top corner of the wall.

Unfortunately for him, that's *my* security feed.

I pivot on the balls of my feet and shove him into the corner. The tall hurricane glass in his hand spills all over his shirt and falls into a potted plant.

"You, fucker! You made me spill my drink. Fuckin' ass—"

He takes a wild swing midcurse, missing me by a mile. When he pulls back to try again, I kick him straight in his knee. He doubles over with a groan and I yank him up by his beads. No doubt he had big plans to throw them and yell obscenities at passersby, but they're not going to be used by anyone but me tonight.

I pull them taut, choking him, before grabbing his sweaty half-buttoned shirt with my other hand and slamming the man against the wall. His eyes bug out and he grabs in vain at the necklaces with his alcohol-soaked hands. His bum leg tries to kick, but he can't control it, and he can't scream out because my grip on the Mardi Gras beads is cutting off his windpipe.

He's too easy.

The thought annoys me, and I almost ignore it as I watch his pale face turn crimson. I could just choke the life out of my prey with all of this stupid fucking plastic and be done with it. Then I could end his miserable existence right here. But my own moral code makes that impossible.

I'll never take down the defenseless. And as drunk as this guy has gotten, that's exactly what he is. Defenseless.

If he were in my dungeon, I'd let him make his choice, trial by water or combat, but he hasn't done anything to warrant that kind of discipline. My gaze darts around, looking for a suitable punishment to fit the crime, and my eye catches on the wrought iron fleur-de-lis spike above the wall.

Perfect.

I meet my prey's terrified red eyes. Snot and tears flow from his nose and eyes. I want to kill him just for his weakness. When his eyes start to glaze over, I know it's time to finish it.

"Never. Put. Your. Hands. On. Anyone. Again. Do you understand?"

He tries to nod but my grip on the beads is too tight and my hold on his lapels too lax.

"Good. Now... fight for your innocence."

I drop him and catch the thick cord of beads with both hands before he falls completely to the ground. Pushing up with my legs, I reach the top of the fleur-de-lis with my stretched arms and hook the necklaces around the spike.

Once I've hung him by the plastic, I let go and watch with satisfaction at the sounds of him struggling for breath and the sight of his body jerking in the Mardi Gras bead noose.

My punishment is just, in my opinion. He used his hands on me, and all he has to do to get free is use those same hands to extricate himself from his necklace.

But he doesn't. Instead, I study my prey as he dangles, slowly losing oxygen while his feet kick feebly. His face turns that pretty shade of strangled purple I so love to see. Since the bastard won't help himself, I have to do the work.

I sigh before yanking him down by his shoulders as hard as I can, popping beads left and right from his neck. He lands hard on his ass, and takes a lifesaving gulp of air. I kneel down in his face, careful not to touch any part of him again.

"Do you know who I am?"

He shakes his head, clutching his convulsing neck, now with bright-red bead-shaped bruises already cropping up.

"I'm going to give you my calling card," I say, twisting my ring on my finger. "When you come to, I want you to ask around about what the symbol on your face means, got it?"

"The... the what—"

I rear back and slam my fist into his forehead, knocking him out flat and leaving a detailed print of a skull on his pale skin. The hit wasn't as hard as possible, but the indent from my ring might leave a scar. If it does, hopefully he'll see it every day in the mirror, and remember his lesson. If nothing else, he'll attribute his wound to the night the Phantom of the French Quarter spared his life.

Before I leave, the light glints on his necklaces and an idea for later sparks in my mind. I remove several of the strands that don't touch his sweaty neck and are less gaudy. The sparkling black ones and the ones with the skulls particularly catch my eye.

As I stand from my kneeling position, I wipe my bloody ring on the guy's shirt. I'll have to wash my hands and beads as soon as possible to cleanse my body of his reeking oils. Using the hand that never touched his skin directly, I check my mask to make sure it's intact. The skin underneath itches from having to wear the prosthetic earlier, but the adhesive is still in place, so I pocket my new trinkets and continue my journey above ground to my meeting.

I weave through the greenery that usually hides the doorway from patrons and emerge into the restaurant's open-air bar. The sports fans are newly disappointed, groaning as I pass by them and the brightly colored water fountain. I slip through unnoticed around tables and waitstaff as I navigate my way to St. Peter Street.

The quicker I move, the less likely I'll be seen. Granted, once my little friend wakes up, the rumors and tall tales will spark up again. Just how I like it.

Once I get out of the busy alleyway, I pivot quickly to Bourbon Street. Almost immediately, all kinds of smoke, alcohol vapors, and body odors burn my nose. The crowds are in full force tonight and any concern that I might be noticed evaporates with the clean air I once breathed. Revelers are dressed to impress or practically not dressed at all. Everyone on Bourbon tonight is here for, and part of, the spectacle and my plain bone-white mask is child's play when people are literally in costume.

My skin crawls as the bodies and fluids around me brush against me, and I barely hold back my revulsion. I want to turn back, but I'm on a mission and I must complete it before Scarlett wakes up. It's one thing for her to joke that I've kidnapped her and hold her against her will. It's quite another to wake up, locked in a dark underground room by yourself. I would die before Scarlett ever felt an ounce of the misery I did.

When I arrive at one of the oldest jazz clubs in the Quarter, I fade into the poorly lit, tightly packed room. The air is sticky with humidity and thick with the music bouncing off the walls. The band on stage in the back is one of the best in New Orleans, and I can't help but imagine Scarlett up there tearing the house down with her soulful voice, just like she did at Masque earlier tonight.

My gaze flicks to one of the cellists and he nods to me before stomping his booted foot in rhythm next to where the large instrument rests, showing off the rubber skull design underneath the end pin. I nod back before pushing open the wooden doors to the bar's back alley.

A short line of patrons grumbles in front of a man wearing sunglasses, despite it being the middle of the night. He's lazily sitting outside a large green slatted door, perfectly acting like he's not guarding it. But this shadow is one of my best. I've never seen him off his game. Raising my hand, I pass by the complainers and show him my ring. His chin barely lifts in acknowledgment and he opens the door behind him.

"Hey, he didn't have to have a password!" One of the women I passed sneers at my shadow as I round the entry.

"The Phantom doesn't need one," he responds simply before closing the door.

I push against a door that is camouflaged to look like the plastered brick wall around it, revealing a hidden open-air staircase. I take the winding red stairs two at a time until I come to the landing that overlooks the courtyard below. The private, password-only lounge is to my right, through the tall white door, but I go left instead onto the skinny balcony outlining the garden square below. I stick to the shadows and when I get to the opposite wall, a woman sidles out from behind a small alcove.

"You're late."

With her revealing herself in the faint city light, I can see her eyes flash as they narrow at me, but I doubt she can see much of me beyond my white mask. Her hair is shaved on the sides and the gel on top gleams in the moonlight, as does the government-issued firearm she's trying to hide underneath her black dress shirt and slacks.

We don't exchange names. We don't need to. As a Sixth District officer from the New Orleans Police Department, she covers the Garden District and knows all about who I am. The Chatelains have made sure of it. Technically, she should be on their payroll, but she's made it very clear to her precinct that she wishes to remain unaffiliated. She's taking a big risk meeting me, but so am I.

The case I'm interested in happened in the Garden District, and as a Bordeaux, anything that happens on the Chatelains' side is strictly off-limits. If she were to go back and tell her captain, Rand would have grounds for retaliation or questioning as he sees fit. I'm potentially betting my life on this stranger's silence.

"Why were you late? Is there something I should know?"

"I had business," I reply, though I don't need to.

I need this woman's information more than she needs me right now. Not to mention that she's sleeping with my second-in-command, Sabine, so I treat her with a little more cordiality than normal. Sabine's as loyal as they come but she's fucking lethal every time she finds out I've been "rude" to people she cares about.

"You have them?" I ask.

"Yup, it's all here for both cases." She hands me a flash drive and I pull out the USB connector for my phone, plugging both in.

Once the options come up, I thumb through the files. Like Sabine said, there are hundreds of videos from a decade ago. But when I get to the single file about a different incident, I frown.

"This is it?" I ask, pointing at the screen.

"Not much to go off of," she explains. "That's why it's a cold case."

I scowl and glance at the file briefly, just to verify it's the correct one. It only takes a few seconds to check the contents and I download them to my phone's storage service before handing back the thumb drive. I swallow my frustration and focus on asking the right questions, just in case there's something missing.

"Since you were on the scene that night, is there anything else you remember that might not be in the case file?"

She sucks her teeth while she thinks and ultimately shakes her head. "Not really. Witnesses heard a girl's scream and several gunshots. Someone from the restaurant nearby called 9-1-1. Vic had two GSWs, one gunshot to the chest and the other in the head."

"Two shots," I murmur and she nods.

"Naturally, he was DOA. Shooter was long gone, though. No idea what direction he went because the restaurant's cameras weren't working."

Of course they weren't. I'd made sure of it.

"And the girl?"

"By the time we arrived, she still had tears on her face, but she wasn't crying anymore. She seemed... pissed. Which, I guess I don't blame her. All she kept saying was that the other guy shouldn't have gotten away. And that he couldn't have been too far."

I pause. "Did she say why?"

The officer shakes her head. "Nope. When we tried to interview her, she clammed up. We never did find the murderer, but with her father's criminal history, we figured it was rivalry based." She gives me a pointed look. "The vic was in a lot of gambling debt. He owed someone money and that's how he paid for it... We thought it was the Phantom of the French Quarter at first."

Gambling debt? Was all this just over money?

I keep my face blank as I point out what should be obvious. "Out in the open isn't the Phantom's style."

The officer shrugs. "That's also why it's a cold case. It was just speculation around the precinct, but believe me, if my guys could've pinned it on him, they would've."

And that's why I don't go into the Garden District anymore. Fucking Chatelains...

"The whole thing was messy with a lot of weird missing pieces," she continues. "The vic had gunshot residue on his hands, but the weapon was nowhere to be found. The suspect dropped his gun before fleeing, but there were no fingerprints."

There wouldn't be. He'd burned them off.

"Did the girl ever ask you for updates?"

"She did for a while, but I think she gave up. Due to her father's debts, she was kicked out of rental housing. I heard she got a scholarship to attend her senior year of school since her father wasn't paying for it anymore. Last I heard, the poor thing went crazy over all of it."

My fists clench. "She's not *crazy.*"

She holds up her hands in innocence. "Whatever you want to call it. Not many people are hospitalized for being *sane.* Is she what this is all about? Do you know her or something?"

"That's enough," I answer. "As always, discretion is paramount."

She straightens at my dismissal. "Of course. If you, uh, need anything else about the case, let Sabine know."

I nod, but don't reply further, leaving her on the balcony. Instead of going back into the street, I take the stairwell all the way down to a trapdoor at the base of the stairs.

Going above ground occasionally is vital so that my shadows can see me out and about. It's easier to trust their boss is watching over them and has their back if they physically see him every now and then. But I've done my duty for the night and I don't need to stay topside on the way back. Without the Bourbon Street traffic, I cover the two blocks quickly and return to my home faster than it took to leave.

When I quietly open the door, slip inside, and lock it behind me, I'm met with complete silence. I gingerly unholster my gun and hide it in the entryway table's drawer. My heart races faster and faster as I tiptoe to my bedroom, but it calms completely when I see Scarlett sleeping peacefully. Before I sink into bed beside her, I go to the hallway bathroom and hop in to take another shower.

I spot clean around my mask the best I can so I don't have to reapply the adhesive. But I thoroughly scrub off the outside world everywhere else on my body.

Once I dry off, I put on a different black, long-sleeve T-shirt and the same silk pants I wore earlier and exchange my painted eye prosthetic for a clear one. The navy color is the most realistic one I have, but it's also my oldest so when I wear it for too long it makes my eye socket ache, and I haven't switched it out since I retrieved Scarlett from her dorm. I'll have to wake up early to swap it out again so Scarlett won't be subjected to it, but I don't mind. I'll do anything to make sure she's never horrified by me.

I'm about to go to bed when my eyes catch on the Mardi beads on the bathroom floor. With a mischievous smirk quirking the left side of my mouth, I wipe them down in the sink, too.

I go to my living room, closing all the doors behind me so I can do some "home improvements" that I can't wait to try out with Scarlett. Once I've finished, I call it a night and head to my room.

The brisk chill of my apartment filters through my long sleeves, hitting my still-damp scars on my back and arm. I quickly slide underneath the covers behind Scarlett to get warm. Her soft disgruntled groan makes me have to hide my chuckle, but the relieved sigh that escapes her once she's nestled in my arms has my chest tightening to the point of pain.

As long as she sleeps, I'll be happy, but I probably won't get a wink.

My mind is humming with theories. I'm dying to read and watch those files immediately, to learn the truth of what happened the night that changed Scarlett's life and destined her to be in mine. But the truth will have to wait while I savor this fantasy, one where I have Scarlett safe and sound, protected in my arms, just like this, forever. It's a dream I wouldn't mind never waking from.

Scene 18

OPEN YOUR EYES

My eyes snap open, but I don't know why.

There's no alarm, but I'm still wide awake at—I roll over and move the white roses aside to see the clock on the bedside table—*six* a.m. I stifle a groan and rub my weary eyes. The last time I woke up this early voluntarily was probably when I was an infant and I feel like whining like one right now. We didn't go to bed too late, so I had a reasonable amount of rest. Still, a tempting part of me wants to roll over and go back to sleep, but another is already trying to figure out what woke me.

I sit up to take stock of my surroundings—trying to find what tripped that wire in my brain—when it hits me.

That seductive Sazerac scent still embraces me, but its owner is nowhere to be found. And the piano music I've craved over the past year is playing, but barely audible, as if Sol's trying to keep quiet.

Ugh, why the hell is he up so early? All I want to do is grab him by his collar and drag him back to bed to sleep. Or hey, if we're in bed, *not* sleeping would be fun, too.

At the prospect of doing one, or both, of those things, I hop out of bed and head to the bathroom to run through my morning routine. Whatever he's working on, I want to listen before I interrupt him, and I'm afraid he'll stop if he hears me moving around.

Once I finish taking my medicine and getting ready, I keep his T-shirt on but find a thong in a small stack of my clothes on a nearby dresser and slide it on. Ready enough, I tiptoe silently to his den where he's playing a beautiful piece I've only heard through the vents in my dorm.

The den is warm and cozy, illuminated by the blazing fireplace and candles from his desk. Sol is so immersed in his piece that I wonder if he would've heard me with a bulldozer. From this view, I can see the expressive side of his face furrowed in concentration. His forehead above his dark brow is wrinkled, his soft lips a hard line, and that midnight eye is ablaze with focus. My eyes can't help but travel farther down his form.

The black long-sleeved shirt hides the tattoos I know are underneath the fabric, but I can still see his shoulder muscles move with every octave change. His biceps stretch the cotton with each chord. He's absolutely mesmerizing.

I stand in the doorway, leaning against the wooden frame, watching him until my eyes flit around the room to the photographs on the wall. The glow from the candles and fireplace flickers over every one, giving each a more mysterious backdrop. They're gorgeous and I'm more than a little jealous of whoever got to be behind the camera lens.

After glancing over all the frames hanging on the walls, I go back to admiring the way his hands fly over the piano until he reaches the lowest octave. His fingers falter on the keys and he stops abruptly, stiffening and staring carefully straight ahead.

"Scarlett, I didn't realize you'd be up so soon."

"Yeah, about that... if you're an early riser, this is so not going to work out. I'm a night owl through and through, mister."

He doesn't chuckle along with me and only keeps staring at the wall. His lack of response makes me frown, but I try a different tactic.

"Did you take the photos? I remember you saying you wanted to travel the world—"

"Ben took them for me," he interrupts. His voice is gentle but his words are clipped. "Listen, I'll meet you in the bedroom. I'm sorry my playing woke you."

"Your playing didn't wake me, but you not being in bed holding me did. Come back and sleep with me for a few hours," I insist and try to step forward, but he flinches and I halt in my tracks. "I, um... I slept really well and woke up naturally. It's early for a weekend but I think with being down here, not having any light makes it easier to fall asleep and stay that way."

He jerks his head once in a nod. "Good... I must've lost track of time, then. I'll meet you in the bedroom. We can talk about today's plans."

"Sol... are you okay? Why won't you look at me?" I inch closer and keep going despite the way his muscles bunch up on his back. "Sol, look at me."

He swallows but remains facing forward. "Scarlett, I—"

"Sol, look at me," I demand, barely resisting the urge to stomp my foot at him.

When he looks up at me, I finally see his face. He's got his bone-white skull mask on still, but an eye patch covers his right eye.

"Oh my god." My hand flies to my lips. "Sol, are you okay?"

He flinches at my question. "Yes, I'm fine—"

I rush to him anyway and reach for his eye patch, but he captures my wrist.

"You said you wouldn't," he accuses, pain clouding his face, as he reminds me of the promise I made to him in bed.

"And I won't. Not your mask, but your eye... are you okay?"

"I'm fine," he growls back, but there's no menace to it. It's more like he's... embarrassed?

"Sol, why do you have an eye patch on?"

He sighs before letting go of my wrist and answering. "You may know that my eye on this side... it's a prosthetic."

I nod slowly. Jaime had said Sol has a fake eye, but I didn't fully know what that meant. I'm thankful he's willing to explain it to me. Maybe one day he'll explain how he got it, but this already looks painful for him to talk about, so I let him take the reins.

"It's an acrylic shell that was fitted over an implant in my eye socket," he continues. "The color prosthetic doesn't fit perfectly. I put one of my comfortable ones on so that my eyelid can still work normally. This one is just a clear acrylic layer over tissue. I'll go change it now—"

"No." Taking a chance, I slide over his lap, straddling him with my legs dangling over the piano bench before he can stand up.

I quickly realize when my core meets the bulge in his thin pajama pants that I didn't think this all the way through.

He's fully dressed in his pajamas and I'm in a T-shirt and panties, but this position is so intimate it doesn't feel like we're clothed. Desire that I try to ignore already twists my lower belly as he settles his large palms around my hips.

Curiosity wrinkles the uncovered side of his brow, reminding me to tug my dirty mind back from the gutter.

My hands drift to his face and I watch his midnight eye as I slowly go to the patch on the left side. His jaw is hard as stone and his cheek tenses underneath my fingertips. I wait for him to relax, like I'm trying to rescue a wounded animal caught in a trap. When his hands lessen their tight grip around my hips, I ask softly, barely audible over the blood rushing in my ears.

"May I?"

He scans my face as if he's trying to assess whether I have an ulterior motive. It aches to know that someone has betrayed him so much in a moment like this that he struggles to trust me now. I keep absolutely still to avoid spooking him. Finally, he sighs heavily and nods once.

My heartbeat is thudding in my chest as I curve my nails underneath the black cloth patch and pull it up. His eyes slam shut as soon as I can reveal what's underneath, and I toss the patch to the side. His fingertips tremble against my skin.

I kiss him softly before whispering against his warm lips, "Open your eyes, Sol."

A breath shudders from him, and I pull back as he slowly lifts both eyelids.

The sparkling midnight one is pleading with me for something. Acceptance? Mercy?

But the other eye... is gone.

His eyelid blinks and behaves exactly the same, but in the place of that dull-blue iris I'm used to, reddish-pink tissue blinks back at me, protected by the clear prosthetic. The bare socket that should contain an eyeball like its counterpart looks vulnerable beneath his thick black lashes.

He looks vulnerable... for *me*.

I keep my gaze on his midnight eye as I cup his maskless cheek with my hand.

"You're safe with me, Sol."

Giving him plenty of time to stop me, I lean in with my lips parted, not sure if he'll welcome my touch. As he meets me halfway and his hand threads through my hair, surprise and relief releases the tension in my shoulders. Our lips brush once until he presses against mine. It's tender at first, and my skin tingles as his other hand travels up my back. But when his fingers fist my hair, those tingles become light pinpricks of ecstasy right before he *devours* me.

Need floods to my core instantly and I moan into his mouth while grinding against his hardening shaft. Every cell in my body wants to show him I accept him for the way he is. To everyone else, he's the Phantom of the French Quarter, but to me, he's my demon of music.

"You don't get to hide from me, either," I murmur against his lips. "I want you."

He growls as he kisses me with an intensity that takes my

breath away, as if my declaration was exactly what he was waiting for.

The hand on my back shifts to my waist and he tugs me down against his shaft to the point that if we weren't clothed, he'd be halfway inside me. My core aches to be filled as arousal dampens my panties. His tangled fingers extricate themselves from my long hair to wrap around my nape and he uses the angle to dive his tongue into my gasping mouth. His length pushes against my entrance, making the head hit my clit just right, but it's not enough right now.

"I need more, Sol, please."

His broad shoulders tilt forward, surrounding me and forcing my back into the piano keys behind me. Discordant notes play against my spine and reverberate from the open grand piano against the stone walls, but the cacophony only heightens our desperation. My thighs hug his waist as I try to ride him, desperately wishing we were naked.

Sol's nimble fingers leave my nape and my head rests against the paper-covered music stand as he strokes my breast.

"Oh, Sol, I'm ruining your sheet music." I try to squirm away, but he licks up my neck, rippling pleasure down my skin before scattering the sheets onto the rug.

"Fuck my music. The only music I want to hear right now are the high notes you hit when I make you come."

His hands dive underneath my shirt before tugging it completely off. He crumples it up like a makeshift pillow, and props it on the keyboard behind my back, protecting my spine from the ivory keys. With my shirt off, he drops open-mouthed kisses along my collarbone down to my cleavage. He then swirls his tongue around my nipple while kneading the other. His fingers roll over each breast, like he's playing a slow song on my skin and he sucks hard on my peak, drawing his name from my mouth in a high-pitched moan.

He encourages me as he switches his mouth's attention from one nipple to the other. "That's it, sing for me, my sweet muse."

While he flicks his tongue over my other bud, one hand skates down my skin to my waist, leaving goose bumps behind it. The other teases my already soaked diamond-hard tip. His fingers stretch across my spine and massage the muscles in my lower back. When his cock pulses against the thin fabric of my panties, I try to circle my hips to create more friction.

"Please. This isn't enough. I need... I need more. I want all of it."

"And you'll get it."

He nips my breast, and I yelp, but he soothes the bite with his tongue before sucking nearly half my other breast into his mouth so hard that he pulls me up from the piano. My hands are in a frenzy, working at his cotton collar, trying to take his shirt off, but he quickly lifts me and plops my ass down onto the keys, blaring more wild notes from the piano's depths. He kicks away the piano bench behind him, giving him more room to kneel between my legs.

When he looks up at me, the candlelight dances on his white mask. His midnight eye is hungry with need, and I stroke his hair back from the right side of his face, uncovering the pink tissue of the bare socket.

"Am I hideous?" he asks in a hoarse whisper, and my heart skips an aching beat.

This huge, strong man—the Phantom of the French Quarter, a King in New Orleans, and my demon of music—is *kneeling* before me, *trusting* me with the pain of his past.

"Outside of your family... how many people have seen you this way?"

He shakes his head. "Only you."

My breath expands in my lungs even as I bend down to meet his eyes. Gratitude over this moment pumps through my veins, and I cup both of his cheeks.

"A sight so precious could never be anything less than exquisite."

His lips lift on both sides, and the genuine appreciation there fills me up like his smile does his face. My demon loves to be praised, it seems.

He reaches up to grab the back of my neck and takes my mouth in a scorching kiss. My curls fall over him like a curtain, hiding us from the world. While his lips move furiously against mine, he slides his other hand up the sensitive skin of my inner thigh, making me shiver. As he moves closer and closer to my center, it's hard for me to concentrate. It's only seconds before those skilled fingers tease my thong-covered entrance, seducing a moan from my lungs.

"So wet for me, pretty muse. Do you want my cock to fill you up?"

"Yes, please, Sol."

"Say it."

Shyness makes me hesitate before I repeat his words back to him. "I... I need your cock to fill me up, *please.*"

"You've never been filled before, have you, *belle muse?*"

"No. Never. You're the one I want first."

He growls against my lips. "This is your only warning, Scarlett. I won't settle for 'first.' I'll be your only. Nothing less."

My stomach flips at the gravity of his promise. When he pulls away from our kiss and spreads my legs, his gaze challenges me to stop him, but I don't.

"Your words don't scare me, Sol. Neither do *you.*"

He smirks as he drapes my legs over his shoulders and fits between my thighs. "Then you won't mind if I make you scream."

He swipes his tongue up my panty-clad center. I moan and clutch the edge of the piano, depressing the keys and making an angry, passionate chord before tilting my head back.

He nips my clit through my panties, sparking a yelp from me and my eyes flash to his.

"Watch me. Tell me how good I make you feel."

"So good, Sol—"

He growls against my thong before hooking his finger in a strap and snapping it off. I cry out at the way it abrades my skin but I forget all about the sting when he blows cool air on my bare pussy. Without wasting another moment, he sits up on his knees, forcing my legs higher over his shoulders.

My heels dig into his shoulder blades as he wraps one arm around my thigh. He spreads me open, revealing my clit for his tongue, and takes one long taste. I watch, trembling with pleasure and mesmerized by that long muscle escaping his lips and swirling around my tiny bundle of nerves, making me tingle inside and out.

He snakes one hand up and probes my opening with his finger, soaking my desire all the way up each knuckle before watching me as he pushes the whole thing inside my channel. I cry out his name and free the piano keys under one hand to pull his thick black hair.

"Sol, I'm so full already. This is so good. So... *amazing.* Your tongue—oh god!" I'm trying to tell him how it feels, but I'm so intoxicated by the rising orgasm his tongue and finger are coaxing from me that my words are a slurred, lust-drunk mess.

His middle finger plays in my arousal too, and just when I think I'm about to come, he pulls out all the way. I groan at the emptiness but he soon fills it with both fingers, making my inner muscles stretch to accommodate his long digits.

"You need to relax, baby. I'm trying to get you used to the feeling, but I'm bigger than just my fingers."

"I... I love it. I just want you."

"The next time you come will be on my cock, I can't stand to think of your tight cunt squeezing anything else." I nod my head in agreement, unable to do anything else while my body is overwhelmed with sensation. My muscles in my lower belly, my arms, my thighs, all tense as I feel the wave rising within me, begging to crash down. I push against Sol's eager tongue, ride his fingers, and tug on his hair, forgetting that I want him inside of me when I come. I'm too consumed with chasing that peak, like a constant scale up and up and up the keys of a piano and just when my body's about to reach the highest note, he stops, withdrawing from my core entirely.

"Sol!" I cry out.

My eyes snap open. I hadn't even realized I'd closed them and it's just in time to see Sol stand and tug his loose pants down, revealing his long, massive cock. The head weeps with precum, and I see the wet stain it's left on the fabric, but my eyes widen at his size and my legs begin to close instinctively.

"Wait... no, you're too big. I can't."

He wraps his hands in my hair and tilts my head up to see the determined look in his eye. "You will take me, Scarlett."

"But," I protest, even as he coats his length through my arousal with his other hand. "I've never... I can't—"

"Shh... shh... shh... pretty muse." He lays his forehead against mine and whispers against my lips. "You will take me, Scarlett. I will stretch this tight pussy, until all you crave is my cock inside you when you come."

He explores my opening with his shaft, pushing in slightly. I shake my head, despite the fact that I desperately want to be full of him. A small whimper escapes me as his thick cockhead spreads me apart.

My inner muscles tighten and his hand leaves his cock to caress my spine, while the other keeps a firm grip on my hip.

"Relax, *mon amour*. I will never hurt you more than this. Not unless you beg for it."

"Please, Sol..." I plead now, although for what, I'm not sure. Part of me desperately wants to come, but I'm also more than a little nervous about my first time hurting like hell.

His hand kneads gently down my spine and rests on my other hip as he rocks in and out, a little deeper each time. I grab the collar of his T-shirt and tug him closer. The trapped air in my lungs escapes on panting breaths.

I tell my body to ease the tension while inhaling one unsteady breath through my nose. On my exhale, Sol's fingers dig into my hips and he suddenly thrusts *hard* inside me. I scream out his name and clutch his shirt. He curses before wrapping his arms around me, as if to keep me from somehow running away from him when he's speared inside me. The strong embrace is surprisingly comforting though, and his warm whispers against my forehead soothe me as my body adjusts to this delicious invasion.

It takes several breaths before I realize he's humming against my forehead and playing with my hair. Calm trickles through me and my heart rate begins to normalize. My knuckles are white against his dark shirt and he gently pulls them apart with one hand before placing my hands on the keyboard. I immediately clutch the lip of the piano and depress the keys. My mind captures several notes and collects them into a chord I'll never forget.

He lifts my chin to meet his midnight eye. "You are ready for me to move, Scarlett."

My eyes burn and my face must show all my uncertainty. I'm still not sure he hasn't split me in half, but if not, one wrong move will definitely do the trick. Even as I shake my head, he uses his thumb to wipe a small tear away and nods back at me.

"You are, *mon amour*. You are mine and you were made for me. Trust me."

My Phantom keeps holding my cheeks as he eases his hard length out and in with a tenderness that I didn't expect, especially not with the desire still burning in his midnight gaze. After a few more gentle thrusts, his hands leave my face and he scoops his arms underneath the crook of my knees. In the next move, he curves into me and—

"Oh... my... *Sol*," I moan, loud and long, wordlessly encouraging him to go faster.

My fingers dig into the keys as he lifts my legs and drives inside me, stroking something in my depths that triggers that increasing octave again.

"Yes, sing for me, my sweet angel. *Sing*."

I hadn't even realized I was still moaning, my mind so lost on the motion between my thighs. His thrusts grow more arrhythmic as I climb that peak and my heels dig into his back again, taking over the task of keeping this angle, freeing his arms.

One hand caresses my cheek and pulls me in for a kiss while the other hooks around the rim of the open piano. The chords and notes we make are loud, chaotic, and reverberate off the stone walls. Our kisses grow just as frantic as his thrusts, until our lips tear apart and all we can do is breathe harshly against each other's lips.

Every muscle tenses again and my palms grow damp on the piano. I release my grip and cling to his shirt instead, shortening the distance between us even more, making it impossible for him to pull out far.

He goes back to latching his fingers around my hip and grinds against my clit. Using his strong grip on the piano rim like a headboard, he pushes deep inside me. His tip massages against a spot that increases the tempo of the pulses in my inner walls.

My entire body is squeezing him, inside and out, and my core tightens around him, trying to keep him inside me. The crescendo my orgasm has been climbing to finally reaches that high note and I cry out his name as I tumble down.

"Fuck, Scarlett. Yes, *mon amour*, sing for me, strangle my cock just like that."

His chest muscles tense underneath my fingertips and he arches his neck back with a curse. The left side of his face flushes and contorts in ecstasy as he looks back down at our connection and grits his teeth. He grips my ass to pull me flush to him before he thrusts one last time. His deep bass croons my name against my neck as we both drift into oblivion.

Scene 19

WHAT ARE WE DOING

J ust hearing my pretty muse's high notes could make me come, but when I'm inside her at the same time, it's a whole different harmony.

Scarlett is still propped up on top of the keyboard, breathing heavily against my chest. The peaks of her bare breasts poke through my shirt and I wish we could be skin to skin.

I've never been fully unclothed in front of a woman before, but with Scarlett, I desperately want to feel her velvet touch against my scars. Her fierce nails would have felt divine embedded in my back rather than my T-shirt. But while she insists that she wasn't turned off by my missing eye, there's no way she'd feel the same if she saw the rest of me. What I have with Scarlett will always be shrouded in darkness, no matter how much I wish to go into the light with her. Phantoms don't survive in the light.

I straighten up, still inside of her, and stroke her glistening alabaster skin, almost iridescent in the firelight. Like the moon.

"You are my moonlight," I whisper against her shoulder in a kiss.

"And you are my midnight," she murmurs back, her silver eyes sleepy from the endorphins her orgasm released, despite having just woken up.

Her declaration sends my heart soaring... and my mind back-tracking. Whatever this is with Scarlett started out as an obsession, but what it is now is so much more, in so little time. And I can't do more.

But I also can't do less.

She is my sweet angel and I am her selfish demon. The spotlight? I can give her that. Nothing makes me happier than seeing Scarlett fulfilling her dream. But I can never give her the sunlight. Letting the world see what the Chatelains did to me is unacceptable. Dark shadows and night are my future. Right now, she's under the spell that my mask radiates. It gives an air of mystery and affords me both anonymity and notoriety, depending on the circumstance. But once the mask disappears, so does the novelty. Especially when the horror of my past comes to light.

My heart twists inside my chest at the thought, stealing my breath. If she glimpses underneath my mask, she'll never be able to look at me the way she does now. It'll either end in disgust, or pity. The second would break me.

I hold her hips as I finally withdraw from her warmth. Scarlett's soft muscles cling to my bare cock as I drag myself out. I've always used condoms, but I won't with her. I'll be damned if I ever put something between us.

The faintest pink tinge glosses my cock in the firelight, and my primal, savage heart thumps like a bass drum roll at the sight of my cum seeping from her swollen lips.

That brief moment of hesitation I had over keeping Scarlett all to myself disappears entirely as I imagine her swollen with my Bordeaux heir. Before I can stop myself, I swipe my cock through our cum, smearing all of mine that I can see back onto my shaft before I sheath myself with her pussy, sealing all of my cum inside of her. I can't waste a drop.

She gasps at my reentry and encircles my neck with her arms. My grip tightens on her thighs and I carry her to the piano bench I kicked against the wall. Once I sit down, I lean my back against the wall and grind up into her more, making sure her pussy swallows every last drop of my seed.

Her hands explore me, dragging down my chest before trying to sneak underneath the hem of my T-shirt. I catch them before they get too far and return them to my shoulders. She doesn't seem to mind my change in course and rests her head against me. Her warm breath sighs against my neck, making goose bumps erupt underneath my shirt. A quick gasp makes me freeze.

"Sol... we... we didn't use protection."

Protection. The word makes me growl. As if she would ever need protection from *me.*

She tries to sit up, but I capture her in my arms and press her entire body flush to mine, allowing her now racing heartbeat to feel the calm, sated one in my chest.

"I'm clean, Scarlett. There's been no one in over a year."

She relaxes slightly, but still clutches my shirt. "Well, that's good. And at least I've got an implant."

"A what?" I jerk back to look down at her.

"A birth control implant. I've got one. So we don't have to worry about any baby Bordeauxs running around."

She says it flippantly, and an irrational sense of betrayal burns in my chest, but I calm my expression.

How the fuck did I not know this?

"Where is it?"

Even as I ask, I know it's a bad idea. Already, I'm having visions of me in a possessive trance, removing it myself before fucking a child into her with triumph.

Her wary eyes narrow. "I don't think I'm going to tell you."

"Excuse me?" I ask, my right brow rising despite the mask adhered to it.

She watches me before finally shaking her head. "Yeah, I'm definitely not telling you. Your face has evil scheme written all over it. I've always wanted a big family, but I'm not having kids until I'm good and ready."

I stroke my finger down her naked arm, mesmerized by the

goose bumps that float in my wake. "I plan to know every inch of your body, Scarlett. I could find it myself, you know."

"I'm sure you could." Her smirk softens and those gorgeous moonlight eyes of hers silently beg me. "But I also think you'll respect me on this. Trapping me won't let you keep me, Sol."

Her words catch me off guard. I open my mouth to argue, but guilt slowly filters through the possessive haze clouding my judgment.

I'd had the urge to do exactly that, trap her into being with me. Fate intervened at the beginning of our relationship, and now that I've had her, I would cut her implant out in a heartbeat. But keeping her would be all the more satisfying if she made the decision.

"What if destiny says fuck your birth control? What would you do?"

She rolls her eyes like I'm not dead serious. New Orleanians are full of their superstitions, and while the Phantom of the French Quarter may be one of them, I still have my own beliefs.

"I can't argue with *fate*. If it decides we're meant to be then I guess you're stuck with me."

A devilish grin lifts my lips as I shift underneath her, burying my cock farther inside her and tempting fate.

"It seems I'm stuck *in* you."

She barks out a laugh and groans at the awful joke. "No one ever talks about the Phantom of the French Quarter's corny sense of humor."

This time, even the right side of my face lifts underneath my mask as my smile spreads. "It's only for you, *mon amour*."

"Don't worry, I'll keep your reputation intact. By the way, did you know that people say the Phantom is a *god* in bed—"

Before she can finish that thought, I clutch her to me and pick her up to lay her back on the piano bench. In that one swift move, I stay flush against her, my stern face filling her vision. My loose pants slip down my ass, but at this angle, she can't see the skin that's been revealed. I never left her pussy, so I shove my half-hard cock as deep as I can go, thrusting inside her until my rage gets under control.

"No, I can't again. Please." Even as she pleads with me not to, her heels dig into my back, begging for more.

"As far as I'm concerned, there's never been anyone but you, Scarlett. No one before you mattered."

Her wide eyes soften but she presses those pretty bow lips together. I grind into her, already feeling her renewed arousal coating my cock. I use my thumb on her clit and swirl the little nub underneath my finger as I lift up her leg and curve my strokes to reach that spot that makes her sing. She finally lets go of a moan and I growl at her again.

"Tell me you understand."

"I understand," she gives in and I begin to pound inside her.

A second time would normally take much longer to come again, if at all, but my cock has been weeping in my hand for Scarlett's tight pussy for over a year now. It's eager to claim her again and already hard as steel.

"Come, pretty muse."

She moans at my command and my spine tingles while the base of my shaft tenses. My finger on her clit works in tandem with my cock to find the perfect rhythm. Pleasure calls to my angel and she's singing for me, contracting her inner muscles around my cock as she comes. Her cunt begs me to fill her up with my seed as it massages my length with its tight grip, daring fate while my orgasm barrels into me and I explode inside her quaking pussy.

Once her contractions are mere flutters and she's squirming underneath me, my thumb finally leaves her clit. I sit up on the piano bench and lean back against the wall with her sated in my arms. She collapses against my chest and I knead her back muscles with my fingers, stealing a glance at my watch. If I'm to go, I need to get ready soon, but fuck, I don't want to leave Scarlett's body yet.

"What're we doing today? It's a Sunday, so I don't have class."

She chuckles against my neck. "Will you even let me go to class tomorrow?"

We.

That's the first thing I hear.

What're *we* doing today.

The way she's already so quickly referring to us as a plurality makes it easier to answer for tomorrow.

"If you feel happy and healthy, like you do right now, then I'll let you go."

She sits up, her pretty lips parted, obviously as surprised by my admission as I am. "Let me go? Seriously?"

"Yes, you're here because I wanted to make sure you didn't hurt yourself. If you feel good tomorrow, there's... no reason for you to stay here anymore."

"No... reason? None at all? You'll just let me go and we'll be done?"

My brow furrows, pulling at my mask. "Done? Oh, no, *ma jolie petite muse.* I'll never be done with you."

She smiles back at me, but a curious narrowing of her eyes betrays her uncertainty.

You and me both.

Whatever this is can't be good for her and it's impossible to maintain for me, but I have no idea how to fight this pull between us, and I don't want to.

She blinks away her hesitance and returns to my chest. "Well, if I'm stuck with you, tell me what we're doing."

I take another glance at my watch and a thought crosses my mind.

"Get ready for the day. There's something I'd like to show you."

Scene 20

SNAPDRAGON SKULLS

I worry the hem of the gray sheath dress Sol set out for me while I showered. Since I don't even own one like this, I suspect Sol's been collecting outfits for me somehow. Maybe sending his more stylish shadows to fetch them.

The dress is going to be hot though. The humidity here in New Orleans makes even the coolest day stifling, and I have to put a ton of product in my hair to keep the curls from acting wilder than normal. It's a good temperature in Sol's Aston Martin and he's looking practically edible in his black designer suit and white button-down, with a gray tie to match.

Instead of my favorite bone-white mask, he's wearing the one that looks like Ben, and his midnight glass eye is back in. More than once, he's scrutinized himself in the rearview mirror, and he seems unable to stop itching around the mask and rubbing his eye. The combined move makes me wonder if he's more uncomfortable physically, or mentally, with them on. If he keeps drawing attention to it, there will be no way he'll fool people up close in the broad daylight. But it's at least less conspicuous than his favored mask and eyepiece.

Not knowing why he's pulling another smoke and mirrors

act, nerves have me brushing away invisible dust from the remnants of my powdered sugar–covered beignet.

When we left, a bouquet of burgundy snapdragons and still-warm beignets were at his door, dropped off by a shadow. At first I thought the bouquet was for me, but he told me to bring it along. Obviously, I couldn't leave warm beignets behind, and I was surprised as hell that he let me eat them in the car with the caveat that he get one, too. I took that deal in a heartbeat, scarfing the other two down in seconds, despite the fact that I was in nice clothes.

It was embarrassing when I got the white sugary cloud all over me, but he only grinned and provided me some napkins from the center console, as if he'd expected my disastrous eating habits, which, I guess after last night's near-catastrophe with my gumbo and satin dress, I don't blame him. Though, I was equally pleased when he didn't bat an eyelash as I dumped the remaining sugar in my chicory coffee.

He slows to a stop on a random side street outside a brick wall portion of St. Louis Cemetery No.1. A man, nearly as tall as Sol, in a hoodie and bone-white skull mask comes to open my door. He takes the bouquet from my hands to help me out, and when Sol rounds the hood, he trades the flowers for the keys.

"We'll be back at the normal time. Do you have your other mask?" The hooded shadow nods and pats his pocket. "Good, drive around with it on."

"Yes, sir," the hooded man responds and slides into the driver's seat, moving almost as gracefully as the Phantom.

"What was that about?" I ask Sol before turning back to the Aston Martin. Sitting in the car now is Ben. Or, the shadow with Ben's face on.

"How many people have one of those masks?"

"Very few. My prosthetist fitted my most trusted shadows with full silicone masks that look like Ben. We authorize them to wear them so they can pass as one of us behind tinted windows or in low light. It's not perfect, but the mask protects people like Miss Mabel, and gives the illusion that we're—"

"—everywhere," I finish.

As I watch the shadow drive away, Sol whispers a kiss against my temple. "Exactly. It's easier to be nowhere when everyone thinks you're everywhere."

"And where are we now?" I ask, leaning into his touch.

"A disguised entrance to St. Louis Cemetery No.1."

"Where Marie Laveau is buried?" I ask about the most prominent name I know entombed within New Orleans' most famous cemetery walls.

His masked side is seemingly disinterested as he nods and I again find myself wishing I could see all of him. Will he ever again be as vulnerable with me as he was this morning? Will he show me the rest of his past?

Is it fair for me to want that, when I'm still not comfortable sharing my own?

"Actually, I have it on good authority, à la Madam G, that the grave everyone thinks is hers is just a front for tourists. The Voodoo Priestess is actually on the much quieter and more peaceful side. It avoids the drunken vandals and any disrespectful tourists."

"Good. It always made me angry to see what's been done to it. I get paying respects—"

"Any respect can be paid to it like an altar, while she can still be left in peace," Sol agrees and spans his large hand across my lower back. "Come, we can't keep her waiting."

My eyes widen and if it weren't for Sol's gentle nudge, I would've stopped in my tracks. "*Marie Laveau* is waiting for us?"

"Of course not." He chuckles. "Here, hold these."

Rather than removing his hand from my back, he gives me the flowers, and uses his newly free hand to fish a big skeleton key from his pocket. He leads me to a section of the brick wall where paint has worn off. After glancing around, no doubt making sure we're alone, he inserts the key into the center of a curvy *X* marking the brickwork. He twists it, and the wall shifts to reveal the outline of a door. Sol easily pushes the door forward and he slides it to the right like a barn door, eliciting a low rumble of metal on metal.

Once it's open, he escorts me through the entry and returns the doorway to its stationary position behind us.

"Come, pretty muse," Sol murmurs.

My inner muscles flutter at his command. I quickly shove my desire to the back of my mind, and enjoy the way he gently guides me with his hand pressing lightly on my lower back. The comforting touch makes me shiver and I notice in the corner of my eye that even the right side of his lips lift up in a smug, crooked grin.

The sun blazes down on us and bounces off the raised brick and stone tombs. I can already feel the sweat prickling on my nape, threatening to slide down my spine.

Sol doesn't seem to mind the heat even in his suit as he leads us through the maze of graves. I resist stopping at each one, although the curiosity in me keeps me lingering every now and then at certain plots.

"My inquisitive little muse," Sol teases when I get too slow. "The way you long to explore the world reminds me of how I used to be. Come on, not too much farther."

His words make my heart twist for him, but I leave it be, for now. When I see the gravestone that's feet taller than the others, I understand why we're here.

Perched at the peak of a gray stone obelisk are two macabre skulls, positioned back to back. One is perpetually in a morbid laugh, while a frown is carved into the other, reminiscent of the theater tragedy and comedy masks.

A figure in black and as tall as Sol emerges from behind another grave and I have to blink a couple of times before I realize it's Ben. His eyes flick to mine and flash with surprise before settling back on Sol.

"Just in time, brother. She's been asking for you."

Sol grunts his reply as we round another tomb. Maggie is on the other side, holding her daughter high up on her hip with a lace fan working away to cool them off. They're both in black, and Maggie's dress flatters her curves while baby Marie's sequins glitter in the sun.

"Scarlett," Maggie whispers with a surprised smile and quickly moves to give me a half hug. "I didn't know you would be here this time."

"This time?"

She nods. "We come with her to his grave every Sunday."

My eyes dart to the tall pillar underneath the tragedy and comedy skulls. Outlining the freestanding family tomb is a short wrought iron fence, about as tall as my shins. The small patch of ground within is filled to the brim with bouquets of dried snapdragon shells. The little tan, skull-shaped husks have holes for eyes and mouths gaping open in silent screams, giving the effect that tiny skeleton heads pile around the grave.

Stone-carved tattered curtains drape the monument, unveiling the name *Bordeaux* engraved on a painstakingly etched stage. At the end of a long list of French and biblical names with English spelling, is one that seems weathered, but more recent than the rest. Ten years ago, from the inscription.

Jean-Pierre Abraham Bordeaux
Loving father, doting husband, dutiful leader
La vie est une grande mascarade, alors laissez les bons temps rouler.

The last part is a popular Cajun French phrase, so I access my freshman French diction class to decipher the rest until I finally figure it out.

"Life is one big masquerade, so let the good times roll."

The tribute to both the Bordeauxs' opera house and the New Orleans motto brings a smile to my face, until I notice the statuesque woman standing in front of it.

Her silver hair is tied up into a sleek chignon on top of her head and a black lace dress envelopes her frail body. Under her breath, she hums to herself an achingly familiar tune. She looks fragile in every way, until her midnight eyes turn to me.

A swirl of madness fights with clarity there, a look I've felt *intimately*, and my heart breaks for the woman. She's clutching a black parasol with a skull handle, and twists a skull ring on her pale, knobby left ring finger with her thumb. The entire ensemble reminds me of the so-called *superstitions* I've always thought my friends had. It finally dawns on me that they might not be superstitious at all.

They're Bordeauxs. People that Sol and his brother have sworn to govern and protect.

The large piece I've been missing in my New Orleans puzzle clicks into place. My mind whirls with theories, but I blink to focus on the older woman before me.

I hold my breath as she assesses me for a painfully long moment. The stifling heat and anxiety threaten to make me pass out.

After centuries of waiting, I'm afraid I've been found wanting, until she holds her hand out for me to shake. In a moment of true embarrassment, I have to quickly wipe my palm on my dress to avoid getting sweat on the poor woman before I take her hand.

It's cool, like she hasn't been baking out in the Big Easy's heat for longer than three minutes. I look like a mess compared to her. But her familiar lopsided grin sets me at ease.

"You must be Scarlett. I am Valérie Bordeaux. Solomon's mother."

GOOD DAYS AND BAD

I can tell Sol's trying not to laugh at my shocked expression and Ben's staring at his brother like he's grown a third head. Ignoring them both, I lightly squeeze Valérie's hand, careful not to break the woman I thought was dead up until two seconds ago, only to have her squeeze the daylights out of mine.

"N-nice to meet you, Mrs. Bordeaux."

She lets go and smiles warmly. "Please, call me Valérie."

The Southern manners I've been around off and on my whole life buck against the request, but I nod once. "Yes, ma'am. Valérie, it is."

She smiles softly before her eyes drift to her son behind me. "Solomon, thank you for the bouquet. It is so good to see you, dear. It's been ages."

Sol winces at her comment before kissing her on each cheek and giving her the most tender of smiles. "Good to see you, too, *maman*."

I murmur out of the side of my mouth to Maggie, "I thought you said you come every Sunday?"

Maggie gives me a subtle nod before sighing and gazing at the Bordeaux family with sorrow in her dark-brown eyes.

"We do," she finally answers with a quiver in her voice that makes tears burn my eyes.

Sol and Ben lead her to the bench across from the raised grave. The men listen to their mother in earnest while she tells them a story in reverent whispers, honoring the dead around us.

"Sweet, isn't it? For the so-called Phantom of the French Quarter? Guess you know all about that now, don't you?" Maggie asks me as she wipes a few glistening drops of sweat from her dark-brown skin and bounces Marie on her hip.

The toddler gives me a gummy grin, showing off two perfect dimples in her light-brown cheeks and the few tiny teeth she already has. Her jet-black curls are loose and less defined than her mother's tight, voluminous ringlets, but her smile is all Maggie. And her eyes... they're Bordeaux through and through. Her stunning twin midnight orbs stare at me, wide and curious.

I smile back at the little girl before glancing to the bench again. Sol holds his mother's hands as if she's made of glass, and murmurs something low, making her laugh.

"It is sweet... *he* is sweet," I say slowly, just now admitting it out loud.

"At least to those he cares about," Maggie offers, dragging my gaze away from the family and back to her. But she's still looking at them, determination on her face. "God help anyone who hurts the woman Sol Bordeaux loves."

"What does that mean?" I ask, but my question seems to snap her out of wherever she was. She shakes her head slightly and laughs.

"Sorry about that. Sometimes I just get caught up in my own thoughts."

I huff a chuckle, but I'm dying to know what she's thinking. She finally turns to me and steers me gently by the elbow, away from the Bordeauxs. Marie gnaws on the teething ring in her mother's hand, not caring what we're doing in the least.

"Hey, listen. I'm sorry about what happened on the stage the other day." She grimaces before exhaling. "I was dealing with

Monty's—" She looks at Marie and mouths the word *bullshit* before continuing. "And then I walked in on y'all's argument. I should've... done *something*. I didn't know what to say at the time, though. I recognized Sol's seal, but I hadn't known he'd been writing you. It was a shock to see and I wasn't sure how to play it, and I played it wrong. I'm sorry, girl."

"Oh, um... thanks," I reply, not sure how to respond.

It makes sense that she and Jaime didn't stick up for me in front of everyone. They didn't have all the facts. I don't blame her, especially since she figured out it was Sol and Sol's her brother-in-law, but it still hurts. I don't know if anything but time will heal that.

And what was Jaime's excuse?

The question whispers across my mind and I push it away. A sneaking suspicion is creeping across my thoughts that I don't want to analyze just yet. Not here. Now that I've cracked the Bordeaux loyalty code, I can't help but wonder... does Jaime work for him? Is he a shadow? If he is... how long has he been working for Sol?

Any of those answers terrify me because it means my best friend, the rock I've leaned on since my father died, could potentially just be a shadow, maybe even a *spy*, and not my *friend* at all—

Jaime's accused me of sticking my head in the sand before, and I'm trying to be eyes wide open, but this is a lot to handle. In a cemetery, no less.

I try to change the subject, not ready to deal with real life just yet. "You mentioned Monty. How's he doing?"

She rolls her eyes but a spark of excitement lights her face. "He's fine. He didn't have a scratch on him. But for the first time ever, he was true to his word. He actually quit. Miss Scarlett Day, you're looking at your new director."

My jaw drops, but I shake my head with a smile. "Oh my god, *Maggie*. That's amazing!"

Ben shushes us from the bench and I cover my mouth, but

Maggie just laughs. "It's been a lot at once, but I'm happy. At first I was afraid people might think I only got the job because of Ben... but then I sat on the stage and imagined a full auditorium, standing with applause for *my* cast and *my* crew, and I thought fuck them—" She slams her hand over her mouth and looks at Marie who's not paying us any attention before she whispers back to me. "*Fuck them.* I earned it so they can just get used to it."

"Absolutely," I agree.

"Oh, but speaking of favoritism." She juts her chin to the Bordeaux family on the bench. "I'll be doing another audition for the role as Marguerite in *Faust*. Just to make sure no one can say Jilliana only got it because of Monty, or that you only got it because of the Phantom. We'll be doing this one the right way, from the jump. Auditions are tomorrow, so bring your *A* game."

"You got it." I smile, wondering if Sol will actually let me even go.

Do I care? I didn't really want that part anyway...

The plan my father made for me has been tossed into the wind ever since I sang Juliet the other night. If I could play venues like Masque, just like my dad did right here in New Orleans, I'd be happy.

"And what about you? How are you doing lately?" She glances around and hushes her tone so that only I can hear her again. "I heard about what... happened."

I startle for a second, trying to figure out what she's talking about. She narrows her dark-brown eyes slightly before filling in the blank.

"Your... medication?"

"Sol *told* you about that?" My heart cracks at the betrayal, but she shakes her head.

"No honey, Ben did. Sol called him when he needed Dr. Portia to leave Valérie and come to you. She's basically a live-in doctor. Runs her business in a shotgun house right down the road and comes to the family wing of the opera house anytime we need her. The good doctor has been getting called *a lot* lately, what with it being the anniversary and all. Valérie always has a hard go of it this time of year."

My head is spinning, trying to keep up, and I blink as I try to piece all this info together. "Anniversary?"

Maggie nods and tries to tease Marie with the teething ring. "Yeah, of their father's murder," she says it so casually but when my eyes pop wide she stills.

"You didn't know?" Her tight corkscrew curls bounce and Marie grabs several in her little fist. "I thought... since you were here.... Damn it, don't mind me. Mom brain." She chuckles nervously and tickles Marie's belly until the little girl shrieks with happiness and sets her mom's hair free from her tiny grasp.

"May I?" I ask, hoping to both coax more "mom brain" confessions and play with a sweet toddler. Being the only child of a traveling musician, I grew up always wanting a huge family and planning to have one of my own. Any chance I can get to hold a baby, I'm there.

"Oh, yeah, sure." She passes Marie off to me and slouches as if it's the first break she's gotten in hours. Maybe it is. "She's teething so if she's a little drooly, just pretend it's 'cause she likes you."

I chuckle as Marie snatches my own hair. She tugs it *hard* and I try to keep a straight face like her mom did, but my scalp is way too tender. Maggie helps me by tickling her belly again and Marie erupts into giggles. Maggie and I still and glance around guiltily at the Bordeauxs while Marie goes back to her teething ring.

Ben is smiling at Maggie, like they're in on a secret the rest of us aren't. Mrs. Bordeaux is grinning wistfully and Sol, hell, the possessive heat in Sol's midnight gaze makes my core clench.

"Oh please, don't stop on our account," Mrs. Bordeaux encourages. "Abraham loved to hear children's laughter. Hearing his beautiful granddaughter would have been his greatest joy."

"We'll still try to keep the giggles to a minimum," Maggie promises.

When the Bordeauxs go back to their conversation, my eyes

catch Sol's lingering on me and I have to fix my eyes on the ground, Marie, anything to avoid the absolutely sinful thoughts I'm having about him in this cemetery.

I glance back to Maggie, who's doing her best to fan all three of us. Even though Maggie cut herself off earlier, I can't get what she said out of my head.

"So... Mr. Bordeaux. He was... murdered?" I mouth the last word.

Maggie winces and nods. "It was when Ben was fifteen and stayed in Europe for spring break, well before he and I started dating. I was around though, because our families have been close since Prohibition."

She darts her gaze to the Bordeauxs on the bench and lowers her voice to barely above a whisper. "In true Bordeaux fashion, they paid the coroner to report that his injuries were... *self-inflicted*. They never released that he'd been shot *twice*. In the heart *and* head."

"What?" My brain short-circuits as my own nightmares cloud my vision, but Sol's dad died nine years before mine did. There's no way they're linked, right?

I shake my wild conspiracy theories away and focus on the conversation. "That's insane. Why would the coroner agree—"

"Because the Bordeauxs wanted to deliver their own punishment," Maggie explains. "And Bordeaux justice—now the *Phantom's* justice—is much scarier than anything the government can do. And everyone who knew Abraham, knew he wouldn't leave his family to fend for themselves. The empire has been up to Ben and Sol ever since."

I nod slowly, taking it all in. "And Mrs. Bordeaux... Valérie. What about her?"

Maggie sucks her teeth. "She has good days and bad days. Sundays are hit or miss, but if we don't come, she gets very upset, so we take the risk. If I were her, *all* my days would be bad. Considering the fact that Ben was in Europe, she was the only one around when everything happened to Abraham and Sol—"

"Sol?" I interrupt, unable to stop myself. "What happened with Sol?"

Maggie's eyes flare and she shakes her finger at me. "Nope. Not falling for it. Telling you about his dad is one thing, but telling you everything else that went down will only lead to trouble. Or at least, a *very* stern talking-to by my husband."

Shit, so close.

A crash makes me jolt and Marie shrieks in my ear.

"Shit," Maggie curses and gently scoops her daughter from my arms before we both turn to see Mrs. Bordeaux cursing and yelling at Mr. Bordeaux's grave. Ben stands off to the side, his eyes wide and glassy, his hand covering his mouth while Sol tries to calm her with his deep, soothing voice.

"Ben has a hard time," Maggie explains under her breath. "It's why we bought Dr. Portia a French Quarter house. Sometimes we still have to call Sol to settle her down. He's just better with her. It's not always like this, though," she reassures me. "Just bad days, like today."

She leaves me and goes to Ben's side to console him, leaving Sol by himself to soothe his mother. I take a ginger step forward... and another... and another, slowly gathering courage even though the wild madness in her eyes makes my stomach twist in knots.

"Scarlett, *mon amour*, can you please tell my mother about your role as Juliet? She loves opera." Sol's authoritative voice is still gentle to me, although he snaps at Ben right after. "Call for your car, brother."

Ben nods and struggles to get out his phone.

I turn to Mrs. Bordeaux's glazed eyes. "Mrs. Bordeaux, do you like *Roméo et Juliette*?" She blinks and shakes her head like she's trying to stay present, so I continue. "My favorite aria is in Act 1. Do you, um... do you want to hear it?"

It's clear by just looking in her eyes that the poor woman is fighting hard for her sanity, but she seems calmer at the line of questioning at least. Going with my gut, I sit next to her on the bench and begin to sing *Je veux vivre* under my breath.

Mrs. Bordeaux's white-knuckled grip on Sol's hand gains color again as her fingers loosen. Those unseeing eyes sharpen in focus. Once I get through the first verse, the madness has already seemed to clear and recognition filters through. Soon enough, she begins to hum with me, already knowing the melody.

I glance to Sol and my chest squeezes. Sweat prickles on his brow, from the sun or stress, I'm not sure. But his midnight gaze is fixed on me, and full of gratitude and sorrow. His jaw is set hard, as if he's trying to stave off the emotions boiling just underneath the surface. One hand holds his mother's while his free one stretches across the back of the bench and squeezes mine.

Together, Mrs. Bordeaux and I get through the entire song, and by the end she seems to be mostly back in good spirits. We talk at length about all things opera and her favorite shows she's seen from her chair in box five. After several minutes, I start to relax but Sol's grasp on my hand is still strong.

"The New French Opera House is my Abraham's, you know. We met in Paris and he convinced me to come to the States with him by bragging about his own personal opera house. He hated the shows, but he'd still see every one of them with me. Now it's my Solomon. He'll sit with his *maman*." She beams at Sol, and my heart skips at the love in her gaze.

He tries to catch her before she pats the mask side of his face, but she makes contact anyway. Her hand suddenly spasms and she begins to whisper under her breath to him.

His grip on my hand disappears.

"Scarlett, go with Maggie."

"What?" My eyes dart to Maggie and Ben. They look just as bewildered as I feel, but when I return my gaze to Sol's, he's focused on his mother. His hands wrap around hers, as if he's preparing to stop her from fleeing. Then I hear it...

That sweet encouragement I thought she was sharing with Sol, is now harsh, unintelligible muttering.

"*Maman*, you're okay—"

"It's their fault," she hisses. Spittle collects on her trembling bottom lip as she stares off into space. "He would be alive if it weren't for them, I know it."

"Who are you talking about, Mrs. Bor—Valérie?"

"*Mon amour*, please go—"

"And what they did to you, *mon pauvre fils*. Solomon... *you* would be different. Your face—"

"*Maman, c'est assez.* That's enough," Sol scolds quietly but she twists to face me again while her voice rises in pitch.

"H-He was here for holiday. Homesick. He should've stayed with his brother. It all changed—"

"*Maman!*" Letting go of her hands, he immediately cups her face to get her to look at him. He speaks French in his low, comforting bass as he tries to catch her frantic gaze.

Her wide eyes narrow, and for a split second I think she's going to calm down again, but she rears back and slaps his face. The mask side.

I glimpse red skin before he twists away from us both. Valérie screeches, looking as if she's fighting with herself over being horrified, or maybe even sorry, but it's all in French, so I have no idea what she's saying.

Maggie curses and pastes a saccharine smile on her face to comfort her teary child. "Marie, let's go see your great-great-great-great grandma, 'kay?"

Maggie scurries farther into the depths of the cemetery, and I stand awkwardly, at a loss of what to do. Ben seems to finally snap out of it as his brother rights his mask. My gaze darts anywhere but on Sol, trying to give him privacy.

When he's finished, the Bordeaux sons lead their mother in a practiced, solemn march as they carefully escort her out of the cemetery. Ben holds one of her arms, while Sol holds the other and presses his mask against his face with his free hand. Despite everything, Sol faintly sings "La Vie en rose" in French, the same song Mrs. Bordeaux was singing when we walked up, and she visibly relaxes against him.

My feet are lead as I follow slowly behind them, my heart

breaking for the pain Sol bears every time his mother is around, never knowing what the day—or even the next moment—will be like. The knots in my stomach writhe like snakes and I feel as if I'm going to be sick. Unable to take it anymore, I lean against one of the tall wrought iron gates surrounding the raised tombs, not caring that the sun has heated it like a fire poker. I welcome the distraction, even though it burns.

A rustling behind me catches my attention.

"Holy shit. *Lettie*? Is that you?"

Scene 22

BRITTLE AT THE EDGES

My childhood friend's shocked baritone reaches my ears and I whirl around to find a concerned expression furrowing his brow, coming straight for me. He envelopes me in a hug, and I pat his back while trying not to inhale his stifling gardenia scent.

"*Rand*? What're you doing here?"

"I... I visit my family's tomb on Sundays," he explains before letting me go and towering over me barely two feet away.

His parents died in a car accident on the Pontchartrain Expressway when Rand was a teenager, and from what my dad told me when I got older, his brother hung himself not long after. So tragic.

"I'm so sorry about Laurent, Rand. I know I never talked about it—"

"How could you?" he asks with a shrug, that charming smile back on his handsome face. "We never talked about it in our emails. And then you stopped writing."

"I'm sorry." I wince. "When my father found out, he made me stop responding."

A huff escapes him. "It's too bad your father didn't understand what we had. Loyalty." My lips purse at his assessment until

Rand backtracks. "Not to say your dad wasn't loyal, of course, but I don't think he'd ever had what *we* had."

He steps forward and I glance around to see if anyone can see us. I *know* I'm doing nothing wrong, but Sol and Rand don't like each other. There's no way Sol will appreciate us being together like this.

"I really should go, Rand. I'm sorry—"

"Wait." He grabs my forearm and pulls me close. His blue eyes are tense as he searches my face. "How are you? I've called you nonstop all weekend only to go directly to voice mail. Haven't you been getting my messages? Are you okay? I've been worried sick about you since I heard you overdosed."

Ugh. That *word*. I hate it so much but I swallow down my pride. It is technically what I did, but it still sucks to hear it thrown back at me. But the few people who are close to me would know not to use that word.

"How did you hear about that?" I ask, unable to keep the suspicion from my voice.

Rand jolts back and shakes his head like I've offended him. "I *care* about you, Lettie. You never replied to my messages, so I had to ask people around town to find out if you were even fucking alive. What's with this attitude all of a sudden?"

I blanch and my face grows clammy. It never occurred to me that Rand would be looking for me, but should I feel *guilty* about it? He's not my keeper.

"Look, I'm fine now. I've been taking it easy the past couple of days. Sol took care of me—"

I try to tug my arm away, but his grip doesn't give.

"What is he to you, Scarlett? Sol Bordeaux? I heard that you were with him," he sneers and I recoil at the disgusted look warring with the concern on his face.

"That's not really your business. Now, please. Let me go—"

He drops my forearm, as if he hadn't even realized he was still holding it. "Do you even *know* who you're getting in bed with?

The monster he is? You're such a good girl, Scarlett. I'd hate to see you get corrupted by someone like him."

I'm not a good girl.

Sol claims to know the darkest parts of me and I've been too afraid to ask what he's referring to. My true darkness has nothing to do with my disorder, and everything to do with the night my father was murdered. Or rather, what I did right after. If my childhood friend knew the type of rage I was capable of, he'd never call me a "good girl" again.

"He's not a monster," I say instead, whispering roughly as I step back. "And who I get *in bed* with doesn't involve you. It never has."

It's a low blow, but it does the trick. He stumbles back, obviously shocked at my defense. But there's an underlying frustration that narrows his eyes.

"Really? You don't know anything about him. For starters, you should ask him about the *real* reason why I have to visit my brother's grave. After that, maybe ask him what happened last year, when one of my men went missing after completing a simple job. Oh, and don't forget about asking him what I found in my garden yesterday." He seems to grow green at the memory and shakes his head. "He's *sick*, Scarlett. Hell, if you need more evidence, you could even ask your so-called best friend—"

"Wait, Jaime?" My heart thunders as my suspicions rear their ugly head. "What does he have to do with all of this?"

"*Or*," Rand continues without answering me, obviously on a roll with his accusations. "Just ask Sol about the *tourist* he beat up for no reason last night. Look—"

Before I can back away, Rand has my forearm in his unrelenting grip again. My head is reeling, so I don't even try to get free, and just wait while he thumbs through his phone until he lands on a news article.

"Rand, what're you doing—"

"Look." He shoves the phone in my face and I have to blink past the sun to see the screen.

A closeup of what looks to be a very hungover tourist is front and center with a towel around his neck and an ice pack lifted to his face. There on his forehead, clear as day, is an imprint of a skull. The headline above says, *Tourist attacked by Phantom... or Hurricane?*, obviously suggesting that the tourist was crazy drunk and just injured himself.

"This was last night?" I ask, unsure what to think.

In the past, I would've believed the potent hurricane drink had been the culprit. Now... I can't deny that the cut looks eerily similar to Sol's ring. But when would he have gone? It's on the tip of my tongue to say that he cuddled me all night, but I keep it to myself.

"Yes. That skull is his *calling card*. And the proof is there in the picture. Ask him about it. And if he doesn't tell you the truth... well, you'll know he doesn't think you're good enough to be trusted."

I school my expression to hide all my uncertainty. Sol's only been good to me, and I just promised myself I would stop questioning him. And this morning, I *know* he was more vulnerable with me than he's ever been with anyone. I could tell. On top of all that, he's been honest with everything I've confronted him about so far.

Our conversation about justice flashes across my brain. It was right before he explained his relationship with Madam G. Rand was wrong about that, could he be wrong now? Or did the tourist have what was coming to him?

"*...I've made sure they deserve it. That's the Phantom's—*"

"*—moral code...*"

I bite the inside of my cheek while my heart races. "Why are you telling me all of this, Rand?"

He sighs, his shoulders sagging as he removes his hand from my arm. But his soft palm holds mine before I realize he's even reached for it.

"For a little over a year, I've been working to come back and finish what my father and brother started. To bring more jobs to

New Orleans and make this city as great as it used to be. Finding out you're still here, even after your father died, was a bonus. But, Lettie, Sol and his brother *hate* me and my family, for no reason. Have you wondered why Sol is interested in you all of a sudden? I told them we were childhood sweethearts. What if he's trying to get back at me by taking you from me? I'd hoped we could pick up where we left off..."

With all my many questions, Rand's theory is revealing uncertainties I didn't realize I had. But at the rest of his statement, my head is shaking before he even finishes.

"Rand, there's no 'picking up where we left off.' We were... whatever we had... it was never appropriate at that age—"

"Well, now you're twenty-two and you have the same age difference with Sol. What's the big deal?"

"I'm sorry, Rand. That was a long time ago." My heart twists when I see the disappointment in his eyes, but I'm still thankful when he lets go of me. "Things are different now."

A frustrated huff blows out of his nose and the look of pity on his face makes my skin crawl.

"Be careful with him, Little Lettie. The Phantom of the French Quarter not only looks like a monster with his mask off. He *is* one. When he hurts you, call me, okay? I'll be there for you... Just as I always have."

Before I can argue with him, he yanks me close to him. I have to stop from folding into him by thrusting my hand into his chest. The scent of stale gardenias tickles my nose, so different than the warm, cozy sugar, whiskey, and leather I already crave. He gives me a kiss on the forehead and murmurs against my sun-heated skin.

"I've always cared for you, Little Lettie. My family took care of yours when they needed to. I'll take care of you again. If you choose me, I can give you everything you've always wanted, you only need to say the words. You loved me once. I know you can love me again."

"Rand, I—"

"Shh... someone's coming. I don't want him to hurt you. He will if he finds out you've been with me. Stay safe, Scarlett. I'm only a text message away."

He lets go of me then and disappears behind a house-sized tomb.

"Scarlett? Did you get lost?" Maggie's kind voice is stunted by the concrete, stone, and greenery and I spin to find her emerging with her daughter from behind another obelisk. "Sol sent me to get you. We're taking Valérie back to the house to rest."

"Right, yes... Um, sorry. I got... caught up. Let's go." I straighten my dress, trying to see if anything is out of place when I realize Maggie is watching me warily.

"Are you okay? I thought I heard you talking to someone."

"Nope," I answer too quickly and point in the direction she came from. "Lead the way through this maze, will you please?"

"Right, so you don't get lost again." She glances behind me before turning to navigate the way through the tombs and I laugh awkwardly.

"Exactly."

When we finally get to the hidden gate, I hear Ben and Sol's heated discussion before I see them.

"You know she's not one of us, Sol. She can't be trusted and you just served our weakness on a silver platter! You can't let this obsession ruin us—"

"Our mother isn't a *weakness*. And Scarlett is more than that, Ben—" My chest lightens at Sol's gravelly confession until he continues. "She's the key to everything."

I stop in my tracks and Maggie looks at me with a wince. "Listen, don't mind them, honey." She slides the gate Sol and I entered through to the side and glances back at me. "It was so good to see you."

Her voice breaks the men apart and Ben makes eye contact with me for a moment before darting down to the ground. Sol oozes fury, whether at his brother or me, I don't know.

A black BMW and Sol's Aston Martin wait at the curb.

Maggie gives me a sweaty side hug and barely prevents Marie from leaving with a chunk of my hair. I laugh as I watch them head to the BMW, where Mrs. Bordeaux sits in the front seat. Ben opens the back door for Maggie to slide in and put Marie in her car seat.

"Thank you for coming, Scarlett." Ben waves as he lies through his teeth.

A brief smile is all I can muster.

The shadow who drove Sol's car is nowhere to be found as Sol opens the passenger door for me.

"Come. Let's go."

I glance up at him. There's a scratch on his neck, but his mask looks intact again. Defeat sags the left side of his face, and despite all my questions, my heart aches for him. I reach for his hand. It clutches mine like a lifeline, but it's the only thing that changes in his demeanor.

"Is your mother okay?"

"She'll be fine. This reaction isn't... unusual. They're going home so she can settle down in familiar surroundings."

I nod and just before I slide into the passenger seat, Sol wraps his arm around my waist and brings me flush to his chest. My body curls into his, but I don't miss his long inhale as he kisses the crown of my head. He pulls away and looks at me, curious.

"You smell different. Like... a garden."

Fuck.

His eyes narrow at the no doubt guilty look I have on my face. "Scarlett, are you hiding something?"

"No, of course not." My smile is brittle at the edges.

I don't think Sol buys it at all but he lets it go with a nod. His face is weary and I'm almost disappointed he doesn't catch me in my fib, but it's for the best.

Now I can focus on figuring out what the hell is going on.

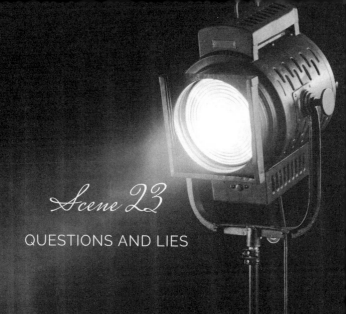

Scene 23

QUESTIONS AND LIES

It's awkward.

It has been since the cemetery. Since I watched Sol's mother's sanity leave her in a blink, right before she slapped her son. Since Rand approached me. Since I caught Sol and Ben arguing about *me*.

We didn't speak on the short drive home, nor through the tunnels. After he fixed me a Cinderella mocktail, he excused himself to go to the bathroom. When he came back, he'd changed into his bone-white mask, but his navy eye remained. The fact that he would rather be in pain than bare himself to me again hurts, but maybe he's just more comfortable around people with it in? More than anything, his mood feels strange, and I can't tell if he's mad at me. Shouldn't I be mad at him?

Now we're in his den while he makes himself a Sazerac and I'm just standing here, sipping my mocktail, trying to figure out what the heck to say.

Awkward.

When he finally finishes pouring his drink the old-school way, from one rocks glass to another, he reclines into the black, high-back leather chair near the gas-log fireplace. The room is only lit by fire and candles, and the way the light glimmers off of his skull mask makes it look like it's aflame. He stares into the blaze for a long moment before patting his lap.

"Come here," he murmurs.

Setting my mocktail on an end table, I obey instantly. Even though my brain is telling me to be careful, to think about what Rand said and what I overheard, my heart and body are still saying screw that, you can trust Sol.

I'm still in my gray sheath dress so I attempt to sit on his lap sideways, but he sets his drink on the side table and picks me up to straddle him in the wide chair. His calloused hands skate up my thighs and I stroke his gray tie until I reach the knot. He lets me loosen and remove the tie, but when I go to unbutton his shirt, he snags my hands before I get too far, and rests them on his shoulders, instead. When he lets go, his hands return to gliding up and down my thighs until his fingertips meet the apex of my legs. I shiver as he repeats the soothing motion.

"You've been so full of questions, *petite muse*. Is there a reason why you're holding back now?"

My eyes widen. "Would you answer them?"

He nods slowly. "Would you answer mine?"

That makes me still. What more could this man want to know? "I thought you knew everything about me." I chuckle.

"Almost." The left side of his lips quirk up. "But I hardly know anything about your dad."

"Oh." I frown. "I'm not sure what you could possibly want to know, but sure. I'm an open book."

"Okay, then. I'll go first. Is there anything you want to tell me? Maybe get something off of your chest?"

"That's your question?" My eyebrow rises.

He shrugs. "Just curious if you had anything on your mind."

Rand found me in the cemetery. He said you were evil and that you're using me to get to him.

Yeah, there's no way I can tell him all that. So I lie.

"No... I don't think so."

Disappointment flits across his face. "Alright then. Your turn."

Wanting to get the question I've had on my mind all afternoon out of the way, I swallow. "I thought... from the way we talked... I thought your mother was dead." I wince, immediately regretting the question.

But Sol doesn't look offended. Although the painful sorrow that furrows his brow makes me feel just as guilty.

"In many ways... she is. Her world died when my father did a decade ago. The woman she used to be is a ghost. We only get glimpses of her every now and then. Music helps bring her back, but you saw today how it's slowly stopped being as effective. We've tried everything. In this case, everything isn't enough."

My heart twists and cracks for him, but he asks his question before I can say anything else.

"Tell me about your parents."

The command catches me off guard, so I think a second before answering. "My dad was a traveling musician and knew every instrument. When he first worked with a band, everyone wanted him, but he could never seem to keep a gig. They always parted ways for some reason. My mom... she was troubled. Let's just say my psych thinks my bipolar disorder is hereditary. My mom died before I could ask her. It was just my dad and me my whole life."

He only nods once in response and I resolve to go in a different direction than my last question. "How many eye prosthetics do you have?"

He laughs. "I have quite a few. Most of them are hand painted and I've needed them since I was fifteen, so I was pretty creative with ideas in the beginning."

"Fifteen? Wow, that's so young. What designs do you have? Can I see? Are they all normal or are they cool?" I ask quickly, my curiosity getting the best of me.

He grins. "I'll show you sometime, how about that?"

A smile spreads on my face at the prospect of him opening up this side of himself to me. I open my mouth to ask more questions, like how it happened, but he beats me to it.

"Why did you come to New Orleans?"

That one's easy. "My dad's first love was jazz music and New Orleans is its birthplace. He wanted to make it here so whenever he could, we'd come back and he'd try to find a professional band gig rather than popping into bars. But again, nothing ever stuck. That's why I came back. My dad insisted I try opera and I wanted to learn from the best music college in the world, in the best city in the world. Plus, New Orleans was the first opera city in the US, so it fit."

"But you don't want to do that anymore?" Sol inquires.

I shake my head. "Growing up, I thought my dad's life was fascinating, but he thought his way was too unstable. Over time, I've realized that Broadway isn't my dream. Now, I'm trying to make my dream my own... Okay, my turn. What about *your* dream? Making music and traveling. Do you think you ever will?"

His fingers tap against my thighs as he searches my face. "Over a year ago, I would've said no. But I've been more... hopeful, lately."

A low current of excitement runs in my veins over his implication. I have half a mind to just dwell on that little tidbit and ask him what he means, but I'm not sure how long we'll be playing this game. My next line of questioning needs to be more serious if I'm going to get real answers.

"What happened the night your dad died, Scarlett?"

I freeze. The irony that I was just about to ask a similarly personal question, *how did you lose your eye*, isn't lost on me. I only wish I'd asked mine first. Now I have to answer the one question I hoped he'd never ask.

"Um... what do you want to know?"

My hands fall from his shoulders, but he grabs them and holds them to his chest over his steady beating heart.

"Everything."

He can't know everything. Never everything.

I focus on my steady breaths for a moment, biding my time to figure out the CliffsNotes version, where to start, and how to end.

"It was a year ago. My dad and I were in the Garden District. He said he needed to see a friend, so we went to that restaurant, Commander's Palace, across from Lafayette Cemetery No.1. He stepped out for his meeting during the main course. By the time it was dessert, he still hadn't come back and I was worried. I paid with some of my stipend money so I could leave and find him. When I got outside..." I swallow and Sol squeezes my hands, but doesn't let me get out of answering the question.

"Sorry, this is the first time I've talked about this with anyone besides the police."

He watches me silently and I'm thankful he's letting me gather my thoughts as I try to remember exactly what I told the police.

"When I got outside, I thought I heard someone talking so I went to see if it was my dad. Then someone came around the corner and..." I pull my hands from Sol's and he rests his on my waist as I cross my arms. "He *touched* me. Put me against the wall and tried to..."

Sol's fingers dig into my waist and I focus on the pain there rather than the restricting agony around my heart.

"I screamed and he... h-hit me. That's when I heard my dad yell for me. My attacker turned and saw him..."

"I've been waiting for you, Gus Day."

Swallowing past the memory, I keep going, not wanting to admit out loud that my dad had somehow known the awful man.

"My attacker dropped me and turned around. He pulled a gun out just as my dad ran after him. Then... he shot him." I gulp as I remember. "Twice. And my dad went down..."

"He shot twice?" Sol asks and my heart races at the question. It's been so long, I've forgotten what I've said and what I haven't.

I hesitate. "Maybe more. It's been so long."

His brows furrow but his hands loosen on my waist and drop

to my hips. "And what happened to your attacker? Your father's murderer?"

I close my eyes, shivering at the burning rage that's branded itself under my skin, remembering the weight of the metal in my hand... the panic and confusion after.

"He ran away," I answer, still trying to make sense of what happened. "Someone inside the restaurant had already called 9-1-1. When the ambulance came, they pronounced my dad dead on the scene."

"So your dad didn't fire his gun?"

My heart stills and I narrow my eyes. "My dad didn't own a gun. He tried his best to clean up his act after I was born, but he was a felon before that. He wasn't allowed to have guns."

Sol watches me carefully and I hate the questions in his eyes. "So when your attacker shot twice—"

"The other guy fired more than that. I corrected myself after you asked me."

Sol nods once slowly and before he can corner me with more questions, I ask the one I've really wanted to know.

"What happened to your eye?"

He scowls at me, no doubt knowing I'm stalling. But it's my turn.

"What do you want to know?" he asks me back.

"Everything."

He searches my face before tossing back the rest of his Sazerac. It's almost as if I can see him having the same internal conversation I did, but I was honest with him. Sort of. Hopefully, he'll be at least that honest with me.

"I was attacked. My attacker left with my eye. I was left with scars."

"Who was it?"

"It doesn't matter. He's dead now."

"How did he die?"

"Scarlett..." he growls, but I keep going.

"Do your scars have anything to do with the Bordeauxs' feud with the Chatelains?"

He stills, as frozen as stone. "Why do you ask that?"

"I'm just curious. Rand says—"

"Rand, and his whole family, are a bunch of liars," he hisses. "You need to stay away from him, Scarlett."

I bristle at the command. "Funny. That's what Rand says about the Bordeauxs."

Sol lifts me by my waist and settles me on my feet before getting up and carrying his empty glass to the bar.

"Well, maybe the Chatelains aren't liars all the time, then."

"What's that mean?" I ask, following him as he makes another drink.

His movements are easy, nonchalant, but his back muscles underneath his white button-down are tense.

"It means... they're right. You should stay away from me."

"Why do you say that? Besides, that's kind of hard to do when you freaking *kidnapped* me."

He scoffs and sips his drink. "You don't know anything about being kidnapped."

"Oh, and you do?"

He slams the drink down and glares at me. The firelight gleams against his white mask, but the rest of him is in darkness thanks to the dim lighting.

Like a shadow.

Like a phantom.

He stands with his legs apart and arms crossed. "Actually, I do. I know what it feels like to be kidnapped, caged, *and* tortured." He prowls closer and I barely resist the urge to both flee and fling myself against him to ease the pain lacing each word. "And I even know *how* to kidnap, cage, and torture."

He's close enough now that I'm sure he can see my pulse racing in my neck, right where his hand goes to grab a curl. He winds it around his finger until it's taut. When he lets go, I feel it brush against my skin as it springs back into a coil, making me shiver.

"Let me know if you'd like a demonstration."

His hand hovers near my cheek and I swat it away. "I don't believe you."

His smile grows cold and mean.

"You don't *believe* me? Which part don't you believe?"

"That you would do those things to me. You didn't even turn me over to a psych ward."

The harsh look on his face falters. "You asked me not to. I know better than most what those places can do to someone."

My breath stops in my chest and my throat goes dry. I immediately know who he's talking about.

His mother.

He shakes his head. "I think that's enough of this game for now. It's time for bed, Scarlett."

"It's not even nighttime yet." I frown. "Besides, I'm not a child, Sol."

"I didn't say you were," he replies calmly. "But you woke up earlier than usual and we both know you need your sleep. I doubt that inquisitive mind ever gets sated."

I tap my nails on his bar cart. "Can you just answer one more question?"

He sighs, and the left side of his face adopts a bored expression, although the way he's fidgeting in his pockets suggests he's anything but.

"What's your question, Scarlett?"

"Why should I stay away from Rand? He was my friend growing up. His family was good to mine. His father even helped mine find work on Frenchmen Street—"

"His father did what?"

My words cut off at the sharpness in Sol's tone.

"H-he... helped my father get music gigs."

"But Frenchmen Street is east of the French Quarter. The Bordeaux side."

"Yeah... is that a problem?"

"The Chatelains have *never* done business on our side without our knowing it. Not even before the city was split."

My brow furrows. "Okay... well they did for my dad, at least. Could you be mistaken—"

"No," he cuts me off. "I'm never mistaken about the Chatelains."

I exhale slowly. "Okay, let me go get my phone and I'll sort this out right now. Rand says he's been calling me—"

"When did you see Rand, Scarlett?" The curious edge to his voice makes me wonder if he already knows.

"I... I didn't. It's just an educated guess—"

"Really, Scarlett? You don't think I know? That I've been waiting for you to tell me since you lied to me at the cemetery?"

My mouth falls open and my heart races. "Wait... you *knew*?"

"Of course I did. What did he say to you?"

"Nothing!" I lie, hoping to derail this line of questioning until I understand what happened myself. "It was barely a few minutes and he was just worried about me."

"I don't believe you..."

I scoff, trying to deflect and play it off. "Is that why we've played this game? So you could try and—I don't know, catch me in lies or something?"

"Are there so many lies that I would have to trick you to tell the truth?"

My lips tighten. "I want to go."

He scoffs. "You want to leave? *Now*?"

"Yes!" I admit. Or lie. Hell, I'm so confused, I don't know what to do or why I'm even really angry right now, but I double down. "Let me go! I'm fine and I don't need you anymore."

"Alright then." He stalks toward the living room door and down the hall. I follow his long strides, ready to fight more, until he presses his phone screen and flings the door open wide. My eyes widen and my heart thunders in my chest, but he just stands there with his arms loosely by his sides, seemingly unfazed by this argument.

"Leave if you're dying to escape your *kidnapper*, Scarlett. Go ahead."

Cool air from the tunnels dries my teeth and I realize my jaw is hanging open.

He's letting me go.

It's not like I ever really felt like a prisoner, but after everything Rand said, I was beginning to question what the hell was going on and why I'm here in the first place.

But now that the door is open...

"Fine." I glare at him. "I'll just leave."

"Go ahead." Sol shrugs nonchalantly. And infuriatingly.

I hesitate for only a second more before I walk out the door—

And immediately get jerked back inside.

The wall is at my back by my next breath and I watch, wide eyed, as the door slams in front of me. Sol cages me in, his hands on either side of my head and the left side of his face is nothing but hard angles and sharp jawline, set in rage. Even the bone-white mask seems to mirror his anger. All I can see is his glaring midnight eye, sparkling back at me. But more than anything, I feel *hunger* radiating from him. The way his chest heaves against my breasts and that intoxicating scent of his sends desire flooding to my core.

"Do you honestly think I'd just let you walk out that door, little muse? You're *mine*."

"Yours? Why? Oh, I forgot. It's because I'm the key to *everything*, right?"

Please, tell me you're not using me to get to Rand...

"You heard that, did you?" He narrows his eyes. "You *are* the key to everything. I don't know how the fuck you could take that as anything but a compliment, but if that's what you're mad about, you'll just have to trust me."

I groan and push ineffectively at his chest. "Trust you? With all your secrets and lies?"

"I've never lied to you, and contrary to what your spoiled ass believes, you haven't earned the right to learn all my secrets."

"But you've earned the right to know mine? That's *rich*. Let me go, Sol."

"No." The intensity in his dark gaze has me squirming and my pussy fluttering, but I hold strong.

"Let. Me. Go!"

He leans in, not letting me look anywhere else as he growls deep from his chest, "*No.*"

I narrow my eyes, but freeze when he bends down and inhales up my neck, ending at my ear with a deep moan.

"Fuck, Scarlett... why didn't you tell me the truth? Knowing *anyone* else touched you today has had me *murderous*, but I've waited for you to come clean. Did you really believe I wouldn't know you saw him? That I couldn't *smell* him on you? I can smell another man on you as well as I can smell your arousal right now. Here—" His hand suddenly finds the apex of my legs and I gasp. His other hand strokes down my neck. "And even here." His sharp inhale against my throat makes me whimper.

I bite my lip to keep from giving in, and I push lightly against his chest. He pulls away to meet my gaze.

"Let me go, Sol. I'll scream. Someone will hear me."

A Cheshire smile lifts the left side of his mouth.

"Oh, you'll do more than scream, pretty little muse. You'll *sing*."

"I'll what—*ah! Sol!*"

I'm suddenly upside down and Sol's—admittedly shapely—ass is in my face as he carries me down the hall. "Put me down! Let me go! I hate you, Sol!"

"Wow, yet another lie. I'm disappointed in you, Scarlett. You just can't stop yourself, can you?"

"I'm not a liar! Drop me right now!" I demand and pound my fists into the backs of his thighs. But it's no use. "I'll scream if you don't!"

"I'll make you sing for me, my angel, my pretty little muse. I'll make you understand the *demon* I truly am. Then we'll see if you still want to run away from me."

I hear him sifting through a drawer before grabbing something.

"Help! Help! Please, somebody!"

I'm screaming at the top of my lungs one moment, and plopped onto my feet in front of the fireplace in the next. Once I gather my bearings, I dig my heels into the soft carpet to run but Sol captures me easily with one arm around my waist.

Pushing and kicking against him is futile. He's bigger than me and actually trained in martial arts, but I flail anyway. While holding me with one hand, he grabs both of my wrists with the other and begins wrapping something hard and plastic around them.

"You know, I wasn't sure how I could use these at first, but I installed this while you were sleeping. And now, you've given me an excellent idea."

"What're you doing? What are 'these?'"

I freeze and try to figure out what is binding me. A thick layer of black sparkling beads and skulls shine back at me thanks to the firelight in the room.

"Are these Mardi Gras beads?"

Before I can register that I need to keep fighting him, he pulls my bound arms over my head to attach the wrapped beads to a hook in the ceiling. I have to stretch and stand on my tiptoes to keep from dangling from the ceiling.

"Very good." He grins wickedly at me. "And make sure you don't try to pull them down or you could fall into the fire behind you."

"Sol! Stop this right now! Let me go! *I want to go home!*"

"No. You will learn your lesson."

"Which is?"

"No more lying."

I bark out a laugh. "That's funny, coming from you."

"I haven't lied once, Scarlett. But you?" He appears in my

vision again, holding an unlit crimson tapered candle by its holder. "You have been full of them today."

"I don't know what you're talking about." I hiss back, trying to maintain my rebellion while also scouring my memory for every time I lied today alone.

"Another one," he tsks. "My mother always said that liars go to hell, Scarlett. Do you know what hell feels like? Because I do." His admission makes me pause at the pain in his eyes, but as he keeps going, all sympathy disappears. "I don't wish that pain on you, but you do need to be taught a lesson. So here it is."

He disappears to stand behind me near the fireplace. It's not scorching but my bare legs are getting warm. Then he steps back into my vision with the tapered red candle newly lit.

"Sol..." I whisper carefully. "What are you doing?"

He looks into my eyes as he passes his hand over the flame and keeps it there.

"Stop! You'll hurt yourself!" I yell. My heart squeezes for him, and tears prickle behind my eyes.

He raises his brow. "I'm surprised you care. I thought you *hated* me."

"I-I do. Hate you," I insist, but my eyes can't leave where the flame licks his palm. He finally takes it away and shows me the light char on his skin. A sickly smell of burned flesh wafts toward me.

"Why would you do that?" Tears stream down my face and his triumphant smile slips.

"Shh. Shh. Oh, baby. Don't cry for me." He steps closer and wipes away a tear with his thumb as he murmurs reverently. "What pretty tears you shed for someone you hate."

My eyes narrow, pushing out more tears despite what I vow next. "Believe me, I won't shed another one for you. Not when you string me up and taunt me about how you're going to torture me."

He kneels and sets the candle on the black marble hearth. "The torture will be so delicious, though, Scarlett. I promise to make it worth our while. I used to be deathly afraid of fire. So much so that I didn't even like candles on my birthday cake. I earned the fear, but then I learned how to beat the fear by conquering the pain fire caused me. Now, I'm its master."

His fingers skim up my thighs until they curl around my panties. He tugs them down and my heart stutters as he drops them to the ground. His gaze seems to catch on a loose thread at the bottom of my dress hem. He grabs the candle again while he fingers the thread, and I still completely.

"Sol..." I whisper but he shushes me again.

"Trust me, Scarlett. Trust the man who is about to torture pleasure from you. Do you trust me?"

"I... I do," I answer honestly, but my bottom lip trembles. "I don't know what you're doing. What if... what if I can't handle it? What if it hurts?"

His brow softens. "Do you really think that? That I'll hurt you?"

"I don't know. I'm just afraid."

Hurt flashes over his face. "Pretty muse, I've told you before that I would never hurt you. If you think I will... well then not only do you not trust me, but you're lying to yourself, too. So now is your lesson. You need to be honest, Scarlett. With me, and yourself. This is a demonstration. All the lies you tell yourself—and me—will go up in smoke... just like your dress."

"No, Sol—please..." I can't stop staring down at him as he holds the candle to the hem of my dress. A spark of fear mixed with intrigued arousal flutters in my core. The last feeling floats all the way up to my chest as I realize... I *do* trust him. He won't hurt me. But self-preservation is still riding me hard, and I can't resist the urge to fight him. "Stop... What're you—"

A tiny flame erupts on the fabric and I shriek. It's small, staying no bigger than an eraser as it burns through the fabric in a rising line. Even though it's nowhere near actually touching me, I try to scoot back to get my skin away from it, but the fire at my back grows hotter against my calves. The flame increasingly warms the fabric and begins to heat my thighs.

Even as fear races in my veins, a much different kind of warmth aches in my center at the way Sol's eager face lights up while my dress continues to disintegrate, revealing more of me to him. The fire rises and the back of my neck prickles with sweat, but Sol's attentiveness burns hotter than anything on my dress. Before I can truly feel it on my skin—or the panic I know I should be feeling—Sol grabs my hips and blows the traveling flame out, snuffing it instantly.

"Shh... Scarlett. You're safe. You're always safe with me."

It's only then that I realize the tears I shed when he hurt himself are still cascading down my cheeks. But now that the flame is gone, so is any ounce of fear I had. My pussy clenches for something to fill it as he looks up at me.

Never breaking my hungry stare, he fists the dress halves, a slit now burned into it, and rips the fabric up the center. He stands as he splits the dress. Every time he jerks the fabric, my body jolts forward, as if it's trying to get free for him. His fingertips are cool compared to the flame, and as they graze my fevered skin, goose bumps bloom in his wake.

The fabric finally parts in two and drapes over me like a short-sleeved cape. While he stays fully clothed, my front is completely open to him, but for my bra. Cool air wafts a chill all over my body, perking my nipples, and adding to the tremble of need thrumming under my skin. After the shit he just pulled, I should be terrified. But with the ravenous way Sol studies my body right now, my core aches for him more than ever.

His gaze finally meets mine and I mewl when my inner muscles quake.

"I've mastered my fear of flame. And now I'll master you."

He steps forward and traces my black bra, starting with my collarbone and going down my strap, curling over my cup, too far from where I actually want him. His strokes are so light on my sensitive skin as he swoops down to the middle and back up my other breast. My legs clench together as I desperately try to keep my desire from leaking down my thighs.

I don't want him to know the effect he has on me, but with the satisfied smile he's boasting right now, he has to know. I'm seconds away from begging him to fuck me right here. When he finally flicks open my front bra clasp, I gasp as my breasts spill free from their confines. He licks his lips and I don't realize I've done the same until he swipes my wet lips with his thumb. His midnight eye follows his thumb's trail as he slides it between my parted lips and meets my gaze.

"Suck, pretty muse."

I'm mad at him. Angry as hell for keeping me, for punishing me, but more importantly, for keeping secrets from me.

But damn, do I need him inside of me right now.

My Phantom has unleashed a desperation inside of me I never knew I had. Until now.

I am his angel, he is my demon of music, and all I want to do right now is sing for him.

Keeping his gaze, I suck his thumb farther inside my mouth, swirling my tongue around it, moistening it with my spit. His other fingers hold my chin as he pumps in and out. My pussy pulses, craving to be filled.

"You're doing so good, Scarlett," he murmurs in his deep voice.

His appreciation washes over me like a cooling wave and my eyes close as he pulls his thumb out. He traces his dry fingers along my jawline, teasing my neck, down my chest, until his wet thumb swirls around my already erect nipple. The wet digit draws my peak into a diamond and he goes to the other to do the same. My head rolls back and I'm not even embarrassed at the throaty moan that escapes me.

"That's it, sing for me."

Something much wetter and softer has my eyes snapping open and I look down to see Sol sucking my nipple into his mouth. He watches me with his midnight eye and I lick my lips again as I watch him circle the pink muscle around my hard nipple. His hands grip my waist as he switches sides and pays attention to the next, laving it with his flattened tongue before flicking the tip.

"Your tongue... it feels amazing."

His lips try to lift on his right side and his cheek raises his mask.

Just that simple show of happiness in my demon makes me shiver. I don't totally understand this torture by pleasure business, but I'm not so sure I'll be learning the lesson he wants me to learn.

His fingers dig into my waist, so long from years of mastering the piano that they nearly span my stomach entirely. My clit pounds with each beat of my heart and I feel my body aching for release, but I know this won't get me there.

"Please, Sol, I need you. I want you inside of me."

"Did you love my cock inside you, pretty muse?"

"Yes! Please! I need it again."

"Have you ever had another cock inside your pussy, Scarlett?"

"No, never. Only yours. I only want yours."

I'm coming to learn that these questions are one of the games he plays with me. He already knows all my answers, but I give them anyway. He takes pleasure in my praise.

He growls low with approval as he meets my gaze. Watching my every move, he slowly rolls his zipper down over the bulge that's grown in his pants and pulls himself free. Precum soaks the swollen head and I swallow the impulse to break free and lick it. His thumb smears the liquid on his tip before he raises his thumb to my face.

"Open."

I immediately accept his offering, swirling my tongue over the salty flavor. He removes it too soon, returning to his cock to mix my spit with his precum. His palm pumps hard, spreading our fluids up and down his shaft.

"Have you ever had a cock in your mouth?"

"No." My eyes flare with interest. The desire to do just that is a tangible throb in my inner muscles right now.

He steps up to me and wraps one arm around my ass while he continues to stroke himself. His free hand caresses my ass and I bite my lip as he brings me closer.

Until he spanks me.

I yelp out and try to squirm away, but he grabs a fistful of my ass cheek. His fingers graze my crease and he whispers against my lips.

"Have you ever had a cock here?"

I shake my head, a little nervous. Sol already feels too big for my pussy. I honestly can't imagine him anywhere else.

"N-no. You know I haven't."

He growls possessively and bites my lip, licking the sting before he pulls my hips against his.

"When I take you there, you'll love that, too," he promises before leaving me entirely. I clutch the beads for dear life, afraid the sudden movement will have me crashing into the fire that's baking me through the part of my dress that's still draped over my back. The heat is nothing like the burn I have roiling inside me, though, but I don't let him know that.

"Please take me down. I need you. I feel like I'm cooking."

He smiles sinfully and grabs the still-lit candle from the floor. "You're cooking all right and I'll eat you soon enough, but for now. I want to play with my food."

"What does that—"

Sol wraps his arm around my hips and pulls me at an angle. He raises his arm high before tipping the crimson candle over my chest. I watch in horror as the small droplets of hot wax fall to my breast.

"Sol! Stop!" I scream out, expecting pain on the sensitive skin, but as soon as it lands, there's only a little sting. He blows against it, cooling it immediately. Goose bumps ripple around the drop as the wax molds and hardens against my skin, and a full-body shiver takes over.

"Feel good?"

"Mmnnn," is all I can manage as I bite my lip. He watches my eyes as he does it again. This time, my body anticipates the burn and the rush before the wax lands. I'm deliciously validated when the bloodred wax drips a light tingle in a line down the mound of my breast. He follows its path with cool breath, steering it to connect with my wet, erect nipple. A low moan pulls from my diaphragm as my clit pulses. "*More.*"

He lets go of my waist to fist his cock as he lowers the candle closer to me by a few inches, allowing it to drizzle molten hot wax down my chest until he drips it over my nipple directly.

"Sol!" My yell echoes throughout his home and my hips thrust forward, seeking him out, as if they can find his cock and force it to relieve my throbbing pulse inside.

The wax drips down my nipple onto the floor and when my hips try to push forward on my tiptoes, the next few droplets miss their mark and land on my lower belly near my trimmed curls. The sudden heat makes my muscles squeeze and contract, the faint promise of an orgasm.

"Please, Sol. Please. I *ache.*" My chest heaves while I plead.

"Does your pussy need my cock, pretty muse?"

"Yes, please. I need it. I need you."

"Does my sweet angel need her *démon de la musique*?"

"Yes. Please!" I beg without hesitation. Sol's lesson was obviously effective since I have no desire to play coy with him. My pride burned with my dress.

"But how can that be?" he asks, an affected confusion tinting the purr in his voice as he places the candle on the mantel. "I thought you *hated* me."

"I don't, oh god. Please. I don't hate you. I never hated you."

"Does that mean you *lied*?"

"Yes. I'm so sorry! I lied. I could never hate you. I *need* you."

He lets go of his cock to thread his fingers through my hair before tugging me forward and growling into my ear.

"Your demon loves it when you beg for him, *mon amour*." He

bites my earlobe, making me cry out, before kneeling and meeting my eyes. "Now sing for me."

In one swift move, he scoops my legs over his shoulders, leaving me bare to his gaze. I hold on to the beads, praying for dear life that they don't break while in this position, but I forget all about it when his tongue meets my clit.

As if the taste was all he needed to break free, he squeezes me closer, both hands gripping my ass, and *devours* me. I cry out his name in a high-pitched moan and encourage him, telling him sweet gibberish to keep him going. He moans his approval against my pussy and laps up my desire before zeroing in on my clit. I clutch the beads so hard that the plastic skulls pinch my skin as I suddenly explode into pieces.

The explosive crescendo catches me off guard, as one loud melodic chord in *fortissimo* resounds through my body. I'm screaming his name as my orgasm barrels through me, tensing every one of my muscles to the point of pain. My legs tremble on Sol's shoulders and when they've finally stopped, he stands, and catches the back of my thighs again. He holds them up at his sides before driving inside me.

"Fuck, Scarlett, your pussy grips me so hard when you come. Do you think my cock can make you come again?"

"Yes, yes, yes. *Please.*"

His hands stroke my sides lovingly as he waits for me to accommodate his size, but I want him to *move* already. My fingers tremble, dying to touch him, to carve my nails into his skin while he takes me, but I'm still hung up by the beads so I clutch them for dear life even though I trust Sol won't let me fall.

"Please let me go. I just want to touch you."

"Not yet," Sol answers before muttering under his breath. "But one day..."

The promise is so low, I can barely hear it, almost as if he's vowing it to himself more than me. I'm about to plead with him again, but he finally curves his hard cock into me and thrusts at a wild staccato beat.

Every pounding thrust pushes me to the verge of another orgasm. He wraps his left arm around my waist to clutch me to his chest. When he pumps in, he grinds against my clit before pulling back out. The move makes it impossible for me to see anything but my demon, his midnight eye full of emotion while firelight dances across the white-skull mask on the right side of his face.

I'm so hot and sweaty, the wax on my breasts and stomach is still soft on my skin. It smears all over his white shirt, but he doesn't seem to care. I stop caring about it, too, when my inner muscles squeeze, threatening to combust again.

"You feel so good, Sol. I'm going to come again," I moan. "I can't wait."

"You don't have to wait. Come, pretty muse. Sing for me, angel."

The words act as a catalyst and I combust. My already spent muscles flutter around him, gripping him tightly and nearly locking him into my body.

"*Goddamn*, Scarlett."

He calls out my name and drives up into me one final time while tugging me as close to his pelvis as possible. The beads above me snap but he catches me before I can drop, cradling my back with his forearm underneath the scrap of dress that still covers me. I lock my ankles and arms around his back and neck to help keep me steady. The beads *tink* and tap around us like rain as they fall on the black marble hearth. I wrap my arms around him immediately as he pumps his orgasm inside of me.

"Fuck your birth control," I think I hear him mutter.

With the covetous, primal way he looked at me while I held his niece, and the absolutely feral way he just took me, I regret the implant at this point. Any arguments I had when I threatened to leave have just been thoroughly fucked out of me. I want a full family one day, and having a bunch of Bordeaux babies running around the New French Opera House is a new dream I'd love to have come true.

Still standing, my legs hooked around his back, he holds me against him, his arm banded around my ass while the other wraps up my back and cups the back of my head. Other than the quiet flames whipping in the fireplace, our deep pants and gasps for air are the only sounds in the room. I feel completely safe, cherished... *loved*. I don't know if the Phantom of the French Quarter can love, but my *démon de la musique* definitely feels capable.

I brush my lips over his. His grip on my nape tightens as he immediately takes control of the kiss. I taste my arousal as he devours my mouth just like he did my pussy. When the kiss melts from fevered need to tender, he leaves my swollen lips to kiss my neck, sending a delicious tremble down my spine.

He squeezes me harder before whispering into my ear, "Never leave me, Scarlett. I couldn't bear it."

My heart squeezes at the vulnerability lacing his full, rich bass.

"What about class?" I whisper back, somewhat playfully, but also slightly worried about his answer.

He stiffens and shifts me so he can look in my eyes. Determination and hesitance fills his midnight gaze. Not for the first time, I wish I could peel off his mask and see the full depth of his emotions. Maybe then he'd not only strip naked for me, but he'd also trust me enough to bare his secrets, too.

"If I let you go tomorrow... you'll come back?" he asks and I can't help but smile.

"Yes, I promise. But only because I want to. Not because you've forced me. Besides, it's not like anywhere I go, you won't go too. You *are* my stalker."

A genuine smile spreads wide across his lips, even the right side, like it's getting used to the muscles again.

"That's all I ask, my muse."

Scene 25

AUDITIONS AND BETRAYALS

"Everyone ready for the *Faust* auditions for Marguerite, take two?" Maggie's timbre quakes as she calls from the auditorium.

Today's her first *official* day as director since Monty quit after the "Phantom chandelier incident." Her nerves are getting to her, I can hear it in her voice, but she practically carried the cast and crew by herself when Monty was in charge anyway. She'll be fantastic.

Me, however? I'm not so sure.

Sol kept his promise to let me leave this morning, but not without trying to entice me back into bed with beignets. He eventually gave up on the ruse and walked me back to my dorm through his tunnels, showing me the quickest route. After I watched him leave through my mirror, I looked around my room feeling... empty. I miss the life Sol breathes into the air around me. His voice, his laugh, his touch, I'm already addicted.

I intend to keep my promise to come back to him. But with the way he's been on my mind all day, I might as well have never left. Even preparing for this audition this afternoon, I've been too busy trying not to think about Sol's earth-shattering tongue. Everything else has been an uninteresting blur.

Part of me feels like this is *way* too fast. But then I remember I've been corresponding with this man for the past year. And whether I knew or not, he's been through it all with me. Ever since my diagnosis, it's been routine, plans, medication, rinse, repeat. I've tried to do everything right for so long, and I've been healthy, sure. But have I really lived?

With Sol? I don't just live, I *thrive*. For once, I'm going with the flow and enjoying things as they come. It's refreshing.

One of the first things I did when I got back to my dorm this morning was check my phone after not having it with me all weekend. There were some worried texts from Maggie, stopping right after my and Sol's performance at Masque. The last message she sent me was, *y'all look good up there.* Her winky face emoji at the end made me smile from ear to ear at the prospect of maybe having another friend to chat with about this stuff. Jaime's perfect, but a girl needs as many *girl*friends as she can get.

Other than Maggie, there was an endless amount of missed calls, voice mails, and messages from Rand. He'd been worried sick, poor thing, but the amount of scrolling I had to do to read all of them was tiring in and of itself. It seems like the guy didn't even take a breath. After that, I read through a very heartfelt apology from Jilliana, which lifted a weight off my shoulders I didn't realize I had.

But there was nothing from Jaime.

At first, I was hurt. But when I texted him and received no prompt "Bitch, WTF have you been doing?" I got pissed. That lasted for about thirty minutes, and now I'm straight up worried. We've never gone this long without talking. Not since he basically attached himself to my hip right after my dad died.

To top it all off, I have auditions for the female lead in *Faust* today and I honestly couldn't care less. That's weird, right? I keep trying to convince myself it's weird, but then the part of me that loved singing in Masque the other night shows up with her logic and reminds me that *this* stage isn't my dream, and what *is* my dream, might actually be in reach. Just downstairs, in fact.

"Hey Scarlett." Jilliana's gorgeous face enters my vision as she peeks into my room, the far-off lights from the stage shine on the side of her head, glowing on her flawlessly curled red hair. "Maggie called for us, but I asked her for a moment. Do you, um... do you mind if we chat?"

"Oh, sure, of course. I finally cleaned my dorm, so there's actually space on the couch this time." I chuckle. "Come on in."

She nods and closes the door behind her. Instead of sitting beside me though, she stands with her back straight, wringing her fingers as she toes the ground. Jilliana and I are both seniors. I've seen her in too many shows to keep track and I've *never* seen her this nervous. I raise a brow when she twists a red curl around her finger until she finally huffs and meets my eyes.

"Did you um... did you get my text? I tried calling to meet for coffee, too."

I wince. "Yeah, um, I didn't have my phone. I just saw my texts this morning and I haven't gotten back to people yet. I'm sorry."

She waves me off. "Oh god, please don't apologize. Are you... are you okay?"

I nod slowly. "Yeah? Why?"

"That's good. That's good. I, um, kind of saw what happened before Jaime slammed the door on us. I was so fucking worried that I was the one who made you—"

"Oh, *that*," I interrupt with a nervous laugh. "Well, I'm fine. No need to be worried," I say carefully, trying to calm her nerves with a smile, but she just shakes her head.

After taking a deep breath, she pinches the bridge of her nose between her fingers. "I don't apologize often. But after the way I acted—"

"Jilliana, it's okay—"

"No," she says firmly, her emerald-green eyes meeting my gaze. "No. Don't let me off the hook. What I did was awful, all because I was afraid the career I had earned... the *wrong* way, was in jeopardy. I... I got mad at the wrong person. And there was no excuse for talking to you like that. I never... I never should've brought up your... disorder." Her face scrunches up as she wrestles her emotions back into composure. "Oh god, I'm the worst."

"Jilliana, seriously, it's okay. I get it."

"If you really believe that, *that's* not okay. No one deserves to be talked to or about that way. It took this weekend of freedom to realize how much Monty... owned me. It makes me sick when I think about how I let him blackmail me like that."

"You didn't *let* him do anything." I scowl. "Jilliana, he was your professor. You were in an awful position—"

She puts her hand up to stop me from consoling her further. "I don't deserve for you to try to make me feel better and I don't deserve your forgiveness. But if you decide to give it to me, I'll be grateful. If you *can* forgive me, I'd love to buy you a beignet sometime and just shoot the shit. Maybe we can even be friends."

A smile curves my lips. "I'd like that."

She releases a breath like she's been holding it for days. "Yeah? Okay, amazing. Well, until then. Break a leg in auditions today."

"About that, I'm thinking of skipping the lead auditions and telling Maggie I'm good for a lesser role, or understudy."

Jilliana's eyes flare wide and she points a long manicured bloodred nail at me. "Scarlett Day, don't you fucking dare."

My jaw drops at her reaction. "What? I thought you'd be happy—"

"Oh, hell no. As soon as I saw the email, I've been busting my ass all weekend, perfecting my audition. This is the first time I've had a chance to really prove—to myself and everyone else—that I deserve to be on this stage. If you bow out, I'll never know if I would've been good enough to be the lead, fair and square. Don't you fucking dare sell us both short."

"Okay... so what *do* you want me to do?"

She huffs and props her hands on her hips. "Bring it, obviously. You're going to sing your pretty little heart out. And then I'm going to do it better." She smiles triumphantly as if she's already won. Hell, with that attitude, she practically has.

What I wouldn't give to have that confidence. Maybe once I start pursuing my own dreams, I will.

Over the past year, I've withdrawn more and more into my shell. The "quiet little mouse" is what Monty used to call me. But I certainly haven't been afraid to speak my mind with Sol. If I can go toe to toe with the Phantom of the French Quarter, everyone else should be a piece of cake. That realization makes tension release in my chest and my lips lift at the corners.

"Jilliana? Scarlett? Are y'all ready?" Maggie calls again.

Jilliana holds out her hand. "Do we have a deal?"

I take hers in mine and shake. "Deal."

"Okay, great. See you out there, Scarlett. Give it your best shot or I'll get sick every show on purpose."

I laugh, but cover my mouth when I hear my name called through Maggie's megaphone, apparently thinking we just hadn't heard her.

"Showtime." Jilliana winks before she walks with me out of my room and to the stage. When I step out, front and center, she points at me. "Your best, Scarlett. I'm serious."

"Wouldn't want to disappoint you, Jilliana." I chuckle and return her wink from earlier.

The first gentle notes of *Il m'aime*, one of the arias performed by the lead female character in *Faust*, begins to play over a speaker system and I do exactly as I promised. I bring it.

While I sing, I can't help but glance up at box five. When I see my demon of music looking on, an actual smile widens across my lips, not just the one I'm wearing for the sake of the audition.

We never talked about it, but I'd wondered if he'd show, and now I know he wants me to see him. The stage lights are dimmer, making it easier to see the auditorium but he sits near the railing instead of blending into the shadows like the Phantom he is. A smile lifts the left corner of his lips and my heart flutters in my chest.

Hell, I debated staying in my own dorm tonight, but there's

no way I can resist going back down to him, especially since I know the way now.

Once I sing the final notes, the music cuts off abruptly and Maggie gives her obligatory claps. She's always tried to be impartial and even if I sang the chandelier down, she'd still give the same emotionless claps.

"Very good, Miss Day. Well done. I'll be posting my decision at the end of the week. Jilliana Cruz! You're up!"

I give one last glance at Sol before stepping backstage and his heated gaze makes my stomach flip with excitement. When I turn around, Jilliana is wearing a playful scowl.

"Good job. You would've brought the house down." Then she breaks into a cocky grin. "Challenge accepted."

She straightens and walks past me to center stage. The same song plays again over the speakers, but Jilliana's performance is undoubtedly better. Her acting is spot on, and I can *feel* her whole heart and soul pouring from her.

The way she gleams looks exactly like how I felt on stage at Masque. There will be no contest between the two of us. She's got the lead in the bag, as she should.

My eyes flicker to the now empty box five. I'm giddy to go see him after this. I have a few classes to prepare for the rest of the week, but the perks of the senior-student life is I'm only supposed to be focused on my equivalent of a senior thesis—a.k.a. participating in this opera—and pursuing my goals for the future.

Thanks to Sol, I'll be doing exactly that this Friday. He told me before I left this morning that he's secured a gig for me at Masque during the Red, White, and Black Party. It's just another step toward fulfilling my dream.

I practically glide to my room backstage to pack an overnight bag for Sol's. As I'm humming and packing, a blur passes by my room and I look up to see the back of someone walking past my open door. I glance out and see Jaime's frame speeding away.

"Jaims!" I call out. He continues as if he didn't hear me until I call for him again. "Jaime! Come here. I have so much to tell—"

When my best friend turns around, I gasp at the welt on his cheek. "Jaime, oh my god, what... what happened to your face?"

The dim hallway makes it hard to see properly, so I rush to him and try to tug him into my room, but he holds up his hands, like he doesn't want me to touch him.

"Jaime, what's wrong? Come talk to me."

He shakes his head and steps back before leaning against the wall. The far-off light from the stage shines down the hallway, illuminating his face, and my heart sinks into my stomach.

His bronze skin usually glows due to his meticulous skin regimen, but he looks *exhausted*. Not only that, but the swollen cut on his upper left cheek looks like... a skull. As if someone with a skull ring punched him in the face. The injury is almost exactly like the one Rand showed me in the cemetery of the tourist Sol supposedly beat up.

I cover my stomach as it begins to turn, as if that could take this guilt and nausea away.

"Jaime... what happened?"

He looks around before he spits back at me, "Why don't you ask your new *boyfriend*?" This angry version of my happy-go-lucky friend is nothing like I've ever seen. He practically spits out each word as he speaks. "I've devoted my whole fucking life to that bastard, and I make *one* mistake and he does *this*!" He jabs his finger at the purple bruise and skull-shaped cut.

"S-Sol did this? No, no way. There has to be a mistake. He wouldn't hurt one of my friends."

Jaime's loud laugh is harsh and hurts my ears. "Scarlett, he would *murder* for you. A punch in the face is nothing."

He would murder for you.

Those words hit me hard, making me stagger back. It was a fact I knew and had told myself I was okay with. I trusted that he only punished people who deserved it. But *Jaime*? What the hell could he do to deserve the Phantom's justice?

I glance down the hallway, checking to see if anyone's around, but it seems like it's just the two of us for now. I whisper anyway. "Why would Sol hurt *you*, though? You're my best friend."

"I don't know. You tell me. All I know is last night, I was getting drunk on Bourbon with some of the cast one second. The next, I was thrown into an alley and got the shit beat out of me by my own boss. Or one of his other followers. I've been loyal for years and this is how he repays me? He's supposed to protect his shadows, not hurt us," he hisses.

My eyes widen and that twist in my stomach hardens to lead as my suspicions from yesterday are finally confirmed. I still hadn't figured out how I was going to broach the subject, but it looks like Jaime doesn't have that problem.

"You're a shadow?"

"Yup." Jaime's voice increases as he gets more upset. "I've been his loyal guard dog for over a year, making sure you're—"

His mouth snaps shut and his brown eyes widen.

My heart stops.

"What about... me?"

Jaime shakes his head. "N-nothing. It's nothing. Forget about it, Scarlo. I'm an actor. I'm just being dramatic. Telenovela at its finest."

He turns like he's going to actually walk away from this conversation, but I clutch his forearm and stand in his way.

"Jaime Rodrigo Dominguez, you tell me right now what the fuck you're talking about."

He winces, looking contrite and like he'd rather be anywhere else. But I don't give in. Not this time.

"Okay, let's go to your—"

"No," I answer, knowing that the *Phantom* could be just one mirror away. "You tell me right here."

He scratches at his five o'clock shadow that's usually never there before sighing. His shoulders sag against the wall as he meets my eyes.

"It all started when your dad died."

Act 4

My triceps, shoulders, and chest strain against my long-sleeved black shirt as I lift the weight in my chest press. It's been days since I've been able to be mask-ess and go without wearing my eye prosthetic, so it's been just as ong since I've worked out properly. With Scarlett hopefully coming to see me again soon, I want to go ahead and get a good one in. It feels good to get some frustration out. Other than Scar-ett's audition, it's been a shitty day.

The shadow who drove my Aston Martin while I was in the cemetery with my family has gone missing. He's one of my best, so not being able to get in touch with him is out of the ordinary. 've reached out to my contacts and while some of them don't know, others sounded... cagey.

My shadows have never had a reason to distrust me. I have to figure out where their wariness is stemming from before Scarlett comes by so I can give everyone my full attention.

That's why I watched Scarlett's audition, not that I could've esisted going in the first place. I had to see her one more time to get it out of my system before I went about my day. She did so well, but for the first time, I was able to see how much she holds back when her heart's not in the song.

I can't wait for her to perform again on Friday at the Red, White, and Black Party. Ziggy Miles, the lead singer of the jazz and blues band, was more than excited to have her perform with them again, and all those details between the band and Madam G have been worked out, too. All Scarlett has to do is show up and bring the house down with her gorgeous voice. I've even already arranged an outfit to be delivered to her dorm. Until now, I've never looked forward to going to Masque, but seeing Scarlett in the dress I picked out for her will be divine—

An alarm chimes on my phone and I rack the bar before sitting up. The cool air in the room nearly makes me shiver as it kisses my damp skin through my long sleeves. My home is exactly the way I want it, but some of my scars are sensitive to the chill that's everywhere but my den and bedroom.

As I pat some of the cool sweat off my forehead, I check the security app I installed on my phone. It's a close proximity alert. Something's tripped a scanner in the tunnels. When I thumb through the security feeds, I narrow my eye to make out who it is.

"What the—"

Scarlett is navigating the tunnels with her cell phone flashlight. If she'd just called me, I would've turned on the lights for her.

"What the hell are you up to, little muse?"

It's not a problem that she's in the tunnels. It's that I've only shown her the path once, and if she deviates from it in the dark, there's no telling which of my traps she might accidentally trip.

The feed cuts off as a phone call comes in. My finger flicks it to answer and I bark into the mouthpiece. "Sabine, what the fuck is she doing down here? She was supposed to call me."

"I don't know, sir," Sabine answers in her alto. "Do you want me to get her?"

"No. No. I'll get her. Watch all the other entrances, I won't have her in danger down here."

"Will do."

We hang up simultaneously and I jump off the bench press,

not wasting time to retrieve a jacket to combat the cold, damp tunnels. I turn on the screen again, just in time to watch her almost land face-first in the channel. My heart thuds as she catches herself, but I quickly activate the tunnel lights so she can see where she's going.

I race through my apartment, locking the door behind me before I navigate the still dim, but much brighter, tunnels to get to her. I hear her cursing before I see her and when I round the corner, I wrap her in an immobilizing embrace to prevent her from doing anything else so reckless.

"What're you doing, Scarlett? You could've gotten hurt," I hiss, my heart pounding as I take deep steadying breaths, attempting to get my pulse under control now that I know she's safe.

"Let me go, Sol! Don't touch me!"

Confusion has me furrowing my brow, and I try not to let my heart ache at her tone. I drop her to her feet and raise my hands at the sides of my head before taking a step back, giving her space.

She brushes off her T-shirt and leggings before straightening her posture. When she finally looks up, she gasps and stutters back, her hand over her mouth.

"Your... your..."

I forgot to put on my mask.

Her eyes are wide and as her hand moves, her lips stay parted. In any other circumstance, I'd think the look was wonder. It morphs into something akin to understanding, and hope takes flight in my chest... Until the horror I feared finally replaces her features.

My stomach churns and I instinctively know that look. It's the same one my mother gave me when I finally fought my way home at fifteen. It's the same one everyone had before I got fitted for prosthetics and masks. But this sinking sensation that makes me feel like I'm falling into an endless pit... that's new. Because for once, I'd let hope get in the way of reality.

I slap my hand over my face to cover my awful shame. My voice is flat when I whisper, "I'd hoped you would be different."

She blinks rapidly, as if she's coming out of a trance, and she shakes her head. "Sol, no... that's not it."

"I'm hideous Scarlett. Believe me, I *know*. I've been horrified and ashamed at what was done to me for over a decade."

"No, Sol, you don't—"

But I can't hear her excuses, not with *that* look still plastered there.

"Why are you down here, Scarlett? You shouldn't be here."

Her gaping mouth finally shuts and her fingers massage her temple. When she finally seems to remember her purpose she gazes up again at me and anger flares back into her eyes.

"When did you start following me?"

Her question catches me off guard and my mind scours itself for reasons why she would want to know that *now*. I come up with nothing so I go back to what I've done all weekend and answer in a way that won't endanger her. Until I find the full connection between Gus Day, his murderer, and the Chatelains, telling her my theories could only put her at risk. Or make her hate me more than it looks like she does right now.

Or worse... Scarlett is loyal and protective to a fault, especially over her father. If I tell her that I suspect he still dabbled in the criminal world, working for the wrong side, and that he could be the reason why she was assaulted and he was murdered, all that could easily drive her straight into Rand's arms.

"When, Sol?"

I swallow and carefully blank my expression. "After your father passed away."

As soon as I see hurt crumple her face after the words fall from my mouth, I know they're the wrong ones.

"When *exactly*?"

My jaw tics. "The night of."

Her eyes flare at that. "Why then? Were you there?"

I keep my mouth closed. There's so much I can't say yet.

She's not one of ours.

She's not, but she's *mine.*

That puts her in even more danger.

But what if telling her will save her?

What if telling her pushes her away for good? In the wrong direction?

"Secrets again, huh?" she tsks. I've never heard her voice with such venom. "Okay. How about this one? When did you *hire* Jaime to be my friend?"

My jaw falls open, stunned, but she keeps pressing.

"When you hired him, did you tell him he was going to be a professional cockblocker? All so what? So my *virginity* would remain intact? For *you*? How fucking disgusting."

My head shakes hard. "I didn't know you were a virgin, Scarlett. Not until that night you told me."

"Oh, right, when you assaulted me while I was drugged."

"You weren't drugged yet," I growl. "It's not my fault you begged a phantom to get you off."

"Ugh, it's only your fault!" she shrieks, tears of fury suddenly spilling down her cheeks.

Her accusation stings, but it's her despair that breaks me. It echoes off the stone walls, crashing back into my chest, pulverizing my weakest muscle. My heart only just started to grow stronger because of her, and now the pain I've caused is crushing it to pieces.

"Scarlett, it wasn't like that—"

"No! You're not getting out of it this time! *All* of this is your fault," she repeats and glares at me. "Me thinking I was going crazy. Me thinking I had started a true friendship—"

"Jaime loves you as a friend, Scarlett," I insist. Deep down, I know this is hopeless, but I won't give up. "His job was to watch you and *protect* you. The way he went about it wasn't part of the job description. Befriending you was true to his nature."

"And what about his 'nature' made it so no guy would look at

me for the last year? Or was that part of his 'job description' only
to sate your jealous obsession? Your... your primitive instincts!"

I step forward, huddling her into the wall. Even though she's
mad at me, and even though I'm horrifying to look at right now,
that small, pink muscle in her mouth darts out to lick her lips as
she holds my heated gaze.

"You crave those primitive instincts, Scarlett. And you love
being my jealous obsession. Don't let your anger turn you into a
liar. Think about it." My voice pitches low and my hope returns
when I cradle her cheek and she shivers with pleasure. "You're
right, I don't want anyone to touch you. You had to be off-limits
or else I wouldn't have been able to control myself. My position in
the darkness would've made you an easy target for enemies to
manipulate my emotions. Beyond that, not every shadow knew
who you were to me and if someone touched what was mine, I'd
have had to hurt them, no matter who they were, and I never
harm my own if I can help it."

Hatred flares in her eyes again and she swats my hand away.
"Not harm your own? What about Jaime then?"

My head jolts back at the topic change. "What about him?"

"He sure didn't look unharmed with the skull imprinted over
his cheek." She grabs my hand and shows me my own ring. "This
size to be exact. Just like that tourist who says the Phantom of the
French Quarter knocked him out."

"Scarlett, I don't know what you're talking about. Only a
betrayal is punished with violence. It's not the Bordeaux way. I'd
never hurt Jaime after everything he's done for me and you, but
the tourist fucking deserved it. How do you even know about
that?"

She falters at that question before blurting out an answer I'm
not sure is totally truthful. "It was in the news! But what about
me? Am I someone you would never hurt? I'm not one of yours.
Your brother made that quite clear."

"You're not one of ours, yet. But you are *mine* and under my
protection."

"What if I need protection from you, hm? So I don't think I'm crazy? So I don't believe someone is my friend for over a year? So I can live my life without being manipulated and tricked? Or can you not let go of your 'key to everything,' yet?"

"Scarlett—"

"You are a monster. Rand was right about everything. Are you using me to get to him, too?"

My eyes widen. "When did he say that? Yesterday? I thought you said you barely talked?"

I knew she was lying to me, but I'd hoped she'd come to me with answers in time. Apparently, our timing fucking sucks.

"He probably would've told me earlier if you hadn't had my phone the whole time! But yes. He bumped into me when he was visiting his brother's grave, which he says you're responsible for, too, by the way."

Alarm bells blare in my head. "Scarlett, we were at St. Louis Cemetery No.1. Rand's family isn't—"

"He said you're using me to get to him. Has this all been to get back at the Chatelains? Because I'm his friend and his family did something unspeakable to your family and vice versa and back and forth until everyone dies, right? Well, at least the Chatelains have only helped me. They supported my dad. Paid for our housing and they were there for me even after my dad died by paying for my room and board for school."

"What the fuck, Scarlett?" I laugh at the absurdity. "Do you really think the *Chatelains* paid for your room and board at *my* family's school? The Bordeaux scholarship you received after your father died set you up in the only room in the New French Opera House that directly tunnels to my apartment. Think about it."

Confusion tries to twist the anger away in her features. I brush a curl from her face and enjoy the way her body still leans into me while her mind fights me.

"Why do you insist on hating me, Scarlett? Why do you insist on seeing me as the enemy when all I've done is protect you?"

"Not protect me." She shakes her head. "You manipulated me."

"I encouraged you."

"You owned me."

"I *love* you."

The angry retort on her lips dies with my murmured confession. She shakes her head and slides along the wall to get out from underneath my direct gaze.

"You're not in love with me. You're obsessed with me," she whispers finally, although she seems much less sure of herself. "There's a difference."

I tilt my head. "There might be a difference, but that doesn't mean I can't be both. You've been in theater for years, so you know. Obsession and love make the best stories."

"Or the most tragic ones."

She drags her hand along the wall as she retreats toward her room. Every step is slow and reluctant. Like she's trying to convince her body to commit to the wrong actions.

"It's up to you to decide which story is ours," I finally reply. "If you stay, I promise to give you the best love story ever told, every day, for the rest of our lives. I was forced into the shadows, and I've made my home here. But I've only ever wanted to share a life with someone. Like my parents shared. The kind of love that consumes you in life and leaves you a shell when the other goes too soon. I used to feel sorry for my mother, but some days she gets to escape to a world where the love of her life still exists. He's not just a phantom, he is her everything. I want to be that for you, with you. I want one love that survives this lifetime."

Her head slowly shakes. "What you're describing is madness, Sol."

"Is madness so terrible, when euphoria is on the other side?"

"It is when you lose yourself in it and it makes you behave in ways you never would otherwise."

"Isn't that the definition of love?"

Her sigh weighs me down and I sag my shoulder against the wall.

"I don't know," she answers. "But I do know that I can't have that with you. The man I'm with won't use me like a pawn."

My heart threatens to burst out of my chest as our gaze breaks, and I grab her hand.

Her moonlight eyes flick to my hand before meeting mine.

"I've never used you, Scarlett, but it terrifies me that you don't realize you're Rand Chatelain's pawn right now. He's playing you. I don't know what happened to Jaime. I'll get to the bottom of it. But Rand feeding you lies? I would think you could see right through that."

"Okay, what happened then?" she asks me. "Did you have something to do with Laurent's death? His parents?"

"Not his parents. His parents' accident was a tragedy to the Chatelains but the Bordeauxs had nothing to do with it, despite what Rand and his brother thought. As for Laurent..." I let go of her and stand straighter. "Yes, I killed Laurent. I killed him for what he did to my family. And to me."

"Rand made it sound like it was a senseless act of violence. Not retribution."

"Not retribution?" I bark. "What about my face?" I point to the scars that web over the right side before I grab the back of my collar and pull my shirt over my head. "What about my chest? My arms? And my back?"

Her eyes flare with heat before I rotate, showing her the cuts, the burn marks, and every inch of the desensitized skin I've tattooed to remind me that my body is mine to mark. After Laurent Chatelain skinned me, sending strips to my brother as a morbid 'proof of life,' he burned me to stop excessive bleeding. It all grew back in jagged, glossy pieces of varying shades of red and white, like a gruesome jigsaw puzzle.

By the time I've done a three-sixty, the disgust I knew she would feel overwhelms her expression. "I told you I conquered my fear of fire. I did it because it was used against me when I was fifteen years old, and I've been like this ever since."

"Laurent... he did this to you?"

"Gladly," I grunt. "Do you still believe what I did was unjustified? Do you still believe that Rand has your best interests at heart? Like I do?"

"Does Rand know? What did he do?"

"Of course, Rand knows. He fled as soon as he could, like the coward he is."

She frowns. "So after you killed his brother and the rest of his family was dead, instead of retaliating, he ran away from the conflict?" When I don't answer, she continues her questioning. "He's back now. Do you know why?"

"I don't know. He says it's to rebuild his family's business—"

"So... not revenge."

"Maybe. I'm not sure. But Rand is Laurent's brother, and Laurent was pure evil—"

"That... that was Laurent, though. Not Rand. Rand wouldn't... he was—*is*—my friend. You can't punish him for what his brother did."

It's not lost on me that I thought something very similarly only days ago, but that was before Scarlett was at stake. Now I don't know what to think.

"I didn't believe it at first, but now my instincts are telling me there's more to Rand. You have to be careful with him, Scarlett. I'm trying to figure it all out. You need to stay away from him until I do."

She scowls and I know I've overplayed my hand.

"It's not your job to tell me what I can and can't do. Listen, I... I have to go. I'm confused and I need to think about all this. Away from you."

"When will I see you again?" I ask, unable to help myself. "You still have your gig at Masque on Friday. Will I see you then?"

"I'll be there. Without you. This... it has to be over."

I reach for her, attempting to console her one last time, but she dodges me, evading my touch. Instead, I carve my hands into my hair and exhale deeply.

"Look, Scarlett, if you really believe I've only hurt you and have never had your best intentions in mind, then you should go." The words rumble out of me like thunder in an approaching storm. "But if you leave now, I'll know you're done with me. And I... I'll be done with you. Like you want." The last words burn as they come out of my mouth and I have to swallow.

Her shoulders heave with her breaths and I know she can sense me so close to her. She shakes her head slowly.

"I'm sorry, Sol. I have to go."

And she walks away.

My muscles, my heart, my very being screams at me to follow her, to pull her back to my chest and never let her go.

But even after everything, she chooses to believe the man whose family tried to ruin mine. Who tried to ruin *me*. If she doesn't trust my instincts on Rand and insists on thinking this is all some pathetic feud, then I can't change her mind. I thought my actions would speak louder than his accusations, but I guess I'm nothing more than some evil creature to her now.

I slide down the wall and sit on my haunches. My heart aches as I listen to her soft footsteps finally make it safely to the mirror door in her room. Once they're gone, it's just me and the soft sounds of the runoff channel in front of me.

My phone buzzes and I pull it out of my pocket and answer it, already knowing who's on the other side.

"No," I say, not waiting for Sabine to ask.

"So you... *don't* want anyone else on her? You're *actually* done?"

"She wants to be left alone, I'll leave her alone." But a thought crosses my mind. "But get me Jaime Dominguez. I need an explanation."

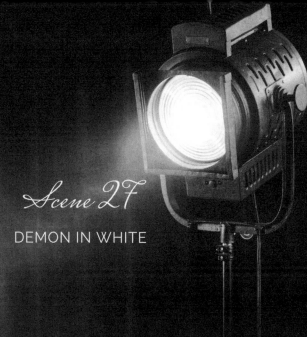

Scene 27

DEMON IN WHITE

One Week Later

M asque is busy again tonight, as usual, but the same thrill I had the night I was here with Sol is gone. All of it is gone.

The music. The roses. The notes. The comforting feeling I'm not all alone in this world.

Gone.

I know I shouldn't care, that I should be grateful he's leaving me alone. Hell, I *asked* for this. But even though it's exactly what I thought I wanted... it still hurts that he truly did just let me go. Our time together was like a match held between two fingers, effortless to light, glorious in the darkness, and painful when it was snuffed out in my grasp. It doesn't matter how long we burned together, I still can't alleviate this sting under my skin.

No matter how hard I try to forget him, I miss my demon of music.

"Ordered your favorite," hot breath whispers against my ear and I shudder before turning to give Rand a bland smile.

He messaged me incessantly after my falling out with Sol. When I finally texted Rand back the next day, Sol's warning was

°

heavy in my mind. But Sol hadn't been able to give me more to go off of aside from what happened a decade ago with Rand's older brother, *not* Rand. And I was so lonely that day, I needed someone—*anyone*—and my childhood friend seemed like my best option. Frankly, my *only* option.

Ever since, Rand has been trying so hard to cheer me up. He's never left my side, always asks me if I'm doing alright, and makes sure Sol hasn't "bothered" me again. At first, I was grateful to not be alone, but now I can't help but be annoyed with his perpetual charm.

"Thanks," I reply and accept my Cinderella mocktail. He frowns from behind his red devil mask when I set it aside, but I told him I only wanted my bottled water and he hadn't listened. My nerves are too shot to hype up with sugar, so I'll have to wait to enjoy it after I sing.

"I saw Jaime at the bar," Rand offers before straightening the lapels of his all-bloodred suit. "Looks like he *really* misses you."

The sarcastic tone has me turning in the direction he just came from.

Sure enough, Jaime is standing at the bar in a dapper silver suit, with a shining silver mask over his eyes, surrounded by members of the cast and crew. Everyone breaks into laughter over something he says, and that gnawing loneliness in my chest digs deeper.

I guess I really was a job to him.

"Looks like it," I mutter, both to myself and Rand.

I've barely seen Jaime since he dropped that bomb Monday. He hasn't talked to me or looked at me during rehearsals and classes. Rand even pointed out just yesterday that the few times we've seen him, he turns the other way.

"What an asshole. You're better off without him, Lettie."

"I don't know," I hedge and rub a pang in my chest. "I kind of miss him."

Rand frowns. "Well, maybe he'll figure out what *he's* missing. And hell, it might not have anything to do with you and Sol.

Maybe he's just jealous of how much time we've spent together. I swear he's into you."

I snort. "For the hundredth time, I'm not Jaime's type. Besides, even if he was interested, *I'm* not. I don't see him that way. He's my friend." I squeeze Rand's hand across the table. "Just like you are. I don't know what I would've done without you if you hadn't warned me about Sol."

His charming smile grows brittle and he pulls his hand out from underneath mine. He sips his scotch before sucking his teeth.

I lean forward conspiratorially. "You know... just because Laurent drank scotch doesn't mean you have to." The grin I receive is much smaller than I expect as he stares into his glass.

"My brother could never find his favorite brand in New Orleans. I think about that all the time. How he tried to make this city better and was never satisfied. I don't prefer the drink, but it reminds me of why I'm here. When I rebuild the Chatelain name, we'll take all of New Orleans, starting with the ports. It'll be better than my brother could've dreamed."

My brow furrows. "I thought... I thought you didn't care about all that stuff. I thought you were back here because it's your home. For the art and the culture."

He shrugs and rolls the bottom of his drink on its edge. "I love New Orleans, but art and culture don't make money, Scarlett."

Frowning, I twist the rose gold opal necklace that was delivered to me this morning by a local boutique. With the necklace were earrings to match and a long, black satin dress. I debated wearing the outfit, since I have no doubt it was meant to be a gift from Sol and he just never canceled the delivery. But after realizing I had nothing else to wear besides theater costumes and leggings, I caved. Honestly, I'm glad I did because I feel gorgeous.

The dress is sleek with a plunging neckline, and an embroidered sparkling black butterfly spans my back. The design looks just like the mask I'm wearing over my eyes.

One of the reasons I *know* it was Sol who left me this dress is that the wrap skirt opens up to a slit that starts right at my right hip bone. Every now and then, I graze my hand over the sensitive skin, imagining that it's his instead.

But no. I did this. I decided that my future would be without Sol, and I need to stick to my decision. He's a ruthless stalker who manipulated me for months.

"I love you."

That admission still shreds my heart and resolve to pieces. I close my eyes and shake my head.

"Hey, you okay?" Rand's hand covers mine, prompting me to open my eyes. His thumb caresses my palm, making my skin itch under the soft touch. But concern furrows his brow, so I resist tugging away. "If this is too much for you, we can go. There will be other chances to sing somewhere like this. These places are a dime a dozen."

"No, no. I'm fine. Just a little headache," I lie.

The truth is, I would like to leave, but Madam G and Ziggy Miles are letting me sing, and I don't want to pass that up.

"Okay, if you say so. I can see why you're getting a headache though. It's dark and musty down here and this theme is gauche. I might get a migraine from these flowers alone." He sniffs the air for emphasis. "Definitely not freshly cut."

He gestures around the speakeasy, at the gorgeous red, white, and black roses everywhere. Another donation from my demon of music, I'm sure. He, however, is nowhere in sight.

My head has been on a swivel looking for him all week with no reward. He probably bought an exorbitant amount of decorative bouquets just to support Miss Mabel and Madam G, but a secret part of me hopes he at least thought of me when he ordered them.

"Really? You don't like the flowers? I think they're gorgeous. And the lady who sells them is the kindest—"

"From Treme, though, right?" He snorts. "Sweet Lettie, I grew up in the gorgeous *Garden* District. These look... sad in comparison."

My jaw drops. He was never this pretentious growing up.

Or maybe I've just idealized him in my head? It's certainly more comforting to remember the good than face the bad.

"The band's pretty good though. Speaking of music... how did your audition go? If you're the lead, I'm sure I can get you in with the best people on Broadway."

I'm shaking my head before he even finishes. "I actually don't want to do theater after I graduate. I think I'm going to stay here. Maybe sing at venues like this. Besides, I didn't get the part."

Jilliana got it after killing her audition. She owns that role now.

Rand frowns. "Seriously? I thought tonight was just a one-off. Don't you think lounges and bars are a little... *humble* for someone with your talent? Wouldn't you want to reach your full potential—"

"We've got a special guest in the house tonight," the lead singer, Ziggy Miles, announces into the microphone. "Miss Scarlett has graced us with her presence again. Scarlett, come on up."

Anxious energy tumbles in my stomach and chest and I look to Rand for encouragement.

"Don't embarrass me." He winks with a teasing grin.

I wince before muttering back, "I'll do my best."

"Lettie, Lettie, Lettie... I'm *kidding*. Can't you take a joke?" He squeezes my hand as a sincere smile finally graces his lips. "You'll be great. Can't wait to hear you."

"Thanks." My lips lift at the corner before I take a deep breath and get up from my chair.

Ziggy's unmasked, wrinkled grin greets me as I navigate through the black, white, and red–clad masked crowd toward the stage. Everyone I pass is clapping and it makes me giddy and nervous at the same time. When I'm nearly to the platform, a white blur catches my attention. My heart races and I stop in my tracks, trying to search for it, but Ziggy reaches down with a hand to bring me up to the stage.

"Come on up here, now, Scarlett. Can't keep your audience waiting."

"Sorry!" I laugh nervously and accept his helping hand to climb onto the stage.

But even after I'm settled underneath the spotlight, visions of a raven-haired Phantom in white keep flitting in the corner of my eye. I can't stop myself from peering out into the crowd, but Ziggy interrupts my scouting when he speaks into the microphone again.

"Miss Scarlett has agreed to sing a song for us all, haven't you, Scarlett?"

I nod quickly and stutter into the microphone. "Yes!"

I'm not nervous exactly, but my excitement is finally back after a week away from Sol. I chase the feeling even if it's muted.

That was the first-time rush, that's all. The second time just isn't as exciting.

I know that's not true. I'm quickly learning that lying to myself hasn't worked before and it won't now.

"Take it away, Miss Scarlett. Let an old man get a drink while you sing the house down." Everyone laughs, although Rand seems preoccupied over at our table near the wall. He's scanning the room, seemingly looking for someone. I ignore him and join in with a chuckle as Ziggy gives me space for the mic.

The band starts playing without my prompting, and my heart freezes in panic because it's a different song than the one we discussed. But when I realize the tune, my pulse stutters back to life.

It doesn't have any lyrics... unless I sing my own.

My eyes search the cozy venue until I finally find the man who wrote the notes for me. His midnight eye sparkles underneath the bar's dim lights. The all-white suit he wears matches his skull mask, and the candles flickering everywhere give him an ethereal glow. My breath escapes me when he tips his glass and head to me.

"Sorry about that folks." The music stops behind me as the pianist talks into the microphone. The band never has to wear a mask, so when I look back at him, I can see the mirth and encouragement on his face as he gives me an out. "We all get stage jitters.

But you can do it, can't ya, Scarlett? We got a special request to do this one just for you."

I bet you did.

"Right, so sorry, guys." I swallow and give an awkward laugh. "Take it from the top."

The band counts down again and plays the song I've only heard echoing up through my vents, the siren call of my demon. I can't help the twist of guilt in my chest over leaving the way I did. The look on his face was one of utter betrayal, which made no sense considering *I* was the one who'd been betrayed by him and Jaime.

Right on cue this time, my mouth opens and I release the words I've only sung for my demon of music. They pour from me, practically unbidden. My lyrics fit perfectly with the low, sensuous melody, and I sing about finding my one true love and him accepting me, my light and especially my darkness. We've written many songs together over the past several months and I know he chose *this* one for a reason.

As I sing, I begin to analyze the lyrics, trying to figure out what my demon is telling me. In them, I talk about how my secrets are buried in tombs like my father's and how I have to hide my emotions behind my own mask. The irony of those lyrics isn't lost on me now. It isn't until I get to one very specific verse that my heart begins to pound with realization. I almost stutter as I describe how it took one night to bury all my secrets, but the next day brought the rest to light...

Does he know?

He said he started watching me the night my dad died. Why? Does he somehow know what I did? Was he there? Did he... *fix* it for me?

My mind is spinning and it takes me getting to the second chorus to realize I've been staring at Sol the entire time. I try to look away but my eye catches on the man in silver next to him.

Jaime?

Why on earth is he with Sol? He sees me staring at him and

raises his flute glass, an apologetic look on his face. The skull on his leather bracelet glints in the bar light and I look away. Rand's all-red suit catches my eye and I almost miss the beginning of the final verse thanks to the look in his eyes.

They're not looking at me. He's glaring at Sol from behind his devil mask, and the murderous scowl on his face sends my protective instincts soaring.

I take a final look at Sol and once again, I desperately wish I could see his whole face. The left side is practiced indifference, making my chest ache, and the other is hidden behind the mask. I can't help but wonder if the light would glint off the scars as beautifully as it did in the tunnel.

When I realized he'd forgotten his mask, his bare face had stolen my breath. The burned tissue and stitched-together flesh shimmered, practically iridescent in the dim lamplight. I'd almost gotten lost in a moment of reverence when he'd stripped his shirt to reveal an intricate patchwork of scars interwoven with tattoos over his arms and chest, the veins of which all lead to a striking skull that takes over his entire back. But then realization hit, and my body had warred with kneeling in awe, and bending over to vomit.

How much pain had he been in? At *fifteen*? He'd said Laurent had done that, but the Laurent I knew was nothing but kind to me when I spent time with Rand during one of my dad's late shows. But you never really know anyone. I'm living proof of that. Everyone wears a mask. Sol is just more up front about his.

The one I've worn the past year hides the secrets and rage boiling under my veins, threatening to ooze from my pores.

Has my demon seen under my mask... and loved me anyway?

"You're my pretty little muse, Scarlett. I worship your voice. Your body, mind, and soul are no different."

"Even the darkness in my mind?"

"Especially the darkness."

I blink as I find the last note and when I've opened my eyes again, my phantom is gone, and so is Jaime. Despite the applause,

I feel more nerves now than before I started. I thank the crowd and quickly make my way off the stage before beelining to the woman's restroom.

People praise me and I smile, but I can't catch enough breath to thank them. I'm about to turn the corner for the bathroom when an arm wraps around my waist. I'm clutched from behind and tugged into a very familiar alcove. A mirror at the end of the diagonal hallway is at the perfect angle, and I can see us clearly.

The white suit jacket is a stark contrast against my satin dress and I fall back into the embrace as a strong hand travels between my breasts and up to my throat. I don't fight when calloused fingers grip my jaw and turn my head to the side as his nose skates up the column of my neck. The scent of whiskey, sugar, and leather is overwhelming in the small space. His other hand dips beneath the slit in my dress and tugs me by my bare hip.

I moan when my demon's lips brush my ear as he whispers. "You were perfect up there, *ma jolie petite muse.* Did you figure out why I chose that song?"

"W-Why?" I ask as his wide hand pulls my hips against his hardening length.

"You wanted to know why I started to follow you? It's because I saw your darkness that night, Scarlett. Your darkness called to mine. My life was pitch black before you. You were the moonlight to my midnight."

His forearm presses harder into my chest and his fingers brush my pulse. "Do you feel it, Scarlett? Close your eyes and feel my heart beat with yours."

I do as he says and swallow past his fingertips as I *feel* our hearts beat together in time. My head nods before I've even decided to agree.

"Listen, pretty muse. Listen to the song my heart beats for you and admit you know its rhythm."

His warm lips caress my cheek and our reflection flashes in my vision. My demon of music in white. His angel in black.

Everything inside me is telling me to give in. To trust this man who understands me better than I do myself. But then my brain fights me, reminding me of the manipulation, his skewed *justice*. And even though my entire body tries to rebel, I shake my head.

"I... I can't, Sol."

Despite my words, I soak up the fullness of his lips against my skin... until it's all suddenly gone.

"So you've made your choice. It's done."

At Sol's deadened tone and the abrupt chill coating my skin, I snap my eyes open to see my reflection in this dark corner.

Alone.

I hold my own silver gaze as my hands slide over my throat and belly, to see if I can still feel where his fingertips caressed me. But I can't feel anything.

I'm numb.

If I didn't smell Sazeracs and leather, and I didn't know for certain that I'm in my right mind, I would've thought I'd made up the whole interaction.

My hands drop from my own body and I collect my breath before remembering what I was even doing in this darkened area of Masque in the first place. Taking a steadying breath, desperately trying to convince myself that I've made the right decision, I step out of the alcove.

"Scarlo!" I stop immediately and spin around at Jaime's tenor voice cutting strongly through the din echoing from down the hall. He's looking sharp in the three-piece metallic suit I saw him in earlier, but his fervent glance around puts me on edge.

"Has he talked to you?" His eyes are wide behind his silver mask.

"Who?"

"Mr. Bor–Sol. Did he... did he explain?"

I purse my lips. "Gonna need a little more to go on, Jaime."

He sighs. "I told him to give you another chance."

"You told Sol Bordeaux, the Phantom of the French Quarter, what to do?"

"I had to. He's convinced you've made your choice. Poor

broken bastard thinks that since you saw underneath his mask that you can't stand him."

"What? That's not it at all. What I couldn't stand is the way he orchestrated *my life*, hired a friend for me, and then punched him for no reason!"

"No, fuck. Listen, Scarlo. He asked me to stay away from you this week, since you asked for your privacy, and I've been trying my best. But you're my best friend, so I've got to tell it to you straight. The way you guys played together last week was incredible. I've never seen you light up like that on any stage or for anyone. If someone in this shitty world can do that for you, you have to keep them."

"Jaime, he manipulated me—"

"Yes, he *protected* you, but he never controlled you or took your decisions away. As for me... I'm sorry I ever made you think our friendship wasn't real. Sol just asked me to watch over you, not steal you as my best friend and never give you up. I did all that on my own. My *job* was to protect you when he couldn't. That's all."

"Okay, so what about punching you?" I ask, my nose scrunched as I try to take all this information in. "Why did he do that?'

"I fucked up. I thought it was Sol because of his ring but I was wrong."

"What? How do you know? Didn't you see his face?"

He sighs and shakes his head. "It was dark and it was my third day straight of getting shit-faced because I felt guilty for not sticking up for you. The guy was wearing a hoodie and a mask that looked like him, so I assumed it was Sol. But see—" He points to his healing bruise where a skull imprint used to be a week ago. "If the Phantom had done it, then I'd still have a nasty skull-shaped scar. He doesn't pull his punches. He also reached out to check on me and—"

I shake my head. "Wait, so you're telling me that there's a... copycat Phantom of the French Quarter?"

"Yeah, I guess you can say that."

"Why would a copycat come after you? And how could he have a mask with Ben's face?"

"One of his shadows has gone missing—" My eyes flare, but he keeps going. "We haven't been able to find him, so maybe someone got a hold of his mask somehow? That's what we're trying to figure out. Whoever this is was trying to turn you and me against him. And it worked."

Hope unfurls in my chest like a flame. I tried to push Sol away from the beginning, never giving him my full trust. And I realized this week that Sol was right about me loving his possessive, primal side. It was finding out he'd hired a friend for me and then beat that friend up that had been my final straw.

But what if he was framed? Knowingly or not, I've been able to trust Sol, my demon of music for almost a year. What if I had trusted him on this? We'd still be together, but now... Could he forgive me for doubting him?

My hand clasps my necklace over my chest, as if it could hold me back from sprinting to him right now and begging for forgiveness. I can't be too hasty, though. There's still one huge question that needs to be answered.

"But... who would do that?"

Jaime's jaw tics as he leans in. "Scarlo, let's be real. I think there's one person in particular who would—"

"Jaime, what are you doing with my date?"

My best friend tenses and sidesteps away from me, revealing Rand. A sour look has his face twisted and his arms are crossed over his red suit. He glances up and down at me. "You okay?"

"Sure she's okay." Jaime smiles and throws his arm over my shoulder. "She's just chatting with her bestie. Got a problem with that?"

"Her bestie? Where have you been all week while she's been upset? And what does your boss think about you being all over his former obsession?" Rand's smug tone slithers up my back, making my stomach knot.

Jaime shrugs. "He couldn't care less about her now. He'll probably be under a tourist by midnight tonight. They've always been his favorite."

His fingers dig into my shoulder, telling me he's lying, but his words still couldn't have cut deeper if they'd been knives. I use all my acting chops to stay blank faced, despite the blood fleeing it.

"Really?" Rand frowns. "I thought he was just being a bastard and not talking to her. But he doesn't care about her anymore? Just like that?"

"Just like that." Jaime snaps for emphasis and I jump.

"Interesting." Rand's brow furrows even more. "Well, if you don't mind, I'd like my date back." He gives me a small smile that reminds me of when we were younger.

My own smile is thin. After experiencing all these emotions whirling in my body, the last thing I want to do right now is be around Rand. But I also don't want to hurt his feelings. He's been there for me since I left Sol. I'll placate him tonight, then go back to my dorm and think over what the hell just happened. Tomorrow I'll face all of this.

Hopefully I won't be too late.

"Oh sure." Jaime beams back at him with a grin he only saves for the stage. "Talk to you later, Scarlo. Text me." His face falls before he bends into my ear with a whisper. "Think about what I said."

I almost ask which part, but he's gone just as quickly as my phantom was. Like the shadow he is.

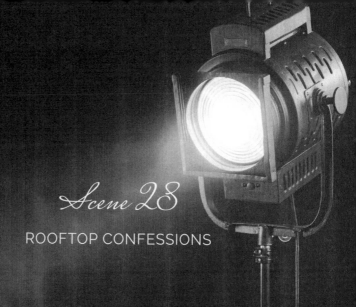

Scene 28

ROOFTOP CONFESSIONS

I wanted to go to the bathroom to get a moment to myself, but now I just want to go to bed.

"Seriously, are you okay?" Rand asks, his frown apparent through his devil masquerade mask.

"Yeah." I nod. "I'm okay. Just ready to call it a night."

"Do you think what Jaime said was true?"

I shrug. "I'm not sure. But can I be honest?"

"Of course." His voice is smooth and coaxing. "You can always tell me anything, Lettie."

Stop using my dad's nickname for me.

It's on the tip of my tongue to say the words, but I bite them back instead. He's been sour all night, and I'd be lying if I said I wasn't grateful for the reprieve in his mood.

"I don't know if what Jaime said was true, but I think I might've drawn the curtain too soon with Sol. I think... I think I need to talk to him. At least apologize for the way I left."

Rand's lips thin as he nods slowly. "Why don't you think on it tonight? I've got something in mind that might cheer you up."

My tense muscles lighten at his suggestion. "Really? What is it?"

"Always so curious, Lettie." He smirks. "I left your drink on the table, hold on for a second and I'll go back and get it—"

"Oh, no that's okay." I wave him off before he turns all the way around. "Let's just go. I'm guessing I'll be getting my surprise somewhere else? I was kind of hoping to just go to bed. I'm pretty wiped."

"This won't take long, I swear. Just trust me."

Those last three words are almost enough to make me say no, but the pleading in his eyes softens the blaring alarm bells in my mind.

Without my answer, he still grabs my hand and guides me through the hallways and staircase that lead up to the New French Opera House. But instead of going toward my dorm, we continue up the stairs.

"Where are we going?"

"There's something I think you need to see."

The speakeasy is meant to be hard to get to and depending on how you get in, you have to go through the inner trappings of the opera house to get there. Bordeaux students have free rein and we've learned the ins and outs, but somehow Rand knows exactly where he's going.

We go up—flight after flight—until we reach the very top roof access.

"The roof? How did you even know there's access up here? Students aren't even allowed—"

He presses his phone screen—an older model than I thought he had—and the door opens with the same kind of whirs and clicks that the doors in the tunnels have. As soon as the clicking is finished, he pushes open the door, revealing the rooftop, and turns with a smug smile.

"There's a lot about the French Quarter that Sol Bordeaux doesn't realize I know."

My chest seizes and I freeze as Rand yanks me through the door and closes it behind us.

"Rand... what does that mean?"

He steps out onto the rooftop and twirls in a circle with his arms out. "Look at it, Lettie. New Orleans in all her glory. The French Quarter in all her splendor."

I follow him to the Bourbon Street side of the building and rotate to see my surroundings. The rooftop of the New French Opera House is flat with a waist-high wrought iron parapet that lines the outer walls of the roof to protect people from falling over. From her perch in the middle of the building, a bronze statue of the Greek goddess Athena stands guard over the city with her circular shield in one hand and her spear in the other. Only a few blocks away, the Central Business District towers in the night sky, and below us, the lights and sounds of Bourbon Street glow and drift up to us.

"It's beautiful," I agree. "But, um, why are we up here, Rand?"

He rips his mask away from his face and finally settles his wild gaze back on me. Apprehension knifes down my spine and my heart thunders in my chest. I have the urge to remove my black butterfly mask too, but I refrain, not wanting to take my eyes off of his with the chilling vibes emanating from him.

The exact same clear blue I remember when I was a kid now glares back at me. The fact that there's no manic insanity there makes his dramatic and loud movements more unnerving.

There are so many people who are afraid of mental illness and the ones who suffer from it. Some even go so far as to believe we're all capable of being monsters. But people who don't require madness to behave irrationally are more dangerous than us all.

"It was my brother's dying wish to own New Orleans, you know. Like the Bordeauxs *think* they do. And I've come back to finally fulfill his dream. But this stupid *truce* is getting in the way. I thought by getting close to you again, I would get underneath Sol's skin. If he doesn't care about you, though... then I get to finish what *I* started."

Icy dread freezes in my veins as I finally realize that the misplaced trust I had as a kid has led me astray once again as an adult. But this time, it wasn't just at my expense. I hurt the one person in my life who has only ever cared for me. I even went so far as to blame him for the very thing that Rand is admitting to right now.

He walks in a semicircle around me and I fight the terrified stiffness in my body to turn with him to keep him in my sights. When my back is to the street, he stops and faces me, evil tensing his handsome features, and I gulp before taking a small step back.

Talk to him. Try to figure out what the fuck he's talking about, then run the hell away.

"Wh-what did you start?"

"Did you know your father worked for mine?"

That makes me still. "He did? I knew your family helped ours when my father was in between gigs—"

Rand snorts. "We don't just *help* people, Scarlett. No one deserves handouts, least of all your father."

I shake my head. "No... my dad was one of the best. That's why your dad sponsored him—"

My former childhood friend barks out a laugh. "He was mediocre at best. You, however, have talent. And yet you're planning to waste your life playing for tips like he did. What I can't decide is whether you're pathetic or delusional for thinking that's a good idea." He pauses and pretends like he's thinking. "Although, considering your diagnosis, probably both, right? Hmm... too bad stealing your meds backfired so badly. I've heard stories of your episodes. That could've been fun to see."

My mouth falls open. "That... that was *you*?"

He smirks, triumph shining in his eyes. "Guilty. Wanted to see how long it'd take for your little Phantom friend to come out of hiding. I hadn't considered he'd kidnap you. Tell me, did you sleep with him, Lettie?"

My eyes narrow. "That's none of your business."

He huffs before shrugging. "Yeah... I thought you might have. I never dreamed you'd be slutty enough to spread your legs and let him ruin you. But hey, I suppose that's just the cost of doing business."

"What do you mean, *ruin* me?" I argue nervously.

"The bastard fucked you and discarded you." He sneers as he throws his arms out to the sides. "I'm sure your sweet, naive little brain believed he thought you were someone special. But you wasted your body on a monster."

"Rand—" My eyes burn and embarrassed anger bubbles in my chest.

He inches forward, his head tilted. "Did he brand you?"

The question makes me blink. "Did he what?"

Rand waves his hand up and down in my direction. "I don't see any skull jewelry or any of those stupid amulets. So did he brand you? Bordeaux followers are barbaric in their loyalty. The most loyal get branded. They can never leave after that. The shadow I tortured for information had one, although it didn't do the Bordeauxs any good. So did Sol do it to you?"

Inappropriately timed butterflies flutter in my stomach at the thought, but I push them away and shake my head.

"Christ. Maybe he doesn't like you as much as I thought," he mutters.

My eyes blink as I try to compute all the information he's spitting at me. "Why are you saying all of this?"

"Because, sweet *Little Lettie*, you're no good to me now. I went to New York to get away from this shithole of a city. But when I got there, I met some people who shed light on all the hard work my brother was doing to get New Orleans under Chatelain guidance. I was studying abroad when Laurent assassinated the patriarch of the Bordeaux family and then decided to use dear, artistic Sol as further leverage for our negotiations. It was genius. He even placated Ben once the fool suggested a truce.

"We split New Orleans to 'avoid further bloodshed.'" He uses finger quotes and rolls his eyes. "Laurent didn't care that we were denied the ports for our particular brand of business, because why would he? He was just biding his time, waiting for Ben to come out of hiding so he could kill another Bordeaux when he had the chance and take over the whole city. But then your fucking father meddled."

"My... my father?" Blood drains from my face and gears begin to turn inside my dizzy head.

"Yes, *your father*. That one took me a while to figure out. It was only after I put one of my best guys on him that I realized what a thief and a con artist he really was. He and my father had an arrangement. If he spied on the Bordeauxs in the French Quarter, then my father would pay Gus Day's bills."

My heart is throbbing in my chest and I want to sit down, but I can't put myself in a weaker position than I already am. Rand, thankfully, seems lost in his story as he continues to expose my father's secrets.

"He was a fantastic snitch, and he rose so high in our ranks that my father confided in him about his plans to take over. But your father betrayed us by telling one of the Bordeaux shadows... and then you guys suddenly moved again and he went AWOL. A week later, my parents died and Laurent had to move up the time frame on their original plan."

"Sol s-said they were in a tragic accident—"

"Bah! That's rich, coming from the professional 'suicider.' Jacques Baron... are you really dumb enough to think he hung himself? No, Sol did it. Jacques was a Chatelain man—"

"Who hurt women—" I spit back, unable to hide my animosity, and Rand glowers at me.

"I don't give a fuck what he was doing to women, he was my second-in-command and my proxy when I was gone."

"Why would you want someone like that to work for you?"

"Oh, like the Bordeaux shadows are angels? Do you really think liquor is the only thing they spill in the streets? They're easy to catch, though. If I hadn't captured the one at the cemetery last Sunday, I wouldn't have been able to teach your stupid friend a lesson, or unlock the roof door to give you this splendid view tonight." He lifts the old phone he used to activate the door and shakes it for emphasis. "The Bordeauxs will never find their missing man though. Unlike Sol, I don't leave my bodies out in the open."

"You're an animal..." I grimace and take a step back. He mirrors it forward, and sweat prickles on the back of my neck.

The laugh Rand lets out makes my stomach churn. "You know who's an animal? Sol. I've seen the footage of what my brother did to him, and the guy howled like a dying cat when he burned."

Vomit builds in my throat and I barely swallow it down.

"Afterward, your beloved Sol *strangled* my brother. It was his first 'suicide,' as reported by the police the Bordeauxs paid off. I was too young and alone to do anything then, but I grew the fuck up while I was away. Now I'm demanding *Chatelain* justice—*true* justice—for everyone who got off scot-free. No more of this Phantom bullshit. The businessmen I made a deal with in New York said I could have it all if I just secured the port for their specific... trade... you could say."

My breaths are coming too quickly, exacerbating my lightheadedness. As I try to force slow inhales and exhales, Rand prowls toward me and I back up just as slowly, my eyes darting around the rooftop for some kind of escape plan.

"The Bordeauxs wouldn't budge and that's when I realized Sol's obsession with you would play in my favor. I thought about having the whole family killed, but Sol murdered our best assassin a year ago, and I couldn't take the chance of fucking up my plans."

"Y-your assassin? Why would Sol care about him?" I question Rand.

"Because Two-Shot killed the Bordeaux patriarch and kidnapped Sol a decade ago. That was Two-Shot's last job, but I brought him out of retirement. And do you know *why* I did that?"

"Why?" Suspicion drifts across my mind and my mouth dries while the answer remains on the tip of my tongue.

"To investigate your father. Once he found out it was your dad that tattled to a shadow about my father's plans and got my family killed, I ordered Two-Shot to take him out." He spits out every word, and each one feels like a slap in the face. "Your father lived unpunished for way too long. And, well, you know the rest. You got to meet Two-Shot up close and personal, didn't you?"

My back hits the Athena statue. Our steps have steadily mirrored each other until now, and he smiles when he realizes that he's cornered me. But his words have flipped a switch in my mind as he rants.

"From what I could tell from the police reports, he got a little sidetracked when your dad tried to hide from him. Two-Shot had a thing for unwilling girls. His fooling around probably cost him his life, though."

Oh, you have no fucking idea.

"If he'd left you alone, Sol wouldn't have had a chance to sneak up on him. He unloaded a gun into Two-Shot's chest. Then, in true Phantom fashion, he strangled him for good measure, just like he did to my brother a decade ago. Shooting isn't his usual MO. The only reason I found out at all was a side street camera that caught Sol carrying Two-Shot into Lafayette Cemetery No.1. My men scoured that cemetery afterward to find his body in a recently open grave. There was no trace of me ordering the hit, so it looked like a personal grudge between my assassin and your father. I'd had to go back into hiding after that to ensure I kept my cover."

As I listen to Rand's version of what happened, realization sets in. He's got some of the pieces jumbled up, but they all start to come together for me.

Pride and gratitude for Sol, mixed with guilt for not trusting him, fill my chest, making it hard to breathe. But I school my face to keep my scared expression as he continues.

"And now that I've gotten my revenge on your father, I've set my sights on *you*. Gus Day destroyed my family, so now I'm going to destroy his. It's perfect timing really. I'll get to kill two birds with one stone by taking out Gus Day's own daughter and Sol's obsession. Let's see if the Phantom of the French Quarter really doesn't care about you. And if he doesn't, I'll just hit closer and closer until I get what I want. I'll take everything from them, like they did me, until I've secured all of New Orleans away from those monsters and under Chatelain control."

Angry tears burn my eyes, and I shudder as he strokes my cheek.

"*You* are the monster."

He smirks and drops his hand, but steps just a foot away from me. "Oh, Scarlett. Didn't you know? I'm a nice guy. And this nice guy is going to finally get what you've been keeping from me for years. You were always such a fucking prude."

"I was *twelve*," I growl.

His face grows red right before he grabs me by my shoulders and slams me into the bronze statue behind me. Stunned by the move, I don't even try to flinch away when he smacks my face, hard enough to make me bite my tongue. My black butterfly mask rips free and drifts to the ground. Pain pounds like a drumbeat in my brain, forcing me to move at a much slower tempo than what is survivable right now.

But the rage that's been simmering in my veins since he began to taunt me with father's murder begins to boil. I try to focus as Rand paws at my dress, but flashbacks streak across my mind.

Hands digging into my skin, under my clothes, scratching and clawing to get what they think they deserve. All the memories come barreling into my brain, in reverse.

Jacques Baron.

My father's assassin.

Rand Chatelain.

The fury flooding through my body energizes me, just like it did the moments after my father's murder. He'd shot the man who'd tried to assault me, wounding him, inadvertently helping me to finish the job.

"I know Sol says he doesn't care about you, but I've known

that bastard my entire life. No Bordeaux likes to share his little toys. I only wish I could see his face when he sees your body after I push you off the roof. No one will question whether the crazy woman committed suicide after her beloved dumped her like the trash she is. It'll break his sadistic heart."

I'm so sorry, Sol.

I space out, staring over Rand's shoulder as he feels up my body and I try to figure out what to do, how to get out of this, how to use my rage to break through the instinct to freeze, like I was able to do the night my father died.

As soon as his murderer had limped away, I'd snapped out of it and grabbed my father's gun. I ran after him and shot him in the back. When he fell onto the black pavement, he rolled over to face me. The way he'd begged for his life filled me with hate because my father hadn't been given that mercy. I'd stared into the murderer's pleading eyes and fired into his chest until the gun clicked in my hands. I'd kicked him to make sure he was truly dead, as if the glazed, wide-open eyes weren't proof enough.

The unmistakable sound of a zipper rolling down finally snaps me out of my fear. A lithe shadow stalks toward us. Hope sparks the fight in me, clearing my mind and making me realize Rand's let go of me to take his dick out. I'm completely free.

Charcoal eyes flicker at me as the shadow nods.

I gather up all the courage I can muster, wanting to make sure that if this doesn't work out, that at least he knows the truth.

"Rand," I shout.

"*What?*" He doesn't even bother to look up from his dick, assuming I'm a nonthreat.

"Sol didn't kill your assassin..." That stops him. He finally meets my gaze, narrowing his eyes as I tell the truth. "*I* did."

I push him back with all my strength, taking pleasure in his stunned face. It hardly makes him move, but it gives me enough room to bring up my leg and kick my stiletto into his naked dick as hard as I can before running.

He's howling as I tear off my shoes and he limps to catch me by my dress strap, ripping the neckline deeper, but a whistle of wind flies by my ear and his howl ends in a scream.

I turn around to see him writhing on the ground, clutching his dick and his shoulder. A long dagger extends out from just underneath his left collarbone and I whip my head around to see Sabine marching toward us.

"I thought he was done with me."

"He took everyone else off your detail but me," she answers as she quickly passes me to get to Rand. "He's been trying to put together why a Chatelain man murdered your father. It seems this one had the missing pieces."

"So... so he didn't know that my father told a shadow about the Chatelains' scheme?"

She shakes her head. "No. I had no idea it was your father either. Mr. Bordeaux kept his informants' identities close to the vest and never shared business dealings with Sol or Ben. He'd wanted to wait until they were adults."

The truth lodges emotion in my throat. "I... had no idea."

I had no idea about any of it. When I went after my father's murderer, I wasn't thinking about how I was killing someone who was fleeing from me. I was thinking about revenge. Sol protected me from getting charged for murder after unloading the gun into the assassin's chest. And I hadn't known it, then, but he'd also protected me from Rand retaliating. I owe him my life.

"Run to Sol," she commands me and points to an open trapdoor in the rooftop. "That will take you the way we went last week. Keep your hand at eye level and never let it leave the wall. It'll keep you from getting lost. I'll text him he's got a new prisoner to deal with in the morning."

My eyes blink and I realize that relief, fear, and rage has finally made the tears that had been threatening to fall stream down my cheeks.

"Th-thank you." I choke out.

Sabine just nods. "I trusted a Chatelain when I was young, too. I was a new bodyguard and pissed that my boyfriend was trying to take down my boss. Laurent insisted on meeting me and I fell for it. Sol was just being a kid and snuck out to watch a band play. His father had to go find him. That's when Sol was kidnapped and Mr. Bordeaux was murdered. I've been wanting to make amends for a decade." She glances back at Rand before walking to him and twisting the knife farther in. Rand shrieks and recoils into a ball before finally passing out. She looks back up at me. "This may be my only chance. Run. Go to him. You need to be there before I text him or he'll go ballistic."

Nodding without another word, I stand up and run barefoot toward the trapdoor to follow her instructions. My ripped dress billows behind me as I race down the wrought iron stairs until I get to the bottom landing. As soon as my feet hit damp stone, I move away from the sound of rushing water on my left and find the stone wall on my right. Dragging my hand along it, I wind through the pitch-black tunnels.

When I round a corner, a dim lamp gleams just in front of me in the dark. I stagger with relief, but my wobbly legs make me trip and fall, landing hard on my knees. I feel for the wall again, finding steel instead.

Still on my knees, my heart pounding in my throat, I bang my fists against the steel and scream.

"Sol! Please help! I need you!"

The door underneath my fingers falls away as it swings open, and orange light glows behind Sol's silhouette, making him look more like my demon of music than ever before. Tall, imposing, and backlit by hellfire.

His face is bare and he's wearing a white dress shirt. His angry keloid and burn scars on his face have a beautiful sheen under the light. Pain and remorse make my insides twist.

I didn't trust him, and he was right about everything. Will he forgive me?

Concern flares over his harsh features as he looks down at me, lighting a fire of hope in my chest. His brows draw together over his midnight eye and the pink socket beside it, and his strong jaw tics.

My breath heaves in my chest as he lifts my chin to turn my face toward the light before growling.

"Who the fuck hurt you, little muse?"

S carlett kneels before me, trying to catch her breath. The view would normally please me and have my cock twitching in my pants, but the look of despair marring her gorgeous face raises the hair on the back of my neck, prompting me to scan the rest of her.

Her black satin dress has a rip in the plunging neckline and a bruise is forming on her cheek. That's all I need to see to know that someone is going to die tonight.

Fury builds in my chest like a wildfire, ready to burn whoever the fuck touched my muse this way. I breathe slow, heavy breaths in and out of my nose, attempting to calm down. She seems terrified enough, and I don't want to make it worse. I tilt her head to examine the damage and use my thumb to swipe a tear trailing down her flushed cheek.

"You were right," she whispers. "About all of it. About Rand—"

Hatred stokes the fire in my chest like gasoline, but I don't say a word. She tries to avert her gaze, but I don't let her, tightening my grip on her chin.

"He's a monster. He said he's behind my father's death. He

tried to—" She swallows. "*Hurt* me. He was going to fake my suicide and then go after your family next."

The blood in my veins burns with rage. This Chatelain fool thinks he can fuck with what is mine? Hurting Scarlet is a direct attack against me and Rand knows it.

It's a declaration of war.

I'd thought Rand was just an insolent fop. I miscalculated in thinking he's the same soft kid I grew up with. Ben was right, he's just as evil as Laurent, maybe worse if I don't remedy this.

My phone vibrates and I check my watch to see a picture of Rand bleeding in my dungeon and strapped to a chair. A message from Sabine confirms that she's secured him and that she and Jaime are keeping watch for me until I deal with it in the morning.

Good.

The tension in my back and chest immediately loosens, knowing I can count on my shadows, and that Rand is no longer out in the world with the potential to hurt Scarlett or anyone else in my family.

"I'll take care of it." The promise rumbles from my throat. "Be careful on your way back to your room."

My fingers disappear from Scarlett's silky skin like it'll singe me. Her jaw falls with the movement, and panic surfaces in her moonlight gaze. I turn to close my front door, leaving her on my threshold, when she reaches out and grabs my pants leg.

"Wait! I-I'm sorry. I should've listened to you, I should've trusted you."

I study her, fighting every muscle that wants to pick her up and take her into my home and never let her leave again. But...

"You made your choice, Scarlett. *Twice.* I lost every time."

"*No!* Please, I made a mistake—"

"No, you didn't," I hiss before leaning down and grabbing her hands. "I opened up to you and you believed I was a monster. Don't feel bad," I sneer. "You're not the first. My own mother couldn't look at my face. It wasn't until I was fitted with a prosthetic that she could stomach speaking to me again. I hate wearing it," I spit out, but she doesn't flinch. "It reminds me of who I could've been if the Chatelains hadn't tried to burn me alive. But I wear it so I never have to see that look on her face again. So forgive me, Scarlett, if I don't want to see that same look on you."

"What look?" she asks, her eyes searching mine. I huff, nearly laughing at the absurdity of her question.

"That horrified, 'what a monster,' look. Believe me, I'm well-versed in it."

She shakes her head hard and her raven curls spill over her shoulder, kissing her cleavage. "That wasn't toward you. I couldn't stomach that someone was evil enough to cause you so much pain. Someone *I* knew. I could never be horrified by this—" Her soft fingers caress the glossy ridges of my scars before I can stop her, and I jolt, realizing that I'm completely bare before her again.

I've never forgotten my mask in the decade that I've needed it, and here I am, forgetting it twice with her in the span of one week.

I don't move a muscle, but I can feel my body tremble as her fingers glide up my cheekbone. My eyes burn at the reverent tenderness in her touch.

"Does that hurt?" she asks and stills. I catch her wrist and gently remove her hand.

"No." My voice is hoarse as I answer and I swallow back the emotion threatening to reveal itself to her. "Get up."

She listens with an eagerness that makes my cock twitch, and quickly gets off her knees to stand.

"Living room, now," I command her.

The urge to go straight to my dungeon and enact my revenge against Rand is a steady hum in my mind. But the need to get to the bottom of things with Scarlett is an unbearably loud drumbeat thumping in my chest.

I lock the door behind us and she follows me into the living room where I snatch up my Sazerac from the side table and pace on the rug in front of my fire. It blazes warm in my hearth and candlelight glows on the black leather furniture and marble.

When I turn around to face Scarlett, the orange and red flames shimmer over her face and the satin dress that hugs her curves. The vision takes my breath away, but I inhale and exhale to center myself before confronting her.

"Tell me this, Scarlett. If you weren't horrified by me, then why is it that when I told you who the evil fucker was, you refused to believe me?"

"I believed you that Laurent did it." She closes her eyes slowly before meeting mine. "But after everything that I'd just discovered about you with Jaime being my bodyguard and his injury, it was difficult for me to wrap my head around the fact that my former childhood friend could be dangerous, too. I'm so sorry, Sol."

"So it took your beloved Rand's confession to believe me, is that it?" I hiss, unable to help myself.

I want to trust that this woman standing before me is actually seeing me for who I am and not the monster I've had to become. But I've been fooled by my blind hope regarding her once before already.

"No! I mean... yes. I don't know. All I can say is that I'm sorry. What can I do to make you believe me when I say that I want all of you? Especially everything under your mask? I... I love you, Sol." The muscles in my chest clench at those words, and I nearly double over. But I remain stoic on the outside. "It took losing the letters, the music, *you*, to realize I've fallen for you. I think I fell for you from the moment I read your first note written as sheet music. But I was too afraid to admit it."

Her shy, vulnerable smile makes my cock twitch. I swallow hard to attempt to get my desire under control.

"Who falls in love with a phantom?" I ask quietly past numb lips.

"I did," she answers, her silver eyes molten and earnest. "I've always felt at ease with you. You've shown me how to embrace myself, to go for my dreams, and to not be afraid of the dark parts of me."

Scarlett inhales a shaky, steadying breath. "It was you that night, wasn't it? You're the one who... when I killed my father's murderer, you were there, weren't you?"

"His name was Two-Shot..." I hesitate for a second before finally admitting the whole truth. "That man killed my father. I tracked him once I was strong and capable in the art of *accidents*. I found him outside Commander's Palace that night and had my rope ready. I'd planned to take care of him there and then stage his body at his own home. But I realized he was waiting for someone, *looking* for someone, and I stayed in the shadows to spy on him. Then you came out searching for your father. You were... captivating. My inability to stay focused almost cost you your life. It was obvious you were innocent in all this, so when Two-Shot attacked you, I almost lost it and blew my cover. But your father finally came out of hiding and took his shot. I was too late to stop Two-Shot from returning fire."

"My father was a Chatelain informant. That's why he began to perform in the French Quarter. It was to get closer to the Bordeaux shadows. Rand said that my father betrayed the Chatelains almost a decade ago, but Rand only found out last year. That's why he sent Two-Shot to assassinate him." She confirms my suspicions with shame heavy in her voice as she lowers her head.

"He tried to do right in the end. But the bullet hit Two-Shot in the shoulder. Your father's shot was wide."

"My shots weren't." Glorious fury glitters in her eyes. Just like that night when her darkness called to me and I answered. "I *knew* he was dead, but when the police came, he and the gun were gone..."

She trails off, her moonlight gaze locks with mine as I continue.

"When you ran to check on your father, I looped my noose

around Two-Shot's neck and made sure the job was finished before hiding him in a nearby grave. I didn't know what the issue between Two-Shot and your father was. Rand may be telling the truth, but if your father betrayed the Chatelains, mine didn't tell us. Ben and I were only fifteen when my father died and he kept the business private because we were minors. I was afraid Rand's proxy would retaliate against you if they found out that you were the one who killed their best assassin. On top of that, you were young and still full of understandable rage. I didn't want them or the police to come after you, or ask you questions about the gun you used since it was a Chatelain pistol—"

"What does that mean?"

"The Chatelains deal in drugs, weapons, and women. I could tell the gun was one of theirs because of the model and the filed-off serial numbers." Her eyes widen. "I didn't want this distraught victim to get caught up in the criminal legalities and questions of a stolen gun. It was better for everyone, and especially you, if the murderer and the gun *disappeared*."

"You protected me that night."

"And I'll never stop. After I witnessed you exact justice on my father's assassin, my obsession with revenge transformed into a craving for you. I haven't been able to resist you ever since. Your light, your darkness, your passion... *you* have consumed me every moment. You became more than an obsession. You became everything. But now you've asked me to leave you alone, so protection is where my obsession ends now."

Her moonlight eyes plead, bright in the golden light flickering around us. "What do I have to do to get you to... to want me again?"

"It's never been a matter of *me* wanting *you*, Scarlett," I growl.

She swallows. "What do I have to do to get you to believe that *I* want *you*, then? How can I convince you to forgive me?"

I watch her carefully as the firelight dances across her smooth alabaster skin before finally making my decision. "If you want me to trust you again, prove to me you don't think I'm a monster."

That sexy plump bottom lip purses in question. "How do I do that?"

"Beg for it."

Scene 30

LIKE SHE NEEDS IT

Her eyes widen with shock and hunger and my cock lengthens in anticipation. An evil smirk crosses my face and I begin to lazily unbutton my shirt. My gaze homes in on her tongue as it darts out.

"B-Beg for it? H-how?"

As I once again unveil the multitude of scars and tattoos I have crisscrossing all over my chest and torso, her expression only gets more ravenous. My muscles and shaft tense, ready to move and thrust inside her when she crosses her legs under her long dress, no doubt trying to keep her arousal from dripping down her creamy inner thighs.

Once I've finished removing my shirt, I toss it onto the couch and study her features. My chest thrums with cautious hope at her expression. There's no horror, only the same starved ache I've had riding me every day I've had to be without her this week.

"Strip for me."

Her cheeks flush as she bites her lip and loops her thumbs under the straps on her dress. My gaze catches the rip in her plunging neckline, and rage has my head pounding and my fists clenching to the point of pain.

I have half a mind to wait and lock Scarlett in my apartment for her safety while I go kill Rand. But I trust Sabine and Jaime to keep him secured for me and I know Scarlett. She needs this right now.

She needs to know I trust her before we separate again. Without that reassurance, her thoughts could spiral while she's alone. And I want her to know I've got her back before we face the monster in my dungeon.

She pulls the fabric over her shoulders and lets go. Satin flutters to the ground, leaving her awaiting my next command in a black strapless bra and thong.

"Strip everything," I specify, unable to produce anything but a growl while I hold myself back from taking her here and now.

She nods once before unhooking her bra in the back. It falls before she slowly slides her thong down her legs, revealing her trimmed patch of black curls. When she's completely bare to me, she steps out of the clothes and pushes them to the side with her toes, and waits.

Her brows are raised in earnest over silver eyes that scream "eager to please." I glance from them to the ground.

"On your knees, *ma jolie petite muse*. Show me how badly you want my forgiveness."

She doesn't even hesitate long enough for me to backtrack on my resolve.

Good.

This isn't for me. She needs to know that she chose me, after everything the Chatelains and I put her through, that *I* was the one she begged for. Not only that, she needs to trust that she's earned my mercy.

She collapses to her knees on the rug and I sweep her soft curls away from her face to better see the firelight glimmering over her skin.

I unbuckle my belt and slide it out of the loops with one hand. The hiss of leather against fabric sends a frisson of pleasure down my spine before I drop it on the marble hearth with a *clink*.

"Take me out, pretty muse." Her face shines up at me, only a little apprehension in her moonlight eyes. "Don't worry. I'll show you what I like."

She nods and hovers tentative fingers over the zipper of my slacks before unbuttoning and unzipping them. I'm not wearing boxers, so my length springs forward, making her eyes widen. She takes a deep breath as her slender fingers pull my hard cock completely from my pants. Her grip is too gentle on my shaft, as if it's a loaded weapon she's hesitant to wield.

"Tighter, Scarlett. Like this." I grab her hair and jerk her head toward me.

She narrows her eyes in challenge, and I can feel her try to nod against my grasp but I don't let her. That determined gaze stays on mine as she tightens her grip and stretches her other hand over my clothed thigh to steady herself. She studies my expression as she fits the tip into her mouth. As she tastes with a tentative tongue, her lips instinctively protect my sensitive skin by covering her teeth.

When she begins to move up and down my shaft, warm ecstasy flushes through my body and my head lolls backward while I cling to her hair. I fight the urge to take over that's thrumming in my veins, and allow her to test her limits before I thrust right past them.

She sets the pace as she sucks me, laving the head with her tongue, swirling around the shaft, and moaning against the tip. The gentle reverberations force me to steady myself on the mantel with my other hand.

"Fuck, Scarlett. Moan for me, just like that, baby. Relax your tongue and throat and suck me down. I want to feel these vocal cords sing just for me."

She does as I demand and slides me farther into her mouth. Her saliva coats my length, enabling her to move me in with ease, but I'm still not all the way inside.

"Use your hand more, baby. Pump me like I do when I'm thrusting into your tight pussy."

She shivers and begins to stroke me with her hand, but I see her other one slide down her naked skin.

"That's right, play with yourself. Caress your clit. You're doing so good for me. You deserve to feel good, too. Explore yourself while you explore the only cock that will ever be inside this gorgeous body. But don't you fucking dare give yourself an orgasm. Do you hear me? That's my job from now on."

She trembles against my hold and I slacken my grip to let her nod. My eye follows the trajectory of her hand as it glides down her torso.

"Widen those soft thighs so I can see you touch yourself."

She obeys and I'm pleased to see that if I tilt my head to the side, the new position exposes the apex of her legs nicely.

"Now focus on your clit so I can see *everything*."

I have the perfect angle to watch as she uses two fingers to zero in on her clit. But I lose focus when she hollows out her cheeks like a natural and moans again. The vibrations send tingles down my spine, forcing me to almost lose all control.

"Mmmm, yes. I love feeling you sing on my cock." I can smell her arousal from here and I lick my lips as if I can taste it in the air. "Are you dripping on my rug for me? Does your tight, thirsty pussy want my cock inside it?"

She mewls her reply, but I can't bring myself to end this euphoria, just yet. I tighten my grip on her hair and shove inside her open throat. Her mouth takes up over half my cock at this angle. She grips my thigh to steady herself while furiously massaging her clit.

"Relax your jaw. Sing for me while I fuck your throat, my angel of music."

She opens wider and her muscles relax around my cock, no longer trying to push me out of its impossibly tight confines. While twisting one hand through her raven black hair at the back of her head, I use the other to clutch the mantel of the fireplace and steady myself. I step into her, forcing her to lean back and cling to my pants.

Once she begins to sing, I ease my cock into her throat until her nose presses against my pelvis and my balls touch her chin. I thrust forward, feeling the gentle vibrations and different notes from her vocal cords against me. As I pump in and out, saliva weeps from her mouth, shimmering down her gorgeous neck in the firelight. Pretty tears sparkle down her rosy cheeks.

The vision I've always had merges into reality, but it's better than anything my imagination could have conjured. My spine tingles and the base of my cock tenses every time her plump lips brush against it. She sings louder, and I can finally tell that the music she's making around my cock is the same she sang at Masque earlier.

For me.

Because make no fucking mistake, while the world may hear them on the stage, these lyrics are meant for me. I've been drawn to her darkness since that very first night, and whether she realized it or not, she wrote that song for us.

My thrusts grow wild with the rising notes. But I don't want my frenzy to drag out too long and damage her pretty voice, so I give in to the urgency driving me. The blinding need to explode spasms through my body, threatening to release.

"I'm coming, sweet muse. Swallow your demon down."

Last weekend, I'd silently promised myself I'd never waste a drop, only ever spilling inside her tight cunt. But I haven't had her in a week and I know I'll be able to go again as soon as I come.

I remove my hand from the mantel so it can join the other tangling in her hair. My ass cheeks clench and my muscles strain as I cradle her head, keeping her teary eyes locked on mine, and I shove my cock to the hilt. Her bright moonlight eyes widen as hot jets of cum shoot from my throbbing tip, pulsing inside her. They glaze over and her tight, velvety throat milks me, drawing out my climax, overwhelming me as bliss tingles underneath my skin.

Seconds pass and she begins to fight my hold to breathe. I withdraw to let her gasp for a much-needed breath, dribbling cum on her lips before I sink back inside.

She mumbles her protest against my staff and clutches my wrists, but I stroke her hair and whisper low. "Shh. Relax, *mon amour*. Relax. Drink me in."

Scarlett follows my directions and her eyes close. Those plump, swollen lips surround my shaft as she begins to rhythmically suck again, suctioning out the last remnants of my orgasm. I murmur low encouragement to her, watching her muscles loosen throughout her body as she calms, as if my voice and cock are soothing the panic she just had over not being able to breathe.

Once I've finally finished coming, I try to pull out, but her nails bite into my wrist and she lurches forward to keep her lips tight around my shaft. A guttural moan escapes me as she repeatedly swallows against my softened cockhead, slowly coaxing it back to life.

"Goddamn, Scarlett. Yes, baby. Suck my cock like you need it, pretty muse."

She milks my shaft, rocking her lips back and forth until I'm back to full mast and straining to come again.

"Enough," I growl, unable to wait any longer.

I withdraw from her and curse as she whines for more and I nearly come at the sight of her spit dripping from my tip. I tug off my pants and kick them aside before kneeling in front of her.

While kissing her forehead reverently, I thread both hands through her thick curls. She rests her hands on my waist and the usually desensitized skin around my scars tingles for her.

When I pull away, I drop my hands from her hair and twist my ring so that the skull is facing inward. I'm sure she can see the heat in my gaze as I scan her body until I find the perfect place for what I'm planning next. The thought that I should warn her flickers across my mind, but ecstasy will be the only way she can get through it. She won't be able to get there if she's nervous. And I won't make her endure the pain unless I know she's absolutely sure.

When I finally meet her silver gaze, my heart thumps wildly in my chest.

"You begged for forgiveness so well. I forgive you, but now I want to hear how good I make you feel when I'm inside your sweet pussy."

She bites her swollen red lip and fights a smile. "I can do that. Easily."

My grin matches hers, tightening the right side of my face.

"Then, turn around for me."

Scene 31

SHE'S A BORDEAUX

My heart is pounding like a bass drum as I position myself on all fours facing the piano. On my right, the fireplace is warm on my skin, and so is Sol when he settles behind me, his hands on either side of my hips. His hard length prods my opening, and he waits for a moment, teasing it until I realize this is my cue.

"Yes, Sol, please fuck me—"

Before I can even finish, he drives in to the hilt. I cry out his name in a delicious mix of pain and pleasure. "I'm so *full*."

"Your pussy strangles my cock, Scarlett. I can't go a week without being inside you again. Do you understand?"

I nod adamantly. "Please. I can't either."

He pumps in and out at a quick speed and the sounds of our skin slapping together makes my clit tingle. I dig my fingers into the rug to meet him thrust for thrust. It takes me no time at all to find that pulsing flame in my core, and it builds into a bonfire. My back curls up like a cat as I try to get him to massage that special spot inside me so I can explode.

Sol pulls my hair like reins, forcing me to straighten, and easily finds that explosive spot, coaxing a moan from my lips. His cock drives into me over and over, taking me so close to my peak. One arm snakes up over my breasts and he suddenly slows, dragging the tip up and down. I cry out at the new, thorough pace and he turns my jaw to the side as he kisses up my neck. His other hand slides between my legs and swirls around my clit. The angle has him so deep inside of me that I can feel an ache in my core every time he thrusts up. The exquisite sensation begins to build and my nipples peak into diamonds against his forearm.

"Whenever you're about to come, your entire body tenses around me. Do you love that feeling, Scarlett?"

His hand drifts down my throat before leaving my skin, while his other keeps working my clit and that exact feeling takes over my body, tightening my muscles in my core, my ass, and my thighs.

"Yes, I love it. And I love that *you* are the one who gives it to me," I answer honestly.

He shivers against my back, still stroking in and out of my pussy. I stretch to thread my fingers through his soft, black strands and tilt to the side to see his midnight eye sparkling at me. My other hand clings to his forearm, and my fingertips move with his muscles as he works to tease my clit. I let go of his hair to caress the sensitive skin on his face. His body vibrates around me as we intertwine tighter and tighter.

He kisses me harshly and his tongue plunges into my mouth to brush mine. I moan at the taste of warm Sazerac, and emotion blooms in my chest as the kiss turns tender. When he pulls away, I meet his gaze again.

"I love you, Sol." His thrusts pause and his finger stills on my clit, so I move my hips to keep going as I confess to him. "I loved you when you were only music sheets, roses, and letters. You've been here for me longer than I ever knew. I never want to let you go again. I want to be yours."

The words feel beautifully final as they leave my lips.

His right hand strokes my jaw once. "Forever? One love, beyond this lifetime?"

"Forever with you, Sol, my demon of music."

His fingers leave my jaw and he leans toward the fire. Before I can see what he's doing, he captures my lips and drives inside me until my orgasm flares to life again. Each thrust is consistent and hard. His fingers swirl quickly over my clit and my inner muscles squeeze around his shaft.

He breaks our kiss and whispers against my lips. "If you make this promise, I'll never let you go again, little muse. You are swearing to love me forever." He pauses briefly before continuing. "You'll have to wear my mark."

"I swear it," I promise instantly before licking my lips and making my decision. "I want to wear your mark."

The words rush out of me just as I reach my peak. A moan escapes me as I come, and he kisses my neck while he leans us upright again and his hand returns from the fireplace.

"Good," he mutters before kissing the tender skin between my neck and shoulder.

I cry out his name as pleasure racks my body with shivers and I fall, fall, fall into bliss thanks to his talented fingers and primal thrusts.

Until searing pain ripples up my body, radiating from the sensitive skin on my right hip bone.

"*Sol*!" I scream his name and scratch at his arms and neck, trying to writhe away from the burn, even while my pussy squeezes him tight as I come.

"That's it, Scarlett. Claw into me, little muse. Give me new scars," he growls against my neck.

He takes my beating and holds on to me with his viselike grip on my hip while still massaging my clit. His guttural groan vibrates against my back and fills my ear while his last thrust spills deep inside me.

My body convulses with agony, but his finger on that bundle of nerves draws out the ecstasy in my orgasm. When I've finally come down, he wraps his arms around me in a tight embrace and the scalding burn in my hip cools to a stinging ache. My orgasm must've helped temper whatever caused it, cloaking it in a veil of pleasure. He pumps gently inside me and it takes me a second to realize he's singing that French lullaby in his soothing bass.

I breathe through the pain and pleasure while he holds me, keeping his cock nestled in my pussy. He maneuvers us to lie on our sides to face the fireplace. I rest my head on his bicep and he leans over me from behind to wipe tears I hadn't known were spilling from my cheeks.

"Shh. Shh. You did so good for me. You're mine now. You did so good."

He traces featherlight circles around the tender skin with his right hand. Even before I glance down, I know what I'll find, but my eyes widen anyway at the puckered indent of a skull above my right hip bone.

"Did he brand you... The most loyal get branded."

"Sol," I whisper. My heart flutters in my chest. "You branded me with your ring?"

As if he's expecting me to flee, his arms tighten around me, locking me against him, and he hums the lullaby louder before answering.

"You promised me love beyond a lifetime, little muse," he reasons. "You're mine now and you can't go back. You said you'd wear my mark, and this is what it takes to be one of ours. To be mine."

I settle in his arms and an overwhelming flood of warmth fills my chest as his words sink in. I'd agreed to wear his mark, although I admit that I wasn't sure what that would mean exactly or when it would occur. The pain isn't gone, but the worst of it was only a fleeting moment thanks to my orgasm. His voice is low but rushed as he keeps going, obviously worried I'll flee or fight him.

"I couldn't tell you or the pain would've been worse. I'm sorry for the deception." He wipes my tears again and I nod, allowing him to curl around me to soothe me. His masculine leather and Sazerac scent fill my nose, helping to calm me, and his cock pulses against my inner muscles.

My skin tingles as I realize that Sol is inside me still, surrounding me with his body, and filling me. He's made his indelible mark on my mind, body, and soul. Now with this brand, I'll be forever tied to him.

Lingering tension in my chest releases for the first time since I left Sol in the tunnels last week. A sense of peace settles over me. I rest my hand over his forearm banded around my chest and squeeze. The hard muscles enveloping me relax as he realizes I've forgiven him, too.

"I love you, my *démon de la musique.*"

"I love you, my muse," he purrs against my neck and kisses it.

I am Sol Bordeaux's, and I can never be free.

And I've finally accepted that I don't want to be.

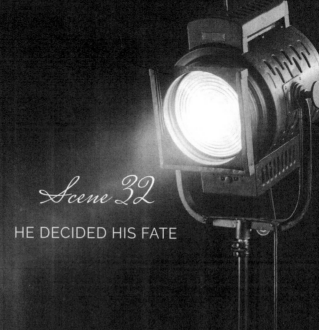

Scene 32

HE DECIDED HIS FATE

Sol pauses outside a steel door in the underground tunnel and takes a deep breath before looking back at me. Concern wrinkles his unmasked brow. Even though it's only been mere hours since we made up and my brand still stings under the bandage Sol tended me with, my lower belly flutters at the intense look in his midnight eye.

"You really don't have to do this. You don't need to see—"

I'm shaking my head before he can finish. "No. I'm here with you. You know my darkness." I reach for his free hand and squeeze. "I can handle yours."

"But my darkness—"

"*Speaks* to mine," I interrupt. "The moon can't glow without her night, Sol."

"And now my night will never be so dark again," he murmurs before pulling me in and kissing my head.

He swipes his phone and shoulders open the newly unlocked door. Cool air blows my hair back from my face and I'm grateful Sol had a long-sleeved black sweater, jeans, and tennis shoes for me to wear instead of my ripped dress. Evidently, he's been compiling quite the collection of clothes for me over the past several months.

The room is dark with stone walls and floors. Next to the door is a large iron cage full of weapons. Along the right side is one of the runoff channels, although this one sounds faster than the others. This room is the closest to the Mississippi, Sol had explained, and I'm sure that open pipe is where the phantom breeze blew from when we first came in.

As soon as we step down the stairs, Sabine and Jaime stand from their chairs on the opposite sides of the room.

"Leave us," Sol commands in a low tone.

Sabine's lips barely lift at the corner as she walks past us. "I think the way I left him is poetic."

Sol rumbles a laugh. "Quite the Shakespeare."

Before Jaime follows her out, he hugs me. "So glad you're safe, *cher*." He pulls back with a smile. "Beignets, soon. Yeah?"

"Yeah." I nod, matching his grin.

"Go," Sol orders and Jaime drops his embrace immediately with a mock salute before meeting Sabine at the door.

When she closes it behind them, a loud *clang* reverberates off the walls and into my chest, making the hair on the back of my neck stand on end. Sol steps to the side, revealing Rand. My eyes widen at the sight of him.

His mouth is duct taped and he's tied to a chair in the center of the room, still fully clothed in his now ruffled red suit. Blood dampens where Sabine stabbed him with her dagger, but the injury doesn't look lethal. Though the same can't be said for the anger that blazes in his blue eyes as they track Sol across the room.

When I step forward, his gaze leaves Sol and lands on me. Even with the duct tape over his mouth, I can easily see the disgust marring his features.

Sol strides across the room and rips off the tape. Rand grunts before sneering in my direction.

"I should've known you'd go back to being the Phantom's whore—"

Sol's fist crashes into his face and the crack of knuckle against jaw bone makes me want to wince. From Sol's hesitant glance back at me, he expected me to, but I keep my face carefully neutral.

I told Sol I love all of his darkness, and I meant it. He's taken off his mask for me, bared himself fully, and I'm not running away this time.

He nods once at me before placing his hands on his knees and leaning into Rand's face.

"You don't get to manipulate Scarlett any longer. You will only speak to her if she wishes. You live if she wishes. Do you understand?" Rand's angry eyes face him and Sol yanks Rand's blond hair up and down, forcing his head to nod. "Good. Glad you understand."

"Fuck you," Rand spits back at him, but Sol takes a step away and casually walks to the steel cage near the door. He opens it with an antique key and hands it to me before casually walking inside the cage and calling over his shoulder.

"Choose your weapon, Chatelain."

"Sword," Rand growls.

Sol laughs harshly. "Typical. You always did like challenging me in fencing class." He lays his phone down on a display of weapons before removing two swords from a rack and walking out of the cage.

"Weapon?" I ask, my voice pitching higher with alarm.

"Everyone who finds themselves in this chair fatally injured a Bordeaux, a shadow, or schemed to. I told you they either swim or fight down here, but I always give my opponent their choice of weapon."

He uses his sword to point at the opposite corner where a desk with paper and pen sits alongside an old-timey telephone.

"This time, I'm giving you another option. Dictate your confession, tell me where my shadow is and who you're working with, or decide your fate by physical means."

"Like I said." Rand narrows his eyes. "*Sword.*"

Sol chuckles harshly. "I'd say I'm impressed with your courage, but I'll hazard a guess that it's your pride, not your bravery, that's fooling you into believing you can beat me in a fight."

"So you don't just... kill him?" A sick, twisted sense of disappointment mixes with the uneasy feeling in my stomach.

"No," Rand answers. "The Phantom of the French Quarter likes to torture—"

"*No*, I don't," Sol hisses and tips Rand's face up with the sword to meet his eyes. "Your brother taught me the importance of a fair fight. Only cowards harm the defenseless."

"Let me guess, true torture is fighting for your life and losing."

"No. That's the last victory and redemption you'll ever have," Sol answers. When Rand opens his mouth to argue, he slides the blunt side of the sword up to Rand's eye. "Torture is never getting the chance to fight."

Before Rand can retort, Sol speaks again. His voice starts off low, as if he's thinking out loud, but it rises as he addresses Rand directly.

"I was tied up just like this." He grazes the blade underneath Rand's eyebrow. Rand shudders, but no blood seeps out. "Do you know what it feels like to have your eye plucked out by a dagger, Chatelain?"

My stomach drops and vomit threatens up my throat again, but I swallow it down. Meanwhile, Sol doesn't wait for a response as he traces Rand's eye.

"Thankfully, your brother decided to stab through the sclera. Apparently the iris and pupil are more painful. That's what the doctor said anyway. And there's not as much blood as you see in the movies. The blade slid into the white of my eye as easy as softened butter. Then he plucked it out and I *felt* my eyeball plop onto my cheekbone, right before your brother severed it from my eye socket. A nearly surgical removal, as if he'd practiced it before. He then privately shipped a fucking eyeball to a goddamn teenager backpacking through the Alps on spring break. Ben hadn't even been told our father was dead yet. He found out after opening his package at base camp. But do you know the worst part of your brother's torture?"

Rand doesn't answer, and my lungs seize. I stopped breathing while I listened.

Sol inhales a deep breath. Rage shudders through his frame on his exhale.

"It wasn't even when Laurent skinned me alive, piece by piece, to send to Ben, and then lit me on fire, all for his sadistic thrill." Sol jabs his finger toward his unmasked face. "No, the worst part happened *after* I twisted his own rope around his neck, strangling him. It was the feeling of power and vindication I felt over his death. Before that, I'd never liked violence or death. My father's business was *his*, and I didn't want anything to do with it. But Laurent changed the way my mind worked, transforming me into something that enjoys the thrill of the hunt, and the high of the kill. And *that* was the worst thing he could've ever done to me."

"Laurent's torture has nothing to do with me," Rand claims.

I open my mouth to tell Sol about how Rand said Laurent was a *genius* on the roof, but Sol beats me to it.

"Now, there's where you're wrong. You see... after you taunted me with Scarlett... I decided to look into you. You were, what, *sixteen* when you were self-proclaimed *childhood sweethearts*? She was twelve. Now I don't know if anything actually happened between you. Those aren't questions I'm going to force her to answer. But that phrase alone makes me want to forego my usual punishment and kill you right here and now."

My stomach knots itself while warmth blooms in my chest. A mixture of shame and gratitude. I've never told anyone about the way Rand touched me. I was too embarrassed and confused then, and I've tried to just forget it ever since. For the first time, it feels like that twelve-year-old girl inside of me is finally getting justice when I've been too ashamed to stand up for it myself. Sol is taking that burden and doing it for me.

"And it got me thinking. *If* you were a goddamn pervert at sixteen, I'd had no idea at the time. You hid it well behind your charming facade. If that was the case, then what else did I miss? That's when I decided to look into the facts of my case a little more, too. Specifically, the videos."

I have no idea what he's talking about, but Rand pales at the last sentence. Sol steps forward and lays the tip of a sword on top of one of the ropes securing Rand to his chair.

"Scarlett, lock yourself inside the cage. The key works from the inside and my phone is in there, too. Call Jaime if things go wrong."

"But, Sol—"

"Please," he whispers harshly before pleading with his midnight eye.

Nodding slowly, I do as he says and scurry toward the iron cage. The door squeaks as I close it, but the antique key turns easily in the lock. I hold his phone for good measure, ready to call my friend, and hoping like hell I don't have to.

Sol cuts the ropes on the other arm of the chair before tossing the sword at Rand's feet. Rand shakes himself free and snatches the sword off the ground, lunging at Sol. There's a clash of steel as Sol easily swats the blade away while his other arm is tucked behind his back. Rand looks much less polished than Sol as he tries to find an opening, but Sol is defending himself confidently —and patiently.

"I had the pleasure of meeting one of your loyal men last week," Sol says, his back tensing.

My heart pounds against my chest as he finally attacks, feinting a swing at Rand's leg and forcing him off balance. Sol's phone creaks in my hand, so I put it back on the display table to stop myself from breaking it.

"He mentioned I should 'watch the videos again,' referring to all the home movies your brother made while I was under his dutiful care." Sol bounces on the balls of his feet, on the defensive again as Rand throws himself with uncontrolled swings. "Imagine my surprise when I got my hands on the encrypted video footage from back then. I was able to watch them this week, and come to find out... while my other eye was blindfolded, *you* were actually the one who set me on fire. *You* made me burn while your brother laughed."

Sol lunges again, sending Rand stumbling backward and closer to the channel's edge. Rand's clear-blue eyes widen with terror.

"He... he made me!"

So swiftly I almost miss it, Sol's sword is somehow under Rand's chin. "Do. Not. Lie. To. Me. I saw the glee on your face. You only second-guessed yourself when you idiotically set my ropes on fire and I was able to get free. What is it like to know that your stupidity got your brother killed?"

"What're you talking about?" Rand asks, attempting in vain to harden his voice. His fist tightens around the sword's grip.

Sol twists his and Rand hisses as a drop of blood falls down the center of his neck. "I'm talking about how I was able to choke the life out of your brother with my own rope because *you* burned it. Funny thing is, even after you foolishly set my binding on fire, if you hadn't been a fucking *coward* and fled, you could have saved Laurent. I barely managed to finish him off with just the two of us. What if you had stayed and saved your brother?" Sol's words drip with venom. "Maybe the Chatelains would've ruined New Orleans, after all."

Rand's shout is his only warning as he flings himself at Sol. My hands fly to my cheeks and I barely resist the urge to cover my eyes entirely. Enraged tears run down the cracks between my fingers, but I don't make a sound, afraid Rand will get the best of Sol somehow. With every word out of Sol's mouth, my anger at Rand boils and boils under my skin. I even look around me to see if there's a weapon *I* can take to finish the job, but I know Sol would never forgive me.

Rand has taken my father, but he tortured Sol, and schemed to take down the entire Bordeaux family and empire. And now he's threatened to do it all again. This is Sol's vendetta, and I am at peace with whatever happens to the man who betrayed me.

A curse pulls my attention away from the weapon rack and back to the combat as Sol stumbles over one of the discarded ropes. Rand leaps at him and stabs frantically. Sol lands in a roll and yanks one of the ropes at Rand's feet. The move sweeps Rand's legs out from underneath him. He falls much less gracefully, while Sol ends his own in a backward roll that nimbly returns him to his feet, sword in hand. Before Rand can get off of his knees, Sol is on him, blade poised at his throat just above his Adam's apple.

"Wait!" Rand cries out just as another trail of blood drips from the new paper-thin slice on his neck. "W-wait! I'll confess. I'll do the confession instead."

"It's too late for that—"

"No, please! I'll do it! Y-your shadow! He's at the bottom of the Mississippi!"

Sol's face morphs into pure rage. "You motherfu—"

Rand shrieks and ducks away. His high-pitched scream cuts off as he tries to bargain with my demon. "Stop! I-I can tell you who I'm working with, too!"

I can see the full breadth of Sol's emotions thanks to his face being laid bare, the confusion, the sympathy, all still mixed with the well-earned hatred I have seeping from my own skin as well.

Sol flicks his gaze to me. "What do you say, Scarlett? I said earlier it's your choice, I meant it. Death or confession—"

Rand swings his sword wildly.

"Sol, look out!"

My blood runs cold, but Sol is too fast. He leans away from the reckless attack as it cuts a thin nick on his arm, but his own blade slices through his attacker.

There's a sickening thump as Rand's head lands on the ground. It slowly rolls away from his body until it comes to rest face up, a look of horror forever frozen in his features.

Like he's seen a ghost.

Or a phantom.

I cover my mouth to quiet my shriek. Sol's chest heaves in his blood-splattered white dress shirt. He swallows and looks back at me. "Are you okay, Scarlett?"

"Am... am I okay?" I sputter. "Are *you* okay?"

I unlock the door and sprint toward him. As soon as I get within a few feet of him, Sol wraps me up in his embrace and I cling to him. My hands worry over his clothes, but he seems fine.

"Don't worry about me, little muse. I only have a scratch."

The air caught in my lungs escapes me slowly as I inspect his arm, confirming that the blade only grazed him. I glance at the severed head, screaming in silence at our feet. My stomach lurches but I swallow back bile to focus.

"What if I'd lost you, Sol?"

"*Jamais, mon amour,*" he answers swiftly and kisses my head. "You'll never lose me. I'm the shadow that will protect you always."

We stand in silence for a moment with only the water rushing by us at the edge of the room. The hammering pulse in my ears almost drowns out the sound. When my heartbeat finally slows, he loosens his hold on me.

"He's really gone, huh?"

"Dishonorable cowards always decide their own fate. Rand Chatelain chose to follow in his brother's footsteps. Death by the Phantom of the French Quarter. It's... it's finally finished. The Chatelains are no more."

I grab his free hand and meet his sparkling midnight eye. "What do we do now?"

"Now?" He inhales and exhales one slow, deep breath, as if the weight of his past has finally been lifted. A small, peaceful smile slowly spreads over his lips, lifting even the right side of his face. "Now I can give you the sunlight."

Reprise

YOU'D LOVE HER

Sol

Heat radiates from the stone, making me sweat underneath my mask. I keep gently brushing the soft bristles over the etching in front of me, thoroughly clearing the crevices to make sure no more buildup from the elements occurs before its next true cleaning is due. When I've finished, I drop the brush into the bucket before standing and dusting off my knees.

I place my hand on top of a stone curtain and stare hard at my father's etched name.

"Oh, Solomon, it is gleaming," my mother calls from her seat on the bench several feet behind me. "Thank you. Your father would be so proud."

Her words of encouragement make me smile, and my chest expands when her brittle soprano begins to sing "La Vie en rose," the song she and my father danced to at their wedding, the same one she sang to us every night. It still brings her back to the present more than any other grounding tool we've used.

A soft hand I already know better than my own folds into

mine. "I didn't know him, but I know you. And *I'm* proud of you. But I think he would be too," Scarlett reassures me and I nod.

"He would be."

She kisses my left cheek and, for the first time in my life, I wish it had been the right one. Her lips on my sensitive skin is pure heaven. She squeezes my hand again and bends to take the bucket, leaving me with my father.

Now that I've cleaned the obelisk, the polished stone is nearly too bright for my eyes, but the comedy and tragedy skulls at the top of the drawn-back curtain look as if they'd been carved today. I trace my fingers over the macabre grave, following the threads of the curtain until I get to my father's name and epitaph.

"It's over, Dad. I'm sorry it took so long, but it's over. The men who tried to take everything from us are gone." I glance back at Scarlett and revel in the adoration welling in her eyes before I return to the grave. "And I found my muse. She is my moonlight when my world gets too dark. You'd love her," I say with full confidence. "She's the one for all of my lifetimes. She's mine."

I trace the word "father" one last time and step back toward my family. Maggie takes my mother by the hand and holds Marie as they sit on the bench Ben and I had installed. Ben stands closer to me to whisper in hushed tones so that none of them hear.

"I've made all the necessary arrangements. As far as the world knows, Rand Chatelain ran off to the Alps to pout after not securing a business deal in New Orleans. He'll inevitably be declared missing, and no one will bother looking in his family's tomb in Lafayette Cemetery. He's the last of his line. No Chatelain will hurt us again."

"And the shadow's family?"

A flicker of emotion passes over Ben's face. It's the same one I've had gnawing at my stomach ever since Rand admitted he'd murdered one of my men. Guilt.

"They're set for life." His voice cracks and he clears his throat. "They'll never want for anything after his sacrifice."

"Good," I reply as Scarlett latches on to my arm and squeezes tightly. I kiss the side of her head before speaking to my brother again. "Scarlett said he bragged about dealings in New York?"

Ben scowls. "I'm looking into it. No doubt traffickers like the Chatelains, but we'll keep our shadows on the lookout and our own wits about us."

"Yes, we will." My eyes flicker to Scarlett, then to the bench where our mother and Ben's whole world sits. "We have to. For their sakes."

Ben gives me a nod before clearing his throat and facing Scarlett directly. "I owe you an apology. I'm protective of my brother, as you can understand. But I should've known from the way you two lit up the stage last week that you were for him. I'm sorry for doubting your intentions."

An understanding smile lifts Scarlett's lips. "You're forgiven."

"Thank you. And be good to him. I think you're the only one who can bring the Phantom out into the light." He returns her grin before joining the others.

I follow him and kiss my mother goodbye. When I'm finished, I meet Scarlett's moonlight eyes and see the wheels in her head still turning from Ben's comment.

"Ready to go?"

She nods before stating her off-topic reply as if she's asking a question. "We should go on a vacation after I graduate."

I jolt back with a chuckle as I lead her toward the gate. "Yeah? What sparked that idea?"

She shrugs. "Your brother says I need to bring the Phantom out into the light. What better way than to travel the world and capture your *own* pictures to hang in your apartment?"

My lips quirk up. "I like the sound of that."

Prosthetics these days can be impressively discreet. I only refused to get them because of my stubborn vendetta. But now that the Chatelains are gone, so is the source of all my shame. I've avenged my family and my injuries. New Orleans is ours, and the world is at our feet, why not enjoy it for once?

When we're about to leave the cemetery through the hidden gate, she suddenly stops and stands in front of me. Sincerity sparkles in her eyes as she reaches up to cup the bare side of my face.

"You're a good man, Sol."

Pride puffs my chest but I try to play it off with a smirk before a faux-serious scowl takes over that side.

"But I'm your *démon de la musique*. The feared Phantom of the French Quarter. You should be afraid of me, *ma jolie petite muse.*"

A brilliant smile flashes across her face. "And you're my Sol. I could never be afraid of the darkness that loves my own."

Her declaration lodges emotion in my throat, and I have to swallow past it before I kiss her on the forehead. My promise comes out in a rough whisper.

"I am yours, *ma belle muse.*"

"And I'm yours, my Sol."

Epilogue
ONE YEAR LATER

The view from box five is completely different from the theater stage. I have to admit, I love this one a lot more, despite the fact my very own demon of music keeps distracting me, not even letting me enjoy the show. Or maybe I love it so much *because* of the way he's distracting me.

I'm sitting just inside the shadows of the box watching the Bordeaux Conservatory perform *Roméo et Juliette*, with my thighs spread wide and my legs draped over my brand-new fiancé's shoulders. He doesn't bother with the mask or the navy prosthetic when it's just the two of us and I love looking at his face while he drives me wild. The dim lights flicker over his scars and the clear acrylic eye, making them shine iridescent, like the diamond he just slipped on my finger without asking.

"You're mine, ma jolie petite muse. My mark etched into your skin promises me forever, but this ring will tell the world."

"I'm yours," I'd replied, right before he lifted the skirt of my black satin dress and swirled his tongue through the arousal already flooding my core. Not wearing panties was absolutely the right decision. All the sneaky touches he'd given me throughout the show so far had built up my desire, and I was more than willing and ready.

The diamond skull glitters on my ring finger as I clutch the armrests and sink lower into the velvet cushion. I'm chasing that peak, trying not to make any sudden movements or show my pleasure. If Sol figures out I'm coming this way, he'll stop. He swore earlier that my first orgasm of the night will be on his cock, not his tongue, but if I have my way...

The orchestra strikes up and I allow myself a little moan that can't be heard over the melody, but my demon leaves my center and stands immediately, making me groan in frustration.

He picks me up and sets me on his thighs so I'm facing the stage before he unzips himself. His hard length brushes against my ass as it pops out from its confines. I lift myself up on the armrest and slide my soaked entrance over his cock until he grabs my upper thighs and pushes all the way into me in one swift stroke.

He doesn't stop to let me adjust. We both know we don't have time. Instead, he drives upward in his seat as soon as the soprano starts singing, making the chair creak underneath us. Sol spreads my legs obscenely, hooking them over his wide-open thighs. One arm wraps around my waist and massages my clit with two fingers as he pumps his cock in and out.

I do my best to ride him, but he keeps me still, licking his fingers before playing with my nipple through the thin fabric over my breasts. My lower belly begins to tense and my inner muscles squeeze tight, ready to combust. Slowly, my back begins to arch against him and my toes curl, pushing my feet off of the ground. The few inches up gives him more room to pump into my core. His arm leaves my waist and grabs on to my hip. His fingers caress the brand he's so obsessed with.

Weeks after he marked me, I found out from Maggie that I could have chosen simple jewelry, like she did, but I'd just laughed at her suggestion. Of course my demon would never let me get off that easy. And I wouldn't want to.

The part in the aria is only a few measures away, and Sol's thrusts grow harsher. We are loud, but the orchestra is louder... I hope. It's not like anyone can kick Sol Bordeaux out of his own opera house.

My muscles are getting tighter and tighter as my clit flutters against his fingers, until finally Sol's deep voice whispers roughly in my ear.

"Sing for me, my angel."

I only have to wait one more measure for the soprano to hit her longest note before I *let go*.

Whatever high note my moan hits, I have no idea as I come in waves down the scale, my orgasm driving through me as Sol squeezes me and kisses my neck while caressing the skull on my hip and swirling around my clit.

"Yes, sing for me. Strangle my cock, *belle muse*. Tell the world you're mine."

He curses against my neck and digs his fingers into me while he comes. Spots form in my vision from the pleasure vibrating through my body as I cascade in my demon of music's arms.

When we're finally both spent, I sag against him. The orchestra finishes their final measure and the audience breaks out in applause. All the while, he holds me, caressing my inner thighs and stomach under my dress. I move to get up but he locks me in place with his arm up between my breasts and his hand on my neck. If he has it his way, he'll soak his cock inside me for the remainder of the performance. He tilts my jaw so I can look at him through my sated eyes.

His midnight eye sparkles with hope that makes my chest expand.

"Do you think we did it that time, Scarlett?"

I smile and wrap my hand behind his head to tug his hair hard enough to pull him down to kiss me. He pulses inside my core, no doubt trying to make sure my pussy drinks him dry. It's why he doesn't let me orgasm until he's coming at the same time. I got my birth control implant removed months ago, and he's convinced us coming simultaneously is a surefire way to get me pregnant with his Bordeaux baby.

He might be onto something.

I break away from his warm lips and smile. "I hope so, my Sol."

Both sides of his lips lift high now that the right side has gotten more used to smiling. A year of travel, singing and playing together on stages all over the world, and just being in love has given those previously unused muscles a workout.

It's made me healthier too. Sticking to my routines and medicine while we're on the road was a challenge at first, but we figured it out together, and I've been in remission for months.

He wraps his arms tighter around me to watch the rest of the show just like this with him nestled inside me. I almost want to tell him there's no point.

But I have a plan.

For the first time, the Phantom of the French Quarter has been taking his vacation days. We're mostly nomads at the moment, but we still use his old apartment every time we're back in town. We'll use the Prohibition tunnels to go down there so I can change, but then we're attending the Masque after-party. While we're there, we'll meet Ben, Maggie, and Jaime for drinks like old times, and then I'll perform for the rest of the night while Sol plays for me. It'll be hard keeping the secret to myself for so long, especially when I get to look at him while he eye fucks me the entire show.

In the last song, our song, I've added new lyrics. It'll be then that I tell him all his hard work has already paid off.

I'm pregnant with my demon of music's baby. He's my fiancé, and I'm living the life I've always dreamed of. Where happiness is just happiness and his darkness sings to mine.

I am his muse, and he is mine.

My Phantom of the French Quarter.

My demon of music.

~ Fin ~

Also by Greer Rivers

Conviction Series

Escaping Conviction

Fighting Conviction

Breaking Conviction

Healing Conviction

Atoning Conviction

Leading Conviction - October 4, 2022

Standalones

Catching Lightning

An Enemies-To-Lovers College Sports Romance

Phantom

A Dark, Modern Phantom of the Opera Retelling

A Tempting Motion

An Enemies-To-Lovers, Office Romance Short Story

Thank you for reading!

Please consider leaving a review on Amazon, Goodreads, and Bookbub!

Just one word can make all the difference.

Be a Dear and Stalk Me Here

You can find all things Greer Rivers here:
https://bit.ly/StalkGreerRivers

Acknowledgments

Hi! If you're new here, this is the part where I ramble on and say thanks a million times and it's still not enough! You obviously don't have to read this, but you can if you want to! Hell, you might even be in it. But the tl;dr version is: if I know you, I am thankful for you, more than you'll ever know.

First, and almost foremost (sorry, the hubs is always my #1), thank you READERS! The dream makers, the spicybooktokers, and the Boss Ass Bitches! I know your time is precious, so to have you spend it on something I wrote is a true honor. Let me just tell you that you make an author's world go 'round. Hanging out with y'all is why I do this and I love hearing from readers! All you beautiful words of affirmation people who reach out to me to tell me pretty things: You rock my world with your encouragement and I'm truly so surprised every single time someone says something nice about my words. I wouldn't be able to pursue this dream without y'all so thanks for making my dreams come true!

The wonderful women of Give Me Books Promotions: Thank you so much for all you did to share Phantom!

Samantha and Brittni and the rest of The Smuthood: Thank you for everything you do to share spicy books with the world! You ladies are amazing and it's so fun to be a part of something so uplifting!

To Barista Alley and your avocado toast and hot chocolate.

To Cat at TRC Designs: GIRL. You are an amazeballs HOOMAN and your covers are pure art!! This is 10000% my fave cover. Congrats on making a milestone in your own personal life and thank you so much for putting up with my extreme perfectionist tendencies. You truly are an angel!

Many thanks to Ellie McLove, my editor at My Brother's Editor, and Rosa Sharon, the Fairy Proof Mother: Y'all are the freaking best and I'm so thankful to keep working with MBE. Thank you for working around my crazy schedule!

To Phantom's alpha and beta readers:

A.V., Ashleigh, Pascale, Kristen, Carrie, Sierra, Whitney, Randi, and Salem

You put up with my last minute BS and I can't thank you enough!! I'm so thankful that y'all have been on this wild ride with me!

A.V.!!! Avie, Avie, Avie you are magnificent. Thank you so much for reading on my crazy schedule and always providing amazing feedback. We started this journey together and I've loved growing with you! As always, I agreed with every comment and I'm so grateful to you for helping me become a better writer, but I'm most thankful for our friendship. I can't wait to read what you have in store and see where our journeys go!

Ashleigh, thank you again for squeezing me into your schedule! I appreciate you in all the ways and your hype queen energy!

Pascale, your feedback was epic! I've been brainstorming a "the phantom wins" book for ages and you reaching out to me about a book rec months ago helped motivate me to write it! Thank you also so much for reading on such a tight deadline when you've got so much big girl job stuff going on. I'm excited to see where your writing journey takes you!

Thank you betas for telling me pretty things. I love you all and I'm so appreciative of the friendships we've developed.

Kristen and Whitney, thank you so much once again for your awesome feedback! I used everything, obviously, and I'm so grateful to you!!

Carrie, Sierra, and Randi, I've always been so thankful for your constant support. I'm so excited for what's to come next for y'all, too!

Salem, you and I've been through it since the beginning, too! I absolutely love that I can get through the book and make it prettier by the time you get it because your feedback is *everything*. I'm so glad we're friends and that you're okay with me hermiting away in my writing cave half the time.

Moral of the story: I've made some great friends with all of you and that means everything.

Thank you Bre and Carlie! I'm super excited to have a PA TEAM now and I'm so grateful for your help and support. It means THE WORLD and I can't thank you enough! Also please stay on me about manifesting because that stuff is the bomb dot com.

To my TikTok author friends: Many of you have been encouraging as hell and also hilariously fun to get to know. Booktok is my people and I'm so glad I joined and met all you other thirsty bitches. This has been such an incredible journey and I am so very grateful to call y'all my friends! Thank you so much for putting up with me while I took thousands of pictures of buildings and signs and asked questions incessantly in NOLA! Speaking of NOLA...

Thank you James, the tour guide, for answering all those questions! Thank you to the psychic in the hidden speakeasy we went to who told me all the pretty things. It was the jumpstart I needed. Thank you to Southern Charm New Orleans for keeping me in the know and excited about the setting, Pat O'Brien's alleyway, Fritz's European Jazz Club, and the vampires of New Orleans. Thank you also to Jarrett Stod on TikTok. You don't know this, but I watched every single one of your videos to make sure I got down the personal perspective about Sol's eye.

To KK: Whoa. THE JOURNEY WE HAVE BEEN ON... girl. I'm excited. Before we know it, we'll be writing something else together! I'm so excited about the stories and adventures we've cooked up. Also, thank you for knowing when and when not to tell me pretty things. P.S. I'm still on board with the guest bedroom thing, and I can't wait to go to that bar in Savannah.

To my OG BABs/Dinner Divas: Katie, Sydni, Liz, and Lauren: As always, please never stop hanging out with me even though I disappear. Y'all are seriously ride or dies and I'm so grateful for you. Also I loved Camp. It was delicious and I'm all about going a million more times and eating several courses of apps again. I can't wait for Wilmington!

Thank you, Katie, my bestie who is okay with driving me around when somehow both of my cars don't have air conditioning at the same time and it's 100 degrees outside.

Thank you, Sydni, my bestie who is going to have the BEST time celebrating her bachelorette weekend with a bazillion people! I seriously am so excited!!

Thank you, Liz, my bestie who I totally need to go buy a baby gift for right after I finish writing this! You are going to be the best mom to the cutest little BOY!

Thank you, Lauren, my bestie and future roomie who I can't wait to make up totally bizarre rumors with to keep the snitch squad busy! I'm looking so forward to that trip for many reasons but now also because I know I'll have a partner-in-crime!

To my wonderful family, my momma, sisters, BIL, and precious baby angel face niece and the FUTURE precious baby angel face niece we'll be adding soon: Your support means everything and our lives are busy and hectic, but I'm so blessed that I get to share them with you! Menee and BG I had the best time taking a break from editing to go to the park with y'all and Baby J. Momma, I'm so glad you were able to go on that river cruise and I loved seeing the pics while I wrote this! BIL, dude, drink water and rest! You deserve it. Once again, I *never* expect y'all to read my books, but if you do, I hope you at least enjoy them!!

To Maria: I firmly believe that when everyone is born we should be assigned a therapist and I'm so grateful I lost my mind at the perfect time that I got to have you as mine. You're one of the few who can tame Athena.

Speaking of which, Athena, you crazy bitch. I hope you enjoyed the flashback in the prologue and scene 10. This is the book I've wanted to write you since 2015, and even though you stress me out and make my life truly terrifying sometimes, thank you for making me, me.

And finally, to the hubs: WE DID IT. I honestly felt like at one point you were helping me write 3 books at one time and that can't happen again (*sweating emoji*). Writing one book is going to be a dang dream. You are my "Mighty Alpha," first reader, last reader, all the readers in between, business partner, co-owner, manager, TikTok approver, cliff jump pusher/catcher, favorite encourager, IRL book boyfriend, best friend forever, and the love of my life. Thank you for reading this book even though it's not a suspenseful as the Conviction series. Thank you also for sitting with me and dealing with me even when weeks like the last two weeks have been hellish globally and personally. In happier news, I'm super excited for mountain drives and more Barista Alley Fridays. Your pretty words fill me up and give me the courage to do all the scary things in this world. Walking and plotting with you are two of my favorite things and quite literally keep me sane. As always, I am so incredibly thankful for you believing in me 100% and taking hugenormous leaps of faith with me. You've saved my life and you've changed it for the better. I wouldn't want to spend a moment of it without you. Thank you for making every day an HEA.

And last, but not least, to the United States Supreme Court: fuck you.

Love,

Greer Rivers

All About Greer

Greer Rivers is a former crime fighter in a suit, but now happily leaves that to her characters! A born and raised Carolinian, Greer says "y'all," the occasional "bless your heart" (when necessary), and feels comfortable using legal jargon in everyday life.

She lives in the mountains with her husband/critique partner/irl book boyfriend and their three fur babies. She's a sucker for reality TV, New Girl, and scary movies in the daytime. Greer admits she's a messy eater, ruiner of shirts, and does NOT share food or wine.

Greer adores strong, sassy heroines and steamy second chances. She hopes to give readers an escape from the craziness of life and a safe place to feel too much. She'd LOVE to hear from you anytime! Except the morning. She hates mornings.